The Skylark's Secret

OTHER BOOKS BY FIONA VALPY:

The Dressmaker's Gift

The Beekeeper's Promise

Sea of Memories

The French for Love

The French for Always

The French for Christmas

The Skylark's Secret

Fiona Valpy

LAKE UNION
PUBLISHING

This is a work of fiction. Names, characters, organizations, places, events, and incidents are either products of the author's imagination or are used fictitiously. Any resemblance to actual persons, living or dead, or actual events is purely coincidental.

Published by Lake Union Publishing, Seattle

www.apub.com

ISBN-13: 9781542005159
ISBN-10: 1542005159

Cover design by Emma Rogers

Printed in the United States of America

For the people of Loch Ewe,
then and now.

When I'm lonely, *cridhe gaolach,*
Black the night or wild the sea
By love's light my foot finds
The old pathway to thee.

From 'The Eriskay Love Lilt',
traditional Scottish song

Lexie, 1980

It's one of those days, on the cusp of early summer, when the sky and the sea alike are awash with sunlight. Days like this are rare enough up here in the Scottish Highlands to be remarked upon and stored away in the memory, hoarded as talismans against the long darkness of the winter. I button Daisy into her coat and pull a woollen tammy over her curls. Even though there's warmth in the sunshine, the wind on the hills above the croft can still nip noses and chill ears, turning them cherry pink. Then I buckle her into the carrier and hoist it on to my shoulders. She chuckles, loving the sensation of height, burying her fingers in my hair, and we set off up the path.

Climbing steadily, leaving the waters of Loch Ewe behind us, my breath becomes more laboured as the path steepens, twisting through the pines alongside the burn that chatters and babbles companionably on its way down the brae. Finally, we emerge from the darkness that pools beneath the trees, into the sunlight of the higher ground. Calf muscles burning, I stop for a moment, my hands on my hips, taking gulps of air that is as clear and cold as the water in the stream. I turn to look back the way we've come. The clusters of whitewashed croft cottages fringing the road here and there along the lochside are still just visible, but in a few steps more they will disappear as the heather-clad arms of the hills fold us into their embrace.

Along the edge of the path, half-hidden among the scrub of rowans and birches, primroses turn their faces to the sunshine while shy violets attempt to hide theirs. The climb evens out a little and Daisy and I sing as we go, our voices chiming in the clear air.

'*And we'll all go together*
To pull wild mountain thyme
All around the blooming heather,
Will ye go, lassie, go? . . .'

Higher still, when we run out of songs of our own, a lark bursts from the cover of the yellow-flowered gorse, soaring like a tiny skyrocket into the blue above us. Against the silence, its song seems to hang, suspended, each note cut with perfect clarity, creating a necklace of sound. I stand stock-still and Daisy and I hold our breath, listening, until the bird is a tiny dot, high above the hills and its song is stolen away by the wind.

The path becomes a narrow, grassy track, more accustomed to the hooves of sheep and deer than to the soles of walking boots. At last, we turn the corner and there is the lochan, sheltered in its dip in the hillside. Daisy waves her arms in delight and laughs at the sight. Today, the water of the pool is scarcely visible. In a magical transformation, its peat-blackened depths are obscured by a coverlet of white waterlilies whose petals have been coaxed open by the sun's warmth.

I ease the carrier from my shoulders, rubbing the ache where the straps have pulled, and lean it against the lichen-spotted remains of one of the stone walls of the old bothy as I undo the buckles, lifting Daisy out. She immediately takes off on her sturdy little legs, red wellies sinking into the mossy ground, and I grab her, hugging her close and burying my face in the warmth of her neck. 'Oh no you don't, Miss Speedy! Water can be dangerous, remember? Here, hold my hand and we'll go and have a look together.'

We potter at the water's edge, peering between the reeds and the broad blades of yellow flags at the spot where an otter's tracks scar the damp ground, the telltale furrow of a heavy tail winding between the scrapings of the animal's sharp claws in the mud.

Once we've finished exploring the bankside, we settle ourselves in a little moss-lined hollow and sit on my coat, side by side, out of the wind in the shelter of the bothy's gable wall. The roof of the ancient building – once someone's home, perhaps, or a summer shelter for a hill shepherd – has fallen in completely, leaving only the collapsing shell of the walls and a blackened hearth beneath the chimney. While Daisy plays at making a cup and saucer with the waterlily that I've picked for her, humming busily to herself as she pours out imaginary pots of tea for me, I gaze out from our hillside perch beside the lochan to where the wider waters of the sea loch spread out below us. The light skims across its surface like a skipping stone, splintering into fragments that dazzle eyes more used to the grey of the winter sky.

It must be a trick of that same light because, for a moment, I imagine I see the hulks of great ships anchored there. Perhaps they are ghosts, shadows left behind from those years when the loch was a secret gathering place. I blink and they disappear, leaving only the water and the island with the open sea beyond.

A cloud passes across the face of the sun and, as the light shifts, suddenly I become aware of the deep, dark waters of the lochan, hidden beneath their drift of lilies. On the crest of the hill above us, a red deer hind watches silently, slipping away when I lift my head to meet her gaze. And then the shadows pass and the sunlight is back. From the slopes above us, I can hear the lark's song again. I wish it had words so that she could tell me all she knows.

For this spot, too – hidden above the sea in the arms of the hills – is a place of secrets. This is a place where lives began and lives ended. A place where the only witnesses were the skylarks and the deer.

Lexie, 1977

As I hurry along the street, weaving in and out through the crowds, the clock at Piccadilly Circus tells me what I already know: I'm late. And this audition is my big chance, a shot at a major female lead in a West End production. In my haste, I catch the platform toe of my boot on an uneven paving stone and trip, gasping with the sudden pain of it, stumbling against a passer-by.

'Sorry,' I mutter, but he doesn't even raise his head to acknowledge either the contact or the apology and we both hurry onwards, caught up in the rush of our busy lives.

I'm used to it now, the impersonality of the city, although at first, all those years ago, I found the move to London pretty tough. I missed Keeper's Cottage so much it hurt. And I missed my mother even more. She was my friend, my confidante, my greatest supporter and I thought of her often, alone in the little whitewashed house beside the loch. The city was full of people and lights and the sounds of the traffic. Even a cup of tea didn't taste the same as it did back home in the Scottish Highlands because the kettle in the galley kitchen in my digs was encrusted with phlegm-coloured limescale that tainted the water as it boiled.

But, at the same time, a part of me was relieved to have left Ardtuath. The anonymity of the city was welcome after the claustrophobia of living in a tiny community where everybody made it their business to know your business and no one was ever backward in coming forward with their considered opinion on it. My new life gave me a freedom that I'd never had at home and I was determined to move forward into my bright future without so much as a glance back over my shoulder.

I'd soon made friends at the stage school I was attending as a scholarship student and begun to adapt. The long hours of gruelling classes – dance, singing, acting – and the novel excitement of my urban life quickly replaced my old reality with a new and far more superficially glamorous one.

Of course, that reality wasn't really so glamorous at all. Up close, the costumes and make-up lost their magic under the glare of the spotlights, revealing their makeshift tackiness. We would change in cramped dressing rooms, vying for space in front of the mirror among a clutter of clothes, eyeliner and hairpins, where everything was covered in a fine layer of the powder that we used to set our make-up and kill the shine. The air would be heavy with the smells of sweat and stale perfume and the damp soot carried in on our coats from the London streets, and we would snap at each other, releasing little bursts of pre-performance nerves. But all of that would be forgotten in an instant with the adrenaline rush of the five-minute call.

Little by little, I've grown accustomed to walking for miles along streets where the air is filled with the stale breath of seven million people and the sky above is cut into dirty grey rectangles, glimpsed here and there between the buildings. It's a far cry from the skies over Loch Ewe, which arch from hills to horizon in an unbroken sweep. I've grown used to the London weather, too. Or rather to the lack of it. The seasons in the city are marked by the changing of the displays in the shop windows rather than any real climatic shifts: even in the middle of winter the city seems to generate its own heat, rising up from the damp pavements and radiating from the brick walls of the houses. Occasionally at first I used to miss the sense of wildness that the Scottish weather brings, the unfettered power of an Atlantic gale, the breathtaking chill of a clear, frosty morning and the first faint, elusive warmth of a spring day. But I quickly buried my hand-knitted jumpers at the back of the chest of drawers in my bedsit and replaced them with the figure-hugging cotton tops and floaty cheesecloth shirts that the other students wore, more suited to the fug of audition rooms and more likely to catch the eye of an agent or a producer. And I learned to drink coffee instead of tea, even though a cup cost more than a whole jar of the instant stuff that Mum would buy from the shop in Aultbea.

I duck into the alleyway that runs down one side of the theatre and shoulder open the stage door. My stomach churns with nerves and I swallow the bile that rises in my throat, which isn't going to help my voice one bit. The last few months have been stressful, finishing my run in *Carousel* and starting the whole gruelling process of going for auditions again. I've not been eating or sleeping very well. I tell myself the anxiety is entirely understandable, given the work situation and worries about how I'm going to pay my rent as my bank balance dwindles. But underneath that lies another horrible realisation that has dawned slowly but inexorably over recent weeks: Piers is losing interest in me. Maybe, just maybe, if I land this role then he'll love me again. Maybe we'll be able to recapture the passion and the excitement of those early days and everything will be all right.

I join the others who've already gathered backstage and shrug off my coat, running my fingers through my hair to smooth the unruly red-gold curls back into some semblance of order. 'Sorry,' I mouth at the production assistant, who ticks my name off on her clipboard. She flashes me a smile, too brief to be real, and then turns away. I recognise one or two of the others: the world of musical theatre is a small one. But we avoid meeting each other's eyes, concentrating on keeping our nerves under control and listening to the first hopeful to audition for the female lead. Competition for the role is going to be keen – the press is already buzzing with news of the Broadway revival and the London show is selling out.

I try to take deep breaths and focus on channelling the role of Mary Magdalene, but my attention wanders back to another audition, two years ago, in another theatre. It was for a production of *A Chorus Line,* directed by the brilliant Piers Walker whose star was in the ascendant on the West End theatre scene.

He singled me out at the audition. At the end of the exhausting day, he asked me to join him for a drink. He told me that he wanted me in the show even though I was more of a singer-who-could-dance than a dancer-who-could-sing, which was what they'd originally been looking for. He told me I had a luminosity, that I reminded him of a red-headed Audrey Hepburn. Later that evening, he told me he'd never met anyone like me. That I had a rare talent. That he could help me with my career. And that night, as we lay in the tangled sheets on the bed in my dingy digs, he told me I would be his muse and that together, we would blaze a trail to the very top of the industry.

I drank in his words as thirstily as I'd downed the glass of wine in the pub behind Drury Lane. How naïve I was: they both went straight to my head.

The infatuation has worn off now, two years later, and the reality of life has kicked in. Recently, Piers has been coming home later and later from the theatre, more than once mentioning the name of a new starlet who, he makes a point of telling me, really *gets* his vision and is a total *dream* to direct. I've begun to realise that he needs the affirmation of an audience far more than I do. Life is a performance for him and, like the productions he directs, each of his relationships seems to have its run before the novelty wears off and he moves on to the next one. I'm still clinging to the hope, though, that I will be the one to change all that. That I will be the one who makes him want to stay.

The constant anxiety is taking its toll. Sleepless nights and a feeling of nausea in the pit of my stomach have had an effect on my voice, although I'm not admitting that to anyone. Perhaps I've overstrained it a bit, trying out for several parts that have stretched my vocal range. But I can't afford to let that doubt affect me now. I need to push through today and put in a performance that will land me the female lead in *Jesus Christ Superstar.*

'Alexandra Gordon.' The production assistant calls my name. And so I step on to the stage and take a deep breath, determined that, even though my heart is fluttering against my breastbone like the wings of a trapped bird, my voice will soar free again, as effortlessly as the skylarks that fly above the hills surrounding my former home.

I land the part. And for a few weeks, Piers is as attentive as he used to be, bringing me flowers and taking me out for a celebratory meal. It's going to be all right, I think, breathing a big sigh of relief. But once rehearsals begin, I seem to be struggling more and more to reach the high notes. The director is concerned, and when he talks to me I can see his eyes flicker with the doubt that he's made the right choice for the role. Then one day a voice coach takes me aside and asks me if I'm okay.

'Fine,' I say, forcing a smile that's a good deal brighter than I'm feeling. 'It's been a difficult couple of months but I'm getting back on track. I've had a bit of a stomach bug, too, but I'm getting over it now. I've just been a little off form, but my voice will be fine once I'm fully recovered.' I hope I manage to sound convincing. Actually,

I've been feeling horribly queasy after downing a piece of toast and a cup of coffee this morning, but I've ploughed on determinedly and come in to work.

'All right.' She looks at me doubtfully. 'But Alexandra, I've seen this happen once before. I hope you don't mind my asking . . . are you pregnant?'

The second she says it, I know. It's as if I'd known already, I just hadn't admitted it to myself. Automatically my hands go to my belly as the blood drains from my face. A pregnant Mary Magdalene isn't going to look the part on stage, despite it presumably having been a hazard of her profession. I sway as the walls seem to collapse in around me.

The voice coach sits me down on a stool at the corner of the rehearsal room and presses my head towards my knees to stop me from fainting.

'It can happen,' she explains. 'In pregnancy the hormonal changes can cause the vocal cords to swell. It can affect your range. You've been straining to reach the notes and that can cause a bleed. You should see a specialist, get it checked out. And definitely rest your voice for a while.'

Piers's fury erupts with the force of an Atlantic storm. 'What a complete disaster,' he says when I tell him that evening, having seen a doctor who has confirmed both that I am pregnant and that I have what looks like a lesion on one of my vocal cords. I reach out to put my arms around him, desperately needing the reassurance of a hug, but he shakes me off.

'You'll have to get rid of it,' he says, the heat of his rage turning to a cold, hard anger as he turns away to pour himself a large Scotch.

For a moment I'm confused and think he's talking about the lesion. But then I'm dumbstruck with horror as I realise he means the baby. Abortion's been legal for ten years now, but I haven't even considered it as an option. I feel a connection to this child already, at once fiercely protective and lovingly tender.

He takes a gulp of whisky and goes on, 'Get rid of it and then if you need an operation on your throat they can sort that out. You don't want to lose this role.'

My head fills with white noise and I can't think straight. And then, through the confusion and the fear, I hear a thread of my mother's voice, singing the words of songs of love and loss in the kitchen at Keeper's Cottage:

'*Will ye gang love and leave me noo?*

Will ye forsake your ain love true?'

I know the answer to that question: there's no doubt what Piers is going to do. He has already left this relationship.

And then the noise in my head clears and there is no doubt in my mind, either. I'm going to have this baby and I'm going to raise it on my own. Perhaps my voice will mend in time. The voice coach said there was a chance it would, as long as the damage I've done to it isn't too bad. I'll need to see a specialist to know. But now that will have to wait a few months. I have some savings set aside which, at a pinch, I can live off until the baby is born and then I can get my career going again. It isn't over, just on hold. After all, other singers have combined children and a career. Why shouldn't I?

The Scotch has loosened Piers's tongue by now and when I tell him to leave he lets fly a stream of invective so bitter it makes me frightened for what he might do to our baby. He tells me he wants nothing to do with me ever again, that I am selfish to make this decision, that I'm just as self-centred as every other actress he's ever met. 'It's probably not even my child.' He pulls on his jacket and as he wrenches open the door, he flings back at me, 'It's not surprising they gave you that role – they clearly know a whore when they see one.'

I shut the door on his hateful words with a thud. The finality of the sound echoes off the walls. And then I collapse to the ground and lie curled on the grimy tiles of the hall floor, my knees drawn up to protect the flicker of new life in my belly as I sob into my hands. I feel completely alone.

But one thing's for sure, my life is in London now. There's no way I'm going back to Scotland.

Lexie, 1978

Thankfully Daisy's slept, strapped into her car seat, ever since we passed Inverness. I know that means it won't be easy getting her off to bed tonight, but I'd rather have the peace for the final miles. I turn off the cassette player, having grown heartily sick of our combined collection of nursery rhymes and West End show tunes over the two days that we've been in the car. The radio reception up here is non-existent, so I'm left with the humming of the engine and my own thoughts as the twisting road draws us north-westwards.

A sense of dread lodges itself in the pit of my stomach as we begin to approach the coast. I haven't been back once since I left Keeper's Cottage more than a dozen years ago. Of course, Mum came to see me several times during my career and from the way she went on about it, you'd have thought the journey down on the sleeper was the big event rather than watching her only child perform in *Oklahoma!* and *Carousel.* I suppose I always took it for granted that she'd be here, in the little stone croft house on the shores of Loch Ewe, if I ever wanted to come back. But coming back was something I definitely never wanted to do. I didn't even have the strength to arrange a funeral service in the kirk when Mum died in the hospital in Inverness. It was easier – and far more practical – to have a simple service at the crematorium in the city. I could sense the disappointment and disapproval among the small band of villagers who made the journey to say their final farewells to Flora Gordon even as they shook my hand and muttered their condolences on that awful, empty day.

So now I am returning, at last, reluctantly, having run out of options. And it's too late. Mum has gone. I still can't really absorb the finality of those words. How can I carry on without her? The two of us were a team. As long as we had each other, we never needed anyone else. She was the one who gave me the confidence to leave, encouraging me to apply to the stage school and helping me pack my suitcase when the time came. I always knew that even though we were so many miles apart, she was always right there with me in spirit when I stepped on to the stage to sing. But now I'm on my own, with my baby, whom I know will be referred to behind my back as a *fatherless bairn*. There are worse insults, of course, and I've no doubt those will be put to good use, too. There will be the whisper of gossip in the lane, and the tutting of tongues at the kirk gate. And they will say that history has a funny way of repeating itself, and what would you expect from a girl who was born out of wedlock herself and went gallivanting off to the theatres of the big city? *She had the voice for it, though*, they'll admit; but then they'll shake their heads and say *for all the good that's done her*.

Daisy wakes up, startled from her sleep as the car rattles over a cattle grid with a clatter. She wails in dismay at finding herself still strapped into her car seat, and squirms, straining to get out, building up to a really good tantrum.

'Okay, sweetheart,' I say. 'We're nearly there. We just need to stop at the shop for a few things.'

It's sorely tempting to drive on through the village, past the old gateposts that mark the entrance to the long-deserted Ardtuath Estate, going straight to Keeper's Cottage so that I can hang on to the precious, final shreds of anonymity for a few more hours. But I'm dying for a cup of tea – and something stronger, too. And I'll be needing food for supper. There'll be nothing edible in the house, which has been empty for months.

If I'm being totally honest, the thought of unlocking the door and stepping over the threshold into the chilly, darkening silence of rooms that were always so full of life and light terrifies me. Stopping to do some shopping will delay the moment when I have to confront the bare truth of the things I've been trying so hard to ignore for so long. Loss. And guilt. And grief.

I pull up in front of the shop and groan, catching a whiff of a decidedly less-than-fresh Daisy, who's now screaming at the top of her lungs. 'Sorry, precious girl, you'll just have to wait a few more minutes till we get to the house.'

I balance her on my hip, sending up a quick prayer that the shop will be deserted. I push the door open and the bell pings, although it's drowned out by Daisy who is doing a much better job of announcing our entrance. My prayer has obviously gone unheard, as they mostly do. Several heads turn.

'Och, Lexie Gordon, it's yourself. Come home to Ardtuath at long last!'

Daisy's wails have ceased for a moment as she takes a gulp of air and so the greeting is loud in the sudden silence that has fallen, reminding me that Alexandra Gordon, star of the musical stage, whose name was once printed on West End show bills, is long gone: here, I am – and always will be – Lexie.

'We were just saying that we couldn't recognise the car, thinking it must be some incomer. And look at this bonny wee lass, the pride and joy of her granny – may her dear, departed soul rest in peace.' Bridie Macdonald bustles towards us, her flow of words washing over me like a wave. When she finally pauses to draw breath, she recoils slightly, nostrils aquiver, as the rich smell that has escaped from Daisy's nappy reaches her.

'Hello, Bridie.' I nod a vague greeting towards the others, too, a blur of faces assembled by the till, too harassed to be able to single out individuals among the group. I juggle Daisy on to my shoulder, reach for a basket and begin to trawl the cramped aisles of the shop for what I need. Bridie follows close on my heels, asking a stream of questions and clucking distractions at Daisy who's started screaming again.

I answer as civilly as I can manage. 'Yes, I'm back. Yes, it has been far too long. Yes, I'm afraid she's not very presentable after a day in the car. I've just stopped in to pick up these few bits and pieces, and then I'll get her up to the cottage and sort her out.'

I chuck in some tea and biscuits, my progress hampered by Daisy's squirming, Bridie's questions and a cluster of shrimping nets on bamboo poles that I knock over as I try to manoeuvre past them to reach for a pint of milk.

'No, I'm not sure how long I'll be staying. No, I've no particular plans at the moment. No, I'm still not singing again. Yes, I'll need to do some clearing out of Mum's things. That's a very kind offer, but I'll probably be able to manage on my own, thank you. No, I've no particular plans to sell Keeper's Cottage just yet.'

Bordering on desperation now, I throw a few more items into my basket – four shrivelled carrots and a tattered leek, and then a bottle of tonic water. I search for a lemon but there are none, save the ones made of bright yellow squeezy plastic. There are no potatoes left either, so I grab a packet of Smash and, because I am already beyond cooking anything from scratch, a tinned steak and kidney pie.

Finally, I reach the till. The assembled group there has been in no hurry to move on, happy to let Bridie ask her questions and to listen with interest to my answers. Their judgement hovers above my head like a sparrowhawk intent on its prey. I set the basket down and adjust my grip on my soggy, smelly daughter, thankful that she's fallen quiet at last. When I glance over my shoulder I realise that her silence is a result of the chocolate buttons Bridie is feeding her, which Daisy is dribbling down the back of my suede jacket. I bought this jacket in another lifetime, when I had money and a lifestyle that went with such luxurious garb. Now I wear it because I can't afford to buy anything more practical. I'm aware how it must look, though. Like its owner, this jacket doesn't belong here.

I smile at Morag behind the till. The group of women watch, assessing each item as Morag rings it up and then packs it into a cardboard box, emblazoned with a logo, which reminds me . . . 'Oh, and a bottle of gin, too, please.'

She reaches one down from the shelf behind her and I carefully avoid catching the eye of any of the other women. Their unspoken judgement hangs even more heavily in the air. I pay and then look up at last with a defiant smile at the assembled company.

'Hello, Lexie,' says a blonde-haired young woman with a push-chair, from which an immaculately dressed toddler, just a little older than Daisy, watches the scene with wide blue eyes. It takes me a second to recognise her.

'Elspeth? Hi. It's good to see you. And you have a wee one too now?'

We were friends at school, but lost touch when I moved south.

She nods. But makes no further attempt at conversation.

Awkwardly, I bend to gather up the cardboard box of groceries, balancing the weight of Daisy in my other arm. She smiles beatifically at Bridie, Morag, Elspeth and the other womenfolk, her cheeks flushed, her eyelashes spiky with her recent tears.

'Here,' says Bridie, 'let me give you a hand with that.'

She tries to take the box of groceries from me, but I shake my head. If she sees that my car is packed to the roof with my worldly belongings it'll be a dead giveaway: as well as clearly doing a very poor job of raising my fatherless child, she'll know that I have slunk back to Ardtuath, homeless, my tail between my legs, my career in tatters, several months too late to care for my poor abandoned mother in the last days of her life.

'Don't worry, I can manage. If you could maybe just open the door for me? Thanks.'

As I balance the box on the bonnet of the car and dig in my bag for my keys, the tinned pie topples and clatters on to the tarmac. Behind the window of the shop, several faces turn in our direction.

I open the door and bundle Daisy into her car seat. Not surprisingly, she makes her thoughts on this outrage known at the top of her lungs. I wrestle the straps over her flailing arms without a word because if I open my mouth I'm not sure I'll be able to restrain myself either from swearing loud and long or bursting into tears.

I turn to pick up the pie from the road. But Elspeth stands there, her big-eyed baby gazing up at me inscrutably from her pushchair.

'Here,' she says, holding out the dented tin.

'Thanks. Not much of a supper, but it'll have to do for tonight.' My embarrassment and shame make me babble nervously.

Elspeth nods, glancing through the windows of the car, taking in the box of kitchen stuff and the desk lamp that are wedged against the glass. She looks as if she's about to say something, then thinks better of it and turns her pushchair around. 'Be seeing you.'

'Yeah.' I stand there lamely for a moment, watching as she wheels her fragrant, neatly dressed baby back along the road, turning in at the gate of one of the houses that overlook the harbour before manoeuvring the pushchair through its yellow-painted front door.

Then I ease my stiff limbs back into the driver's seat and take a deep breath before turning the key in the ignition. 'Right then,

Daisy,' I say, as cheerfully as I can, hoping she doesn't hear the wobble in my voice, 'Keeper's Cottage, here we come.'

The sound of knocking awakens me the next morning. After being up into the small hours, the pair of us had at long last collapsed and fallen into a deep, deep sleep before the dawn began to suffuse the sky beyond the hills.

Our disrupted night owed a good deal to Daisy's refusal to go to sleep in the silent and unfamiliar darkness: she'd been used to the background hum of traffic and the glow of a light-polluted city diluting the blackness to the colour of weak orange squash, tucked into her own cot in her own bedroom. By the time I'd changed her and fed her, waiting for the immersion heater to warm the water enough for a shallow bath, and then got her ready for bed, she was wide awake, enjoying the novelty of the tiny cottage filled with my mother's things. To prevent her from wreaking destruction among the ornaments and photos that cluttered the sitting room, I attempted to remove the lid from the battered pie tin at the same time as juggling Daisy on my hip.

After wrestling for several minutes with the ancient tin opener and the dented metal encasing my supper, and having ripped a gash in my finger that dripped bright blood everywhere, eventually I admitted defeat. Wrapping a wad of loo paper around my wound, I turned off the oven and poured myself a gin and tonic instead. Then I took Daisy through to the bedroom and made up the bed, an awkward job with my injured hand. Someone must have been in, as the mattress had been stripped and the linens laundered and stacked back neatly in the airing cupboard.

I knew there was an old wooden cot in the attic, the one I'd slept in at the foot of this same bed in this same room when I was a baby, but by now I was beyond fetching the ladder from the shed, finding the cot and bringing it down, then assembling it. So I tucked Daisy into a nest made out of blankets and curled up on the bed beside her. But she was having none of it. Clean, cosy and well fed now, she was a new woman and ready for some fun and games after her long and boring day in the car. Even in my exasperation, I couldn't help laughing as she rolled herself over and over, tangling the bedcovers around us both.

I tried singing softly to her, but the sound of my cracked voice brought the tears to my eyes and so I stopped. I fished her favourite Blue Bunny out of the bag of her toys and found a picture book. But gymnastics were more what she had in mind and so I bounced her on my tummy, her little legs working like pistons, in an attempt to wear her out. After half an hour, my arms were aching almost as much as my head. The gin was a bad idea, I decided, and I scooped up both Daisy and my half-full glass and went back through to the kitchen. I left the glass on the table next to the gin bottle, then wandered through to the sitting room to gaze out of the window.

The old windowpanes had always let in a bit of a draught and so I wrapped Daisy in the shawl Mum had knitted for her when she was born, its pattern of scallop shells as delicate as the finest lace. I stroked her back, trying to lull her into sleepiness, the white wool soft beneath my fingertips. For a moment, an image of my mum sitting beside the fire, the cobweb-fine skein of this same wool in her lap as her knitting needles flew, threatened to overwhelm me again. I shook my head and blinked back the tears, too tired to cry any more today.

The moon was rising behind the cottage, casting a path across the loch. It was high tide and I could just make out the water lapping softly at the sand beyond the road's edge. Oblivious to my maudlin weariness, Daisy cooed and chattered, pointing a chubby forefinger at the window and naming each new sight in her own matter-of-fact way. 'Dat,' she said, and, 'Dat.'

The silence of the night was broken occasionally by the cry of a curlew from the shore. As I spoke softly to my baby daughter, kissing her freshly washed hair and rocking her gently on my shoulder, the quiet sound of an engine out on the loch made us both look up. A small fishing boat slipped across the sliver of moonlight, leaving a streamer of stars dancing in its wake where the propeller had stirred up the phosphorescence.

'Dat,' said Daisy, with emphasis.

'I know, it's beautiful, isn't it?' I replied. 'A boat.'

'Bat,' said Daisy, and I laughed.

'That's right, clever girl.'

We watched until the lights in the water stopped their dance and all became still once more. 'Come on, sweetheart,' I said. 'It's bedtime now.'

But Daisy had other ideas.

By two in the morning both of us were reduced to exhausted tears. It was only after she'd sobbed herself to sleep that I dried my own eyes on the hem of the sheet, curled myself around her, pulling the shawl over us both, and sank, at last, into oblivion . . .

The knocking at the door that awakens me is muffled by my dreams at first, and I surface slowly from the depths of sleep, floating towards the surface and the daylight as the noise persists, drawing me upwards.

Carefully, so as not to disturb Daisy, I untangle myself from the blankets and pull on the dressing gown that hangs on the back of the bedroom door. I fling open the front door, ready to confront the inconsiderate person who's making such a din at this unholy hour of the morning.

The words die on my lips, though, at the sight of the man who stands there, outlined against the steel-grey waters of the loch, the wind ruffling his hair.

Taken aback, I run a hand over my own dishevelled curls and pull the dressing gown cord a little tighter about my waist.

'Can I help you?' My voice is icy, despite the warmth of his smile.

'Hello, Lexie. I'm Davy Laverock.' He pauses for a moment, as if the name should mean something to me. There's an awkward silence while I rack my brains. Nope. Nothing. Other than '*laverock*' being the Scots word that Mum used to use for the skylarks nesting in the hills above the loch. I stare at him blankly.

He looks away, his smile faltering slightly, then holds out a carrier bag. 'Bridie said to bring you these.'

I take the bag from him and glance inside. It's heavy with a haul of squatties, the langoustine-like squat lobsters that fishermen often catch in their creels. My mouth waters at the sight of the tangle of coral carapaces: there's no commercial demand for them but they are absolutely delicious boiled in a pan of water drawn from the loch and served with a dish of mayonnaise or garlic butter. The hard work involved in extracting the meat from their armoured tails is well worth a broken fingernail or two.

'Thank you,' I say. 'And thanks to Bridie, too.'

'She said you'd just arrived back. Thought you could use them.'

The gossip-wires are already humming, then.

We stand there awkwardly, and I scan his face again, looking for any clues that will help me place him. He has the open, buoyant expression of a man completely at ease with himself, slate-blue eyes set in a weather-beaten complexion. He clearly belongs to the area and thinks that I will know who he is, in the taken-for-granted way that everyone here knows where they – and everybody else – fit in.

'Sorry about your mum,' he says at last. 'Is everything okay in the house? I know Bridie's been in to check a couple of times. But if you need a hand with anything, just let me know.' He glances past me as he says this. His expression flickers and I sense that his attention has been caught by something behind me. Looking round, I realise it's the sight of the gin bottle standing next to a half-empty glass. I know what he must be thinking. And at this time in the morning, too. Then I catch sight of the kitchen clock and see it's later than I thought – nearly ten. But even so . . .

I look back at him defiantly. 'Yeah, that's not what it looks like. It's about as far as I got with supper last night.'

He shrugs. 'I'm not judging.'

Aye, right. I give it half an hour, tops, before that titbit is fed back to Bridie.

'Anyway, enjoy the squatties. If you'd like more ever, I'm out most days with the creels. Leave me a message on the jetty.'

I relent a little, realising how ungracious I've been. 'Thanks, really. I'll enjoy these.'

'No bother. Well then, be seeing you around.'

I watch as he strides back to a Land Rover parked at the side of the road, whistling a snatch of a tune as he goes. He has the broad shoulders and loping gait that are typical of a fisherman. I recognise the song as it's the one Mum used to sing so often. He gets in and starts the engine, glancing briefly back towards the cottage and raising a hand in salute as he pulls away.

I tip the flat remnants of last night's drink into the sink and stow the gin bottle away in a cupboard. Then I stash the bag of squat lobsters into the fridge, and find that I'm humming a verse of the song he was whistling, which is now running on a loop in my head. I even try a few words of the chorus: '*Will ye gang love . . .*' But I stop when my voice cracks with emotion.

Something stirs in the depths of my memory. Maybe there *was* something familiar about those slate-blue eyes of his, but I can't quite place him. I reach to grasp at dim thoughts, but they dart away, just beyond my reach, slippery as fish.

I fill the kettle from the tap and set it on the stove to boil. As I take the old brown teapot down from its place on the shelf, a breaker of grief crashes over me, knocking the breath from my chest. Mum's voice seems to fill the kitchen around me, singing that same song, and I hug the pot to my heart.

'Oh dig my grave both lang and deep
Put a bunch o' roses at my head and feet
And in the middle a turtle dove,
Let the people ken that I died o' love . . .'

She always had a pot of tea on the go, forever bringing me a mug whether I wanted it or not. But the sight of that old teapot makes me realise that they were never just cups of tea she was giving me. They were some of the punctuation marks that helped make sense of our story together – those little pauses and connections that I took for granted. Those cups of tea were just one of the ways she let me know she loved me, several times a day.

With the words of her song still echoing in my head, I go through to the sitting room and take the photo of my dad off the mantelpiece. His dark eyes are unfathomable, hidden in shadow in the picture, which is the only one I have of him. His name was Alec Mackenzie-Grant, he was in the navy, and he died before I was born. But I know little else about him. When I'd pester Mum to tell me stories of him she always spoke of his kindness, of how he'd loved her and how he would have loved me had he known me. But when I pushed her to tell me more, when I asked her about his parents – my grandparents – and his life as the laird's son up at the big house, she'd been evasive. She'd always change the subject, saying, 'Did I tell you about the time Alec and your Uncle Ruaridh went out in the boat to catch mackerel and saw a basking shark?' And although I'd heard the story a hundred times, I'd let her tell it again.

It was only as I grew older that I realised how hard it must have been for her, contemplating the life she might have had as mistress of Ardtuath House and perhaps regretting the life she'd not been able to give me. And so I learned to stop asking those questions, which only made her look so sad. But I always wondered about my dad – who he really was and why Mum was reluctant to talk about his side of the family. Her stories were of the innocence of childhood, an innocence that the tides of war must have swept away. It's understandable that there were things she wanted to protect me from, things she wanted to forget. But now I regret not asking her again. I regret not knowing their story. I regret that it's a part of my own story that is now lost to me.

I set his picture back in its place, next to the one of my mum. I don't even have a photo of the pair of them together and that thought saddens me even more.

The kettle whistles as the water comes to the boil, calling me back to the here and now, and I wipe a tear away on the sleeve of my dressing gown. Back in the kitchen I warm the pot, spoon in the leaves from the tin caddy on the counter and let them steep. A proper pot of tea, just the way my mum, Flora, always made it.

And then I hear Daisy stirring and I hurry back to scoop her up from the bed and make her day begin with a smile.

Flora, 1939

Flora Gordon added peat to the range and set the kettle on the stovetop to boil. The waters of the loch were just beginning to turn pearly-grey in the light of the dawn. Her father would be home any minute, back from giving the animals their early feed, and he'd be needing his breakfast and a warming cup of tea.

She heard his boots on the path, accompanied by the lighter patter of Braan's paws. The black Labrador was always at his side, whether he was checking on the ponies in the field and the working dogs in their kennel behind the steading, or out on the hill keeping an eye on the game birds and deer for which, as keeper on the Ardtuath Estate, he was responsible.

She hummed a tune softly under her breath and the kettle joined in, muttering and whistling to itself. She set the pan of oatmeal that had been steeping all night on to the heat, adding a pinch of salt and giving it a good stir. Then she warmed the brown teapot and spooned in the leaves from the caddy, her movements quick and deft with the efficiency born of habit.

Braan bounced through the kitchen door, tail wagging, looking for a pat from her before burying his snout in the tin bowl containing his own breakfast.

'All right, Dad?' she asked, expecting that the answer would be his usual silent nod as he took his seat at the head of the table and stretched out his feet in their thick woollen socks towards the warmth of the range.

But this morning he went instead to stand at the window looking out across the loch. 'Looks like we have visitors,' he said, nodding towards the water.

Drying her hands on the cloth that hung beside the stove, Flora joined him.

In the silence of the early light, a line of ships slid into view. Their grey hulls moved slowly, but with a power that parted the waves with ease. The air around them appeared to vibrate, agitating the seabirds that wheeled above them. She counted five vessels. They seemed to have materialised like leviathans risen from the waters of the loch, awoken from their slumber by the declaration, just ten days ago, that Britain was now at war with Germany.

Her father picked up the pair of binoculars from the windowsill and looked through the sights. Wordlessly, he passed them to Flora. The ships bristled with guns and antennae and as they drew closer she could hear the thrum of their engines.

'That'll be the Home Fleet then, I reckon,' her father said.

Flora shivered with a mixture of excitement and apprehension. 'But what would they be doing here? The war is hundreds of miles away.'

Her father looked at her shrewdly from beneath his shock of white hair. 'It *was* hundreds of miles away, lass. But not any more.'

'Might Ruaridh be on one of them, do you think?' Flora's heart leapt at the thought. Her brother had joined the Royal Navy two years before, and she sorely missed him. Like so many lads who'd grown up on that coast, he was as at home on the water as he was on the hills.

'I doubt it. His last letter said he was in Portsmouth, assigned to destroyers. They're smaller than those battleships out there. He could be deployed anywhere by now.'

As they watched, the leading ship manoeuvred slowly to a halt and dropped anchor with a rattle of chains audible even at this distance. Flora handed the binoculars back to her father. 'What do you think they're doing here in Loch Ewe?'

He shrugged. 'Your guess is as good as mine. I'm sure we'll find out soon enough.'

He turned away from the window, but not before she'd glimpsed the look in his eyes. Although his bearing was as upright as ever and his manner as calm as usual, she could tell the war filled him with dread. He was fearful for what it meant for his son, far away in England, and now the arrival of these warships in the peaceful waters of the loch below Keeper's Cottage had brought that sense of dread right up to their front door. The presence of her tall, capable father who was so at ease in these hills – a man trusted by the laird to oversee the Ardtuath Estate and a figure so respected in the lochside community – had always made her feel safe. But that glimpse of fear in his eyes made her feel that a fault line had cracked open in the ground beneath her feet, disturbing the equilibrium of their lives.

As if sensing her uneasiness, Braan pushed his nose into the palm of her hand, reassuring her. And then she turned away from the window and dished the porridge into the waiting bowls.

The post office was so busy that the queue doubled back on itself in the crowded space of the little shop. It seemed that half of the village either had a letter to post that morning or a sudden need to buy an envelope and a stamp or two. Flora joined the line, but no one was in any great hurry to reach the counter to be served by Miss Cameron, the postmistress. Instead, there was a hum of conversation that revolved entirely around the arrival of the Home Fleet on their doorsteps.

'That big ship in the middle is HMS *Nelson* and they have Mr Churchill on board.' Mrs Carmichael was a fount of knowledge on most matters, not only restricted to those directly relating to her pivotal role as chairwoman of the local branch of the Scottish Women's Rural Institute. With all three of her sons off to the war with the Argyll and Sutherland Highlanders, it was generally acknowledged that she was entitled to hold forth on military matters, too. And now that her husband, Archibald Carmichael, had assumed the role of air-raid warden, her source of local information was second to none.

'What is it they're doing here in Loch Ewe?' asked Bridie Macdonald, who had reached the front of the queue and was busy licking stamps. She handed her letters back to Miss Cameron for the postbag. 'A quarter of pan drops, too, please.'

The postmistress reached the tall jar of sweets down from the shelves behind her and weighed them out, tipping the mints from the scales into a white paper bag and twisting the corners to seal it. 'There you go.' She sorted the coins Bridie handed over into the till.

'It's top secret, Archie says,' Mrs Carmichael replied.

'They're probably scouting out places to base the Fleet, ready to defend us if there's an invasion of U-boats from the north.'

'Wheesht, Bridie, you know what they say . . . *careless talk costs lives.*'

Bridie was about to point out indignantly that Mrs Carmichael had just announced to any German agents who happened to be waiting in the queue for stamps and sweets that the First Lord of the Admiralty himself was on one of the ships out there on the loch, but she thought better of it and popped a mint into her mouth instead. Mrs Carmichael was, in build and in temperament, not unlike one of those battleships and Bridie was neither brave enough nor foolish enough to give her any cheek.

'Instead of standing about gossiping, you can come along to the hall this afternoon and lend a hand. The Rural is knitting scarves for our boys at the front and we need all the help we can get. Can I count you in? You too, Flora?'

It was impossible to say no to Moira Carmichael. Both girls nodded obediently. 'Very good. Three o'clock sharp. Bring your own needles. Wool will be provided.' She picked up her basket as the door pinged. 'Ah, Mairi, I hope we can count you in as well?'

Flora turned to greet her best friend with a smile.

Mairi Macleod shrugged cheerfully. 'Count me in for what?'

'We're knitting scarves for soldiers,' Bridie chipped in, the pan drop in her mouth clicking against her teeth. 'Three o'clock sharp, in the hall.'

'I'll expect all three of you girls to be there then,' said Mrs Carmichael, sweeping regally out of the door.

The queue shuffled forward, filling the not inconsiderable gap.

'Any word from Ruaridh?' Mairi asked.

Flora shook her head. 'Not since last week.' She held up the envelope she was carrying. 'I'm just sending him a letter now.'

Glancing out of the window toward the hulks moored in the bay, Mairi said, 'I wonder how long they're going to stay?'

One of them had a plume of dark smoke rising from its funnel and from another, small launches were being lowered into the leaden water. There were signs of activity on the decks of the others as well, figures hurrying purposefully to and fro.

'I've no idea,' Flora replied. 'Maybe they're just passing through on their way to somewhere else.' But Bridie's words still rang in her ears. Could they be scouting for places to harbour ships? Was this something more permanent? Only time – and perhaps Mrs Carmichael – would tell.

Flora and Mairi sat by the range, chatting companionably as their knitting needles flew. The balls of grey wool that had been handed out at the meeting of the Rural two days before were rapidly being transformed into scarves, made to Mrs Carmichael's exact specifications.

'This grey is a bit drab,' sighed Flora, setting her knitting aside to put the kettle on.

'I know,' agreed Mairi. 'But I suppose it's regulation issue.'

'Ach, surely a little bit of colour can't hurt. Look, I have this remnant of red. I'm going to add a wee stripe of colour, just at one end. That way, whichever soldier ends up wearing it will know we wanted to cheer him up.'

Mairi laughed and dug into her workbasket, holding up a skein of daffodil-yellow wool. 'Good idea. Even just a row or two will make it a bit more personal.'

From the loch, the blast of a ship's siren caused a flurry of sandpipers to rise from the shore, taking fright. Over the past couple of days, more ships had arrived, including one that was said to be laying anti-submarine nets across the mouth of Loch Ewe.

'What's going on now?' Mairi raised her head from her work, craning her neck to see out of the kitchen window.

'More ships coming in,' said Flora, absent-mindedly tucking a strand of her russet-gold hair back into the braid that hung down her back. 'Maybe Bridie's guess was right the other day. There do seem to be an awful lot of them now.' The stretch of water between the shore and the island teemed with vessels of all sizes, from the great battleships with their vertical prows and towering turrets to smaller and faster destroyers and cruisers. The launches that buzzed back and forth between the gathering fleet appeared tiny alongside the imposing grey hulks.

Slower and more cumbersome than the launches, two fat tugs chugged back and forth in the distance, out towards the mouth of the loch. They were rumoured by Bridie, who'd heard it from Mrs

Carmichael, to be laying a boom that stretched from the end of the island across to the rocks on each of the opposite shores in order to protect the harbour, keeping out any U-boats that might manage to slip past the nets fixed across the mouth of the loch.

Flora set the tea to steep and picked up her knitting again, splicing in a strand of the red wool and deftly working another row of neat stitches. When the front door opened she barely glanced up, expecting Braan to come bouncing in ahead of her father, the pair of them just down from the hill. But the next moment she had jumped to her feet, knitting thrown aside, and flung her arms around the young man in his blue and white naval uniform who stood in the kitchen doorway.

'Ruaridh!' she cried. 'Oh, we hoped you'd be on one of those ships. Dad will be so pleased.'

Her brother grinned, picking her up and swinging her around until she couldn't tell whether she was giddy with the whirling or with the joy of seeing him. Setting her back on her feet, he reached to give Mairi a hug, too. 'Glad to see you're keeping yourselves busy. Any chance of a cup of tea?' he said matter-of-factly, as if he'd just popped out that very morning instead of it being nearly three months since his last leave.

'How long are you here for?' asked Mairi.

'Not long at all. I've managed to wangle an hour ashore, that's all. We've come to accompany the *Nelson* north. We'll be leaving tonight.' He settled himself at the table, stretching out his long legs.

'Which is your ship?' Flora asked, passing him a cup.

'The *Ordie*. She's over there towards the island. See those three destroyers? She's the one on the right.'

'Will you be coming back?'

'Hard to say.' He blew on his tea and then took a sip. 'It all depends on where the action is. But for now it's just great to be sitting here at home with my two favourite lassies.'

'Didn't you meet anyone in Portsmouth then? A girl in every port, as they say,' teased Mairi. Although Flora had used to secretly hope that one day her best friend and her brother might become a couple, she knew that Mairi was more like a second little sister to Ruaridh.

'Och, they kept us far too busy with our training for boring things like war, so I'm afraid I have nothing to report on that front.'

Just then the door was pushed open and Braan burst into the kitchen, giving a yelp of joy at the sight of Ruaridh who leaned forward in his chair to fondle the Labrador's ears. 'Good dog, Braan. Where's your master then?'

'Here,' said Iain Gordon, pulling the tweed deerstalker from his head and stuffing it into the pocket of his jacket as he stepped across the threshold. 'I knew there was something up when Braan turned and raced down the hill. Thought it might be you, son.'

Ruaridh stood and embraced his father and Mairi began to roll up her knitting, stowing it in her basket.

'I'll be off now,' she said. 'Best be getting back to help Mum with the supper and the weans.' Mairi was the oldest of six, her siblings ranging in age from fourteen years down to five, which possibly accounted for her reserves of patient good humour. Her parents were hard-working farmers, with sheep and a herd of milking cows that kept the Macleods busy from dawn until dusk every day. Flora envied her and her sprawling family, but Mairi always joked that she'd happily swap them for a big brother like Ruaridh who could introduce her to his friends. 'Take care of yourself, Ruaridh Gordon. And I hope we see you back here before long.'

'Bye, Mairi. It's been good seeing you.' He glanced at his own watch. 'I'll not be able to stay long, Dad, just a few minutes more. I've to report back on board by five. But I couldn't pass up the chance to come home, even just for half an hour.'

Once he'd downed the dregs of his tea, Ruaridh got to his feet, setting his cap firmly back on his head and bending to give Braan's silken ears one last stroke. 'Be seeing you then, Dad.'

'Aye. Soon enough.'

Flora sensed the ocean of words, unspoken since they had no need of saying, that surged and tugged beneath the surface of their matter-of-fact parting. She fetched her thick gansey down from the hook by the door. 'I'll chum you back to the jetty,' she said, wanting to spin out the precious time they had together for as long as possible.

And then the brother and sister set off down the track, turning on to the road that skirted the water's edge. There was more traffic than usual – a purposeful to-ing and fro-ing of jeeps and trucks filled with soldiers and sailors – and they constantly had to step aside on to the grassy verge to make way for the speeding vehicles. Ruaridh was telling her about life on board the ship and his job as a signalman as they passed the main gates of the estate, when the hoot of a horn made them turn and look up the drive. A sleek burgundy-coloured saloon car was bouncing over the potholes towards them.

'It's Alec!' Ruaridh sprang forward as the car pulled up alongside them, reaching to shake the hand of the young man, also in naval uniform, who had hailed them.

'Ruaridh. You're here too! And Flora.' He shook each of their hands in turn. 'It's been years. But it's so good to see you both again. Allow me to introduce my fiancée, Diana Kingsley-Scott.' The elegant young woman sitting in the passenger seat looked a little bored, but waved a languid hand bedecked with a large sapphire engagement ring in their direction.

'Congratulations! We hadn't heard the news.' Ruaridh clapped Alec on the shoulder.

'I only popped the question last week. We thought we should come and tell my parents before the official announcement appears in *The Times* tomorrow.'

Alec Mackenzie-Grant's smile hadn't changed a bit since the days when the three of them had spent hours together as children, making pirate dens in the copse above Ardtuath House and sailing paper boats down the burn. He hadn't been like the other boys in the playground at the tiny primary school they'd all attended, who'd ignored Flora, deeming her beneath acknowledgement on the twin counts of being a year younger and a girl. She remembered how he'd included her in the boys' games, how he'd run over to back her up when she'd confronted Willie McTaggart over his bullying of Bridie, and how he'd picked her to be on his team for sports day. He and Ruaridh had been best friends during those carefree years, before Alec was sent away to prep school when he turned ten. And although their educational circumstances had separated them during term-time from that point on, the laird's son and the keeper's son had remained firm friends in the school holidays until the time came when Alec went off to university and spent his time at the family home in London or visiting friends in England in the breaks. Even though they'd drifted apart, the years seemed to fall away now that he was back.

'Where are you headed?' Alec asked.

'Back to the jetty at Aultbea,' replied Ruaridh. 'I just managed to grab an hour ashore to come and see Dad and Flora. We sail tonight as escort to the *Nelson*.'

'Well, that's reassuring to know.' Alec grinned. 'I'll be on board. You're on one of the destroyers, are you? Fantastic. Hop in, we'll give you a lift. Unless you'd rather walk, of course.' He shot a look at Flora. 'And you're welcome to come, too, if you want. I know how precious time with family is.'

'All right, and then I'll stretch my legs on the walk back,' she answered.

The Gordons climbed into the back of the car, which smelled of new leather.

'I'm just running Diana back to Achnasheen to catch the train,' Alec said.

'Where is home for you, Miss Kingsley-Scott?' Ruaridh asked politely.

'Kensington,' she replied. The flatness of her tone didn't invite further questions.

There was a moment's awkward silence and then Alec said, 'Diana's thinking of getting a job in the diplomatic service. Doing her bit for the war effort.'

'Flora's been knitting all afternoon, doing her bit, too,' Ruaridh said.

Flora blushed with shame. It sounded very tame in comparison with 'getting a job in the diplomatic service'.

As Alec drove she sat in silence, listening as the two men compared their experiences in the navy so far. They'd missed each other in Dartmouth, where Ruaridh had recently completed his signalman's training soon after Alec had passed out from the Naval College as a sub-lieutenant assigned to the Home Fleet; and they must have overlapped at Portsmouth just last month, although their paths hadn't crossed there among the melee of gathering ships.

On the headland before Aultbea, Alec pulled off the road and cut the engine, rolling down the window to let the sea air fill the car. In the sudden stillness, the four of them sat in silence, listening to the sound of the water's quiet surge and the cries of the seabirds. For a few moments no one spoke. Diana tapped a manicured fingernail impatiently against the crocodile-skin handbag cradled on her lap.

Flora glanced across at her brother's profile. The breadth of his shoulders was emphasised by the wide collar of his naval tunic and beneath his cap his sandy hair was cut short, making a stranger of him as he sat watching the distant bustle of activity in the loch.

She switched her gaze to Alec's back. His shoulders were equally broad, but his cap lay on the back seat beside her and his straight black hair was ruffled by the breeze. The thought of them boarding their ships and facing the dangers out there on the cruel, unforgiving sea filled her with fear. She swallowed to try to relieve the tightness of her throat as she pictured them leaving the safe embrace of the hills surrounding Loch Ewe and heading northwards into the swell of the open sea. Blinking to clear the tears, she caught sight of the reflection of Alec's smile in the car's rear-view mirror. He was watching her watching them, his eyes still those of the childhood friend who had always been her champion and protector.

He turned to face her, resting his arm along the back of the driving seat. 'How's your father?' he asked.

In the early years of his youth, Alec had spent more time with the keeper of the estate than he had with his own father. Sir Charles was only ever interested in shooting and fishing with the friends he invited up from London when he came north, and was very often absent from Ardtuath on business in England, leaving Lady Helen and his son to their own devices.

'He's well.' Flora smiled back at him, suddenly conscious of the bagginess of the woollen gansey and the unruly, wind-blown strands of hair that had escaped from her braid. She tucked a wayward lock behind her ear. 'Busy, now he's doing the factor's work, too, but he enjoys having charge of the estate, I think.'

When Sir Charles's manager had left to join up a few weeks ago, Ruaridh and Flora's father had quietly stepped in to keep everything running smoothly for Lady Helen in her husband's absence.

Alec nodded. 'Ma said he's doing a great job. My father will be up again soon. Ma's trying to persuade him to spend more time at Ardtuath. She worries for his safety down in London.'

A blast from a ship's horn across the water made him turn to face straight ahead again.

'Time we got going, I think,' Diana said, pointing at the slim gold watch encircling her wrist.

With a nod, Alec turned the key in the ignition and reversed the car. They drove the final stretch to the jetty in silence and then Alec drew up alongside a pile of creels to let the Gordons out. He shook hands again with Ruaridh. 'Be seeing you at the other end, then. It'll be good knowing you're not far off.' At the same time, he turned and reached his left hand back towards Flora, mooring the three of them together for a moment. He gave her fingers a reassuring squeeze. 'Keep safe. And knit me one of those scarves, if you have the time. It'll certainly be welcome up there on the northern seas.' With a salute, he turned the car and drove away, leaving Flora and Ruaridh to say their own goodbyes.

After she'd waved her brother off, Flora watched from the jetty until the launch had heaved-to alongside the *Ordie*, and then she turned away. The breeze had stiffened with the chill of evening and she hugged the folds of her jumper around her as she walked back in the direction of Keeper's Cottage. At the little cemetery, she pushed open the wishing gate and went in, past the wind-sculpted yew tree, picking her way through the clusters of granite gravestones to one that stood a short way up the hill.

She knelt among the tufts of cotton grass that bowed their soft white heads over the mossy blanket covering the grave.

'Hello, Mum,' she said. 'Ruaridh came home today. He's looking well. He's off tonight on one of those ships out there, headed north.' She cleared a wisp of moss away from the headstone, tracing with the tips of her fingers the incised letters spelling out her mother's name and the name of the baby sister she'd never known, who had died together when Flora was two years old.

'Alec came back, too.' She paused, adrift in her thoughts.

Then, just before she turned to go, she whispered, 'Keep them safe.' And the wind snatched up her words, casting them out on to the darkening waters of the sea.

Lexie, 1978

Daisy loves the graveyard. The moss is soft beneath her hands and knees as she crawls through the grass, chuckling at the tufts of bog cotton that tickle her nose and make her sneeze. I'm trying to have a serious conversation with the stonemason about what to put on Mum's headstone. 'Just *Flora Gordon* and the dates, I think.'

'Ach, d'you no want some sort of a message? *In loving memory of a beloved mother and grandmother*, maybe? *Gone but never forgotten*, that sort of thing?'

I can scarcely afford the bare minimum and he charges by the letter, so I politely decline. The undertakers have already arranged for the urn containing the ashes to be buried alongside the grave where Mum's parents lie. Her stone will be set next to the one with the three names – Seonaig and Isla and Iain – commemorating my grandparents and an aunt who died before she was as old as Daisy is now, a thought that unsettles me to the very core of my being.

He shows me some samples of lettering and I choose the one that's closest to that on my grandparents' stone. Then he gets me to write down Mum's name and the dates in a notebook before he leaves, with a cheery wave to Daisy who ignores him as she tries to pull herself up to standing using the granite headstone for leverage. Her legs wobble and she collapses with a bump, her nappy cushioning her fall, then mutters softly to herself as she crawls off to explore further afield.

I walk across to scoop her up from the damp ground. She's sitting gazing up at an elaborately carved stone angel that stands guard over the family memorial of the Mackenzie-Grants.

'That's your grandpa's name there, see?' I tell her.

I trace the lettering of my dad's name – his and mine so alike – with my fingertips. And I remember how, on summer Sundays when I was little, Mum and I used to come to lay posies of wildflowers by our own family stone and how she would always take one flower – a harebell or a tuft of sea pink or a white ox-eye daisy – and lay it at the feet of the angel.

It's a bright, breezy day at last, and a relief to be outdoors again. Daisy and I are both suffering from a severe dose of cabin fever after almost a solid week of rain, which has assailed the windows of Keeper's Cottage from every angle. I've used the days to get things sorted in the house. I've brought the cot down from the loft and set it up so that we can both get a little more sleep, and I've wrapped most of Mum's ornaments in newspaper and packed them away in boxes, safely out of the way of inquisitive little fingers. I've also managed to sort and stash away many of my own belongings so that the cottage doesn't feel so cluttered. The attic is crammed full, but at least the boxes are out of sight. The sorting, unpacking and repacking and wrestling of boxes into the loft has made me feel as stale and dusty as the boards of the attic floor. I'm still stiff, the aftermath of the long drive as well as from ferrying everything in from the car and climbing up and down the ladder. But my physical aches and pains are nothing compared with the ache of the emptiness I feel, which seems to have embedded itself in my very bones.

Thankful to be out here on the hillside, I take a deep breath of the seaweed- and peat-scented air and then tilt my head back to follow the flight of an eagle whose feather-fringed wings are spread wide, catching the wind as it describes sweeping circles above us. It swoops low enough for me to be able make out the hook of its beak and the markings in its undercarriage. Instinctively, I scoop Daisy into my arms, hugging her tight. I point out the bird to her and we watch as it soars off, far out over the loch.

Then she points a chubby finger towards the water. 'Bat,' she says.

'Yes, clever girl. It is indeed a boat.' I wonder whether it's Davy's. Those squatties he gave us were absolutely delicious. Perhaps we should walk down to the jetty and leave him a message, asking for some more. I still can't quite place him, although I definitely feel like I know him from somewhere. Maybe the next time I see him I'll just ask him outright.

Flora, 1939

'Fill that urn with water would you, girls, and get it on the stove.' Mrs Carmichael was in her element, bustling about the village hall and marshalling her troops. The Rural were out in full force, getting ready to welcome the busload of evacuees who were on their way from Clydeside. Some of the children had relations on Loch Ewe and would naturally be staying with them, but others were arriving as part of the government's scheme to evacuate children to rural areas, away from the cities. Glasgow's shipyards would be an inevitable target for German bombing raids and families had been urged to act now, before any attacks.

Moira Carmichael's heels tapped officiously across the floorboards as she hurried about, consulting the clipboard she carried and making sure everything was in order, issuing instructions to her deputy, Marjorie Greig, the wife of the local doctor, who – in Mrs Carmichael's opinion – was one of the few women who could be relied upon in a crisis.

The door opened, letting in a gust of sea air. 'Ah, there you are, Mairi. And is that the churn of milk from your father? Thank you, dear. Put it through in the kitchen, please.' She ticked an item off on her list and then hastened back to where Flora and Bridie were wrestling with a long trestle table. 'Set those tables up over here! No, not like that, put them end to end. And then put out those chairs, please.' She strode off to check on the supplies of extra rations being unloaded from a van at the door.

'She sounds like a garron in those shoes,' whispered Bridie with a giggle as she and Flora rearranged the furniture.

'Wheesht, Bridie, you know she has the hearing of a wildcat.' Flora couldn't help laughing too, though. Mrs Carmichael's progress around the room did sound a little like the clopping hooves of the sturdy Highland pony that her father used to bring the deer carcasses down from the hill.

At last everything was ready and a big pan of potatoes was simmering on the stove. Mrs Carmichael summoned the women of the Rural for a final briefing.

'Right, ladies, are we clear? Each child is to be given a bowl of soup, and then once they've finished that you two will be serving the mince and tatties. One large spoonful of each, in the bowls they've used for their soup. Margaret, you can bring round the cups of milk and the bread and butter. Only one slice each, remember, or we'll run out. Marjorie and Jean, you'll be handing out the Red Cross parcels to the host parents. Here's the list: two tins of milk, one of those tins of corned beef, one bar of chocolate and two packets of biscuits per child. That should help see them through until we can sort out their ration books. I'll be at the table by the door, directing operations and making sure the right families end up with the right children. Girls' – she beckoned to Flora, Mairi and Bridie – 'you come and stand beside me. No doubt it will be chaos when they arrive and I'll need you as my runners. You can help wash their hands and faces, too. Heaven only knows what sort of a state they'll have been sent to us in.'

The flow of commands was interrupted suddenly by a loud crash from outside the hall.

'What on earth . . . ?' Mrs Carmichael bustled out of the door, followed by the rest of the Rural ladies.

At the back of the hall, a troop of soldiers were unloading sheets of corrugated iron from the back of a lorry.

'Sergeant, what do you think you're doing? Don't you know we're expecting a busload of children to arrive any minute?'

'Sorry, ma'am, just following orders.' The sergeant grinned cheerily at Mrs Carmichael, not the slightest bit cowed.

'Well, why are you dumping all this metal here? You have a whole camp along at Mellon Charles. Don't you have better places to store it there?'

'It's not being stored, ma'am. It's for the new extension. To the hall.'

'Extension? I haven't been told anything about an extension! Who gave you these orders?'

'The camp commander, ma'am. Her Majesty's navy has designated this 'ere 'arbour Port A. For the Fleet. Assembly point and what not.' He waved a hand in the direction of the loch, where the number of ships had continued to increase on a daily basis.

'Well, honestly! Someone might have said. We're about to house thirty children from Clydeside and now Loch Ewe will become just as much of a target for enemy bombs. You can't just go designating places as ports willy-nilly. People live here, you know.'

'I understand that, ma'am. But you'll have to take it up with Mr Churchill. He's the one what's done the designating.'

There was silence for a moment as Moira Carmichael thought carefully about taking on the First Lord of the Admiralty.

She sighed heavily. 'Very well then, what must be must be. We'll just have to make the best of it, I suppose. After all, there *is* a war on.'

The sergeant saluted and turned back to his men. 'Right, lads, look sharp. Let's get these materials unloaded before the kiddies arrive.'

Mrs Carmichael turned on her heel and flapped her hands to usher the ladies of the Rural back inside. But she relented enough to say to Flora, Mairi and Bridie, 'While we're waiting for the bus, you might as well make a tray of tea and take it out to them. I expect they'd appreciate a cup once they've finished the job.'

As Bridie set tin mugs out on a tray, she speculated about the extension to the hall. 'You know what this means, don't you? There'll be lots more soldiers and sailors. There might be dances. Imagine!'

'Bridie Macdonald!' Bridie jumped, clattering the cups, as the strident tones boomed across the hall. 'A little less imagining and a lot more concentrating would do you no harm,' Mrs Carmichael declared from her station at the door.

'Golly, you were right, Flora,' Bridie whispered. 'She really *does* have the hearing of a wildcat!'

The bus pulled up in front of the village hall two hours later, disgorging its weary, travel-sick cargo. The winding roads had taken their toll. The driver and the women who'd volunteered to accompany the children to their destination clambered out first, taking thankful breaths of the fresh West Coast air. It had been a long day, involving an early start followed by seemingly unending hours spent incarcerated in the wet-wool-and-vomit-tinged reek that was the inevitable consequence of transporting thirty children, already on edge with nerves and excitement, over the hills and around the sea lochs fringing the jagged coastline.

Mrs Carmichael clapped her hands. 'To your stations, ladies!' She then hurried forward with her clipboard to direct the children into the hall, checking the brown labels pinned to their coats and ticking off their names as they filed through the door. Her nostrils flared as she bent closer. 'Flora! Mairi! Bridie!' she called. 'Take the children and wash their hands and faces before they sit down, please. You'll need to use some of the hot water. And don't spare the soap!'

Flora smiled at two small boys as she led them to the sink. The elder one looked about eight, but the younger of the two was scarcely more than a baby – no more than three or four years old, she guessed. Their hair straggled in unkempt wisps over their ears and their knees were chapped and bruised where they protruded from beneath short trousers that were shiny with wear. She helped them push up the frayed cuffs of their coats and then dabble their hands in the basin of warm soapy water. With a flannel, she wiped the crusts from their eyes and noses, gently drying their hands and faces with a towel, trying not to rub the sore-looking, reddened skin where chilblains had nipped their fingers. She did her best to clean up the younger boy's coat, which bore the evidence of the effect the west coast roads must have had on his stomach.

'There you go. Good as new. Now, come and let's find you a seat at the table and get you something to eat.'

'Please, miss,' the larger of the two said, 'are you going to be our new mammy?'

Flora's heart swelled with compassion for the two wee scraps. She shook her head. 'I'm afraid it's not me that you're coming home with,' she said. 'It'll be one of the other ladies. There's no room in our cottage.' She stooped to read the names on their labels. 'Stuart. And David. The two of you will be just fine, don't you worry. Now, sit yourselves down here and we'll bring you a bowl of soup and some mince and tatties. You must be hungry after your long journey. Then the lady who's going to be looking after you will come and find you and take you to your new home.'

She hurried off to help with the next children in need of some freshening up. But as she worked, she was aware of the boys watching her, two pairs of round, grey-blue eyes peering over the rims of the cups of milk they'd been given.

Once their hot meal had been consumed and the bowls scraped clean, the children began to leave in twos and threes, gathering up bags of belongings and boxes of rations, having been claimed by their host families. Mrs Carmichael continued to direct operations from the doorway until, at last, the hall was empty apart from the two little boys left sitting at the table. The younger of the two – David – had fallen asleep, propped against his brother's shoulder, worn out by the long day's journey from home to this strange new place. But as she finished drying up the cups and plates, Flora noticed that Stuart still maintained a wary eye on the proceedings in the hall as he watched over his little brother.

At last, Moira Carmichael left her station at the door and bustled across to make sure everything had been put away properly. 'All finished? Well done, girls.'

'What about those two?' Flora nodded discreetly towards the forlorn-looking pair at the table.

'Don't you worry about them,' Mrs Carmichael said. For all her outward bluster, Flora knew she had a heart of gold and that a bedrock of kindness lurked beneath her bossiness. 'Stuart and David are coming with me. You wouldn't expect me not to do my duty, would you, with my own sons' rooms to spare in the house? Right then, boys, pick up your things. Let's get you home.'

Flora smiled encouragingly at the pair as they turned to look over their shoulders at her, following like a pair of bedraggled ducklings in Mrs Carmichael's wake. With a cheery wave of her damp dish towel, she said, 'Bye then, boys. I'll see you around.'

Stuart draped an arm protectively around his brother's shoulder, ushering him on towards their first night in a strange bedroom in an unfamiliar house. And her heart swelled again with emotion as she remembered how Alec and Ruaridh used to do the exact same thing when they were young, on the football field or plotting their next adventure in the den among the trees: another pair of brothers-in-arms.

Lexie, 1978

On the days when the weather allows it, Daisy and I have got into the habit of walking down to the jetty. Or rather I walk and Daisy commands which direction to take from her perch in the baby carrier on my shoulders. There's always plenty to see. She likes to check up on the sheep in the field behind the hall, leaning out of the carrier to peer behind the corrugated half-cylinder of the hall's wartime extension and watch the flock diligently cropping the grass.

'In the springtime, there'll be lambs,' I tell her.

'Lat,' she says, approvingly. Her speech really is coming on in leaps and bounds.

When we first got here, I would walk with her on the more solitary path that leads from Keeper's Cottage up through the pine trees to Ardtuath House. The 'Big Hoose', as it's known locally, is shut up most of the time, only used very occasionally for shooting or fishing weekends. But there was something so bleak about the façade of the deserted house, with its forbidding, darkened windows and air of abandonment, that it made me want to seek out happier places to walk. My mood is low enough already without any additional dampeners. And so we've taken to heading towards the village, the risk of having to be sociable being a lesser evil than the risk of complete and utter despondency.

We walk past the row of cottages, where we are usually accosted by someone weeding flowerbeds or trimming hedges in their front garden. Daisy enjoys the attention, even if I do not.

I nod and smile, responding to the social niceties. 'Yes, she's getting bigger every day. Yes, thanks, we've settled in fine. I know, isn't it a grand day for a walk?' And all the time I'm hoping that my smile is doing a good job of hiding how desperately lonely I feel. While I know I should value these simple daily connections, to my mind they only serve to emphasise my feelings of being an outsider.

Bridie Macdonald is almost always around. Sometimes she's pottering in her garden, but occasionally she's indoors and will rap on her window as we walk past, shooting out to join us, as she does today. 'Good morning, Lexie. And Daisy – look at these rosy wee cheeks! It's surely doing you both the world of good being up here in the fresh air. Much nicer for kiddies than a city, eh, Daisy? I was just about to pop to the shop for a pint of milk so I'll chum you along the road. Wait there a moment while I get my purse.'

Inwardly I sigh, knowing that our progress will be even slower as she questions me about all manner of things, from the state of Keeper's Cottage to the whereabouts of Daisy's father (boundaries being an unknown concept to Bridie Macdonald). And the inquisition will be interrupted at regular intervals as she stops to hail a neighbour and exchange snippets of local news. 'Have you heard, Marjorie's off for her operation next week? I know, it's taken long enough to get a date. And apparently they're fixing the road over at Poolewe. There'll be all sorts of hold-ups, so leave time if you're going that way. Has Euan got that boat of his back in the water? Oh, he's off out in it today, is he? Is it scallops he's after? Well, tell him I'll take half a dozen if he has them. You know Lexie Gordon, don't you? Yes, she's come home – back where she belongs at last. And this is wee Daisy – isn't she gorgeous!'

There's something proprietorial in the way Bridie says all this. I feel myself bristling slightly and have to remind myself that she was one of Mum's oldest friends and has always been a lynchpin of the community. It's only natural, and she means well. Behind my smile, my defences are well and truly up, though: the emotional brick wall that I use to keep people out.

We amble onwards, along the road that winds its way beside the loch.

'So, Lexie, will Daisy's daddy be joining you here soon?'

'No,' I reply. 'His work keeps him in London.' At least I can say that in all honesty.

'Och, that's a shame. You'll be missing him.' Her eyes dart again to the third finger of my left hand, which is very obviously lacking any sign of a ring – engagement, wedding or otherwise.

I decide I might as well come clean. At least then it'll put an end to Bridie's questions. 'Actually, we're not together any more. He turned out not to be the paternal type. We split up before Daisy was even born.'

We walk on for about ten paces while Bridie digests this. I'm bracing myself for more questions, but in the end all she says is, 'Well, I'm sorry to hear that. It's hard bringing up a wee one alone. Of course, poor Flora knew that as well as anyone.'

Seizing this welcome tangent, I divert Bridie with a well-placed question of my own.

'I've been wondering about that,' I say. 'You must remember the war years, how my parents met. Everything that happened. Mum never spoke about it all that much. I know my dad was in the navy and he died in the war, but that's about it. Apart from his photo on the mantelpiece and his name on the Mackenzie-Grants' stone in the graveyard, there's not much I know about him. Could you tell me, Bridie?'

For once, she's silent. Maybe I'm imagining it, but it seems to me that something in her usually open expression closes in on itself. It's fleeting – a wary look in her eyes as she inadvertently glances towards the hills above the loch. Something about it reminds me of the look in my mum's eyes when I'd ask her questions about my dad.

Then she pulls herself together. 'Of course, darlin'. You bring Daisy over to mine sometime and we'll have a cup of tea and a chat. I'll be happy to tell you about Alec and Flora. They really were the golden couple. Well, here's the jetty – you'll be taking Daisy to look at the boats, I expect. I must be getting on.'

I stand and watch as she hurries on towards the shop. She turns to look back, giving us a wave, before she ducks through the door.

Is it my imagination, or do I get the impression that when I asked her to tell me about my parents, she was choosing her words very carefully? That caution – and the momentary silence that preceded it – are enough to pique my interest. Is there something there, something that concerns my own past?

Because, for once and most unusually, it seems to me that there's something that Bridie Macdonald is NOT saying.

Flora, 1939

The ebb and flow of the navy's ships in and out of Loch Ewe continued as winter drew in. Along the shore, wisps of peat smoke rose from the chimneys of the little white croft houses, the soft, familiar scent mingling with the sharper smell of fuel oil as tankers replenished the grey hulks on the water.

It was a clear, still morning, and although the December sun lay low in the sky it had managed to flood the loch with light for a few precious hours. Flora was making the most of the good weather, at work in the patch of garden alongside Keeper's Cottage. Her fork plunged easily into the dark soil. It had been worked for generations, enriched with seaweed from the shore and rotted manure from the stables up at the big house, and it provided them with a good supply of vegetables under Flora's careful stewardship. Digging up potatoes, she transferred them, still covered in a powdering of black loam, into a bucket. The tatties rattled against the tin sides of the pail, quickly filling it. Then she heaved it to the store behind the house and emptied it into the larger wooden crates where the harvest would keep through the winter. Ruaridh had suggested that they turn the storehouse into an Anderson shelter, as some of the other crofters had done in case of air raids, but her father had just shrugged and said it didn't seem worth the fuss. Looking out across the water on that calm winter's day, Flora tended to agree with him. The war still seemed very far away. And, after all, the secrecy afforded by Loch Ewe's secluded position was the very reason for its use as a safe harbour.

Coming to the end of the heaped row, she straightened up, hands in the small of her back, and pushed a tendril of hair from her eyes with her wrist. Two small boys were walking along the road and she waved to them as they drew nearer.

'Hello there! Stuart and David, isn't it? How are you getting on?'

They wore clothes that were a size or two too large, jumper sleeves rolled up and short trousers hanging below their knees over thick woollen socks. Moira Carmichael must have kitted them out in her sons' outgrown clothing. Despite the poor fit, the things were of good quality and looked a good deal warmer than the few clothes the boys had brought with them from Glasgow.

Two pairs of round blue-grey eyes regarded her solemnly. 'Hello, miss,' said Stuart, the elder of the two. 'We've to go for a walk and get out of Mrs Carmichael's hair.'

Flora smiled at the words, clearly repeated verbatim. 'Well, it's a good day for it. How would you like to give me a hand getting the last of these tatties out of the ground? And then we can find you a glass of milk and maybe a bit of bannock indoors?'

Two heads nodded and they came up the path to where she stood.

'Can you manage the fork, Stuart? Dig like this, see? If you just turn the ground over, David and I can gather the tatties into the pail.'

She smiled at their amazement as the first forkful unearthed a heap of potatoes. 'Get them all up, that's it. Don't bother to rub the soil off, it helps them keep.'

With the two extra pairs of hands, the rows were quickly harvested. By the time they'd finished, the boys' cheeks glowed with their exertions and the sea air.

Flora set aside a handful of potatoes and dug up a couple of neeps to take into the kitchen. Once boiled and mashed, they would accompany the venison stew that she'd prepared earlier, which simmered slowly on the stove so it'd be ready for her father's supper when he came off the hill.

She ushered the boys into the cottage. 'We'll leave our boots at the door, that's it. And then let's wash the dirt off our hands.'

Sitting at the kitchen table, the boys seemed to relax a little as she set cups of milk down in front of them. 'There you go. You've earned that.' She buttered wedges of oatmeal bannock and spread them thickly with bramble jam before passing them across.

Stuart took a bite and washed it down with a gulp from his cup. 'Mmm, that's good. Our mam used to make bannock sometimes. But at Mrs Carmichael's we mostly just get bread and dripping.'

'So are you settling in all right? It must be a big change for you, coming away from the city.'

'Davy doesn't like the dark. The house is awful big and there's all sorts of noises in the night. School's nice here, though. We're all in the one room, so I can look out for him and make sure the other boys don't bother him.'

'*Do* they bother you?' Flora asked.

'No, not really. It was worse in my old school. But it was easier to bunk off there, 'cause no one really paid any notice. We tried bunking off here one day, but Mr Carmichael was putting up notices about what to do if the air-raid sirens go and he saw us fishing off the jetty and gave us a skelping. We'd to go straight back to school and apologise to Miss Anderson.'

Trying to keep a straight face, Flora said, 'Well, you do need to go to school. My brother always wanted to be out fishing, too, but he knew to do it at the weekends and in the holidays.'

'Where's your brother now, miss?'

‘He’s in the navy. Off on one of those ships out there.’ She had no idea where Ruaridh was at the moment. She hoped he was moored up safely, and she tried not to think of him patrolling the hostile northerly waters where U-boats lurked unseen in the depths.

‘I want to join the navy when I’m grown,’ Stuart said. ‘Davy can come, too, and we’ll be on a ship together. Maybe we can be on the same ship as your brother.’

‘Well, maybe. As long as you stick at your studies. You’ll need to know all sorts of things if you’re to join up.’

She cut them each another slice of bannock and refilled their cups, recalling how Ruaridh and Alec had sat at the table just like this at the same age, wolfing down their food before running back outside to continue whatever adventure they’d embarked upon that day. She was just reaching again for the pot of jam when a muffled boom made them all turn towards the window.

‘What was that?’ Davy asked, startled into finding his voice at last.

‘Was it a bomb, miss? Are the Germans invading?’

Flora peered out across the loch, but couldn’t see any obvious signs of an explosion at first. As she watched, though, a plume of dark smoke appeared out beyond the island, and several ships were changing course, heading in the direction of the mouth of the loch.

‘I don’t think so. But something’s going on. Don’t worry,’ she said, catching sight of the fear on Davy’s face. ‘We’re better protected here than pretty much anywhere else in the country. The navy will look after us. Let’s put our boots on and go and see what’s happened. Here, you can take this with you to eat on the way. Don’t let it spoil your lunch, though, or Mrs Carmichael will be after me!’

There was a buzz of activity around the loch, but it was impossible to make out exactly what was going on. The main focus seemed to be on a point out beyond the mouth of the loch, obscured by the island. They walked towards the jetty, overtaken by a series of military vehicles that sped past them in the same direction.

A small crowd had gathered near the pier. Flora caught sight of Bridie and Mairi in the throng. 'What is it?' she asked.

'They say it's the *Nelson*. She's hit a mine.'

A jolt of panic flooded Flora's veins. Alec's ship. 'How bad is it? Has she sunk?'

'Don't think so.' Bridie shrugged. 'But the ship's holed. It's going to take them a while to bring her in.'

Flora blanched at the sight of a fleet of ambulances driving fast along the road from the camp. They pulled up at the end of the jetty and several uniformed men jumped out, hurrying to throw medical supplies and equipment into a waiting launch. They clambered down the ladder on the harbour wall and the boat sped out into the loch as soon as the last of them had taken his seat.

'That doesn't look good.' Mairi frowned.

Flora wrung her hands in frustration at not being able to do anything, not knowing whether Alec might be among the casualties.

'Clear the way now! Go back to your homes! All non-naval personnel are to leave the area immediately.' Mr Carmichael bustled forward importantly, his ARP helmet firmly on his head, asserting his authority. Then he caught sight of the two boys who were hopping from foot to foot, caught up in the excitement of the drama unfolding on the water. 'Stuart and David Laverock, what are you doing here?' he bellowed. 'Get yourselves home immediately.'

Flora gave them a sympathetic smile and nodded her head. 'Best get back now. Mrs Carmichael will be worrying about you. And it's nearly lunchtime.' She shooed them gently towards the house next to the jetty.

She and Mairi walked with Bridie as far as the Macdonalds' house, where they stood at the gate for a moment, watching the activity out on the loch. Painfully slowly, and listing heavily to one side, the bulk of the *Nelson* drew into view, closely flanked by two destroyers, making for the harbour.

'You know, we should join up,' Bridie said. 'One of the sailors I was talking to on the jetty said they're recruiting Wrens. Apparently they need drivers and all sorts.'

'But we can't drive,' pointed out Flora.

Bridie waved a hand dismissively. 'We can learn. And there must be other things we can do, too.'

Mairi nodded. 'She's right. After all, we can't just sit by and watch while ships are being blown up right on our doorstep.'

Flora thought of the ambulances speeding towards the jetty. If either Ruaridh or Alec needed help, she'd be one of the first to respond. Her heart lurched again as she sent up a silent prayer that Alec wasn't among the casualties on the wounded vessel as it crept towards the shore.

The thought of the injured men decided it. 'All right. We'll go this afternoon then. Come and call for me after lunch and we can walk over to the camp and ask.'

Lexie, 1978

Every surface of Mum's sitting room is filled with photos in frames. Before the arrival of Hurricane Daisy, they were interspersed with herds of china animals and hordes of glass knick-knacks, but those have now been packed away for safekeeping. Daisy has mastered the art of a surprisingly fast commando crawl and the ability to lever herself on to her feet if there's anything to hang on to, so everything precious and breakable on the lower shelves and the coffee table has been moved to higher ground out of the way of her exploring fingers.

I've just left one of the little china ornaments out, a tiny white horse that was always Mum's favourite. I pick it up and stroke the lines of its long mane with my forefinger before carefully replacing it between two of the picture frames.

Many of the photos are of me, at every stage of my childhood and then on into my stage career: I talk Daisy through them and she looks politely at each one as I hold it up for her to see.

'There's me with my bucket and spade on the beach at Slaggan Bay. We'll walk there one day in the summer and take a picnic, shall we? And this is your mummy in the school show, singing a solo. One of my earlier stage appearances. This one looks like *Carousel* – a publicity photo of me as Louise Bigelow. And here's a nice one of your mummy and your granny in London, see?'

'Mmm?' Daisy asks, pointing at the picture.

'Yes, that's right. That's Mummy. And your granny, Flora.' It strikes me that we could almost pass as sisters, Mum looks so young in the photo. We shared the same russet-gold curls, in her case faded a little and drawn into a neat sandy braid, whereas mine tumbled over my shoulders. We were outside the Theatre Royal in Drury Lane, standing in front of the poster for Piers's production of *A Chorus Line* in which I'd just landed my role. If you look closely you can just about make out my name, which Mum is pointing at. My London name, that is. Those dance classes were killers, I remember; my legs were sore for months. But it was worth the pain. My career was on an upward trajectory then. I was being given bigger roles, expanding my repertoire.

In this photograph I can see that I look radiant. My happiness had something to do with the new production. It had a lot to do with the fact that my mum had come to visit and I always enjoyed showing her London, sharing my new life with her, which was hundreds of miles – both literal and metaphorical ones – from Keeper's Cottage on the shores of Loch Ewe. But most of all, I remember, I was overflowing with joy because I'd so recently met Piers.

Looking at my face in the photo, I feel sorry for that girl now, the girl I once was. She felt invincible, golden, chosen from among so many other singers and actors. She was oblivious to the fall that was to come.

The show was a hit. With my first pay packet, I went shopping and bought the beautiful suede jacket that I'd coveted in the window of the boutique I passed each day on my way to the theatre. The minute I slipped it on I felt like a star. Like someone who'd made it, a girl who had successfully shrugged off her previous persona and become somebody else altogether. And now it hangs in the back of the wardrobe, a useless piece of clothing that's entirely unsuited to the place I've washed up in, creased and stained, as forlorn as its owner. I should really take it to be dry-cleaned, but that would involve a day's trip to Inverness and another day to go and pick it up: the thought of the petrol and the cost of the cleaning and the effort it would take to bundle Daisy into the car defeat me.

I sigh and settle the photo frame back in its place on the sideboard.

Daisy begins to fuss, as if she can sense the slide in my mood. I pick up another photo. This one is of Mum and she's wearing the dark uniform of the WRNS. The severity of the tailored uniform contrasts with the informality of her pose, leaning against the bonnet of a military jeep, her hair blowing in the wind. She'd have been about twenty then, I suppose. The most striking thing about the picture, though, is the expression in her eyes. Just like my own in the previous photo, they are shining, radiating the purest joy as she gazes at whoever is taking the picture. I swallow hard as tears threaten to spill on to Daisy's rose-gold curls. Mum looks so carefree, even though they must have been hard times, those war years. I feel almost certain that the person taking the photo was my father, even though I know so little about him. I remember my conversation with Bridie Macdonald on the road the other day and wonder again what it might be that she is so loath to reveal. Next time I'm passing her house, I'll invite myself in and get her to tell me what she knows, I resolve. It's my history, after all, my parents' story.

I run the tip of my finger over the outline of my mother's face, gently tracing the contours of her smile.

Yes, I think, my dad must have been the one behind the camera. Because I know how much she loved him. There was no one else who could have made her look that way.

Flora, 1939

'Gently lift your foot off the clutch and press the other one down on the accelerator at the same time.'

The truck lurched forward, taking out a couple of the oil drums that had been set out to mark a course for steering practice.

'Oops, sorry,' Bridie said cheerfully.

The lieutenant in the passenger seat sighed deeply, grabbing the handbrake to bring the vehicle to a standstill before its fledgling driver could wreak any more havoc. 'I should be paid danger money for this job,' he grumbled. 'Teaching you Wrens to drive is far more dangerous than being out on the deck of a pitching ship in a Force 8 gale, if you ask me.'

In the back, Flora and Mairi clung to the edge of the bench seats that ran along the sides of the truck and tried not to shriek with a mixture of laughter and nerves.

'Right, let's try that again. Think about how your friends did it. Slowly and gently. I said SLOWLY!'

This time, with a loud crunch of the gears, the truck jolted towards the group of Nissen huts at the edge of the parade ground, swerving just in time to miss the camp's commander, who had stepped out to watch the proceedings.

'Och, I think I'm getting the hang of this double-declutching thing now,' Bridie called out over the roar of the motor as she stamped both feet down on the pedals. 'Just let me try that again.'

The lieutenant sighed once more. It was going to be another long afternoon. 'Let's take a break,' he said. He turned to address Flora and Mairi. 'You two can go and report to the office. You've passed.' He signed his name on the bottom of a couple of forms and handed them over. 'Give these to the officer at the desk. He'll let you know which detail you'll be assigned to. Now,' he said, bracing a hand against the dashboard and turning back to Bridie, 'let's give it another go . . .'

It was dark inside the tin hut, where a makeshift desk had been set up next to a small window that allowed a square of winter light to enter. It took a moment or two for Flora and Mairi's eyes to adjust. They stepped forward and proffered the forms to the orderly sitting at the desk. He took them without a word and began writing the girls' details on to cards for filing. Once he'd finished, he looked up at them. 'Miss Gordon. Miss Macleod. Report to Hut Eight. They'll sort you out with your uniforms. You'll be assigned for general driving duties on a day-to-day basis and ambulances when needed. Welcome to the Wrens.'

Blinking as they stepped back out into the open air, Mairi grinned at Flora. 'We did it!' They watched for a moment as out on the parade ground, Bridie appeared to be making headway with her driving, too, negotiating the oil drums without sending them rolling in all directions now. 'Looks like she might be joining us soon. And there's Hut Eight.' She pointed to the row of newly constructed buildings at one side of the small bay.

The toot of a horn made them look round. A car had pulled into the camp, and a uniformed figure waved to attract their attention.

'It's Alec!' Flora exclaimed, joy brightening her face like sunlight on water.

He strode towards them, arms outstretched. 'Flora, Mairi, have you joined up? That's wonderful news! I'm glad I've run into you because I have something to tell you, too. I'm being assigned to duties here, helping to commission the port. We're needing a good signalman and I've suggested Ruaridh, since he knows the lie of the land and every inch of the loch like the back of his hand. It's not definite yet, but I'm hoping he'll be transferred.'

The surge of hope in her heart was so powerful that Flora couldn't speak.

Alec smiled down at her. 'Wouldn't that be something? All of us back here together, just like old times? He might even be home in time for Christmas.'

'That would be the very best news possible,' Flora replied, finding her voice again. 'Having Ruaridh back. And you, too, Alec. Thank goodness you weren't one of those hurt when the *Nelson* was blown up.'

Against the grey of the sky and the waters beneath it, her face and hair glowed, lit by her smile. Alec glanced down at the toes of his boots, apparently self-conscious all of a sudden, his usual easy confidence deserting him. But then he raised his eyes to hers again and plucked up the courage to say, 'There's to be a dance at the hall on Hogmanay. Will the two of you be going? I could come and pick you up, if you like.'

Flora hesitated. 'Will Diana be coming up for it?' she asked, keeping her voice light.

Alec's eyes went back to his boots and his face flushed slightly. He shook his head. 'I'm afraid to say Miss Kingsley-Scott has broken off our engagement. She's met someone else in London, someone rather more important than a mere sub-lieutenant assigned to the sticks.'

Flora tucked a stray strand of hair back into her braid. 'Well, I'm sorry to hear that.' Her words belied the rush of relief she felt.

She was a little surprised at the strength of that feeling, but told herself it was just that Alec surely deserved someone with a bit more warmth about her. She and Mairi exchanged a glance, and Mairi nodded. 'The dance would be grand. Thank you. And Alec—' Flora broke off, trying to find the words, overcome with emotion once again. Had to make do with a simple, 'Thank you for recommending Ruaridh, too. It'll be good to have the pair of you safely back on dry land.'

He saluted them smartly, then turned on his heel and marched off to report to his commanding officer, only once turning back to glance over his shoulder at the girls as they made their way across to the other side of the camp to collect their uniforms.

On New Year's Eve the hall filled up rapidly as more and more of the men arrived, having stopped off at the bar in the Aultbea Hotel for a pint or two, shouting greetings and slapping the backs of their shipmates. There were some faces that Flora recognised from the camp and many others who were strangers, recently returned from duties out at sea.

Alec had very gallantly collected Flora, Mairi and Bridie for the Hogmanay dance and driven them to the hall, preserving their newly waved hairdos and carefully pressed skirts. He found them chairs and brought them drinks, introducing them to some of his fellow officers. A small band began to tune up at the far end of the hall, the notes of a fiddle rising above the hubbub of voices.

Flora's face lit up at the sight of her brother entering the hall with a girl on his arm. So that's where he'd disappeared off to earlier; she'd thought he must be heading for the hotel, whose recently rechristened 'Jellyjar Tavern' had become a popular gathering place for naval personnel. The jelly and jam jars in question had been pressed into use when the hotel had run out of glasses, to satisfy the increase in demand from thirsty soldiers and sailors, so the men had begun bringing whatever they could lay their hands on to be filled with beer. Ruaridh had told her that one especially enterprising sub-lieutenant had managed to persuade Miss Cameron, the postmistress, to part with one of the large sweetie jars that were now sitting empty on the shelf in her shop since sugar rationing had come in. The jar could be filled with several pints of beer and passed around between those who hadn't managed to find a suitable drinking vessel of their own.

As Ruaridh and his date approached, Alec stood and shook his hand.

'Hello, Alec. Mairi. Bridie.' Ruaridh nodded towards the girls. 'This is Wendy. And that's my sister, Flora. Wendy's a Wren, too.'

'Pleased to meet you all,' she beamed. 'I've heard lots about you.'

Flora wondered briefly when the pair had found time for such discussions. Ruaridh seemed to have been very busy of late, at his post at the signal station on the hill beyond Tournaig Farm at all hours, relaying directions to the mass of ships manoeuvring in the loch below.

'Wendy's a meteorologist,' he explained. 'She has to take the weather readings up at the signal station. That's where we met.'

Flora smiled, the penny dropping.

The band struck up a dance tune and Alec held out his hand. 'Would you honour me with the first dance, Miss Gordon?'

'Why, I'd be delighted to, Lieutenant Mackenzie-Grant,' Flora replied, laughing at his formality.

They joined the general surge on to the dance floor, which was quickly packed with couples. Flora smiled over at Mairi and Bridie who were dancing with a pair of officers. Following her glance, Alec bent close to her ear and whispered, 'Good. Now I don't have to be polite and ask them, too. I'd much rather spend the evening only dancing with you.'

Flora hoped that the flush on her cheeks would be attributed to the dancing and the heat in the crowded hall. She'd found herself thinking about Alec a great deal lately, looking out for him at the camp when she was ferrying personnel back and forth to the jetty and hoping that one day he might turn out to be the passenger she was collecting. There was no one else she wanted to dance with, either. He held her hand a little more tightly as the current of the dance carried them along in its flow.

The noise and the heat reverberated in the tin-roofed hall as the evening wore on and midnight approached. Then the band leader stopped the music and everyone shouted out the countdown as the hands of the clock ticked towards 1940. And then there was cheering and kissing as a piper joined the band and struck up 'Auld Lang Syne'.

'A good new year,' Flora whispered to Alec.

Without a word, he drew her close, his arms a quiet haven in the midst of the voices raised in song and celebration, and for a moment she imagined them to be alone, the pair of them marooned on their island of silence in a sea of sound.

'Come and look at this!' came a shout from the door, and the partygoers tumbled out from the loud lit interior into the frost-stilled night. Out beyond the shore, on the darkness of the loch, lights flashed from every ship moored there. It was a fleeting display – they couldn't risk giving away their position, even on New Year's Eve – but a brilliant one.

Although it needed no deciphering, Ruaridh translated their message. 'Happy New Year.'

In the hall, the band continued to play and some of the revellers went back again to dance on already tired feet. Others began to drift away.

'Would you like to stay on?' Alec asked Flora.

She shook her head. 'I can't. I promised Dad I'd be home. I know he'll be waiting up so I'd best be getting off.'

'Come on then, I'll drive you back. I know, let's first-foot him together!'

Flora laughed. 'He'd love that. But we have neither cake nor coal nor whisky so it'll not be much of a first-footing.'

'We'll stop off at my house on the way past and pick some things up. We'd better do it properly if it's to bring luck to Keeper's Cottage for the year ahead. Come on, let's go!'

Ruaridh, Bridie and Mairi all declined the offer of a lift home, preferring to stay on at the party, which was showing no signs of ending just yet, and so Flora and Alec climbed into his car and sped along the empty road to Ardtuath House.

Even though the gates to the big house were rarely closed, their formal grandness was a stark reminder that it stood apart from the whitewashed cottages that were its nearest neighbours. Towering pines lined the drive, blotting out the night sky with a darkness of their own, concealing the house from the community surrounding it.

At the top of the drive, Alec killed the engine, glancing up at the windows, which to Flora's eyes seemed to brood behind their blackout coverings. 'Best not wake my parents if they're in their beds already,' he whispered.

They crept in through a side door, stepping from the crispness of the clear night air through a darkened boot room and into the warmth of the vast kitchen. From across the hall, the faint sound of music made them both pause. Putting a finger to his lips, Alec beckoned Flora to follow him. She hesitated before stepping through the doorway into the more formal part of the house. It felt strange being there with him now that their relationship was changing. He was so confident, so self-assured in his grand home, while the ornate cornicing and heavy antique furniture in the hall seemed to press in on her from all sides, stifling and constraining her usual sense of ease. But she took a deep breath and crossed the divide, the green baize door swinging shut behind her with a soft thud.

He pushed open the library door and the strains of a Debussy nocturne drew them across the threshold into the room. In an armchair beside a fire whose embers burned low, Alec's mother sat with her hands folded in her lap, her head resting against one wing of the chair as she listened to the gramophone.

'Hello, Ma,' said Alec softly.

She turned to face them, the distant – and rather sad – look in her eyes transforming into a smile at the sight of her son.

'Alec? And Flora too – how lovely.'

'A good new year, Lady Helen,' Flora said, feeling she had intruded on a private moment. In the firelight, she noticed a few strands of silver gleaming in Lady Helen's hair, smoothed back into its usual elegant chignon. There had been a look of loneliness in her dark eyes that had surprised Flora. Surely she must be feeling less isolated now that her husband had come back to Ardtuath House?

'And to you both too, my dears. How was the dance?'

'It was fun, thank you,' replied Flora politely.

'Is Father in bed already?' asked Alec.

His mother nodded. 'He was tired. He's been so busy in London since Christmas, closing up the house there.' She turned to Flora. 'I'm sure your father's told you my husband has decided to stay up at Ardtuath now, which comes as a big relief to us all. London's such a target for the Germans. What a luxury it will be for me, having both my menfolk home. At least this dratted war has one or two advantages.'

Alec crossed the room to his mother and stooped to kiss her cheek. 'I'm just going to take Flora home. But we thought we'd stop off here on the way to collect some of the Christmas cake and maybe a dram of whisky for first-footing Iain.'

'Good idea. Help yourselves; the cake's in the larder.'

The record ended, the needle crackling faintly, and she reached to switch it off. From upstairs came a series of heavy footsteps crossing the floorboards. At the sound, Lady Helen froze for a moment. Then she stood, lowering her voice as she said, 'Don't disturb your father though, Alec. You know how he can be. I'd better be getting off to my bed, too. Good night, Flora.' She hesitated, then stepped across to a side table where bottles and glasses stood on a silver tray. 'Here,' she said, picking up a bottle of whisky. 'Give this to Iain. He's certainly earned it, with all the extra work he's been doing around the estate. Heaven knows how we'd be able to manage without him now we've no factor.'

Flora whispered a thank you and then Lady Helen quietly ushered them back into the kitchen, softly closing the door behind them. They heard her making her way upstairs and then the low rumble of Sir Charles's voice, questioning, followed by the soft, placatory tones of her reply.

Alec cut a generous slice of fruit cake and put it in a wicker basket, then added a lump of coal from the scuttle next to the range, wrapping it in a piece of newspaper. Flora nestled the bottle of whisky in alongside the cake and nodded as Alec gestured silently towards the door.

Stepping outside, their breath hung in white clouds on the cold night air. They got into the car and Alec let off the handbrake, freewheeling down the drive beneath the canopy of dark pine branches, only starting the engine once they were almost at the road.

As they emerged from beneath the trees, turning northwards, both of them gasped in astonishment. For while their backs had been turned, the black of the night sky had been draped with curtains of light that billowed and surged above the far horizon.

Alec pulled in to the side of the road. 'How's that for a Hogmanay show?'

Flora's eyes shone as the sheets of colour turned from green to silver and back again. 'Even the blackout can't stop the Northern Lights.'

Still looking straight ahead to the northern horizon, she slipped her hand into his, and his fingers curled tight around hers as they sat in silence, watching the display. The ethereal glow bathed the landscape, transforming the familiar hills into a mysterious otherworld surrounding the waters of the loch, which reflected the swirling colours in their depths.

At last the dancing swathes of light began to fade, becoming fainter as the night stars reclaimed the sky, and the final reflections of the coloured strands sank into the darkening water.

Alec turned in his seat to look at Flora, watching as she gazed on the last of the pale green glow as it died away.

'Would you come out with me? The next time we both have a day off? We could go to the beach at Firemore, or Slaggan Bay perhaps, if it's fine. Do you remember when we walked there with your dad all those summers ago?'

She nodded. 'It was August, I think,' she recalled. 'Just before you were about to go away to school for the first time. Ruaridh fell in the burn and was soaked. We'd to spread his things on a rock to dry. But then we all ended up in the sea anyway. It was a warm enough day that it didn't matter.'

'Well, we won't be swimming at this time of year, that's guaranteed, but we could take a picnic if we wrap up well.' He was silent for a few moments, lost in thought. Then he asked her, 'Do you still have the wee china horse?'

'Of course,' said Flora. 'I keep it on the mantelpiece.'

There was no need to say more, although she remembered clearly the day all those years ago when she'd gone to collect pine cones for the fire in the wood above Ardtuath House. She'd heard a noise, a stifled sob, coming from the stables, and had peered in to find him sitting with his back against the rough boards of the garron's stall, his face buried in his hands. It was the day he was to be sent away to a prep school in the south, the local primary no longer being deemed suitable for the son of the laird.

As she approached, the white pony had hung its broad muzzle over the half-door, as if trying to comfort the sobbing boy. Wordlessly, she had sat down beside Alec and put a hand on his shoulder. He'd raised his head then, dragging the back of his hand across his eyes to dash away the tears that stained his face, angry and embarrassed at having been seen.

'It's never going to be the same again, is it?' he'd asked her, his anguish fraying the edges of his voice. 'Everything's going to change.'

'Maybe some things will change. But this will always be here,' she'd said, pointing to the view beyond the stable door. 'The loch and the hills. And we will always be here, Ruaridh and the garron and me.'

He'd nodded slowly, then swallowed hard and squared his shoulders. 'Please could you not say you saw me here?'

She didn't speak, just reached for his hand and squeezed it by way of a reply.

He'd stood up then, brushing the straw from his jacket, and summoned a watery smile. 'See you at Christmas?' he said.

She'd nodded. 'It'll fly by, you'll see.'

When he'd returned for the holidays, he had indeed changed. He seemed more assured, chatting happily about his new friends at school, the trials and tribulations involved in having to learn Latin and French and his hope that he'd be selected for the Second XV rugby team. Neither of them had ever mentioned the encounter in the stable again. But on that Christmas morning when Flora went to bring in a handful of sticks for the fire, she'd found a small pile of clumsily wrapped gifts on the doorstep. There was a wooden boot-jack for Iain that Alec had sweated over in his woodwork classes at school and a neat horn-handled penknife for Ruaridh. And for Flora, there was the little white china horse with a blonde mane that she'd treasured ever since.

Now, he brought her hand to his lips, kissing it gently before drawing her to him and kissing her more deeply. Then, with a sigh that was a strange, shuddering mixture of joy and regret, he restarted the car. 'Better get you home, or Iain will be out looking for you with his shotgun. I wouldn't want to be the man in his sights!'

She laughed softly. 'I think you're probably the only man he wouldn't shoot at. He trusts you.'

'And you, Flora? Do you trust me, too?'

She looked into the ink-black depths of his eyes and replied, 'Always, Alec. I have always trusted you.'

Lexie, 1978

On my next walk to the shop, I make a point of stopping in at Bridie's. She looks a bit startled to see me standing at her door. I'd been hoping she might ask us in, fussing over Daisy as usual, and sit me down so that she could tell me her recollections of the war years – and my mum and dad's story in particular – over a cup of tea. But my suspicion that she's avoiding that particular cosy chat crystallises a little bit more when she doesn't do so. Instead, she reaches her coat down from the hook beside her front door, saying, 'What good timing! I'm just away to the jetty to see if I can catch Davy before he takes the boat out. He'll put out a line for some mackerel if I ask him. We can get some for you, too, if you'd like? And wee Daisy, would you like a nice fresh fishy for your tea? You're growing so fast, so you are, so you are!'

I get the sense again that this is not just her usual chattering. It's not at all like Bridie Macdonald to pass up the chance to find out more about the sorry set of circumstances that have washed me back to the shores of Loch Ewe. So my interest is piqued even more keenly as to what it is she's hiding from me.

Up until now, I've felt a bit like a limpet when in her company, clamping down hard on my own sense of shame as she's tried to prise more snippets out of me. But she is, apparently, equally adept at clamming up. It's going to take a little more patience to coax information out of her, I can see. I am shamelessly prepared to use my daughter as bait, if need be. So, as we walk along to the jetty, I make my move.

'Bridie, I'd love to bring Daisy to yours one afternoon. She gets a bit bored stuck in the cottage when it's an indoor day.'

'Well, we've certainly had a few of those this past week,' she replies. 'What a gale it was blowing at the weekend! I didn't set foot out of my front door.'

Refusing to be deflected so easily with talk of the weather, I plough on determinedly. 'Yes, so could we come over sometime? Just say whatever day suits you – I have nothing going on. You were so kind as to offer. And it would do me good to have some grown-up conversation for a change.'

Pinned down now, and unable to resist the thought of time with Daisy, she bites. 'Och well, I'd love to see the pair of you, of course. What about Thursday? You could come over about three, once this wee one has had her after-lunch nap?'

'Thursday at three would be perfect. Thanks, Bridie.'

'Good, that's settled then. And here's Davy, look. We're just in time.' She waves energetically to catch his attention as he prepares to cast off from the quayside. He stands on the deck of his boat, whose name I now see is the *Bonnie Stuart*, dressed from head to toe in a serious-looking set of oilskins topped off with an orange life jacket.

'Good morning, ladies,' he greets us, with a shy smile.

The boat tugs at the rope, which he holds taut around the mooring bollard, as if the vessel is impatient to get going out into the waves tossing their white heads beyond the lee of the island.

The brisk breeze smells of seaweed and the recently passed rain; it blows Daisy's curls every which way where they escape from beneath the woollen tammy that I've pulled down firmly to keep her ears warm. She chuckles and reaches her hands towards the boat, enthusiastically repeating her favourite word: 'Bat.'

'There's the clever girl,' Bridie coos. 'D'you hear that, Davy? She's starting to talk now.'

He reaches to shake her hand, her fingers looking like a tiny starfish as they clutch his broad, weather-worn thumb. 'Well, one of these days when the weather's a bit gentler I'll take you out for a turn on the water, maybe. If you'd like to?' He glances at me, uncertain.

'We'd love that.'

'Lexie was just telling me she's longing to get out a bit more now that she and Daisy are settled,' Bridie chimes in enthusiastically.

I try to refrain from shooting her an irritated glance at this rephrasing of my recent admission to her that cabin fever has been setting in up at Keeper's Cottage.

'Aye well, there's surely nothing like an hour or two out on the loch to blow away the cobwebs,' Davy says. 'I'll let you know when there's to be a calm window in the weather.'

Bridie issues her order for a couple of nice fresh mackerel for each of us and Davy nods and waves as he casts off.

'There now,' Bridie says, evidently pleased with her morning's work. 'Well, I'll be letting you get on to the shop. And I'll see the two of you on Thursday, like we said.'

'Thanks, Bridie, I'm looking forward to it.'

As I turn to open the door of the shop, I glance back along the road, and can't help noticing that instead of continuing towards her house, Bridie Macdonald has turned in at a neighbour's gate and is hurrying with purposeful steps up the path to knock at the yellow-painted front door.

I arrive promptly at three o'clock on the Thursday, as arranged, with Daisy in her pushchair. But as I turn in at Bridie's gate, I realise that I've been outmanoeuvred. Sitting at the front door is another pushchair. I should have known: we limpets don't give up our secrets easily. I knock, and Bridie flings the door open.

'Come in, come in! And look, Elspeth and wee Jack are here too. I thought it would be nice for Daisy to have a pal of her own age to play with. And, of course, you and Elspeth go way back. I remember seeing the two of you getting off the school bus and standing chatting for ages at the stop, rain or shine, before you went your separate ways home to your mammies. Such great friends, you always were.'

Looking at the politely bland expression on Elspeth's face, I wonder whether she's been press-ganged into this jolly afternoon play date or whether she came willingly. Because we *were* good friends, once. We sat next to each other in the little primary school in the village, the only two girls in our year group. We held our own against the bigger kids when the going got boisterous and we moved on to the big school together, sharing the morning and evening bus journeys as well as our packed lunches and the answers to our homework. In the school show, she was always there in the chorus behind me when I sang my solos and it was her encouragement, in the form of a dare, that had made me try out for one of the main parts in the first place.

At seventeen, our lives took us on to separate paths, though. Mine was the road to London and a scholarship place at a performing arts school; hers was the lochside road that was already so familiar to us both. She got a job behind the bar at the hotel and did a correspondence course in bookkeeping in her spare time, working her way up to a better-paid administrative position behind the reception desk. We lost touch soon after that, although I'd heard from Mum about her engagement and marriage a few years ago to

Andy McKinnes, who'd been in the year above us at school, and the subsequent arrival of little Jack.

Seeing Elspeth now, kneeling on the yellow-and-brown swirls of Bridie's sitting room carpet as she shows her son the pictures in a book of nursery rhymes, I feel guilty in all sorts of ways. I feel guilty that I left and she stayed. I feel guilty that I haven't been a better friend – I never once invited her down to stay with me in London. I feel guilty that I was the one who stopped writing, responding to her lengthy letters with briefer and briefer notes, and then just occasional postcards depicting Big Ben and Carnaby Street, before our correspondence dwindled and died altogether in the absence of any common ground. Remembering our encounter in the shop a few weeks ago, I feel guilty, too, that her calm, competent mothering skills put mine to shame. And, as the tiny solitaire diamond in her engagement ring catches the light when she turns a page of the picture book, I feel guilty that she's done the whole engagement–marriage–baby thing in the socially accepted manner, whereas I've succeeded in making a complete mess of it.

She smiles up at me, tucking her hair behind her ear in a mannerism that I remember vividly from our teenage years, her coolness thawing just a tad at the sight of Daisy balanced on my hip.

'Hello, Lexie. And hello, Daisy sweetheart – would you like to come and look at this book with Jack?'

Daisy surveys the pair of them, round-eyed and serious, before arriving at the decision that this looks like the opportunity for some fun and reaching her arms towards the floor. I kneel on the carpet, too, and Elspeth turns the book so that Daisy can see the pictures.

'Isn't that grand! I knew they'd get on like a house on fire,' Bridie clucks from the doorway. 'Now then, the two of them can get acquainted while I make the tea.' She bustles off into the kitchen, satisfied that her social get-together has begun so well.

Naturally, with Elspeth here I won't be able to quiz Bridie about my parents' history as I'd hoped to do. In fact, she's cleverly managed to turn the tables on me. With the help of an ally who knows me so well from years before, this is the perfect opportunity for her to question *me* about my recent past.

Grudgingly, I have to hand it to her. Bridie Macdonald is no fool. But the way to prise a limpet off a rock is to catch it unawares, so perhaps one of these days I'll get the truth out of her, when her guard is down. I just need to be patient and wait for the right moment.

Forcing myself to smile, I gather Daisy on to my lap and softly join in a round of 'Pop Goes the Weasel', conscious of the roughness of my singing. If Elspeth is surprised that this is all that's left of the voice that once filled West End theatres, she is polite enough not to show it. Bridie, as she comes back with a tray of teacups and a jug of orange squash, is less tactful.

'It's lovely to hear the room filled with the weans' giggles,' she says, pouring juice into the baby beakers that we've brought with us. 'And your singing again, too, Lexie. I remember when you sang the solo at the Christmas carol concert when you were just seven. Your mammy was so nervous for you that first time, I thought she'd burst. And by the time you'd finished there wisnae a dry eye in the hall. You were note perfect!'

I help Daisy lift the cup and drink, careful not to spill orange squash on the swirly carpet. 'I'm afraid nowadays my singing brings tears to people's eyes for the opposite reason,' I say, trying to deflect the anguish I feel with humour.

'What happened?' asks Elspeth, matter-of-fact.

'I overstrained my voice. Developed lesions on my vocal cords. I had an operation, but it didn't work, left too much scar tissue. So that's it, my singing career over.'

'Will they recover in time?'

I shake my head silently, not trusting words.

'That's a shame,' Elspeth says, the tone of her words softening a little. 'A tough break.'

I turn towards Bridie, who's fussing with the teapot, grateful for the distraction, which gives me a moment to blink the tears from my eyes. 'Just milk, thanks, Bridie.' Turning back to mop Daisy's chin with a tissue, I say, 'It'd all have changed in any case with this one on the way. There are plenty of singers queuing up to step on to the West End stage who aren't either pregnant or tied down with a baby.'

Bridie settles herself on the sofa, and I get the impression that she's preparing to launch into a series of questions that would make the Spanish Inquisition look like a cosy fireside chat.

Unexpectedly, though, Elspeth comes to the rescue, tactfully changing the subject and getting me off the hook. 'You know, there's a playgroup you could bring Daisy to if you'd like, just me and a couple of other young mums who get together at one another's houses on a Friday morning. Tomorrow's my turn to host, so you'd be welcome to come along.'

I shoot her a grateful glance. 'I'd love that. And I know Daisy would too.'

Jack is busily posting puzzle pieces into the right-shaped holes in a plastic ball with the confidence of familiarity, while Daisy helpfully offers him pieces of Lego by way of her own contribution. He ignores her at first, intent on his work, but eventually gives her a shy smile and takes the proffered block, popping it through one of the holes. Daisy immediately offers him another one and he chuckles, realising that here is a good new game.

'They're getting on well, right enough,' says Elspeth with a smile, and I feel the ice thawing between us a little more. Life may have taken us in different directions for a while, but perhaps those years apart can slide away and our babies bring us back together, rekindling the easy warmth of our own shared childhood.

Later, once the orange squash has been finished and both children have happily slobbered sugar-iced Playbox biscuits down their fronts, we gather up toys, cups and books and prepare to head homewards.

'Thanks for the lovely tea, Bridie,' I say, hugging her and meaning it. It's been a surprisingly enjoyable afternoon after all, in spite of the fact that I'm no further forward in learning anything more of my own family history.

Elspeth and I strap our babies into their pushchairs and stroll a little way along the road together before we take our leave. The children are quiet, worn out with all that socialising, and we walk in silence for a few moments, each lost in our own thoughts. When we reach her gate, stopping to watch the sky as the setting sun begins to edge the clouds with red and gold, I turn to face her and say, 'I'm sorry about the way we lost touch. When I bumped into you in the shop I wondered if you were angry with me because I left?'

She gazes out across the darkening waters of the loch for a moment, considering. Then she says, 'No, Lexie, I wasn't angry that you left. I was angry because you came back.' She looks me squarely in the eye. 'You were my hope, you see. The proof that there was a world out there, and it might not have been one I could ever have been part of, but you still linked me to it, even after we lost touch. I kept all your letters and cards. I've still got some of the programmes from your shows and that signed ticket stub you sent me after you went up on stage during *Godspell* and met David Essex.' She smiles a little sadly. 'When I saw you in the shop that day, it was like I'd finally lost the link to that other world. Like a door had slammed shut once and for all. Sorry I wasn't exactly welcoming. I know it must have been hard for you, coming back.' She reaches across and gives me a brief hug, then she turns Jack's pushchair and begins to wheel him up the path to the yellow front door.

'Elspeth?'

She glances back over her shoulder.

'Thanks.'

She nods, rummaging in her pocket for her key. 'See you tomorrow.'

As I walk back along the road to Keeper's Cottage, I find I'm humming softly, almost under my breath. And once Daisy is fed and bathed, I hold her in my arms and sing her a lullaby, to the accompaniment of the shushing of the waves.

'*Hush ye, my bairnie . . .*'

While the notes may be cracked and broken in places, it still feels good to use my voice again, watching her rose-gold lashes flutter on her cheeks as I sing my baby daughter to sleep.

Flora, 1940

It was March before there was a day when they were both free that was calm enough for Flora and Alec to pack a picnic and explore some of their childhood haunts. She was just wrapping some corned beef sandwiches in newspaper when his car pulled up at the cottage gate. She watched him cover the path in three loping strides before he caught sight of her through the kitchen window. His face lit up and he gave a jaunty salute as she flung open the front door. She stood on tiptoes, her lips meeting his halfway as he stooped to kiss her.

'I just need to put my boots on. I've got sandwiches and a bottle of water there on the table.'

'We'll add them to the hamper. I've managed to wangle the use of a tender for a few hours, so we can get out on to the loch. I thought we might take a turn across to Firemore Bay, if you like. The road round is closed off with a checkpoint but we can get to the beach by the water, so long as they don't take us for invading enemy agents and shoot us!' Catching sight of her anxious expression he gave her a hug. 'I'm joking. Don't worry, I've squared it with the officer in charge and got permission to take the boat over.'

As they took the supplies from the car to carry them to the jetty, Moira Carmichael came out of her house. 'Good morning, Alec, Flora. Isn't it a lovely day? And where are you two off to?'

'We're just going out for a turn about the island. And yourself, Mrs Carmichael?'

She raised her bag – from which a pair of knitting needles protruded – with a flourish. 'I've some new recruits to the Rural over at Poolewe who need to be shown what to do.' She fluttered her eyelashes at Alec, surprisingly flirtatious. 'No rest for the wicked, as they say!' Craning her neck to look down towards the jetty wall she then shouted, with more of her usual force, 'Stuart! David! I'm away now. There's some bread and dripping for your lunch. I'll be back by three. Mind you get the vegetable bed dug over like I asked you to by the time I get back.'

Two small figures, sitting side by side at the top of the slipway where they dangled handlines into the water, turned and gave her a thumbs-up.

'Honestly, those boys will be the death of me,' she grumbled. 'Archie and I have our work cut out teaching them even the most basic of manners, I can tell you.'

'What word is there of Johnny, Matthew and Jamie?' Alec asked.

She beamed. 'I've had letters from Johnny and Jamie just this past week. Nothing from Matthew but then he's off who-knows-where on some training exercise with the second battalion, his brothers say. They're all fit and well though, thank you, Alec. Give my best to your mother, won't you, dear? And please thank her for her very generous donation to the canteen fund. It makes such a difference, being able to provide a bit of home cooking to those who are so far from their homes.'

'I know how much the lads appreciate it,' Alec agreed. 'Ma was only too pleased to be able to offer a little support.'

'Well, mustn't dilly-dally. There are socks to knit.' Moira stowed the bag of knitting in the basket of a bicycle that leaned against the fence and then, settling her hat firmly on to her grey curls, she mounted it somewhat unsteadily and wobbled off along the road.

Alec carried a wicker hamper to the jetty and set it down next to Stuart and Davy while he went to bring the boat round.

'Hello, boys,' Flora greeted them. 'Have you caught anything?'

Stuart shook his head. 'Not a nibble.'

Davy chipped in, 'We're trying to catch a fish for Mrs C so she'll not be so cross. It's not easy having two extra mouths to feed.'

'Wheesht, Davy,' his brother admonished him. 'She'll be even crosser if she catches you saying that.'

'But it's what she says all the time,' protested Davy, squirming out of reach as his brother tried to give him a cuff around the ear.

'She's not really cross with you, you know. She's just anxious about having her own boys away at war.' Flora smiled at them reassuringly. 'She's taking good care of you, isn't she?'

'Yeah, she is, I s'pose,' said Stuart, pulling in his line to untangle a skein of weed from his hook. 'She makes really good mince and tatties. And when she has the time, sometimes she bakes us scones.'

Flora unbuckled the hamper and brought out a bottle of ginger beer. 'Here you go, why don't you two share this while you're fishing? Or you can save it to have with your bread and dripping if you like.'

'Are you off out for a picnic?' Davy asked. 'Can we come too?'

Drawing the boat alongside them, Alec laughed. 'Sorry, lads, I could do without the extra competition. This outing is just for me and Miss Gordon.'

'Is he your sweetheart then?' Davy asked Flora, looking just a little bit crestfallen.

'He's a very old friend of mine,' she replied with a smile.

'And yes, I hope I am her sweetheart as well, because she's certainly mine.' Alec grinned. 'In any case, I wouldn't like to have to answer to Mrs Carmichael if that vegetable patch isn't dug over by the time she gets back.'

Flora passed him the hamper, which he stowed against the transom before handing her into the boat. Pushing off from the jetty, they waved to the boys and then Alec steered out on to the loch, heading for the northern end of the island. They picked their way past the battleships at anchor in the bay. A refuelling tanker churned the oil-slicked surface of the water and the fumes rasped at the back of Flora's throat, but once they reached the point of the island, the wind picked up a little and the air was fresh again with the smell of salt and seaweed. Flora pulled off her woollen tammy and let the breeze wash over her bare head, teasing tendrils free from her braid.

'Oh, it feels so good to be back out here. If you don't look back towards Aultbea, you can almost imagine there's no war on at all, with the loch and the hills as wild and empty as they ever were.'

Silently, Alec pointed to the sky above, as an eagle launched itself from a small stand of trees on the island and soared away across the dancing waves, heading west. They watched it until it was swallowed by the hills towards Melvaig. 'At least some things remain unchanged. But the war is coming closer now. Did you hear about the air raid on Scapa Flow two days ago? The Luftwaffe managed to sink the *Norfolk*. The Home Fleet is dispersing from there now – so Loch Ewe's about to become even more crowded, I reckon.'

Flora nodded, then took his hand in hers. 'Let's not talk about the war today, please, Alec? Just for an hour or two, let's pretend we're as free as the wind and the sea.'

He smiled, entwining her fingers in his before raising them to his lips and kissing them. 'Agreed. Today is a carefree day. And spring is on the way. Look there, the spruces are getting their new needles. I love how bright they are among the darkness of the pines.'

As the shoulder of the island hid the ships in the harbour at Aultbea from view, it really was possible to imagine that they were the only boat on the water that day and to forget, for a little while at least, the transformation that had been wrought upon the tiny lochside community. Each time the bows of the boat met a wave, wings of fine sea spray flew along the gunwales, making Flora feel she was soaring, joining the birds overhead in their flight.

Alec steered the boat towards the white sands of the beach at Firemore and pulled in alongside the rocks. In the shelter afforded by the headland, the water here was as calm as a hillside lochan, making it easy for Flora to scramble ashore. She balanced at the top of the boulders, reaching back so that Alec could hand her the hamper and, while he made the boat fast, she spread a plaid rug on the dry sand a little higher up the beach. Raising a hand to shield her eyes against the dazzle of the spring sunlight on the water, she smiled as Alec approached, his boots crunching on the black tangles of bladderwrack that festooned the bay. He threw himself down on the rug beside her and lay looking straight up into the sky above, which was the same colour as the delicate harebells that grew here and there along the roadside in summer.

'We're being watched.' He pointed upwards and she lay back, too, to follow the lazy circles that the eagle drew as it spiralled ever higher, climbing on a thermal over the hills. Alec reached for a pair of binoculars that he'd tucked into the hamper alongside the sandwiches and ginger beer. He handed them across to her and she focused the sights, just able to make out the graceful, finger-like primary feathers at the end of each wing. She passed the binoculars back and Alec took his turn. After a few minutes, he sat up and scanned the hills on the far side of the loch.

'That eagle's not the only one watching us,' he said with a grin. He pointed towards the shoulder of land above the eastern shore, where she could just make out the grey walls of a concrete hut, one of many that had sprung up around the loch in the past months. 'That's the signal station. I'd better be on my best behaviour, because your brother is keeping an eye on me.' He handed the binoculars back to her.

'How do you know Ruaridh is on duty today?' Flora asked, squinting through the scopes to try to see.

'Look to the left, just beside the hut. What can you see?'

'There's what looks like a signal flag tied to a stick. A blue cross on a white background. What does it mean?' Flora asked.

Alec laughed. 'It stands for the letter X. Which is also used to signal the message "*Stop carrying out your intentions and watch for my signals.*" It's your brother, all right. See, he hasn't run it up the official signalling mast. It's meant just for us. Or, more probably, for me!'

'Well, what a cheek! I'm sure your intentions are nothing but honourable.'

Alec propped himself on one elbow, watching her profile as she scanned the landscape with the field glasses.

'They certainly are honourable. But I do have intentions, you know, Flora, where you are concerned.'

She set aside the binoculars, laughing. 'And may I ask just what those intentions might be, Alec Mackenzie-Grant?'

His expression was suddenly serious as he reached out a finger to brush a tendril of hair from her cheek. 'I intend to spend the rest of my life with you, Flora Gordon. If you'll have me, that is. I can't give you a formal proposal just yet, as I have a few hurdles to cross before I'm in a position to do so. But once both of our families have realised how serious I am about you, once I've had a chance to square it with your father and mine, I'll be asking you. Just so's you know, in case you were in any doubt.'

She lay on her side, facing him, watching the play of sunlight and shadows on his face, and then she said, 'I have no doubts whatsoever where you are concerned, Alec. But you were engaged to another woman just a few months ago. I'm not at all sure this is very proper.'

He picked up a fistful of sand and watched it trickle through his fingers, opening his palm to let the wind scatter the last grains across the beach. 'I'm ashamed to say that I allowed my father to talk me into the idea of marrying Diana. A very suitable match, he said it would be. My heart was never in it. And clearly neither was hers, given the speed with which she replaced me once she got back to London. I won't make a mistake like that again.'

'Yes, but I don't think your father will feel I'm the least bit suitable. The keeper's daughter? For the son of the laird? We're from two different worlds, you and me.'

He shook his head, his dark eyes alight suddenly, with the strength of his feelings. 'This war has changed everything. There is only one world now, a world united in this fight. Don't you see, Flora – the barriers have come down? And it's made me realise what I really want in life.' He hesitated, then reached for her hand, his fingers meshing with hers. '*Who* I really want. It's you, Flora. It has only ever really been you.'

He gathered her close and she pressed her hands against his chest, feeling the warmth of his skin and the beat of his heart through the rough wool of his jersey. And then she raised her lips to his and sealed their promise of a future together with a kiss.

After lunch, they climbed back into the boat and Alec steered a course that hugged the western side of the loch, below the white cottages at Cove where the road became a rough track. They waved to Mrs Kennedy who was pegging her washing on the line in front of her croft house, white sheets billowing like sails in the stiff breeze, and then Alec brought the boat in close to the rock arch so that they could get a look at the nesting gulls whose calls filled the air and whose droppings whitewashed the dark craggy rocks in streaks and splashes.

Finally, as the sun slipped behind the hills of Gairloch and the waters of Loch Ewe began to darken, they turned the boat homewards.

The jetty was deserted as they offloaded their belongings. Alec made the boat fast and then they made their way back to his car. As he stowed everything in the boot, Flora glanced upwards, her attention captured by the sound of tapping from a dormer window on the top floor of the Carmichaels' house. Following her gaze, Alex grinned and waved at the sight of Stuart and Davy, who had their noses pressed against the glass. With a struggle, Stuart managed to free the catch on the window and push it open.

'Be careful,' Flora called. 'Don't lean out like that; you might fall.'

'What are you two rascals up to?' Alec asked.

'Nothing much,' answered Stuart with a shrug. 'We forgot the time when we were fishing and we didn't get the digging done, so Mrs C has locked us in our room with no tea. We're starving, 'cause we didn't get much lunch neither. Mr C and her are away out now, for a meeting at the kirk. Davy's been crying,' he added.

'You'd be greetin', too, if your belly was hurting something cruel like mine is,' his brother retorted. Then he leaned on the windowsill again, craning his neck to get a clearer view of the couple. 'That ginger beer was awfy good,' he said wistfully. 'Is there any left?'

'Sorry, no. I'm afraid we drank the other bottle. Tell you what, though . . .' Alec rummaged in the hamper. 'There's a corned beef sandwich here, and a hard-boiled egg. We just need to find a way to get them up to you.'

'Wait a sec,' shouted Stuart, excited now. 'I've got my fishing line here.'

A minute later, the line descended and Alec was able to catch the end without snagging himself on it. He wound the line around the neck of a paper bag containing the remnants of their picnic and secured it with the hook. 'Easy does it! Wind it in slowly, that's it.'

Triumphantly, the boys hauled in their catch with a cheer.

'Don't you go telling on us now,' laughed Alec. 'I wouldn't want to have Mrs Carmichael after me.'

'And just you remember to make sure you do as she says next time, boys,' Flora warned.

'We will, I promise. And we'll not say a word. Thanks, Miss Flora, and Miss Flora's sweetheart. You've saved us from proper starvation,' Stuart called back.

'His name's Alec,' she told him, smiling.

As they pulled away, Alec remarked, 'So I'm officially Miss Flora's sweetheart now, am I? Well, this certainly has been a red-letter day, despite the best efforts of Signalman Gordon.'

By way of a reply, she rested her head on his shoulder and he drove her back to Keeper's Cottage in contented silence.

Lexie, 1978

Daisy enjoys herself thoroughly at Elspeth's when we go to the playgroup. To my surprise, so do I. I feel a little awkward at first when Elspeth introduces me to the others, my years away making an incomer of me and a stranger in my own community. But children are a great icebreaker, and by the time Elspeth brings through the mugs of coffee on a tin tray we've already bonded over the sharing out of toys and a packet of sponge fingers. Daisy sits regally in the middle of a tartan rug, sucking the sugar from her biscuit, while Jack hands her a series of wooden animals from his Noah's Ark. She sets each one carefully in her lap, unsure of what to do with them but pleased with the gifts nonetheless.

The other children are a little older, three self-assured toddlers who push cars up and down the ramp of a wooden garage and build towers of plastic blocks that can be knocked down with cries of glee.

'Typical boys,' smiles Elspeth. 'It's nice to have Daisy here to tip the balance a bit.'

One of the other mums pats her belly, which is swollen with pregnancy. 'Maybe this one'll be a lassie, too,' she says. Then she turns to me with a grin. 'It's about time. I've three boys already.'

I kneel on the rug to remove a lump of soggy sponge finger from Daisy's curls, and Jack – ever the perfect host – brings me a brightly coloured xylophone. I take the sticks that he proffers with it and pick out the opening notes of 'The White Cockade'. He looks surprised at first, then grins as I softly hum the tune for him and Daisy beats time with the sticky remnants of her biscuit.

When I hand him the sticks to have a go himself, he passes them back to me. 'More,' he says, firmly.

'Okay,' I say, and sing the opening lines of 'The Skye Boat Song'. It doesn't seem to matter to Jack and Daisy that my voice is a little rough around the edges. One by one, the other mums join in with the familiar words, '*Speed, bonny boat, like a bird on the wing . . .*' And their boys put down their cars and bricks and come to listen.

'Would you look at that?' exclaims Elspeth when we finish a repeat of the final chorus. 'It's said that singing will charm the seals from the loch but I never thought it could bring the wee boys away from their games. They love it.'

'Och, all kids love music,' I say, passing the xylophone to one of the toddlers who is showing a keen interest in the sounds it makes.

'It reminds me of how we used to hear those songs sung when we were wee. Our parents' generation was brought up with them – playing, too. My dad learned the fiddle when he was tiny but somehow he never had time to teach me, or if he did, I didn't have the inclination to learn.' Elspeth rummages in the toy box and brings out a tambourine, which she hands to Jack.

'They're not taught at school either these days. There's not so much time for music in the curriculum now,' chips in one of the mums.

'More's the pity – look how much they enjoy it.' Another of the mums nods at the group of toddlers who are now enthusiastically banging on anything they can lay their hands on in an attempt to continue the singing session.

'Maybe we could include some of the songs whenever we get together? Teach them ourselves?'

'Great idea,' says Elspeth. 'Lexie can keep us right.' She gives my arm a pat. 'You know the tunes, after all, and you can remember way more of the words than I can. I've forgotten half of them these days.'

'I'd need to brush up a bit,' I reply. 'But I'm sure there's an old songbook of Mum's at the cottage. I'll dig it out.'

Elspeth nods. 'Your mum was the one who *really* knew all the songs. I remember how she'd sing as she cooked the stovies for our tea on days when I came back to yours to do our homework together.'

Soon after that, playtime descends into chaos as the children grow hungry and tired. I scoop up my dishevelled daughter, who is now attempting to chew the head off a wooden giraffe, wiping the gummy residue of biscuit from her fingers. 'Time to go home, Daisy-Mae.'

At the door, I thank Elspeth for the morning. She gives me a hug, closing the last few inches of distance between us.

'See you next time. It's good having you home, Lexie,' she says.

And those words make my heart feel as if it were a balloon on the end of a string, lightening my steps as I turn Daisy's baby pushchair towards Keeper's Cottage with a final wave to the others.

As we pass the jetty, another figure waves to us from beside a pile of creels. I raise a hand in salute.

'Bat,' remarks Daisy, approvingly.

'Hello, Davy.'

His long legs, clad in his usual oilskin bib-and-brace trousers, cover the distance between us in just a few strides. His Land Rover is parked outside the house beside us, I realise. It's one of the larger homes in the village, with dormer windows below its slate roof and a well-tended garden behind a wooden gate.

'Hi, Lexie. And hello to you, too, Miss Daisy. Been socialising over at Elspeth's, have you?'

I nod. And realise that I don't mind that he knows how I've spent my morning. For a change, it feels reassuring rather than claustrophobic, the way that this small community watches over me and my daughter.

'Well, I'm glad I caught you,' he says. 'The weather's set fair for a couple of days. If you're free tomorrow it'll be an opportunity to come out in the boat. If you'd still like to, that is.'

'Bat,' Daisy says again, beaming at him and kicking her feet in the air.

We both laugh.

'I'll take that as a yes, then.' Davy grins.

'Okay,' I say. 'What should I bring?'

'Just make sure you're both warmly dressed. It's always a wee bit chillier once we get out on the water. Pack some extra layers too. Some juice for Daisy, maybe? I've got life jackets and everything else we'll be needing. We can leave mid-morning and have a bit of lunch on the boat if you're happy to stay out a wee bit longer. But we can play it by ear, let you get your sea legs and see how the two of you like it.'

'Thanks, Davy, that sounds great. It's a date.' I say the words without thinking, then catch myself and blush furiously. 'I mean, it's not a date-date, obviously. I just mean we'd love to . . . we'd really enjoy . . .' I tail off in confusion.

His grey-blue eyes crinkle in amusement, but he keeps a straight face, kindly pretending not to notice the fool I'm making of myself. 'I'll come and pick you up at the cottage, then, shall I? About ten-thirty?'

And I smile and nod again, thankful for the breeze from the loch that cools my blazing cheeks. As I push Daisy homewards, I find that the balloon-on-the-end-of-a-string feeling is still with me and realise that under my breath, I'm humming to myself again.

True to his word, Davy pulls up in front of Keeper's Cottage at ten-thirty sharp. He strides up the path, whistling, and I hurry to open the door. I pull on my wellies and jacket, scooping up Daisy who is already bundled into so many warm layers that she resembles an overstuffed teddy bear, her arms sticking out almost at right angles from the sides of her well-padded body. Davy stows the bags containing extra clothes, hats and gloves, nappies, a changing mat, a double-handled cup with a spout, two bottles of milk, a carton of apple juice, a bunch of bananas and a packet of custard creams into the back of the Land Rover.

'I was only planning on going as far as Firemore Bay,' he says cheerfully. 'Looks like you're ready for an Atlantic crossing!'

The loch is calm beneath a wide blue sky, its shallows and depths casting shot-silk stripes of light and shade across its surface. Along the shore, oystercatchers step purposefully across the sand, intent on picking out cockles or searching for mussels among the rocks to feed their young. Davy points out a pair of red-throated divers, who lift their long beaks skywards as we pass, showing off the silvered patches on their snakelike necks that will turn to blazes of scarlet in the summer.

The *Bonnie Stuart* is already tied up alongside the jetty and Davy jumps on board first, reaching back to take Daisy from me and then offering me a steadying hand as I step on to the deck. 'Here you go,' he says, handing me a pair of life jackets, one small, one large. 'You can sit over there, if you like, and I'll get us underway.'

I perch on the wooden bench that runs along one side of the boat and fasten the clips on Daisy's life jacket. She waves her starfish hands happily at the gulls that swoop and circle in the blue above us in anticipation of a feeding opportunity as Davy starts the engine.

'I've a few lines of creels to check and then we'll head for the western shore,' Davy calls over his shoulder from the wheelhouse. I nod and give him the thumbs-up, settling Daisy in my lap and holding her safe in the circle of my arms as we pull away from the jetty. Her eyes grow big and round as she watches a broad stretch of water begin to unfurl between us and the land. I plant a reassuring kiss on her forehead and she turns to give me her biggest smile, happy to be exploring this new element. The *Bonnie Stuart* cuts an easy path through the water, leaving a ribbon of lace foaming in our wake.

First we head towards the southern end of the loch, where a high pier juts from the shore beneath the pine-clad hills. It's one of the few wartime installations that's still in use, Davy explains, as a refuelling point for naval vessels. He points out some of the other remnants of the war – the grey stumps of concrete lookout posts, a signalling station and the anti-aircraft positions that once ringed Loch Ewe, protecting the ships that gathered here as the convoys mustered. And he shows me the black tideline that rings the rocks of the loch shore, where a slick of oil that floated on the water's surface from all those ships once painted an indelible Plimsoll line, separating the tufts of heather and lichen above from the bare grey rocks below. It's hard to picture how it must have looked when the loch was jam-packed with ships. Nowadays the water is crystal clear again, and its mirror-like surface reflects the hills around us.

'It's fine and calm today,' he remarks. 'But we'll still stick to the shelter of the loch. Even on a day like this, there'll be more of a swell out there on the open water. The Blue Men of the Minch never rest for long.'

He notices my quizzical look. 'Och, and you call yourself a local? Have you never heard that particular piece of folklore, Lexie

Gordon? The Blue Men are storm kelpies, sea spirits who inhabit the stretch of water out there that separates us from the outer isles. They're always up to no good, looking out for sailors to drown and ships to sink. They're said to have the power to summon up storms. The waters of the Minch are some of the most treacherous in the world: I've seen currents in the sea out by the Shiant Isles that flow like raging rivers when the tide is running. The Blue Men are supposed to inhabit caves in the islands' cliffs. It's certainly no place to try to land a boat.'

But those spirits seem far away today. The water beneath us rolls as smooth as an unfurling bolt of silk as we glide through it, watched by a heron poised on one slender leg in the shallows.

Slipping the engine into neutral, Davy lets the momentum of the boat carry us alongside an orange float that bobs on the surface of the water near the entrance to a small rocky inlet. With a boathook he catches the rope attached beneath the float and runs it through a pulley. As he winches the handle, the rope begins to tighten and a creel emerges from the depths, black and dripping. He leans over the side to haul it on to the deck and shows us the catch. There are half a dozen squatties, a large crab and a small lobster. He keeps the crab and the squatties, sorting them into separate buckets filled with seawater, but returns the lobster. 'It's on the wee side, that one, so we'll let it grow.'

Daisy is fascinated by the catch and I have to grab her hand as she attempts to give the crab an exploratory poke. 'Oops! Careful, those claws can pinch,' I explain.

Davy hauls in the rest of the line and declares it a satisfactory catch. He has two good-sized lobsters and a sizeable cluster of squatties to add to the buckets. Then he rebaits the creels with mackerel heads and sets the boat moving slowly forward again so that the line plays out. Each creel lands in the water with a splash that makes Daisy giggle and clap her hands together, until, sinking slowly, the line has been reset. As we set off again, only the orange float remains bobbing on the surface, marking the spot.

We carry on, following the sweep of the shore westwards until we reach the headland at Inverewe. The exotic trees planted in the gardens of the estate, which are able to flourish this far north in the milder air swept up here from lower latitudes by the Gulf Stream, stand out against the Forestry Commission plantations of dark pines and the bare hills that surround the rest of the loch. Towering rhododendrons paint the rocky promontory with splotches of deep crimson and brilliant scarlet.

'They used to store ammunition in the cove on this side,' says Davy, pointing to a secluded inlet, almost hidden by a line of rocks. 'But nowadays there are other inhabitants hiding here.' He switches off the engine and the sudden silence is broken only by the whisper of wind in the trees and the peeping of a flock of sandpipers on the shore.

Then Davy begins to whistle a tune. Daisy looks up, startled at first but, after a glance up at me for reassurance, waves her arms in time to the lilt of the music. Davy gestures to me to join in and I sing the words, keeping my voice soft to stop it from cracking.

'*Heel ya ho, boys, let her go, boys,*
Heave her head round to the weather,
Heel ya ho, boys, let her go, boys,
Sailing homeward to Mingulay . . .'

Then I stop in amazement as three dark rounded heads appear in the water. Davy gestures to me to keep singing and the seals draw nearer. Then he points behind me and I turn to find two more pairs of eyes gazing at us. I hold Daisy up so that she can see them, too. Her eyes are almost as wide as theirs.

'Look,' I say. 'We sang the seals to us!'

She points a finger at them. 'Sea?' she says.

'Yes, seals.'

One of them dives, its sleek back rounding as it disappears beneath the boat, only to emerge on the other side a few seconds later. The others watch, heads bobbing in the water like black floats.

Davy grins before starting the engine again. As we chug slowly away, the seals watch us from their secret cove and then, one by one, disappear back beneath the water.

On the far side of the island, Davy hauls in two more creel lines. There's another good-sized lobster (plus one whose undercarriage is covered in eggs, so Davy carefully puts her back so that she can have her babies and help keep the stocks replenished), and two more brown crabs, as well as more clusters of squatties and a cross-looking dogfish that Davy throws back. 'That's a pretty good haul for today,' he declares. Then he glances at his watch. 'How are you two doing? Happy to go a bit further or would you prefer to head for home?'

'I think we're very happy to keep going,' I say with a smile. The sun bounces off the water, dazzling our eyes and lifting our spirits. Neither Daisy nor I am ready to return to land yet.

With a nod of approval, Davy turns the *Bonnie Stuart* northwards and we follow the western hills to where a stretch of white sand fringes the shore, turning the waters the turquoise of a travel poster.

He throttles back the engine, then puts down an anchor and, as he plays out the rope, we drift gently towards the beach until we can see the scallop shells on the sea floor beneath us through the crystal-clear water.

'Time for some lunch,' Davy declares, dragging a wicker basket from beneath the bench. He brings out some greaseproof-paper-wrapped sandwiches. 'I wasn't sure what you'd like, so there are some ham ones and some with crowdie which I thought Daisy might manage.'

The soft cream cheese meets with Daisy's approval and she stuffs the morsels of sandwich that I hand her into her mouth with gusto. We sit, basking like seals in the sunshine, eating our lunch and letting the light soak into the skin of our faces. Then I give Daisy some banana and a bottle of milk, after which she settles herself into the curve of my arm with a contented sigh and drowsily watches the patterns that the light throws on to the door of the wheelhouse.

Davy sets up a small camp stove and puts a kettle of water on to heat.

'What luxury,' I say. 'This is a very fine restaurant indeed.'

'Glad to hear it measures up to your fancy London eateries,' Davy says with a smile that makes his grey-blue eyes shine. I notice how white his teeth are against the weathered tan of his skin. Then his expression grows more serious. 'You must miss it all, that life you had down there.'

I consider his words – more of a statement than a question – as he puts teabags into mugs and pours water from the kettle.

'Not really,' I say, nodding as he holds up a jam jar filled with milk and raises his eyebrows enquiringly. 'Just a dash, please. Thank you.' I take the tin mug he hands to me and blow on the surface to cool it. 'I thought I would miss it terribly when I left London, but I really don't. In fact, having Ardtuath to come home to has turned out to be the best thing. For Daisy and for me. The one thing I do miss is being able to sing. But that ability seems to belong to someone else now – the person I was in another lifetime.'

'It must have been really hard, losing your voice like that.'

I nod, taking a sip of my tea and settling Daisy a little more comfortably as her eyelids begin to droop. 'It was. At the time it was the end of my world. It was all I had. My voice had become my whole identity. I went from rising star to forgotten nobody in the space of a few weeks.'

Davy sits in silence for a moment, watching a bird of prey that's circling high above the hills. 'Are you always so hard on yourself?' he asks at last, the tone of his words light so that I can't take offence.

'I suppose I am,' I reply. 'But then, so I should be. I've messed everything up so badly.'

He laughs. 'There you go again, proving my point. From where I'm sitting, you've done pretty well so far. You've achieved things that most people only dream of, and now here you are with a daughter of your own to raise, which seems to be another pretty good thing.'

I look down and stroke a fingertip against Daisy's cheek where the sunshine and the sea air have blushed it rosy pink. She's fallen asleep, lulled by a full belly and the peaceful drift of the boat.

He watches me, then asks gently, 'Is Daisy's dad on the scene at all?'

Without raising my eyes, I shake my head, unable to speak. At the time, Piers's words were horrible. But his silence and his complete rejection of me and Daisy ever since have been even worse.

I don't tell Davy about all of that, though. I just shrug at last and say, 'No, Daisy's dad isn't part of our lives.' The understatement of the year.

'I see. His loss, then,' Davy says quietly. From the look he gives me, I can see he understands. And maybe Bridie's told him what Mum had already surmised: that Piers wasn't fit for fatherhood.

'Does it hurt when you sing now?' he asks, after a pause.

I shake my head. 'No. But my voice has deepened and my range has diminished. It's a bit rougher, too, sometimes. Certainly no good for the stage any more.'

'You've a great tone, though,' he says. 'It holds a lot of feeling. If you like the old songs, you could come along to the bar on a Saturday night sometime. There's a group of us who play. Anyone with a musical bone in their bodies is welcome to join in.'

'What do you play?'

'Guitar. And mandolin.'

I nod. 'I'd like that.' Although I'd need someone to mind Daisy and I panic a little at the thought. I've never been out without her.

I finish my tea and Davy holds out a hand to take the mug. He packs everything away in the basket and then, as Daisy begins to stir, checks his watch. 'Time to be getting back, I reckon. We'll go just a wee bit further so you can see the rock arch and then we'll head round the north point of the island and back to Aultbea.'

Back at the jetty he makes the boat fast and then helps me ashore as Daisy stirs in my arms. He scoops a few handfuls of squatties into a carrier bag. 'These'll do for your supper. I'll drive you home, then come back and sort everything out here,' he offers, carrying my many bags to the Land Rover. I laugh when I see he's left it sitting outside his house with the key in the ignition.

'What?' he says with a shrug. 'We all do it. You're not in London now, remember.'

We unload everything at Keeper's Cottage. 'Thanks for a wonderful time,' I say. 'It was great to be out on the water.'

'No bother. Glad you enjoyed it.' He turns to go.

'Davy,' I call after him, 'would you like to come over for supper tomorrow night? We could share these?' I hold up the carrier bag.

'That'd be grand,' he says. 'Thanks, Lexie. See you then.'

'See you,' I agree.

And as I start to hang up our coats and hats and put away the gloves that we didn't need, I begin to sing the song that we entertained the seals with earlier while Daisy keeps time with a cup of juice.

Flora, 1940

The sun was slow to set in the days of high summer, seeming scarcely to dip below the western horizon an hour or so from midnight before it reappeared in the east in the early morning hours. In the evenings, when they'd been released from their duties, Flora, Alec and Ruaridh would take their trout rods and climb into the hills to fish. Their catch provided a welcome addition to the rations, both at the scrubbed pine table in the kitchen of Keeper's Cottage and on the polished mahogany one in the dining room of Ardtuath House.

From the hills above Aultbea and Mellon Charles, they could glimpse the constant buzz of activity on Loch Ewe, where ships moved ponderously like a huge grey shoal and their tenders sped in between them like the insects that skated over the surface of the lochan where they fished. They preferred to turn their backs on the busyness of the naval manoeuvres, though, and watch the calm waters cupped within the folds of the hills, where white water lilies drifted among the reflections of the clouds, hiding brown trout beneath the broad pads of their leaves. The three of them would set down their packs beside the old bothy and then spread out, each finding their preferred spot on the bank of the lochan from which to cast. Little was said, apart from the occasional quiet comment when a fish was landed. The song of the skylarks and the plaintive cries of the curlews from the moor above them filled the summer evenings with their music.

On one such evening, Flora was just about to cast her last fly into the deeper corner of the little loch where the rushes grew tallest, when she was surprised by Corry, Sir Charles's spaniel, who came bouncing through the starry sphagnum moss that grew thick on the hummocks of the hill surrounding the lochan.

'Hello, boy.' She bent down to stroke his silky ears and he wagged his whole body enthusiastically. 'Where's your master?'

A moment later the laird appeared, carrying his own fishing rod. 'Aha, I see you lot got here before me. Have you caught all the good ones already?' Sir Charles's deep baritone reverberated in the evening air, silencing the larks. He strode across to where Flora stood, her catch laid out on the mossy bank. 'Not a bad evening's work, Miss Gordon. I see you've managed to beat the boys.' Two of her three trout were larger than the single fish that Ruaridh and Alec had each caught.

She smiled and nodded. 'Alec will bring those two back to the big house. They should make a nice supper for you all.'

Sir Charles scarcely acknowledged her remark, turning towards his son. 'Pack your things away now and get on back to the house. Your mother is fretting because we have the Urquharts arriving tomorrow for the weekend. We've a day's fishing planned for them and the Kingsley-Scotts invited to dinner afterwards. Take her those trout – she'll be glad of them – and see what you can do to help. You know how short-handed we are these days. Although I certainly don't intend to let standards slip, just because there's a war on.'

At the mention of the Kingsley-Scotts, Flora stiffened slightly, shooting a quick glance at Alec. He hadn't mentioned that they'd be there. She wondered whether Diana would be coming with her parents. She put her catch into the willow creel and handed it to Alec, not quite meeting his eye.

'Here,' he demurred, trying to give her back the three smaller fish, 'you take these for your own supper.'

'No,' she said, firmly replacing them in the basket. 'It sounds as if you're going to need them if you've all those visitors coming.'

'Thank you,' he whispered. 'I didn't know he'd invited the Kingsley-Scotts.' He put a hand against Flora's cheek, reassuring her, and stooped to kiss her.

'You'd better get going, Alec.' His father's voice was sharp with impatience. 'In fact, since you and your friends have been so kind as to do my work for me this evening, I think I'll accompany you home. We can both give your mother a hand.' He shouldered his rod and called Corry to heel. 'Good evening, Ruaridh, Flora.' He gave them a curt nod and she saw how cold his eyes were; his earlier joviality had evaporated. 'Tell your father I'd like to speak to him tomorrow morning about the arrangements for the weekend.'

Alec hesitated, reluctant to leave, but his father snapped, 'Come on, man, I haven't got time to waste.'

Wordlessly, Ruaridh and Flora watched the two figures striding back down the hill. Then they gathered together their things, securing their hooks in the cork handles of their rods and pulling on the jackets they'd discarded earlier, before following more slowly in the footsteps of Alec and Sir Charles.

Flora was washing up the breakfast things when her father came back from his morning briefing with Sir Charles up at the house. Outwardly, his expression was as calm as ever, but she could tell he was out of sorts by the way he dragged the deerstalker from his head and threw it on to the table.

'Are you in for a busy day with the guests?' she asked him, drying her hands on the pinny tied around her waist. His duties as keeper had been unofficially expanded to those of ghillie as well, but she knew he'd rather be out on the hills than standing on a riverbank or rowing a boat while instructing inept guests on how to cast for salmon.

'Aye,' he grunted, his tone gruff, 'but I'm not the only one. Sir Charles has asked for you to go up and help out with the dinner this evening. He wishes Lady Helen to accompany the fishing party, too, and so he wants you to finish off the cooking. I'm not happy about it. It's not your duty. But you know how short-handed they are now.'

Flora nodded. The housekeeper had left at the end of the previous month, returning to care for her mother back home in Clydebank where there were well-paid jobs to be had in the munitions factories and the prospect of a far livelier social life than was to be found in the kitchen of Ardtuath House. And so, apart from Mrs McTaggart from the village who came in to clean in the mornings and do a little light cooking, Lady Helen was having to manage things on her own.

'Don't fret, Dad. I'm not bothered. I'll be happy to help out. It'll be good for Lady Helen to be included in the party for once – she never usually goes out with the rods.'

Flora's words belied her conflicting emotions. It would be a chance to see Alec and she wanted to be of help, but she was all too aware that this was an opportunity for Sir Charles to put her firmly in her place.

'It's ridiculous, Himself carrying on inviting those people. The world's changed for everyone except His Lordship, apparently. It's not right that they expect you to skivvy for them.'

'But Dad, we have our home because of him. And Lady Helen's always been so good to us. I don't begrudge them a helping hand every now and then. I wasn't intending on doing anything else tonight, in any case.'

Ordinarily on a Saturday evening, she and Alec would go to a dance or a film in the hall at Aultbea, or for a picnic with Mairi, Bridie and Ruaridh on the rare occasions that they were all off duty at the same time and the weather was fine. But that evening Mairi was helping her mother at home, and Ruaridh had a date with Wendy. And she'd known for weeks that Alec would be expected to attend the dinner with the house party staying at Ardtuath.

'Well, I still don't like it,' Iain grumbled, reluctantly going to gather up the rods and reels needed for the day's fishing. From the boot room he called, 'You're to go up to the house after lunch. Lady Helen will leave you instructions in the kitchen.'

As if sensing his master's fractious mood, Braan pressed his wet nose against Flora's hand and she scratched behind the black velvet of his ears to reassure him. 'Honestly, Dad, don't worry,' she called back. 'I'm glad to be helping out.'

Settling his tweed deerstalker back on to his head, her father shot her a fond look as he called Braan to his side. 'You're a good lass, Flora,' he said softly. 'I just hope they all appreciate that, too.'

Ardtuath House was silent when Flora walked up the drive. The building had a handsome, pleasingly symmetrical façade, the original two-storey hunting lodge flanked by twin towers in the Scottish Baronial style that had been added a century ago by Sir Charles's forebears. Automatically, she walked round to the back and retrieved the iron key from its hiding place behind the stone trough by the door, letting herself in. The cavernous kitchen was stuffy with the heat from the range, which muttered away quietly to itself, and she pushed open a window to let in the fresh air. On the broad table in the centre of the room sat a bowl covered with a clean dishcloth, and a note in Lady Helen's flowing hand written on a sheet of cream notepaper.

Flora, dear, thank you for helping.

There's a salmon in the larder, which I've already poached. It just needs the skin taking off and some decoration on the platter (cucumber in larder, too, for this purpose).

You'll find a haunch of venison there, for roasting. Please put it in the oven about five o'clock with some juniper berries and a little of the claret that you'll find in the dining room. There are potatoes and carrots in the store room to accompany it.

Mrs McTaggart has made pastry (in bowl) for a rhubarb pie, if you wouldn't mind preparing that, too.

Thank you again for all your help.

H. M-G.

Tying her apron, Flora set to work, fetching the ingredients and utensils she'd need to prepare the meat first, a fine haunch from a stag that her father and Sir Charles had shot a couple of weeks ago, with Ruaridh along, as usual, to lead the garron. Just the other day at Keeper's Cottage, she'd made a stew from the tougher offcuts that her father had brought home, once the carcass had hung in the game store. The finer cuts were always saved for the house, of course. The game from the estate made a big difference to their rations, although her father always shared their allocation with others in the community who needed a little extra.

Setting the haunch in a large roasting dish, Flora added a handful of juniper berries and some dried mountain thyme. Then she went along the corridor and through the green baize-covered door that led to the front of the house. The air there was perfumed with the smell of the beeswax used to polish the rich mahogany of the furniture, overlaid with a faint scent of wood smoke. The dining room had been prepared for the evening, the table draped with a white damask cloth and set with silver cutlery and candlesticks. An arrangement of roses and trailing swathes of ivy from the walled garden formed a graceful centrepiece – surely Lady Helen's work. On the sideboard stood several bottles of red wine. Flora uncorked one, carefully pouring most of the contents into a crystal decanter, and then took the remainder back through to the kitchen to pour over the meat before letting it rest in its marinade back in the larder again.

Once she'd peeled the vegetables and prepared the fruit for the pie, Flora set the kettle on the range and made herself a cup of tea before rolling out the pastry. She worked steadily and methodically with the capable neatness of one well used to such cooking, humming to herself to dispel the heavy silence that seemed to hang suspended within the walls of the empty house.

Just before six o'clock, as she was checking the roasting meat, she heard the sound of cars drawing up in front of the house and the voices of the returning fishing party. A minute later, Lady Helen hurried into the kitchen, pulling her broad-brimmed hat from her head and smoothing her hair into place.

'Flora, dear, it all smells wonderful! You are a gem, stepping in like this. My husband was adamant that I should accompany them today so I couldn't have managed without you. What can I do to help?'

'Nothing at all, Lady Helen. I hope you had a good day's fishing? I have everything in hand, so you have time to go and dress for dinner.'

Sir Charles's voice boomed down the corridor, calling his wife back to the other side of the green baize door, and she gave Flora an apologetic smile before hurrying away.

A moment later, the kitchen door was flung open and Alec strode in, dressed in his tweeds and still wearing his tall fishing boots. Without saying a word, he gathered Flora in his arms and kissed her. She breathed in the scent of the hills and the river from his jacket.

'My darling, I'm absolutely furious with my father over this. He had no right to demand that you do the cooking for tonight. They should have asked Mrs McTaggart to stay. Or paid someone else to come in.'

'Och, I don't mind a bit. I've enjoyed preparing the meal and it means I get to see you too.'

He gazed at her fondly and gently wiped a smudge of flour from her cheek with his thumb. 'Let me do something to help? Washing up? I'm a dab hand at that, though I'm afraid my cooking skills leave much to be desired.'

She shook her head. 'It's all done. Honestly, Alec, I'm fine. You'd better go and get changed. Dinner will be ready in an hour and you don't want to keep your guests waiting.'

Reluctantly, he allowed her to shoo him out once he'd stolen another kiss from her, and she smiled as she listened to his footsteps retreating down the corridor to the boot room. Then she busied herself with the final preparations, setting plates and gravy boats to warm and sharpening the knife ready to carve the venison.

When Lady Helen reappeared in the kitchen to let Flora know that the guests were seated in the dining room, she was transformed. Her dark golden hair, shot through with those few strands of silver, was drawn back from her face with a pair of diamond clasps, highlighting the delicate structure of her cheekbones. Her fishing tweeds had been replaced with an evening gown the colour of the sea, embellished with crystal beading that sparkled softly, reminding Flora of moonlight on water.

But Flora's eye was drawn to a brooch pinned to the dress. It was far less opulent than the rest of the costume, a simple silver depiction of an anchor surmounted by a crown, set in a wreath of acanthus leaves.

Lady Helen noticed Flora looking at it. 'It's rather pretty, isn't it? It's a Royal Navy sweetheart brooch, given by my father to my mother. He served in the Great War. I know it doesn't quite go with the rest of my get-up, but it's far more precious to me than these diamonds.' She gestured to the hair clasps, the rings on her fingers sparkling as their facets caught a ray of evening sunlight that glanced through the window behind her.

She reached for the heavy serving plate on which Flora had arranged the salmon, decorated with thin slices of cucumber to look like fish scales. But as she tried to lift it, she winced with pain.

'Are you all right?' Flora asked.

'Silly me – I sprained my wrist a few days ago and it still doesn't seem to be working properly.' Lady Helen gently probed her arm with her fingertips. Flora noticed that it was swollen, and the delicate skin on the underside was discoloured with an angry-looking purple bruise.

'Shouldn't that be strapped up?' Flora asked. She'd done some first-aid training as part of her ambulance driving course and was eager to try out some of her newly acquired skills. So far she'd only been able to practise on Mairi and Bridie, but here was what looked like a bona fide injury.

'It'll be fine, Flora dear, really, I don't want to make a fuss.' Lady Helen waved her away.

'Well, at least let me carry that through,' Flora said, picking up the platter. 'You need to rest that wrist to let it heal. And you don't want to risk spilling anything on your gown.'

In the dining room, the conversation was already animated, the guests having whetted their appetites with generous drams of whisky and glasses of sherry in the drawing room. A quick glance around the table told Flora that Diana wasn't there, although Mrs Kingsley-Scott was holding forth about the difficulties of planning a wedding at the family estate in the Borders with the war on.

The talk among the men was of the day's fishing, with speculation as to the weight of a salmon landed by Sir Charles and tales of other fish caught on other rivers.

One of the men boomed across the table, 'That ghillie of yours isn't exactly a talkative chap, eh, Charlie? Bit of an old curmudgeon, what? But he knows his stuff, I'll give him that.'

Lady Helen shot Flora an apologetic smile before quietly saying, 'Set it on the sideboard, dear. I'll get Alec to help me serve.'

He had already pushed his chair back from the table and was quickly at her side, taking the heavy platter from her. 'You should be seated next to me, not having to wait on us,' he muttered.

She smiled at him in gratitude, but shook her head and hurried away, preferring the peace and quiet of the kitchen, thankful for the green baize door which deadened the racket from the dining room.

She took the meat from the oven, setting it to rest on a warmed platter, then began to make the gravy with the juices in the pan.

It was bubbling nicely, and she was just draining the vegetables and putting them in their dishes when Alec appeared, carrying a pile of fish plates. He set them on the table and put his arms around her, burying his face in her hair.

'How's it going?' she asked, reaching to fill the gravy boats.

'They loved the salmon. Absolutely delicious. Here, let me carry the venison through – save you the ordeal of having to listen to their inanities.'

'Don't worry, it doesn't bother me. I'll bring the rest,' she said, setting things on to a tray.

'Alec!' Sir Charles's voice was sharp and harsh, making Flora jump so that she almost spilled the gravy. She glanced over her shoulder to see him standing in the doorway. 'Get back into the dining room at once. It's extremely rude of you to neglect our guests.'

'But Father, Flora can't manage everything on her own.'

'Nonsense. The girl's perfectly capable of serving a meal. What she doesn't need is you hindering her in her duties.' He stood to one side and gestured for Alec to leave the kitchen, turning abruptly and following on his son's heels.

Flora's cheeks burned with a mixture of the heat from the stove and the humiliation of the laird's words. But she picked up her tray and walked through the baize door with her head held high, setting the dishes on the dining table and shooting Alec a reassuring smile as she did so. He was sitting back in his place between two of the female guests, looking utterly miserable as they chattered across him about Mr Churchill, the new prime minister, and his wife, who wore the most beautifully tailored coats and such very elegant hats.

Lady Helen caught her wrist as she passed. 'Flora, dear, go home now. You've done more than enough. I'll manage the rest.' She spoke discreetly, her words soft beneath the guffaws and shrieks of laughter as Sir Charles regaled the table with another of his fishing anecdotes. From her beaded reticule, she slipped a small brown envelope into the pocket of Flora's apron. 'Here, for all your hard work today.'

Flora shook her head, trying to hand the envelope back, but Lady Helen held a finger to her lips, gently shooing her away.

'Thank you,' Flora said, keeping her voice low, too, understanding that this gesture was not something that would have had Sir Charles's approval. It was intended as an act of kindness, but at the same time it made her feel even more wretched about the role she'd been forced to play in the evening's proceedings. 'The pie's in the warming oven and there's a jug of cream in the larder to go with it.'

With a nod and a gentle pat on her hand, Lady Helen dismissed her and she hurried back to the kitchen. Before she left, Flora scraped and washed up the fish plates and cutlery. The rest would have to wait for Mrs McTaggart, who'd be coming in the next morning to make the breakfast, but she left everything as neat as she could.

She fished the brown envelope out of her pocket and then folded the sheet of cream writing paper containing Lady Helen's instructions around it. With a stub of pencil she wrote, *Thank you, but I was pleased to help.* She tucked it under the cake slice that she'd set on the table for cutting the pie, so that Lady Helen would be the one to find it.

Carrying her apron, Flora quietly closed the back door behind her and walked down the drive to where the path led into the pines towards Keeper's Cottage. A pair of tawny owls called softly to one another in the trees. Her eyes adjusted quickly to the moonlight and she took several deep, grateful breaths of the night air. At the turning, she paused for a moment, letting the slight breeze cool her face and neck, and glanced back towards the house. Behind the blacked-out windows, she could just make out a glint of candlelight, and another gust of uproarious laughter silenced the quiet conversation of the night birds for a moment. Then she turned her back on Ardtuath House and her face towards Keeper's Cottage, where she felt she belonged.

Lexie, 1978

Daisy's tucked up in her cot by the time Davy arrives for supper and, for a change, the sitting room in Keeper's Cottage feels almost like the sort of place two adults could have a civilised evening together over a glass of wine. I've packed away the toys and put the picture books on a shelf, and I've changed out of my jeans and baggy jumper, digging a skirt out of the wardrobe and a long-sleeved T-shirt out of a drawer.

As I prepare a bowl of garlic mayonnaise to accompany the squatties, which I've cooked and heaped on to one of Mum's dishes, I try again to remember where Davy fits into the life of Aultbea. I have a jumble of indistinct memories that I stored away in a corner of my mind when I left for London, like the jumble of belongings stashed up in the attic. Something tugs insistently on a strand of those memories, trying to untangle itself. Even after our outing on the boat, I've still not been quite able to place him. But there's been a familiarity in his eyes and an assumption of friendship in his manner from the first day he appeared on my doorstep, dispatched there by Bridie.

I hear the door of his Land Rover slam and then there's a snatch of his habitual whistling as he comes up the path to the door, which I open before he has a chance to knock.

He hands me a mandolin-shaped bottle of Mateus Rosé. 'The finest the shop has to offer,' he says with a grin.

He settles himself in one of the armchairs and crosses his long legs. 'This is nice,' he says, looking around at the room. 'It still feels like your mum's, but Daisy and you have made your mark as well. Last time I was here, Flora was sitting where you are now, pouring me a cup of tea.'

'It was good of you to visit her.'

'Ach, I did no more than any of the others. Bridie was here the most, of course. If she spotted a job that needed doing she'd let me know and I'd come and fix it for Flora. She was a lovely woman, your mum. I always felt no matter how much I did I could never repay her kindness to me and my brother when we washed up here in the war.'

Those memories shift and stir, becoming clearer as the mud that clouds my mind begins to settle a little. 'You were evacuees?' I ask.

Davy nods. 'Stuart and I were sent with about thirty other kids from Clydeside. We were billeted with a couple in the village. When the war ended we went home.'

'How old were you?' I ask.

'I was just four when we were sent here . . . nine by the time the war ended. My brother was a few years older, though. He always took care of me.'

He leans forward and takes the photo of Mum from the mantelpiece. 'This is a great picture of her. That's how she looked when I first saw her, not that she ever changed much. And she died far too young.'

I take a sip of my wine. 'She'd have been sixty this year.'

He sets the picture back above the fireplace and raises his glass to it. 'Here's to her, then. Flora Gordon: much loved and much missed.'

At his words, a sudden surge of grief threatens to overwhelm me. In order to cover up the sudden dampness in my eyes, I pass him a bowl of Twiglets and change the subject. 'Thanks for yesterday. It was great to get out on to the water. A magical day.' The memory of the sunlight on the sea and the seals coming to listen to our song is still vivid in my mind.

'It was good having the company. I'm glad we had the weather for it. It's not often we get a day as calm as that, even in the shelter of the loch.'

As I set the dish of squat lobsters on the kitchen table, next to the jug of white campion and dog roses that Daisy and I picked earlier, I steer the conversation back to Davy's story, still trying to unravel that tangled skein of memory.

'So when was it that you returned to Aultbea?'

'I came back in the early sixties. You would have been about sixteen or so, I suppose. It was just about the time you were setting off to London. Everyone was talking about how you'd got a place at stage school. You were the toast of the community. Bridie and your mum couldn't have been prouder of you.'

The strands of long-forgotten memories resurface at last. 'Oh yes, I remember now. You moved into your house that year, I think.' I dimly recall the gossip that heralded his arrival – something about his having inherited the house that he'd lived in during the war years. 'Of course. It used to belong to the Carmichaels.'

He nods. 'It felt like a homecoming to me, being back in Aultbea. And I was lucky to have a home to come to. Glasgow was a tough gig. Even though it was hard coming away from the city when we were so wee, being refugees turned out to be the best thing that ever happened to me and Stuart.'

'And where is Stuart now? Still in Glasgow?'

Davy's eyes cloud over and he ducks his head. Then he says, 'He died. He was stabbed in a fight after a football match.'

'I'm so sorry.' I reach across and put my hand briefly over his.

He shakes his head, remembering. 'We were on our way home after the game. We ran into a group of rival fans. They started in on me. Stuart stepped in, looking out for me as usual. Someone drew a knife . . . It was all over in seconds.'

'That's awful. I'm so sorry I never knew him.'

Davy gazes out to the waters of the loch, which are turning to gold in the evening light. 'He loved this place,' he says. 'He'd have loved the fishing. I named the boat for him. And for my mam. She's gone now, too.'

'Bonnie? That was her name?'

'Aye. She tried her best to be our mammy, but she was on her own and life was tough and when we came away so young she hit the bottle hard. She tried to shake it when we came back to her, but she never quite could. Losing Stuart tipped her right over the edge.'

We're both silent for a few seconds: him lost in his grief, me lost for words.

'I couldn't rescue either of them. And that's something I've had to live with ever since. So I painted their names on the boat when I came home to Loch Ewe, and they sail along with me when I'm out there.'

'And ever since then you've turned your attention to rescuing everyone else you could, looking after Bridie and my mum and anyone else who needed a helping hand?' The words are out of my mouth before I can stop them. I mean them kindly, but they come out sounding wrong.

He gives me a long look. Then says levelly, 'I'm not so sure that's true. It's just the way it goes around here. We all look out for each other. Maybe that's something you forgot in all those years you spent in London.'

Anger rises in my chest, but then I realise he's entitled to defend himself against my bluntness. 'Okay, good point,' I concede. 'I've got out of the west coast ways and perhaps that hasn't been for the best.' Admitting that comes as something of a relief I discover, cutting through the bramble hedge of defensiveness that I've grown to protect myself from my own guilt.

He pours water in my glass. 'Sorry, Lexie. Maybe you've got a point, too. Perhaps I do have a tendency to try and rescue people.'

I raise my water glass to his. 'Here's to both our guilty consciences then.'

He clinks his glass against mine and sings the line of a song.

'*When all is guid an' fresh an' pure –*

Nae guilt the heart to sting.'

I raise my eyebrows enquiringly.

'An old, old nursery rhyme,' he explains.

'Part of your repertoire on a Saturday night?'

He laughs. 'Not usually. We aim to create a slightly cheerier atmosphere. We don't want to have our audience walk out on us in a gloom.'

I pass him the dish and he piles another handful of squatties on to his plate.

'So when are you going to come along and listen?'

I shrug. 'Not sure. I'll need to try and find someone to mind Daisy.'

'Bridie's already offered,' he responds, grinning as I automatically bristle slightly at the fact that they've been discussing my hypothetical social life and putting plans in place to make it a reality. 'Och, would you get over yerself, Lexie Gordon. Let your friends help you every now and then. It'll not kill you.'

I laugh, holding my hands up in defeat. I know I'll enjoy having an evening in the bar listening to music, and I know Bridie and Daisy will have a fine old time of it themselves here at the cottage.

'That's settled then,' he says. 'This Saturday it is.'

'How do you know I don't already have something else on this weekend?' I ask, in one last futile attempt to regain control of the conversation.

'Just a hunch,' he says.

'Based, I suppose, on the common knowledge that I haven't had anything on any weekend since I got here?'

'Something like that,' he says, and refills my wine glass. 'Now, tell me about all those grand theatres you've sung in down there in London. What was the biggest one?'

Somehow the next time I glance at the kitchen clock it's nearly midnight and we've talked for hours. Davy drains the cup of coffee that I made ages ago and pushes his chair back from the table.

'Thank you for a lovely evening, Lexie. It's been grand sitting at Flora's kitchen table again, hearing her daughter laugh a bit. This house was always filled with song and good cheer.'

When he leaves, the cottage seems too empty. I've enjoyed his company and now I've been able to place him, I remember that Mum used to mention his name every now and then. As I clear the cups into the sink, his words echo in the empty kitchen. The range ticks softly to itself as it cools for the night and from the hill behind the cottage comes the ratcheting call of a corncrake. I wander through to the sitting room and pick up Mum's picture from the mantelpiece. 'I think it's time this house was filled with song and good cheer again,' I tell her.

And she smiles her approval back at me as I resettle the picture in its place and turn out the light.

Flora, 1940

On the Sunday evening, the day after she'd cooked for the fishing party at Ardtuath House, Flora sat on the bench in front of the cottage letting the sun bathe her in its light, its rays setting the red-gold tints in her hair afire as it traced a languid path across the western sky. She had her mending basket beside her and was sewing a button on to one of her father's shirts. Securing it with a few quick stitches, she snipped the thread and folded the shirt neatly, setting it to one side. Before reaching into the basket for the next item, she relaxed for a moment, leaning her head against the cottage wall behind her, closing her eyes and lifting her face to the warmth.

Despite the peace of the day's end, thoughts buzzed in her head like flies, irritating and persistent. The news on the wireless that morning had been deeply unsettling: only last week thousands of troops had been evacuated from Dunkirk in the face of the German advance, the Netherlands having fallen and Belgium having surrendered a few days earlier; a British aircraft carrier had been sunk off Norway by German battleships; Paris had been bombed, and Italy was issuing increasingly belligerent declarations. It had been a relief when the news bulletins had come to an end and the music programme had begun. But even singing along to the familiar tunes had failed to lift Flora's spirits much. And then, as a reminder that the war affected those closer to home, too, she'd bumped into

Bridie on a walk after lunch, who'd told her that a family at Poolewe had just received a telegram to say their son's plane had been shot down over the Channel and he was missing, presumed dead. Bridie said, too, that while the evacuation from Dunkirk had saved many lives, news was filtering through that the 51st Highland Division had been trapped inland and many of the men taken prisoner. The threat of the war, which at first had seemed to lie far off beyond the wall of hills, had begun to insinuate itself into the little white croft houses along the lochside now, casting an ever-present shadow of fear even on days when the sunlight sparkled across the water.

It dominated all their thoughts these days, making Flora's private concerns seem petty in comparison. And yet she still couldn't help mulling over Sir Charles's behaviour towards her yesterday. He'd been so cold. Usually he treated her with a brittle joviality, at best, or a casual disregard. But something had shifted since he'd become aware of the closeness between her and Alec. Her pride was still stung by the way in which he'd humiliated her. She tried to push those thoughts aside. She knew Alec loved her, but would he defy his father if it came to it? She'd sensed his anger yesterday and yet he'd been helpless to act. Both he and his mother were held fast in the steely grip that Sir Charles exerted on his family. Was their love strong enough to withstand that force?

She sighed, opening her eyes at the sound of a blast from a ship's whistle out on the loch. Another battleship had pulled into the harbour, manoeuvring as it dropped anchor, and a tanker was drawing alongside to refuel it. Tomorrow morning she'd be back on duty at the camp at Mellon Charles. At least that would be a welcome distraction, knowing she was doing her bit for the war effort.

She reached into her mending basket to pull out a sock in need of darning and began to thread a thick needle with a strand of Lovat green wool. The sound of footsteps on the path behind the house made her turn, expecting it to be her father back from seeing to the garron. But it was Alec who appeared, his face creased in a frown. His expression melted into a broad smile at the sight of her sitting there and he threw himself down on the bench beside her, sweeping her into his arms, narrowly avoiding being impaled by the darning needle in her hand.

He was quick to apologise for his father's behaviour. 'I can't believe how awful he was yesterday, showing off in front of the Urquharts like that. Making a point of inviting the Kingsley-Scotts, too. He's been impossible all weekend. Poor old Ma has retreated to her bed with a headache now that they've gone. He just refuses to accept that the war has changed everything.'

'But *has* it really changed everything?' Flora asked, resting her head against his shoulder and gazing out at the vast grey hulks anchored in the bay. 'Is the world now so different that the likes of a laird's son can be with a gamekeeper's daughter?'

He drew back, holding her at arm's length, trying to read her expression. His dark eyes were filled with pain and love. 'Flora, I have never thought of you in that way. Nor your father, nor Ruaridh. They are like family to me, always have been. And you – well, you must know that I've loved you for years. And I want to love you more, for all the years we have left. In this uncertain world, it feels like my love for you is the only certain thing I have to hold on to. Whatever happens, for God's sake, Flora, don't let my father take that from us.'

She lowered her gaze, trying to hide the doubts she still felt. Very gently, he traced the line of her face with the palm of his hand, then tilted her chin upwards so that he could see her eyes again.

'I know it's not easy,' he said, 'but once this war ends, the power my father wields over us will be defused. We'll be free to marry then.'

'What about your mother, though?' Flora knew how Alec worried about leaving Lady Helen on her own at Ardtuath House. Sir

Charles had grown more and more irascible as the way of life to which he'd always felt entitled was further eroded by the war, and more than once, Alec had admitted to Flora that he'd seen telltale bruising on his mother's arms, which he suspected to be marks of her husband's temper. When he asked her how she'd come by the bruises, though, Lady Helen always made excuses, deflecting his questions. Anxious for his mother's safety, he spent as much time as possible at the house, but was torn, too, between the demands of his job at the base and his longing to spend more time with Flora.

He sighed. 'Maybe things will be better for us all once the war is over. My father will go back to spending most of his time in London and it'll be easier for Ma again.' He reached for her hand. 'Please, Flora, you have to believe in us, as I do. The one good thing to come out of my engagement to Diana was the realisation that I could never feel about anyone the way I do about you. Last night was a ghastly ordeal for both of us. But one day, I promise you, you will be the mistress of Ardtuath House and you will take your rightful place at that table.'

By way of an answer, she entwined her fingers in his, tracing the sinews across the back of his hand with her thumb. She felt safe with him here. But as they sat looking out across the loch towards the western hills, the sky there began to haze over as clouds piled in from the ocean beyond, swallowing the sun. In spite of the warmth of the summer evening, Flora shivered slightly. The solid wall of the cottage she was leaning against still radiated the heat of the day. But she knew full well that this home – the only one she'd ever known – could be taken from her just as suddenly as the sea could change its mood, should Sir Charles's anger at their relationship make him decide that it was time to let his gamekeeper go.

Flora's duties at the naval base mainly involved driving officers to and from the jetty, or delivering and collecting the personnel who manned the lookout posts that had been built around the loch. On occasion, too, she drove larger vehicles – trucks and ambulances – when the need arose. She was sitting in the NAAFI with Mairi when the order came to take an ambulance round to Cove, on the far side of Loch Ewe. A Tilly – the nickname they gave to small utility vehicles in the services – had gone off the road and ended up stuck in the ditch, and its occupants had sustained minor injuries.

Flora drove, with Mairi at her side, and they sped along the shore to where the road narrowed to a single track beyond Poolewe. A mile further on they came upon the car in the ditch, listing alarmingly to one side. A sub-lieutenant was trying to wedge a large stone under one of the back wheels. His colleague – an ordnance officer deputed to service the anti-aircraft gun at the lookout point – sat dazed at the side of the road, with none other than Bridie busily attempting to fashion a sling out of what, on closer inspection, appeared to be a strip torn from her petticoat.

The two girls jumped down from their vehicle. 'Bridie! Are you all right? What happened?' Flora asked.

'A sheep in the road,' Bridie replied cheerily. 'Had to swerve to miss it. I got away with just a few bumps and bruises, but I think this poor laddie's arm is broken. The sheep's fine, though,' she added.

'Here,' Mairi said. 'Let me take a look.' She gathered dressings and a proper sling from the back of the ambulance and knelt beside the officer. Deftly, she examined his injury and strapped his arm gently but firmly to his chest to immobilise the wrist, which was already beginning to swell.

Leaving Mairi to attend to the casualty, Flora helped the other young officer to attach a rope to the bumper of the Tilly. Reversing the ambulance, she managed to pull the car free of the ditch, righting it so that they could have a good look at the damage.

'Oops,' remarked Bridie, 'that rear axle doesn't look too healthy.'

'It doesn't look at all safe to drive. We'll need to tow you back and get it seen to,' said Flora.

The young man glanced at his watch. 'I'm overdue to relieve the lookout at the point. D'you think you could drop me there and then come back for this lot?'

'Of course. Jump in.'

She drove past the row of whitewashed crofts at Cove – those same cottages that she and Alec had seen from the water on their visit to the rocky arch beyond Firemore beach in the spring – to where the track petered out just past the concrete shelter that had been constructed as a lookout post at the mouth of the loch. While the sentries carried out their handover, Flora walked to the edge of the clifftop. Far beneath her, the waves crashed against the jagged black buttress of Furadh Mor, a crag that reared from the water a little way from the shore, where the sea surged and foamed over the rocks as if tugging in frustration at the shelter the headland afforded the calmer waters beyond. She knew the power of the waves wasn't the only danger out there in the North Atlantic, where German battleships lurked beyond the horizon and U-boats prowled in packs, hunting down their prey like hungry wolves.

The drive back to the base at Mellon Charles was slow, hampered by the weight of the damaged Tilly, which floundered behind the ambulance on its tow rope like a drunken whale with Bridie at the wheel. The stir of their arrival brought the camp's commander out from his hut. He raised his eyebrows at the sight of the damaged car and they rose further, almost disappearing beneath the peak of his cap, at the sight of the injured ordnance officer.

'Take that man to the surgeon. And you – Miss Macdonald, is it? Report to my hut once you've washed that oil off your hands.'

Flora shot a sympathetic look at Bridie, although her friend seemed unabashed at the prospect of a dressing-down from the commander himself. After all, it wasn't the first time she'd had a run-in with a sheep, and there was also the occasion when she'd met another Tilly head-on and had a narrow miss, although that time it had been the other driver who'd ended up in the ditch.

By lunchtime, Bridie had been reassigned from her driving duties to a role behind the counter in the NAAFI where the scope for wreaking devastation on the camp's fleet of vehicles was considerably reduced. But, as she remarked cheerfully to Flora and Alec later over a port and lemon in the Jellyjar Tavern, she felt it was a role to which she was better suited, having gained valuable experience under Mrs Carmichael and the ladies of the Rural. Everyone came in and wanted to chat as well, so it was a good place to hear all the news.

And besides, the ordnance officer with the broken wrist had been in to see her and had invited her to go to the film show at the hall with him the following week to watch the latest Laurel and Hardy picture.

'Goodness!' said Flora, laughing. 'Who would have thought there'd be so much excitement to be had in Aultbea, of all places?'

Lexie, 1978

By the time I've finished giving Bridie strict instructions about Daisy's bedtime routine – even though I know she's not paying the slightest bit of attention to what I'm saying as she's too busy bouncing her on her knee and telling her stories about her granny – there's already music spilling from the bar when I reach the hotel.

My stomach contracts with nerves as I push open the door and step across the threshold. Maybe it was a mistake to come out tonight. What if there's no one here I know? Will the fact that I'm brazenly walking into a bar on my own reaffirm my status as a fallen woman?

But everyone in the warm fug, which is heavy with the smell of beer and cigarettes, is too intent on enjoying the music even to notice. Then I catch sight of Elspeth and her husband, Andy, and one of the other mums from the playgroup with her partner, sitting at a table in the corner.

Elspeth waves me over. 'Lexie, we were wondering where you'd got to. Bridie told me she's babysitting Daisy tonight – she's been that thrilled about it all day.'

'Hiya, Lexie,' says Andy. 'Good to see you again after all these years. What are you drinking?' He insists on taking my order, and threads his way through the crowded room to the bar, stopping to exchange banter with several other men along the way.

I settle myself in the chair that Elspeth's been saving for me and feel the tension in my shoulders ease a little. Perhaps it's going to be okay after all. I thought I'd be a stranger, but I discover I'm among friends.

I turn my chair slightly so I can watch the musicians. There's Davy on his guitar alongside an accordion player, a drummer with a bodhrán and a fiddler. They're in full flow:

'I've been a wild rover for many's the year
And I've spent all me money on whisky and beer
But now I'm returning wi' gold in great store
And I never will play the wild rover no more . . .'

The music swirls and flows, its tune as easy and as sure as the tides in the loch, rising and falling and sweeping us all along with it. Every foot taps along in time as the whole room joins in the chorus, raising the roof:

'And it's no, nae, never,
No nae never no more
Will I be a wild rover,
No never no more.'

As the song ends there's a whooping and a cheering and then the band takes a break, leaving their instruments to come to the bar where they're passed drinks on the house.

Davy pushes his way through the throng to where we sit and Elspeth shuffles along, making space for him between us.

'So you came after all,' he says, shouting to be heard above the din. 'I thought you might get cold feet at the last minute and I'd be landed with Bridie for the evening instead.'

'She'd have shoved me out of the house if I'd tried to stay. She and Daisy'll be having a party of their own, I've no doubt, involving way too many chocolate buttons and very little chance of getting to bed on time.'

'All the better for you then; she'll sleep later in the morning. So you can have another drink and enjoy yourself. How d'you like the band?'

'They're good,' I say. 'Of course, the guitar player could do with some practice, but the others are great.'

'Watch it,' he replies, laughing. 'We'll be getting you up to sing later and then you might be thankful for a bit of guitar accompaniment.'

I duck my head, regretting teasing him, then meet his gaze and my eyes are wide and pleading. 'Not tonight. Please, Davy, I'm not ready to sing again yet.'

He can see I'm serious. 'Okay,' he says. 'We'll let you ease yourself in gently. Tonight you can sing along with the others. One of these days we'll get you up there though, Lexie Gordon. When you've music in your soul you can't keep it to yourself forever.'

Elspeth nudges him on the other side. 'Give her a break, Davy. She's saving it for her new gig at the playgroup.' She leans forward and tells me that another group over at Poolewe have heard about our music session and have asked to join in. 'We could see if the hall's free one morning and use that. That way more people can come and it'll give the kids extra space to run around, too.'

Davy nods his approval. 'There you go. What did I tell you? Music in your soul.'

The other band members are picking up their instruments again and he gets to his feet. 'Looks like we're on again.'

I watch him play. Despite my teasing, he's really good. Various members of the audience step up at different points in the evening to play, backed by the band. There's a guy with a penny whistle and a woman with a Celtic flute, a harmonica player and a second fiddler, and the girl who's been serving drinks behind the bar steps up to sing a set, too. Davy alternates between his guitar and the mandolin and I'm impressed at how effortless his playing is, the notes flowing from beneath his fingers. The evening passes quickly and all too soon the bell rings for last orders. We sing ourselves hoarse with a last rendition of 'The Bonny Lass o' Fyvie-O' and then it's time to head home, with calls of 'See you next time . . .'

'I'll chum you along the road,' offers Davy.

'It's okay, I'll be fine,' I say.

'I know you'll be fine, but I could do with a walk to blow the cobwebs away. I'll catch a lift back with Bridie, see her safely home too.'

'There you go again, always looking after people,' I say, teasing him again.

'Ach well, you know me.' He shrugs.

We walk the shore road in silence for a stretch, then I say, 'That was a great evening. Thanks for inviting me along. Your band's really good, you know.'

'I'm glad you enjoyed yourself. And now you won't be needing an invitation the next time, knowing you're among friends.'

At Keeper's Cottage the lights are burning in the windows of the kitchen and the sitting room, but when I peep in I see Bridie fast asleep in an armchair, snoring gently. Tactfully, I make a bit of a noise coming in so she has time to wake up and straighten her cardigan.

'How was your evening?' I ask.

'Och, just grand,' she says. 'We had a few games and stories and then she went down without a murmur. How was the music?'

'It was great! But don't tell him.' I nod towards Davy. 'He'll only get too big for his boots.'

Davy grins. 'No risk of that around here with the two of you to keep me in my place. Thought I'd see Lexie back and then chum you home to yours, too, Bridie. You know what they say about two birds . . .'

She giggles, pleased to be referred to as a 'bird'. 'Always a gentleman, Davy Laverock. Night, Lexie, glad you had a good time. Call me whenever you need a babysitter again.'

When they've gone, I creep upstairs and peep into the cot where Daisy lies tucked up in the shell-pattern shawl, her arms above her head in a gesture of utter relaxation. I put a finger into one soft palm and she smiles faintly, her own fingers curling around it for a moment. Then I place a feather-light kiss on her forehead and tiptoe to my own room, the swirl of the music still playing in my head as I drift off to sleep.

Flora, 1941

The rumblings of war continued but they remained beyond the horizon, a far-off storm out across the ocean. Flora gave thanks daily for the hills cradling the loch that gave shelter to those she loved. In the east, Norway fell to German occupation and Hitler was said to be gathering troops along Russia's borders; to the south, beyond the towering walls of the Scottish mountains, English and Scottish cities were being shaken by the Luftwaffe's bombs as the Blitz rained terror from the skies, while their inhabitants remained defiant in the face of the onslaught.

The secluded waters of Loch Ewe still provided a safe haven for the ships of the British fleet, kept secret from the enemy, as well as for merchant ships that gathered there before they made the hazardous journey across the Atlantic to fetch supplies back to Britain from America. But then, one short night in June, that sense of security was shattered.

It was the urgent sound of a whistle from the anti-aircraft battery below the Ardtuath Estate that wrenched Flora from her sleep. As she surfaced from the depths of her dreams, she became aware of the insistent thrum of an aircraft engine drawing ever closer. She hurried to the window and drew back a corner of the blackout. A waning crescent moon cast its light across the water, adding its dim glow to the beam of a searchlight that swept the blackness of the sky. Suddenly, curtains of tracer fire flooded the darkness. Against their glare, she could see the vast barrel of the ack-ack gun turning skywards as its crew set their bearings. With a flash and a boom that shook the floorboards beneath her bare feet, anti-aircraft rounds illuminated the scene. Four planes swooped and then banked sharply, evading the shells that exploded around them. The gunners reset their bearings, following the course of the Junkers as they flew above the ships that lay at anchor in the bay below. They fired again, and the air reverberated with the thud and boom of more shells as the guns at Tournaig sprang into action too.

One of the planes took a hit, lurching and then wheeling off to the north-west, and then another shell exploded close to a second plane that also swerved off towards the Minch, a pall of black smoke obscuring its tail.

It looked as if the gun batteries had managed to disperse the attack but then, to Flora's horror, a fifth plane appeared, its engines silenced, coming in on a flight path that was straight and low while the ack-ack guns were trained on the decoys elsewhere. It let loose its bombs over the ships out in the bay. The explosions made the walls of the cottage shudder and sent a plume of smoke and water high into the air above the loch. Then all the remaining planes banked and turned, climbing rapidly into the night sky, the sound of their engines fading as they fled. She peered into the darkness, straining her eyes for any glimpse of flames.

As the guns fell silent, she padded to the front door, opening it a crack and peering out. Her father and brother appeared in the hallway behind her in their pyjamas.

'What's the damage?' Ruaridh asked.

'It's too dark, I can't see clearly. But thankfully the bombs don't seem to have made a direct hit. I can't see anything's been set on fire, at least.'

'Best shut that door, lass,' her father said. 'You don't want to be standing there if those planes come back for a second go.' He turned to Ruaridh. 'Looks like Jerry has discovered what Loch Ewe's been hiding. Perhaps we'd better get that Anderson shelter built after all.'

Alec came to find Flora at the base the next day and they walked along the shore a little way. 'I just wanted to make sure you were all all right,' he said. 'No damage done at the cottage? The bomb blast brought down a chunk of the ceiling in the dining room at the house. Ma was quite shaken, but my father is more annoyed about the cost of replacing the plasterwork and where on earth he's going to find someone who can restore such intricate cornicing these days.'

'Have you heard what happened?' Flora asked.

Alec nodded. 'One of the supply ships had a near miss, which did some damage, although luckily there were no casualties.' He grinned. 'Looks like Jerry mistook his target in the dark, because the only thing to take a direct hit were the rocks at the top of the island where the boom net is fixed. Their shape makes them look a bit like a boat.' His attention was caught by something in the sky towards the far horizon, and his expression grew serious.

Following his gaze, Flora shielded her eyes with her hand, just able to make out a dark speck against the dazzle of sunshine. 'What is it?' she asked. 'A buzzard? Or an eagle, maybe?'

He shook his head. 'An eagle doesn't fly in a dead straight line like that. It could be a reconnaissance plane. I need to go and report it, in case the lookouts haven't radioed it in already. Tell your dad you'd best take shelter tonight. I reckon last night was just the beginning.'

Sure enough, over the next weeks German planes reappeared sporadically in the summer skies over Loch Ewe. Mostly they came at night and were seen off by the ack-ack guns, whose crews became adept at chasing away the attackers. But one afternoon, when Flora was returning from driving the commander from the base at Aultbea to the officer's quarters down the loch at Pool House, she had to pull in and take cover beneath the branches of a pine tree when a lone German plane swooped from out of nowhere over the loch.

She pressed a hand to her mouth in horror as it flew low over the schoolhouse where the children were out playing in the yard. But to her astonishment, the pilot seemed to feather back his engines and dip his wings in a cheery salute, leaving the shocked schoolchildren frozen as the headmaster shouted frantically at them to get back inside.

Turning westwards, the plane's engines roared back to life as the anti-aircraft guns began to fire. As if in slow motion, two bombs fell from the belly of the aircraft, engulfing one of the merchant ships moored beyond the island. As the plane disappeared beyond the hills, Flora leapt into the car and sped back to the base, from where a rescue operation was being launched to pick up the survivors from the stricken vessel, whose back had been broken by the blast.

After that final incident, though, it seemed the Luftwaffe found other, more pressing targets to pursue on the Russian front, and the air raids stopped. Which, as Alec later commented, was extremely ironic, as just a few days after the last raid, Loch Ewe was formally designated as an official naval base to be known as HMS *Helicon.*

'What on earth . . . ? Look at that,' Alec said, pausing to catch his breath.

He, Ruaridh and Flora had hiked into the hills one October afternoon to help her father stalk a hind. The game larder was empty and Sir Charles had no shooting parties organised until December, when friends would come to shoot game birds in time for their Christmas tables. So Iain had asked Ruaridh and Flora to lend a hand with the day's hunting, with Flora in the role of pony ghillie leading the garron and Ruaridh helping with the guns. Alec, having heard about the outing from Flora, was keen to come too.

Below them, in the field that bordered the loch beside the local telephone exchange, a squadron of RAF technicians were busy inflating a huge silver balloon. As it filled with hydrogen it began to swell and lift away from the grass, turning its nose towards the water as the wind caught its fins. The men battled to keep hold of it until it was full enough with gas to be released skywards, bobbing at the end of the long wires that tethered it to the ground.

'Funny, isn't it?' Ruaridh said. 'We haven't had an air raid for months. It's a bit late to start putting up barrage balloons.'

'But there are so many ships now. Even more to protect if those Jerry pilots decide to come back for another go,' countered Alec.

The airmen began to work on another balloon, spreading out yards of silver material and attaching cables.

Iain shook his head. 'Ach, it's a bit of nonsense, if you ask me. How long do they expect yon monstrosity to last when the first gale starts to blow?' The Highland pony, who'd taken the opportunity of a brief pause to snatch a few mouthfuls of grass from among the heather, pawed at the ground and tossed her long white mane, jerking at the leading rein in Flora's hand. 'Come on now, see, the garron's getting impatient and we've still a way to climb to reach the hinds.'

An hour's walk later, as they approached the higher ground, her father held a finger to his lips and gestured to them to cut around to the south, so that the westerly wind wouldn't carry their scent to the finely tuned nostrils of the red deer hinds. He knew the hills like the back of his hand, his own father having kept the game here before him. They'd seen nothing so far, but were now skirting round beneath a rise that concealed a hollow where the female deer often gathered. He nodded to Flora, the sign for her to stop with the pony. She led the garron into the shelter of a bluff and tethered the leading rein around a jutting rock. She knew this place, having assisted her father and brother on occasion in the past, and sat on a tuffet of dry heather watching the men climb higher as the pony cropped the mossy grass at her feet.

As they reached the ridgeline they dropped to crouch beneath the rise, flattening themselves on to their stomachs. She knew the deer must be in the hollow when she saw Iain gesture to Ruaridh, who passed over the rifle.

Her father waited, taking his time, looking for a clean shot. He would be searching out one of the older hinds, mindful of the balance of the herd. He was always careful to cull in accordance with the traditional ways, once incurring the wrath of Sir Charles when he'd refused to let a guest shoot a stag just one day out of the season.

The gun cracked, making the pony flinch, and Flora heard the sound of hoofbeats drumming away into the distance. As she watched, her father reset the safety catch on the rifle and passed it across to Ruaridh, then stood up and beckoned to her to bring up the garron: he'd made his kill with a single shot.

Once Iain had deftly gralloched the carcass, leaving the innards on a flat rock where the hoodie crows would make short work of them, he resheathed his knife. Then the men loaded the hind on to the deer saddle and buckled the straps to ensure that the weight would be evenly distributed over the pony's back while it made its sure-footed descent to the road.

As they came down from the hill, they were taken by surprise at the first glimpse of the loch. A dozen barrage balloons now flew from ships in the bay, gleaming like a shoal of huge silver herrings swimming in the skies above Loch Ewe. There was even one bobbing from the roof of the telephone exchange. Beneath them, the airmen continued to inflate more of the balloons, suspended at the end of their long cables that would clip a plane's wings if it came in low over a target, bringing it crashing back to earth.

'Whoa there, lass, you're all right.' Flora calmed the garron as it shied at the strange sight.

'They've certainly been busy,' her father grunted, his eyebrows disappearing beneath the brim of his deerstalker.

The path led down to the road, and as they walked back through the village to Ardtuath House several small boys came running.

'Jings, look at that!'

'They shot a deer!'

'Is that your gun, Mr Gordon?'

'Can I have a shot of it?'

'My dad has a gun, too, in the desert in Africa. He's shooting Germans with it.'

'I bet you could shoot a German with your gun, couldn't you, Mr Gordon?'

Iain calmed the clamouring children as they milled about the horse trying to get a better look at the hind's carcass on its back. 'Now, now, lads, keep away from the pony's back legs. She's liable to kick if you give her a fright. Yes, that gun certainly could kill a man, which is all the more reason to stay away from them at your age.'

Flora smiled at Stuart and Davy who hung back at the edge of the group, a little unsure of the garron's evident power. 'Here, look,' she said, beckoning them forward. 'You can give her nose a wee pat if you like. She won't bite.'

Davy hid behind his brother, but Stuart was braver and reached out a tentative hand to stroke the pony's muzzle. 'Why is its hair so long?' he asked, marvelling.

'It's called a mane. It's so she stays warm in the winter and it keeps the flies from her eyes in the summer.'

'C'mon!' shouted the ringleader of the gang. 'Let's go and look at those balloon things again.'

The children swarmed off towards the jetty, but Davy hung back for a moment. 'Miss Flora? What are those big balloons for? Stuart says they're airships and they can go on fire and kill people.'

'They're just barrage balloons, Davy. They're here to keep you safe, in case there's ever another air raid.'

'Mrs Carmichael says there's been air raids in Glasgow. I hope my mammy is safe.'

'I'm sure she will be. Does she write you letters?' Flora asked.

Davy looked doubtful. 'Sometimes. But Stuart says she's busy at work, making bombs to kill the Germans with, so she can't always be writing to us.'

'Here,' said Flora, taking a piece of apple from her pocket. 'Do you want to feed the pony? Hold your hand flat, that's it, like that. There you go, well done, see – there's nothing to be scared of really, is there?'

Davy beamed at her, shaking his head vigorously, and then, hearing his brother shouting his name from the shore, he turned and ran back to join his friends.

Back at Keeper's Cottage, Flora left her father, Ruaridh and Alec to deal with the carcass and unsaddle the garron while she hurried inside to stoke the range and get supper on the go. Out on the water, another silver balloon bobbed into the air, joining the others that swam in their strange shining shoal above the anchorage against the backdrop of the purple hills.

Lexie, 1978

I've managed to coax a bit of information out of Bridie at last, getting her to talk about what it was like when the war arrived in Aultbea. I resorted to stealth tactics, in the end, inviting her to Keeper's Cottage for a regular tea date on Wednesday afternoons, shamelessly using Daisy as an enticement. She's very good company, in fact, and I find myself looking forward to her visits. Offering her tea and a bit of a chat seems the very least I can do when she's been so kind to me. She's rapidly taken on the role of a surrogate mother and granny, something I know my mum would have loved.

Her face lights up when she talks about being a Wren, and she brings an album of photos to show me of her and Mum and Mairi in their uniforms. The three of them laugh out from the pictures, looking neat as pins in their tailored skirts and ties. Their double-breasted jackets have shiny brass buttons down the front and the Women's Royal Naval Service badge stitched to the sleeve, proudly displaying the embroidered emblem of crossed anchors beneath a crown.

'It must have been extraordinary,' I muse, offering her a plate of chocolate biscuits. 'Loch Ewe going from a community of just a few hundred folk to a military base of over three thousand personnel almost overnight.'

She nods, chewing thoughtfully. 'They certainly were extraordinary times. Exciting, too. All those people suddenly arriving from all over the world. We had Poles and Indians, Americans and Russians around the place. And there was great camaraderie in the WRNS. We had lots of girls posted up from England and Wales, so we made loads of new friends.'

Daisy has crawled over to Bridie and pulled herself up to stand, attempting to climb up beside her on the sofa.

'Here you go, darlin', upsy Daisy!' Bridie scoops her on to her lap and Daisy nestles happily in the crook of her arm. 'Of course, there were downsides to having the military here as well. We were issued with security passes that we'd to carry with us at all times. The roads beyond the loch were sealed off at Laide, Gairloch and Achnasheen with checkpoints, and no one was allowed in without showing their papers. I kept forgetting mine, but luckily most of the guards knew me from the NAAFI and let me through. And there were the sad times, too. A lot of our local boys were away fighting the war, and every now and then a telegram would arrive with news that someone had been killed. It hit the community hard, every time we lost one of our own.'

Her eyes mist over as she remembers those losses. But when I try to ask for specifics – especially about my mum and dad – she veers away again like a startled deer, sticking to more general stories.

As I watch her playing with Daisy, I think what a wonderful mother and grandmother she'd have been if she'd ever had children of her own. Her life would have been very different.

'What about you, Bridie?' I ask. 'With all those soldiers and sailors about the place, did you not have any romances?'

Her face becomes radiant for a moment and I catch a glimpse of how pretty and vivacious she must have been back then. But, like a cloud covering the sun, her expression changes again. 'Oh yes,' she says, 'the war brought opportunity for some. But, you know, for every story of new love there are ten more of loss and heartbreak.' She fishes a hankie from the sleeve of her cardigan and blows her nose. Then she turns her attention back to the photo album beside her. 'Now then, did I tell you about how the Arctic convoys started? I'd been transferred to the NAAFI canteen when we heard the news . . .'

Flora, 1941

The wind was bitter that afternoon, sending the reflections of the clouds scudding across the waters of the loch, and the light was already dimming as the short winter's day gave way to another long night. Flora sat opposite Mairi at one of the long tables in the NAAFI, her hands clasped around her teacup, absorbing the last of the warmth from the thick white china.

The canteen was unusually quiet and Bridie had time to come over and join them, refilling their cups from the large metal teapot that she wielded with gusto, and setting down a plate laden with three slices of the dry cake that was staple NAAFI fare. The men referred to it as the 'Yellow Peril', as it was made with dried custard powder and crumbled into sawdust in the mouth, necessitating more gulps of the watery tea to wash it down.

As usual, she was eager to share the latest gossip with her friends. 'All the men have been called to a briefing,' Bridie said. 'It must be something important.'

It came as no surprise that the role of the base might be changing. The war seemed to be spreading like wildfire, and it felt as if the map of the world was changing colour in front of their eyes as more and more countries were consumed by the flames. Only the other evening they'd seen newsreel footage of the aftermath of an attack by Japanese bombers on a place far away on the other side of the world called Pearl Harbor. The images of broken ships, half-sunk in the oil-slicked water, and of stretchers bearing burned bodies had silenced the usually talkative audience in the hall. Although the devastation was thousands of miles away, to those watching beside the anchorage in Loch Ewe it seemed all too close to home. Those ships could have been their own. Those broken and bloodied bodies could have been their friends and shipmates.

'Now that the Yanks are in, maybe we'll be getting some American visitors,' speculated Bridie hopefully. To date all her romantic liaisons had fizzled out, usually ending in tears due to deployment elsewhere or, in one case, the discovery of a fiancée back at home.

Mairi laughed. 'D'you think they'll be a better bet than our British boys then? They're even more likely to be just passing through.'

Bridie took a bite of cake, considering this. 'Yes, but they might bring things with them. Wouldn't it be grand to have some perfume again? And a lipstick? Maybe even some stockings that don't make your legs look like they belong to a heavyweight wrestler?' She sighed disconsolately, scratching at her calf; the thick wool cladding was perennially itchy.

'I'd settle for a bar of soap,' Mairi said. 'It's to be rationed too now, did you hear?'

'That's rich, coming from you, Mairi Macleod,' retorted Bridie. 'You never settle for anything.' Flora knew that in Bridie's opinion, Mairi was far too picky, having turned down several young men who'd asked her for dates.

'There's nothing wrong with waiting for Mr Right to come along,' chipped in Flora.

'It's fine for you to say that.' Bridie sighed again. 'You've already got your Mr Right.'

Mairi shot Flora a sympathetic glance. Her friend had confided that Alec's father was standing in the way of their betrothal. He'd threatened to pull some strings with his friends in high places and have Alec transferred to Portsmouth unless his son's 'absurd liaison' with the gamekeeper's daughter ended. They knew that this was entirely within his powers, as was his ability to replace his keeper, so they met in secret now, being careful not to rock the boat.

The wind had begun to fling scatterings of sleet against the sides of the corrugated tin huts by the time the briefings ended. Those personnel who were off duty sprinted across the dark parade ground to regather in the warmth of the NAAFI and Bridie hurried back to her post behind the counter to brew another gargantuan pot of tea.

Ruaridh and Alec joined Flora and Mairi, removing their peaked caps and setting them on the table to dry, and quickly filled them in on the latest news. With Russia fighting against Hitler's army on several fronts, keeping the Soviet supply lines open was essential. But in the south the borders were controlled by Germany now. The only way to get vital munitions and equipment in would be through the Arctic. Convoys of ships would have to run the gauntlet past the northern cape of Norway, now defended by German battleships and U-boats as well as the Luftwaffe. And Loch Ewe was to be one of the mustering points from which these convoys would depart.

The mood in the canteen – which was usually light-hearted and jocular, the noise of friendly banter mingling with the clatter of cutlery and the hissing of the hot water urn – had become more serious all of a sudden. What they had seen up until now had only been the beginning.

As Bridie topped up their cups, the three girls exchanged a look of fear as they realised that the safe harbour alongside which they made their homes had just become a strategic focal point in a world torn apart by war.

The hilltops were blanketed in a layer of fresh snow the next morning, and Flora blew on her hands to warm them a little. She'd just had to change a spark plug in the ambulance she was to drive that day, which had refused to start, and her fingertips were frozen. She climbed into the cab and tried the engine again, breathing a sigh of relief when it started with ease. Her orders were to transfer two patients from the sick bay at the base over to Gairloch, where the hotel had been turned into a military hospital. She scraped the layer of crisp frost from the windscreen and then, as she waited for her charges to be brought out, thrust her hands deep into the pockets of her navy-issue greatcoat and paced back and forth in an attempt to keep warm. Her attention was caught by the sight of a familiar figure emerging from the command hut across the parade ground.

'Alec!' she called, waving to attract his attention.

He appeared to be deep in thought, but his eyes, which had been fixed on the path, lit up as he saw her.

He hurried over. 'Flora, I'm glad you're here. There's something I have to tell you.' The tone of his voice was flat, and she realised that behind his smile his expression was taut with tension.

'What is it?'

'Well, the good news is that I've been promoted to lieutenant commander.'

'Why, Alec, that's wonderful. I thought you still had two more years to go?'

'I did. They've speeded things up a little.'

She searched his face, confused by the lack of enthusiasm in his blunt response.

'But . . . ?' she prompted.

His jaw clenched as conflicting emotions played out across his features. 'But with my promotion comes a new role. I'm going back to sea again, joining one of the destroyers. They'll be needing them for protecting the convoys to Russia.'

She was silent while she digested this news and its implications, automatically glancing out across the pewter-dark waters of the loch to where the unforgiving sea stirred restlessly, surging and seething among the rocks beyond the point.

'It could be worse,' he said. She could tell he was making a deliberate effort to sound cheerful, trying to reassure her. 'We'll be mostly escorting ships from Iceland, but I'll be back here from time to time so I'll be able to see you still when I'm home. And I'm not leaving immediately. I'll be here for a couple more weeks – until after Christmas, at least.'

She swallowed hard, choking back the anguish that had closed her throat. 'That's something, then,' she replied when she could get the words out, trying to echo his positive tone.

Just then the two patients were brought out from the sick bay, one managing to walk with the aid of a pair of crutches and the other carried on a stretcher by a pair of orderlies.

'Sorry, Alec, I have to go. We'll talk later?'

He nodded miserably.

She longed to wrap her arms around him and feel his warmth, holding him in the safety of her embrace, but constrained by her duty, had to make do with giving him the bravest smile she could manage.

She opened the doors at the back of the truck, helping the walking wounded case to climb in.

Alec lingered alongside the cab, loath to let her go.

'Drive safely,' he said. 'The roads will be icy.'

She caught sight of his reflection in her wing mirror as she pulled out of the camp. He still stood in the middle of the square with his hands thrust into the pockets of his dark blue jacket, his breath hanging above him in a frozen cloud, watching until she lost sight of him.

As she drove along the shore road, she spotted a supply launch as it bounced into the choppy waves from the munitions store in the secluded harbour below Inverewe House, making for one of the ships in the anchorage. Would its deadly cargo be enough to protect the ship if it came under attack from the enemy? And did the men on board know there was another enemy, too, that threatened lives out there beyond the protective arms of Loch Ewe? Quite apart from the Nazi menace, the Arctic seas were treacherous, storm-wracked wastes, cold enough to kill in seconds, filled with swirling, shifting fog thick enough to hide a battleship until it was almost upon its prey.

She knew how brave Alec was, and how capable, too, but the thought of him out there, facing the cruelty of those twin foes without her, froze her blood more than the bitter chill of the day.

The December shooting parties were organised for the second and third weekends of the month so that the Mackenzie-Grants' guests would be able to take home game birds in time for Christmas. Once again, Sir Charles demanded Flora's presence in the kitchen of the big house. She agreed cheerfully enough when her father passed on the request; she didn't mind helping Lady Helen and it just might give her a chance to spend a few extra moments with Alec. Every second they had together was all the more precious with his departure for Iceland looming large.

She arrived early and began setting out the hampers and baskets that would accompany the shooting party to the hill. There were flasks of hot soup to prepare and piles of sandwiches. She cut slices of Madeira cake and wrapped them in brown paper, to be slipped into jacket pockets and eaten in between drives. It was a far simpler picnic than in the days before rationing, but she did her best to make it look as appetising as possible.

As she finished laying it all on the table in the boot room for her father to collect, the kitchen door opened and Lady Helen appeared.

'Good morning, Flora. I'm so very grateful to you for helping us out again. I hope you've managed to find everything? I've come in search of more bread – we're running out in the dining room. Can you spare a few slices of that loaf?'

'Of course,' Flora smiled, wielding the breadknife once more.

She turned, hearing another set of footsteps approaching, hoping it might be Alec. But the smile faded from her face as Diana Kingsley-Scott swept into the kitchen.

'We're out of hot water. I wonder whether your girl might fill this and bring it back to the dining room.' She addressed Lady Helen, but handed the silver teapot she was carrying to Flora, scarcely acknowledging her.

'Certainly, Diana. I'm sorry you had to come through yourself. Would you mind, Flora dear?'

Flora shook her head, not trusting herself to speak. It hadn't escaped her notice that Diana's hands were bare of rings as she took the teapot from her. What on earth had happened? Wasn't she supposed to have had her wedding at the family estate in the autumn? Where was her husband? And – more to the point – why hadn't Alec mentioned that Diana would be coming to stay for the weekend?

She refilled the pot from the kettle simmering on the stove and followed the two women through the green baize door. The hallway, which had seemed so oppressive when she'd been there at Hogmanay, closed around her again, heavy and forbidding. She squared her shoulders as she pushed open the door to the dining room.

There was no sign of Alec, but Diana was seated to the right of Sir Charles, who was digging into a plate of bacon and eggs with gusto as he regaled his houseguests with tales of previous shoots. He glanced up at the sight of Flora.

'Ah, the estimable Miss Gordon. How good of you to have graced us with your presence this morning.' Flora knew his bonhomie was false, an act for the sake of his audience. 'Tell your father that Miss Kingsley-Scott is going to require the Beretta, would you?' He turned towards Diana. 'As it's your first time out, we'll start you off with something a little lighter, my dear.' He glanced at his watch. 'I wonder where Alec's got to . . . although after that jolly good dinner last night, it's not surprising he's having a bit of a slow start this morning, what?'

Flora's hands shook as she set the teapot on its stand on the sideboard, fully aware that Sir Charles was making a point for her benefit. She left the dining room with as much dignity as she could muster. In the hall, she almost collided with Alec as he hurried down the stairs. He wasn't paying attention to where he was going, intent on fastening the buttons of his tweed shooting jacket.

'Flora!' he exclaimed. 'I didn't know you'd be here this morning.'

'No, but here I am. Your father asked me to come. You know I'm always happy to help your mother out when she has so many guests staying.'

He moved towards her as if to give her a kiss, but she ducked her head and turned away.

'I'd better get back to the kitchen,' she said. 'And you'd better get in there.' She pointed towards the dining room as a gust of laughter escaped from behind the closed door.

He reached for her hand. 'Flora, wait, I . . .'

But whatever Alec had been about to say was cut short by the appearance of Diana.

'Good morning, sleepyhead,' she teased him. 'It's a good thing you're up. Your papa's just sent me to knock on your bedroom door and tell you to get a move on if you want any breakfast before we get going.'

Flora spun on her heel and hurried back to the kitchen, her cheeks burning. She was furious that Sir Charles had managed to remind her, yet again, of the difference between her world and Alec's. And she was angry at herself for being manipulated in that way. She tore off her apron and let herself out through the back door.

'Whoa there, what's the great hurry, lass?' her father said, steadying her as she collided with him on the path.

She shook her head by way of reply, breathless with anger and humiliation. Then, swallowing, said, 'They're almost ready for you. The picnic's in the boot room. And you're to fetch the Beretta for Miss Kingsley-Scott.'

And as she strode along the path back to Keeper's Cottage, she dashed furious tears away with the back of her hand, not sure who she was angriest at: Sir Charles, or Alec, or herself for ever thinking she might one day fit into Alec's world.

Lexie, 1978

It's a wild, wet day. The tail end of an Atlantic storm drives sheets of rain across the loch, sending squalls barrelling across the water to whip the waves into a seething chop. Days like this are a reminder of how quickly the conditions can switch from benign to tempestuous. One day all is calm, the next it's hard to imagine that the sun will ever shine again. There's a west coast saying that if you don't like the weather, wait five minutes and it'll change. I'm starting to get used to it again, accepting that the elements dictate the day's plans. Here, sunshine is a precious commodity.

This morning, Elspeth has booked the hall and we're running an extended playgroup there to include a music and movement session. Mothers and toddlers are coming over from Poolewe and even as far as Gairloch. I'd originally planned to walk along to the village, with Daisy in her pushchair, carrying the musical instruments and tape player that I was going to use. But the weather has put paid to that, and instead I'm going to need to dash back and forth to the car, trying to keep everything dry and get Daisy into her car seat without turning into a drowned rat myself in the process.

I take down one of Mum's old coats from the hooks at the door, one more suited to the stormy conditions than my own London coat. Putting it on, I shove the car keys into one of the pockets and pick up a bag containing the cassette player and tapes. I leave Daisy sitting in her high chair finishing off a slice of toast and honey in the warmth of the kitchen, and hurry down the path to the car. Groping in my pocket for the keys, my fingers close around something else. I draw out a small brooch. It's ornately cast, a crown and anchor set in a wreath of leaves. It's badly tarnished, but when I rub it with my thumb a glint of silver shows through the layer of black. As I stand there with it in the palm of my hand, the rain drips from the hood of my coat and glistens, like tears, on the scrolls of the leaves. This was the coat that Mum wore every day. She would have put her hand in the pocket and held this brooch, closing her fingers around it as she walked to the shop or went to visit Bridie.

A gust of wind buffets me, so strong it almost blows me off my feet, reminding me to get a move on. I put the brooch back in my pocket and fumble for the car keys. I'll show Bridie the brooch next time she comes for tea. Maybe she'll be able to tell me more about it.

The playgroup in the hall is the perfect way to spend a morning when the wind and rain keep us indoors. There's a good turnout, and the children seem to love listening to their mums singing, accompanying them on drums, xylophones and rattles. Those who don't have an instrument dance about while they wait their turn. By the end, everyone is laughing and breathless as we share out drinks and biscuits.

Elspeth and I are tidying everything away afterwards and a couple of the mothers have stayed behind to lend a hand.

As one of them helps me stack chairs, she says, 'Do you think you'd maybe come and run something like this over in Gairloch sometimes? We've a playgroup there and I know the kids would love it. You could charge a fee – we'd be happy to pay, to cover your time and your petrol.' She scribbles down her phone number on a scrap of paper. 'Give me a call and we'll get it organised.'

Elspeth grins at me. 'Well, I would say that was a success. It was good getting so many of the young mums together, too – it can be lonely for them. We could see if the hall is free on a regular basis . . . maybe do this once a fortnight.'

As I drive back to the cottage, Daisy sings in her car seat, kicking up her legs in time, making me laugh. The lowering clouds crack open for a few moments and a shaft of silver light makes the waves sparkle. Instantly, my spirits lift like the seabirds that soar on the wind above us, buffeted by the gusts of the storm but still flying high.

Flora, 1942

Flora had hardly had a chance to see Alec after the shooting party, and when she did, she'd been unable to contain her feelings.

'But Flora darling,' he'd remonstrated, 'Diana is nothing to me. It was my father who invited her up for the weekend. I didn't even know she was going to be there until she appeared with her parents. She's had a bit of a hard time of it, being jilted only a month before the wedding, although I'm sure she'll find someone else now that she's back in London.'

Instead of reassuring her, every word Alec spoke seemed to fan the flames of Flora's insecurity. She was well aware that if Sir Charles had anything to do with it, Alec and Diana would be engaged again in a heartbeat. But she'd relented a little on his last day, not wanting to wave him off with that horrible distance yawning between them. She'd told him she loved him and allowed herself to relax in the circle of his arms.

But now that he was gone on duty with the convoys, she bitterly resented having argued with him at all. She missed him dreadfully, she confessed to Mairi as they crossed the parade square at the base, making for the canteen.

When they walked through the door, Bridie hurried out from her place behind the counter, her face pinched with grief. She was wiping her hands on a teacloth and continued to twist it in her distress as she told them the news.

'The Carmichaels have had a telegram. I saw the postie knocking at their door on my way here this morning, so I popped in to ask Miss Cameron about it and she said it was bad news about Matthew, but she wouldn't say if he was captured or hurt. He's the one who was out in the Far East, isn't he?'

Mairi nodded. 'Last we heard. His battalion was in Malaya and then they were forced back to Singapore. I know she was worried about him when news came through of the surrender there. Mum was talking to her about it just the other day.'

'Do you think we should call in after work?'

'Let's leave it until we know more. Mum'll have gone round, I expect. We'll hear soon enough.'

Flora reached over and gently took the dish towel from Bridie. 'Sit down for a moment. This is a shock for us all.'

Matthew had been in the year above them at school, and his younger brother, Jamie, had been in their year. Johnny, the eldest, was three years older. All three of the Carmichael boys were courageous and skilful shinty players. In her mind's eye Flora could see them practising with their sticks on the beach, their long limbs stretching with athletic ease as they flicked the ball from one to another. Loch Ewe was a far cry for the three of them now: Johnny and Jamie were fighting in the desert in North Africa. She tried to picture where Matthew might be – in a prisoner-of-war camp, perhaps, among his friends from the Argyll and Sutherland Highlanders. She pushed away another image, a more haunting one, of a body spreadeagled on the jungle floor, helpless beneath thick green foliage whose shade could offer no respite from the tropical heat.

Once their shift was over, the three girls decided to walk into Aultbea to see whether Mairi's mother had any news. On the way,

Flora spotted the Laverock boys down on the shore. They had makeshift catapults and were practising aiming pebbles at a larger rock.

'Stuart! Davy!' she called, hurrying across the damp sand.

She saw Davy flinch at the sound of his name, and wariness was written on their faces as they turned towards her. Both boys were shivering in the damp chill of the February dusk.

'Hello, Miss Flora.' Stuart relaxed visibly at the sight of her, although his face was pale in the fading light.

'We heard there was a telegram for the Carmichaels this morning.'

Stuart nodded. She could see from his expression what he was going to say next. 'Matthew's dead. Mrs C went to pieces. We didn't want to go back there after school, so we stayed out here instead.'

Davy held up his slingshot. 'We've made gutties from a bit of one of those balloon things. We're practising so that if the Germans come we can get them.'

True to Iain's prediction, the barrage balloons hadn't lasted the winter. They'd bobbed over the loch for a few weeks, but the merciless westerly storms had ripped them from their cables, scattering tattered sheets of the material far and wide. It wasn't uncommon now to see a shed with a silver roof, or a haystack cover that gleamed in the watery sunshine, where enterprising crofters had put the remnants to good use.

'Well, it's time you were home now. No matter how upset she is, Mrs Carmichael will be worrying about you. Here, we'll take you back.'

Reluctantly, the boys wound up their catapults and stuck them into their coat pockets as Flora shepherded them back to the roadside, where Bridie and Mairi waited. Catching her friends' eyes, Flora pressed her lips together and shook her head, that single gesture telling them all they needed to know. Bridie's breath caught in a sob and Mairi took her arm to steady her as they walked along the road, a ragged cluster of figures who dragged their feet, their sorrow a heavy load to bear.

Flora knocked on the Carmichaels' front door. The blackout had already been closed, giving the windows the appearance of unseeing eyes that had turned inwards on a house frozen with grief. It was Archie Carmichael who opened the door. He seemed to have aged in a day; his cheeks were sunken and his normally brisk and capable manner was gone.

'Ah, there you are, boys,' he said, his voice wavering. 'Come away in out of the cold. And you, too, Mairi, Flora, Bridie. How good of you to have brought them home.'

'Thank you, but we won't stop,' said Mairi. 'We just wanted to chum Stuart and Davy back safely and to say how very sorry we are for your loss.'

'Och well, that's very kind of you, lassies . . .' His words petered out as his eyes glazed over. With an effort, he pulled himself together. 'I'll tell Moira you came by. She'll be pleased that you did. I'm afraid she's not herself just at the minute . . . Doctor Greig has been and he's given her something to make her sleep.'

'Of course. If there's anything we can do, please just say.' Mairi laid a gentle hand on his arm.

'So very kind of you,' he repeated, his words automatic. 'Your mother's been round and has been a great comfort to Moira, I'm sure.'

Flora cast an anxious glance at the boys who stood in the doorway, reluctant to enter the house. 'Can we bring you something for your supper, maybe?' she asked. 'I'm sure you'll be needing something to eat.'

'Don't you worry. We've some soup that Mrs Macleod brought with her. We'll be grand now, won't we, boys?' He made an attempt to sound reassuring. 'Will you come away in out of the cold?' he asked, repeating himself again, his eyes far away.

It broke the girls' hearts to turn away and walk down the path, the door closing quietly behind them on a house to which one of the young men who'd called it home would never return.

From the kitchen window at Keeper's Cottage, Flora watched as day by day the merchant ships began to gather on the far side of the island. Some had sailed up from the south, hugging the safer shores of the east coast and then facing the unforgiving seas of the Pentland Firth to reach the haven of Loch Ewe. Others had braved the Atlantic, bringing supplies and equipment from America. These ships travelled in convoy and had already risked being hunted by the packs of U-Boats that roamed the ocean, looking for prey. At least out there the predators had had thousands of miles of water to cover and so the convoys had a better chance of slipping past undetected. But some of those ships would now join the Arctic convoys, running the gauntlet through a relatively narrow corridor of sea, hemmed in on one side by ice and on the other by German attack planes and battleships stationed on the northern cape of Norway. And Alec would be out there, too, as part of the small escort sent with a convoy to defend the merchant ships.

He'd told her about the destroyer he'd been assigned to, reassuring her that its defences were impressive even if its open bridge left the ship's crew exposed to the bitter Arctic weather. But Flora had overheard two of the officers she'd been driving just the other day discussing how vulnerable the convoys would be without air cover.

'Sitting ducks,' one of the men had said.

'I hear they're putting guns on some of the merchantmen,' replied the other. 'Although that's a bit like giving a child a popgun and telling him it'll protect him against a Messerschmitt.'

'Our boys are going to have their work cut out for them if Jerry gets wind of the flotilla.'

'Not if, but when. They send out spotter planes from their airbases in Norway every darned day. They're already keeping an eye on Spitsbergen and Iceland. So they're going to be very interested when they see a dozen ships heading for Russia's back door, accompanied by some of our finest.'

Flora's fingers had gripped the steering wheel, her knuckles whitening as the full implications of the risks that Alec was about to face had sunk in. No matter how difficult it was for them to be together, she knew she loved him and believed him when he told her that he loved her.

She was still shaken when she returned to the base at the end of her shift. Mairi and Bridie were finishing up for the day, too, but Bridie was keen for her friends to come with her to the Jellyjar Tavern that evening. She'd been standing in front of a couple of Americans from one of the merchant ships in the post office queue and had got chatting.

'They asked what there is to do about these parts, so I told them about the films and the dances. Then one of them asked if there was anywhere a sailor could buy a girl a drink! Can you imagine? Right there in the post office in front of Miss Cameron! Anyway, they're going to be at the hotel tonight and I can only go if the two of you will come too. Mother would have a fit otherwise. Please will you?'

Mairi had to nudge Flora to get her attention. She'd been distracted by the sight of a destroyer waiting out near the mouth of the loch as the tugs manoeuvred the boom nets to allow it to enter the harbour. She couldn't make out which it was, but was hoping Alec might be on board.

Mairi nudged her again. 'What do you think?'

'Hmmm?'

'About chaperoning Bridie with the Yanks tonight?'

'Oh yes, all right. I'll see if Ruaridh can come, shall I? He'd enjoy meeting the Americans, too.'

'Good idea. And there's safety in numbers, in case one of them tries to sweep Bridie off her feet and take her away to New York.'

'Chance'd be a fine thing!' Bridie retorted, although the hopeful look on her face gave away the fact that she'd already been imagining exactly such a scenario.

As they came in out of the frosty night, a cosy fug greeted them in the packed tavern, the atmosphere heavy with beer fumes and cigarette smoke. Ruaridh pushed his way through the throng, the girls following close on his heels. Men were standing three-deep at the bar and the cacophony of voices was a rich blend of accents and languages: Flora picked out Scots, English, Welsh, American, Polish and French, as well as some other foreign languages she couldn't identify. Just as they were despairing of finding a seat, they heard a shout of, 'Miss Macdonald! Over here!'

A tall, blond-haired American was waving them over to a table in the corner that he and several friends had commandeered. Three of the men stood, offering their chairs to the girls, as Bridie's new friend made the introductions.

'It's swell you came. Quite a joint you got here. We weren't expecting Scotch hospitality to be like this!' The sailor pumped Bridie's hand enthusiastically before turning to Flora and Mairi. 'Hal Gustavsen, pleased to meet ya. That's Stan, Greg and Ralph.

And that there' – he gestured towards an even taller young man with the same flax-coloured hair – 'is my big brother, Roy.'

Hal insisted on buying the next round of drinks, refusing Ruaridh's offer. 'No way, buddy. The drinks are on Uncle Sam tonight.'

The Americans' easy manners and generosity had infected the whole room. Several merchant ships were in port and their crews were happy to have a few days' respite after the perils of the Atlantic run. The Arctic journey loomed ahead, but tonight they could relax and enjoy themselves. Hal monopolised Bridie, and Flora and Ruaridh chatted with the others, answering their questions about the best places to play golf and the best beaches to walk to in the area.

'February's not exactly the best month for exploring, though,' Ruaridh pointed out.

'After our Midwest winters, this feels like kinda gentle weather you got here,' laughed Ralph, undaunted. 'We're more used to snowdrifts as high as your head. And we've been cooped up on that ship for weeks. It'll be good to stretch our legs on dry land for a coupla days.'

In the corner, Mairi sat next to Roy, who seemed a good deal quieter than his exuberant younger brother. But they soon discovered a mutual interest in dairy cattle – Roy and Hal having lived on their parents' farm in Wisconsin before volunteering for the Merchant Marine when America joined the war – and were deep in conversation by the time Hal and Stan fought their way back to the table with the second round of drinks. The farm boys had grown up surrounded by an ocean of land. Mairi and Flora were fascinated as Roy described the endless prairies with their seas of waving wheat. 'We'd never seen so much water as the day we embarked from New York. We thought Lake Michigan was big until we saw the Atlantic! There were days when I thought we'd never see land again.'

'You must miss the farm,' Mairi said.

'Sure do. But we have a job to get done, helping you Brits keep the Russkies supplied so they can stop Mr Hitler in his tracks. Besides, when Hal here volunteered, there was no way I could let my baby brother pull such a crazy stunt on his own. I promised Mom and Pop I'd keep an eye on him for them.' His face grew serious as he described what it meant to them to be playing their part. 'My grandparents emigrated to the States from Norway. So it'll be good to sail past the old country, even if it is occupied by the Nazis now. All the more reason to do our bit to free them again. Those are our people, right there, and it hurts real bad to know they're suffering.'

Late in the evening, the revellers began to disperse back to their ships and their homes. Hal and Roy insisted on walking Bridie and Mairi home, even though Flora and Ruaridh were passing their doors on the way back to Keeper's Cottage. Ruaridh had promised to walk up to the lochan to fish for grayling the next day with the brothers and whoever else was free.

Flora glanced back after they'd taken their leave at Mairi's gate. In the darkness, she could just make out the figures of Mairi and Roy, still deep in conversation.

She smiled to herself as she walked on. Because she couldn't have sworn to it, and maybe it was a trick of the shadows, but it looked as though Roy had reached out and taken both of Mairi's hands in his, his fair hair gleaming pale in the moonlight as his head bent towards hers.

Lexie, 1978

We've all arranged to meet at the bar tonight and Davy and the band will be playing as usual.

Bridie comes to babysit. 'Have fun celebrating,' she says as I pull on my jacket.

'Celebrating what?' I ask.

'Och, Lexie, have you forgotten? It's Elspeth's birthday today.'

Of course. I should have remembered. It was a date I'd always known when we were at school. I'd made her cards and spent my pocket money on bath salts or make-up or sweets for her (knowing she'd share them with me anyway), and she'd done the same when it was my turn.

I'm kicking myself as I walk along the shore road to the village. I can buy her a birthday drink, at least, but that hardly seems enough of a present for someone who's been a friend through thick and thin.

The bar's packed out and the skirl of the music seems more joyous than ever this evening. As I pick my way back to our table, carefully carrying a large round of drinks on a tray, I stop to have a quick word with Davy, handing him the pint I've got in for him.

My heart is pounding with nerves as I sit through the next set, and then Davy steps up to the mic and calls for quiet. 'Tonight we're saying Happy Birthday to our very own Elspeth McKinnes.'

Raucous cheers and whoops fill the room and Davy raises his hands, waiting for them to subside. 'And a good friend of Elspeth's is going to join us now, to say Happy Birthday in her own way.'

I get to my feet and walk across to the band, swallowing hard, wondering whether anything is going to come out of my mouth at all as it's suddenly gone so dry. My throat seems to close in on itself, tightening with the fear that I'm about to make a complete fool of myself. I take my place beside the fiddle player and he nods, raising his bow. All of a sudden I feel myself sway as a wave of dizziness washes over me, panicking as I remember the voice coach shaking her head when she listened to me try to sing again after my operation. 'I'm sorry, Alexandra,' she'd said. 'It's just not working. I think the damage you've done is permanent. You won't sing on the stage again.'

But then I look over and see Elspeth's smile, which stretches into an even wider grin as Davy hands me the mic. His hand squeezes mine for a second, steadying me. Elspeth nods encouragingly and I close my eyes for a moment, telling myself to pretend I'm singing to the toddlers at the playgroup or the seals in the hidden bay.

The fiddle starts to play the lilting notes of the introduction and, taking a deep breath, I begin to sing.

'*Oh rowan tree, oh rowan tree*
Thou'll ay be dear to me
Entwined thou art wi' many ties
O' home and infancy . . .'

The other instruments join in, and my voice rises, growing in confidence as the familiar strands of the tune weave themselves in and out through the accompaniment. I can hear that my singing is a bit scratchy, the words a little rough around the edges, but that only seems to add depth to the simplicity of the song. And then, one by one, all the others in the bar begin to sing along softly until our individual voices blend to fill the room.

When the final notes die away, there's a moment of complete silence. And then the cheers and whoops erupt.

'Will you sing another?' Davy asks, leaning close to be heard above the din.

I smile and shake my head. 'Not tonight. That was for Elspeth. I'm leaving the rest of the evening to you boys.'

When I get back to the table, Elspeth hugs me hard. 'Best present you've ever given me,' she says.

'What, even better than the bright green eyeshadow and the quarter-pound of treacle toffees?' I say, referring to the last present I'd bought for her.

'They come close.' She smiles. 'But that song was beautiful.'

As I sit back down and take a sip from my drink, I reflect that I seem to have been singing quite a lot recently, for someone who's supposedly lost her voice.

Catching my eye across the room, Davy raises his glass to me and then picks up his guitar, and the band swings into the next set.

Bridie comes for tea as usual the following Wednesday, and I show her the brooch I found in the pocket of Mum's coat.

Her face lights up when she sees it. 'Alec gave her that. It's a sweetheart brooch – belonged to his mother originally, I believe. Soldiers and sailors used to give them to their girlfriends and wives so they could keep their loves close to their hearts even when they were apart.' She takes her hanky out from the sleeve of her cardigan and gives the brooch a rub. 'See, it's silver. Just needs a bit of a polish and it'll come up like new. Your mammy always wore it or carried it with her in her pocket.'

I decide to tackle her elusiveness head-on. 'Bridie, what happened with my mum and dad? You've told me bits and pieces, but I want to know everything.'

She glances up at me, startled.

'There's something you're not saying, isn't there?' I persist.

'Well now, Lexie, there's a story there, all right. But I'm not sure I'm the right person to tell it on my own.'

I can't help but let my exasperation show. 'If not you, Bridie, then who else?'

'Mairi would be the one.'

'But she lives in America!'

'She does.' Bridie calmly reaches for another biscuit. 'But she'll be here soon enough. She always comes back once a year to visit her sisters and brothers. I've told her you've come home. She's looking forward to seeing you.'

Flora, 1942

It was a crisp morning, the air as pure as the water in the burns that ran off the hills, when Mairi and Bridie met Roy and Hal at the jetty to show them the way to Keeper's Cottage.

Flora was pleased they'd be able to spend time together that day, although she couldn't help missing Alec all the more. As she tidied away the things she'd used to bake a batch of scones, she tried to shake off her own preoccupations, smiling at the sound of Bridie's voice approaching on the road.

In the cramped kitchen, Iain shook hands with the Americans and showed them the flies that were best for tempting graylings while Ruaridh prepared rods for them. They were just gathering everything together in preparation for the walk into the hills when there was a knock at the door.

'Alec! You're back!' Flora flung her arms around his neck and he hugged her tightly to him. All her doubts and fears seemed to dissolve in his embrace.

'We got in in the early hours. The convoy leaves tomorrow so I've not got long. I wanted to spend every minute I could with you.' He was more than happy to join the fishing expedition, and stuck the tin of flies that Iain gave him into his jacket pocket.

The grass crunched underfoot, each blade sugar-coated with frost, as the small group hiked up the path alongside the burn, their laughter disturbing a stag that had been nosing the wintry ground in search of forage and causing him to bound away, his hooves drumming on the frozen earth as he tossed his antlers in annoyance.

The waters of the lochan were still and black when they reached the heights, but the weak sun had melted the frost and Flora was warm from the climb. She'd thrust one hand into her coat pocket and Alec held the other tight, the heat of his skin mingling with hers to keep her fingers from being nipped by the chill.

They set down their gear in the shelter of the old bothy and Alec helped Mairi and Roy tie flies to their lines.

'Back home we like nothing better than to spend our summer evenings fishing in the ponds in the slough on the farm,' said Roy. 'Not that you need fancy flies for perch – they'll eat pretty much anything you care to put on your hook.'

'What's the trick with these here graylings then?' asked Hal.

Bridie, who'd refused a rod, settled herself next to him on the bank.

'You need to cast out towards the deeper water. They'll be down in the depths, where it's a wee bit warmer.' Ruaridh pointed out the best areas, away from the skeletal, winter-bleached reeds at the water's edge.

The group spread out and silence fell as they concentrated on casting, the only sounds the hissing of the lines through the air and the quiet hum of the reels, overlain by an occasional stamping of feet in heavy boots to keep the circulation going. Even Bridie sat quietly, contented to gaze at Hal as he watched the water. At first, nothing stirred. But then the mirror-like surface broke as a fish rose, tempted by the feathered flies that had begun to land there. In a flash of silver, it reached for Ruaridh's hook, but missed and disappeared back into the depths, leaving ever-widening circles that spread across the lochan.

'That's good,' Alec commented quietly. 'At least we know they're there.'

Hal was the first to hook one, giving a whoop as the tip of his rod bent with the tautening of the line.

'Well done,' called Alec. 'Play it in gently now, they're soft-mouthed.'

Bridie ran to get the landing net and carefully scooped in the catch.

'That's a good-sized grayling,' Ruaridh said, with a nod of approval.

A couple of hours later, once they had four fish in the wicker creel, the short-lived daylight began to dim, fine wisps of cirrus cloud veiling the weakening sun as it drifted towards the western horizon, heralding a change in the weather.

'Brrr.' Bridie shivered. 'I'm frozen stiff.'

Hal grinned, wrapping a long arm around her shoulders. 'Here you go, let's get you all warmed up!'

As they reeled in their lines for the final time, Flora and Mairi exchanged a smile, noticing that Bridie was in no hurry to pull away from Hal's embrace.

Back at the cottage, Flora set the kettle on the stove while Mairi put out cups and Bridie buttered a plate of scones. The fishing party sat round the kitchen table, stretching sock-clad feet towards the warmth of the range to thaw out frozen toes.

Roy smiled at Mairi, cupping his mug of tea. 'That sure was a great day. It's been good to feel life is normal again, just for a few hours.' He carefully set down his cup and reached to take one of her hands in his beneath the cover of the table.

The others all pretended not to notice, and reached out eagerly as Bridie handed round the plate of scones again.

As she leaned against the range, waiting for the water to reboil so that she could top up the teapot, Flora watched the group gathered in her kitchen, filling the room with their easy words and ready laughter that warmed the soul. Today had indeed been a good day, one to treasure. Because tomorrow Ruaridh would climb the hill to his post at the signal station and Alec, Roy and Hal would be back on board their ships. And then, when the time came, the tugs would draw back the boom nets and the signal would be given. The ships would slowly get underway and the convoy would begin its perilous journey, slipping from the safe embrace of Loch Ewe and plunging into the ice-grey grip of the Arctic sea.

Alec stayed on when the others had gone. It was already dark outside when Ruaridh went to help Iain check on the garron. Flora gathered up the teacups and carried them to the sink. As she began to wash them, Alec came and stood behind her, wrapping his arms around her waist. He buried his face in her hair for a moment before picking up a dish towel and beginning to dry the cups. When they'd finished, she took the towel from him and wiped her wet hands on it before clasping them around his neck and kissing him.

His dark eyes shone with love as he gazed at her, taking in every inch of her face. 'This is the image I'll carry with me when we leave tomorrow,' he told her, gently brushing back a tendril of copper-gold hair from her cheek. 'Your smile will get me through the roughest seas and home again.'

He relinquished his hold on her for a moment and reached into the pocket of his tweed jacket. 'I have something for you.'

The silver sweetheart brooch with the anchor and crown lay in the palm of his hand. 'Ma wanted you to have it. She said it's only right that you should wear it now.' Carefully he pinned it to her jumper, above her heart.

Flora couldn't speak for a minute or two as her emotions overwhelmed her. She knew how much the brooch meant to Lady Helen, and that this was a sign that she approved of Flora's relationship with her son even if Sir Charles did not.

'I'll wear it every day,' she said at last, 'and treasure it as your mother has done. As we both treasure you.'

'You're my girl, Flora. The only one for me. Let's not say goodbye. We'll just say, "I'll be seeing you."'

She stood in the doorway as he walked slowly away up the path towards Ardtuath House. As she watched, she ran her fingertips over the brooch, which sat like a shield over her heart, tracing the outline of the anchor and the crown above it.

'Come back safe to me,' she whispered. 'I'll be seeing you.' And her words followed him into the darkness of the winter night.

The three girls watched from the pier at Mellon Charles as the convoy sailed. Flora's expression was outwardly composed, but she had wrapped her arms around herself, pulling the sides of her dark blue uniform jacket tightly across each other as though by doing so they might physically hold her together.

Mairi's face was tense and pale as the merchantmen began to move slowly into their allotted positions, as if they were playing a sinister, slow-motion game of follow-the-leader. 'Wheesht, you're crying, Bridie,' she said gently. 'It won't be doing him any good now, will it?'

'Oh, how on earth can you both stay so calm?' Bridie wailed, fumbling in her pocket for her handkerchief and blowing her nose long and loud.

As she replied, Flora's eyes never left the *Isla*, the destroyer leading the string of merchant ships from the loch, knowing that Alec was on the bridge and would surely know she was there. 'We have to stay calm, Bridie, to help them be strong enough to leave. And, let's hope, to help them be strong enough to face the journey ahead of them and come back safely, too.'

Lexie, 1978

Mairi is at the same time a stranger and so familiar that the tears spring to my eyes as we embrace. I remember her, of course, from my childhood. Even though she'd left the family farm for a new life in America at the end of the war, she returned to Aultbea now and then and always came to see us in Keeper's Cottage, bringing with her toys and huge boxes of excitingly foreign candy. Apart from the fact that her hair is now a white that's as pure as the first snow on the hills, she looks exactly the same: warm brown eyes and a complexion as radiant as it was in her twenties.

She's brought with her a pair of extremely cute pink-and-white-striped dungarees for Daisy and a large album of photos and newspaper cuttings. 'Flora sent me these over the years. She always kept me in touch with all the local news. I thought you might be interested to see them.' Despite all those years away, her accent still lilts with the soft inflections of the Scottish Highlands.

She and Bridie take it in turns to cuddle Daisy, who laps up the attention from her two surrogate grannies, charming them with her very own style of conversation.

'Look,' Mairi tells Daisy, 'here's a picture of your mummy when she was wee, making sandcastles on the beach. And here she is on her first day at the big school. See how smart she looks in her new uniform? And this is her singing a solo in the school show.'

'Mum,' Daisy says, pointing a chubby forefinger at the album.

'Clever girl,' coos Bridie, offering her a Liquorice Allsort, which Daisy pops into her mouth with a cherubic smile.

I'm fascinated by the photos, poring over them. My mother took these images, documenting my childhood. She put them into envelopes and sent them across the sea to the other side of the world, where Mairi kept them so carefully, lovingly preserving them in this album. It's a little overwhelming, feeling this loved.

'Here are some of Flora's letters, too.' Mairi takes a little bundle from her handbag, tied with a length of tartan ribbon. 'I thought you might like to read them sometime.'

'Thank you.' I set them aside politely, although the urge to look through them immediately is strong – maybe they'll offer more clues to whatever it is Bridie's been keeping from me.

As if she can read my mind, Mairi says, 'Bridie tells me you've been asking some questions about your father's family.'

'I have. I suppose having Daisy has opened my eyes a bit to what it must have been like for Mum, raising me on her own. She never said much about my dad. And neither has anyone else. I'm curious to fill in the gaps, so I can pass it on to Daisy when she's older.'

Mairi nods, holding out her arms to take Daisy from Bridie to give her a rest and let her drink her tea. 'That's only natural,' she says. 'I know Bridie's been telling you a lot about the war years, how our lives were turned upside down. I'm happy to tell you all I can remember. The album and those letters will be a good starting point. And then you can ask us any questions after you've had a chance to look through them. I'm here for a while, staying with my brother at the farm. We'll have plenty of opportunities to chat.'

'Thanks, Mairi,' I say. 'I'm grateful to you both.'

I go through to the kitchen to refresh the teapot and as I wait for the kettle to boil, I think how easy it will be now to put in place the missing pieces of my family history. As I come back into the sitting room, though, Mairi is murmuring something to Bridie, who is shaking her head vehemently.

They look up as I come through the door, falling silent, and it seems to me their expressions are a little guarded. They're both quick to smile again, but I get the impression that those smiles are just a little too bright to be entirely natural.

Hmmm, I think. Perhaps piecing together my mother's story might still not be quite such a doddle after all.

Flora, 1942

'They made it safely! They're on their way back.' Bridie's face was alight with joy and relief as she passed on the news to Flora and Mairi. A first lieutenant who worked in the wireless station had told her that the first of the convoys to leave from Loch Ewe had had a safe run to Murmansk, making it through the narrow corridor of sea between the Arctic ice and the north cape of Norway without encountering any enemy action from either the waves beneath them or the skies above.

'They've still a way to go until they're safe though,' said Mairi, reluctant to let down her guard until she saw the ships back in the harbour with her own eyes.

'Yes, but he said they're almost south of Jan Mayen Island already. If this weather holds they'll be here within the week. And they're getting close enough to Iceland now for our battleships to defend them. That should deter the Germans, too.'

Automatically, Flora's hand went into the pocket of her jacket where she kept the sweetheart brooch when she was on duty. It was her link to Alec out there on the unforgiving seas and she clutched it as tight as a lifeline. For the first time in a month she allowed herself to breathe a little more easily, as a swell of hope surged in her heart with the thought that she'd soon see him back home safely.

It took an age for Alec to disembark when the *Isla* finally tied up alongside the pier at Mellon Charles. Flora had just finished her shift and she stood on the damp sand at the corner of the bay waiting for him to appear, as the crew made the ship fast and finished up their duties on board. She pulled the sweetheart brooch from her pocket and pinned it to the lapel of her jacket, then blew on her fingers to warm them.

Everyone on the base was overjoyed that the first convoy to leave from Loch Ewe had been successful and all the ships had returned safely. That afternoon, the tugs that operated the boom had drawn back the nets, and the line of ships had sailed slowly into the calm waters without ceremony. The merchantmen dropped anchor on the far side of the island and Mairi and Bridie had cycled off to welcome back Roy and Hal.

The evening chill seeped from the ground through the soles of Flora's shoes and she stamped her feet, to dispel her impatience as much as to keep her circulation going, as she scanned the faces of the disembarking seamen searching for the one that would make her heart leap with joy. And then there he was at last, and in a few strides he'd covered the final yards between them and was holding her tight. She breathed in the smell of the journey from his thick duffel coat – the damp salt of the sea mingled with the chemical tang of fuel oil – as she lost herself in his kiss.

'Come back to the house with me,' he said. 'I can't bear to spend another evening without you. It was bad enough being miles away out at sea, but it'll be torture knowing you're just down the path while I'm at Ardtuath.'

She hesitated, freezing at the thought of going back there. 'Will that be all right with your parents?'

He took her face in his hands and kissed her again. 'It'll have to be. I've been thinking about it – being on watch at two in the morning gives you quite a bit of time for that. My father's going to have to get used to the idea of us from here on in.'

Ardtuath House was completely dark as they walked up the drive, its turrets black against a sky hung with stars. Flora felt herself tensing in anticipation at having to face Sir Charles on the other side of the blackout and reached for Alec's hand. But the front door was locked and Alec's knock echoed in the darkness, met with a resounding silence.

'Looks like they're not here,' he said. 'Come on, we'll go round the back.'

He unlocked the kitchen door and they stepped into the stillness of the empty house. The range had been left to go out and it was barely warmer inside than out.

'Perhaps they're at the Urquharts',' Alec commented. 'Come on, let's light the fire in the library and see what we can forage in the larder.'

Half an hour later the logs were blazing cheerfully in the hearth and they'd spread out a makeshift picnic before it. The atmosphere in the house was completely different when Sir Charles wasn't there. Flora eased off her shoes and knelt on the rug to toast some slightly stale bread on the flames, wriggling her toes in their thick stockings as she luxuriated in the warmth. Once each slice had browned, she removed it from the toasting fork and passed it to Alec to spread with butter while she made the next piece. They ate it with slices of ham and washed it down with a couple of bottles of ale that they'd found lurking in a forgotten corner of the larder.

'Best meal I've had in ages,' Alec grinned. 'But that may have as much to do with the company as it does the menu.' He stretched out contentedly in front of the fire and rested his head in her lap.

'So what was it like? Out there?'

She stroked his hair, watching the firelight dance across his face as he gazed into the flames and told her about the journey. He described the mixture of fear and excitement as they'd set off, which had soon turned into a kind of dull dread as they faced the monotony of the grey Arctic waters, day in, day out, never knowing whether they were being watched and what might be lurking below the waves.

A storm had blown up a few nights in, sending towering waves of icy green water crashing over the deck of the ship. In the bitter temperatures, the water had frozen, forming a thick shell of ice on the windward side of the ship. They'd taken it in turns to tie on a lifeline and brave the treacherously slippery, listing deck as it pitched and rolled, taking an axe to the ice to prevent the build-up of weight from capsizing the ship.

Radio silence had to be maintained so that the German listening stations didn't pick up the convoy's presence, so although they travelled as a group with each ship holding its position in the line, there was a sense of isolation that was only amplified by the sight of the Arctic ice floes in the distance. That winter ice narrowed the channel available to them, forcing them to navigate a fine line between icebergs to the north and the German-occupied Norwegian coast to the south. But the short winter days brought fog as well, which covered the sea in a low-lying blanket – so thick, Alec said, that you could hardly see the jackstaff from the bridge of the *Isla*. Ordinarily they'd have cursed it as another hazard to be negotiated, but in those dangerous waters they'd given thanks for the white shroud that concealed them and allowed them to slip past the north cape undetected. Finally, with relief, they'd turned their bows to the south-east, hugging the Russian shore as they entered the Kola Inlet which led to the port of Murmansk.

Flora passed Alec her glass and he raised himself up on one elbow as he replenished it from the bottle. Then he reached across and fished another log from the basket, throwing it on to the fire where it settled in a cascade of sparks as tongues of flame licked around it.

'What's Russia like?' she asked.

'Cold. Dark. Vast. But with a terrible sort of beauty as well. We were met by a pilot vessel to guide us in and were pretty pleased to see it, I can tell you. It's a deep fjord but the channel's so narrow there you need to keep your wits about you. We had steep mountains to starboard and were jolly glad to think that they stood between us and the Germans. And the most extraordinary thing happened as we neared Murmansk . . . All the upper works of the ships, the masts and the yards, suddenly started to glow with a white flickering light. I'd heard of it before – they call it St Elmo's fire – but that's the first time I've ever seen it. In the mist, everything becomes charged with static and it discharges from anything that has a point. It was like our own personal lightning show. We were mightily relieved that it hadn't happened off Norway, I can tell you. We'd have been lit up for the Jerries like Christmas trees!'

'The Russians must have been glad to see you, with all that equipment for them.'

'I suppose so.' He paused to take a sip of beer. 'Russian dockers are not exactly effusive. In fact, once the cargo was offloaded, one of them said, "Is that all you've brought us?" But it's a tough life for them away up there in the Arctic Circle. At this time of year they only get an hour or two of daylight and the weather is brutal. I think they pretty much survive on vodka to get them through. The war's brought awful suffering to their country as well. Ever since the German advance last year there's been bitter fighting in the south and some of the men working on the dockside had seen action there. They're hard as nails.'

'Well, thank goodness you all got back safely.'

He nodded. 'We were lucky. We picked up a German weather plane on our radar once, thought they might have spotted us, too. But we got away with it this time.'

The words 'this time' made Flora flinch. 'Do you know when you'll next be sailing?'

He shook his head. 'Not yet. It'll take a bit of time to muster the next convoy. Could be a month or so, I imagine. At least the weather should be improving by then. And as the ice retreats we'll be able to give the north cape a wider berth.'

Flora was silent. She knew he was putting a brave face on it, because the hours of daylight would be lengthening, too, and the convoys would be at sea for longer if they were sailing that much further north. It was a double-edged sword: the changing of the seasons would simply bring different risks, making the journey no less perilous. She tried not to think about that tonight, though. He was here, and she was safe in his arms beside the warmth of the fire. She knew that this was a memory they'd both treasure and so she leaned down to kiss away the lines of tension from his brow, her red-gold hair catching the dancing reflections of the firelight in its depths.

Roy and Hal's ship remained at anchor in the loch alongside the other merchantmen just long enough for them to have a couple of days off. They spent every moment they could ashore with Mairi and Bridie. The noise levels in the Jellyjar Tavern reached new heights as the safe return of the convoy was celebrated on the first night, and the brothers spent the next day with the girls, walking on the shore and visiting Bridie and Mairi's homes. Their families were impressed at the good manners and easy humour displayed by the Americans, although Flora overheard Mrs Macdonald telling Bridie that she oughtn't to set her heart on a Yank who most likely would disappear one way or another before the war came to an end.

Two days later, the merchant ships were refuelled and made ready for the Atlantic crossing once again, ordered to return to the States to pick up another cargo.

Bridie wept uncontrollably as they waved them off. Flora handed her a hankie and put an arm around her shoulders, while Mairi stood shielding her eyes as she tried to keep sight of Roy. He'd disappeared round to the starboard side as he helped his shipmates weigh anchor, but he emerged again to salute her and to blow her a kiss, his blond hair glinting in the silver light that bounced from the surface of the water as the ship's propellers began to turn, churning the loch into turmoil.

'They'll be back,' Flora said. 'You know they promised they'd try and get another Arctic run so they can see you again. That shows how much they must like you both – most men probably wouldn't be too keen to do both the Atlantic and the Arctic runs again so soon . . . if ever.'

'Oh, oh,' sobbed Bridie, 'it's so dangerous out there. It feels so wrong to wish them to come back when it's putting their lives in danger. But I can't help it . . .' The rest of her sentence was lost as the ship's whistle blew, its call answered by the other ships in the convoy so that for a minute the hills echoed with the sound.

The three girls watched as the convoy sailed, this time turning westwards from the mouth of the loch. Once the last ship had departed, the tug pulled the boom net closed behind it and the waters of Loch Ewe slowly settled, becoming calm again.

The girls trudged back towards Aultbea, each of them lost in her own thoughts, but then the clouds parted just a little and a ray of spring sunlight shone through.

'Look,' Flora nudged Bridie. She pointed to where the sun had coaxed the first primroses of spring to push their heads out from under their mossy coverlets in the sheltered spots alongside the burn and begin tentatively to unfurl their petals. The sight lifted their hearts, just a little, and Bridie began to talk again, more hopefully now, about the picnics they'd be able to go on when the Gustavsen brothers returned.

Lexie, 1978

It's another diamond day, the loch sparkling after a long spell of rain that has cleared at last. A few fluffy white clouds scud across the blue of the sky, looking as freshly washed as the sheep in the fields below. I'm walking home with Daisy, the pushchair laden with shopping and playgroup paraphernalia, as we've spent another morning making music in the hall. It's lunchtime, so the road is empty, and she and I are both singing one of her favourite songs as we go:

'*You'll take the high road*
And I'll take the low road . . .'

As we approach the pier, a third voice joins in, adding a tenor harmony to Daisy's piping soprano and my slightly rough-around-the-edges alto.

Davy hails us. 'Ahoy there!' Only his head and shoulders are visible where he stands on the deck of the *Bonnie Stuart*, hoisting creels up on to the rough boards of the jetty.

When we reach him, Daisy strains to be released from the straps confining her and I let her out so she can toddle over to inspect the morning's catch. Davy holds up a huge brown crab, its powerful-looking claws safely bound, and lets her touch the carapace, glossy as varnish. The boat bobs restlessly in the breeze, tugging at the mooring lines tethering it to the cleats on the jetty's edge, bouncing gently against its fenders. With a satisfied nod, Daisy allows him to replace the crab in its bucket of seawater and potters over to pick up an oyster shell dropped on to the boards by some passing bird.

'Everyone enjoyed hearing you sing the other night,' he tells me. 'You should make it a regular thing. We'd be pleased to have you do a set with the band if you wanted.'

His eyes meet mine, his gaze as clear as the waters surrounding us. I find it unsettling, as if he can see right into my soul, to the places I try to keep hidden from the world, those dark neglected corners where grief and guilt and pain lurk. I look away, pretending to be fascinated by a clump of seaweed that trails its knotted fingers in the ebbing tide.

'Really,' he insists. 'Do you not miss it, Lexie – the singing? When it's in your blood, surely you're denying a big part of yourself if you're not making music.'

'I *am* making music,' I say, gesticulating towards the bag of instruments hanging from the handles of the pushchair. It comes out a little sharper than I'd intended.

'Yes, for others,' he replies. 'But what about the music you make for yourself? I know I couldn't live without it. It'd be like cutting off a limb if I ever stopped playing and singing.'

A surge of annoyance rises in me, rearing its head like a wave nearing the shore. I'm fed up with everyone judging. I know he's only trying to be encouraging, but it feels like criticism to me – of my choices and decisions, of how I'm trying to live my life.

I'm about to retort that I'm taking my time, that I may never want to sing publicly again, and how could he possibly know what I'm feeling?

The words are in my mouth. But the sound of a splash interrupts them.

In a panic, I look across to where Daisy should be busily posting pebbles through the gaps in the boards, and in the same moment Davy yells her name. There's the sound of another splash and he disappears over the side of the boat.

For a split second I stand, frozen, alone on the jetty. And then Daisy's name tears at my throat as I scream it over and over. I fall to my knees, frantically trying to hold the boat away from the wooden edging, desperately trying to keep it from crushing my baby or from pinning her beneath the water: from sealing the gap into which she's tumbled, the salt water swallowing her whole.

A silence fills my head, the noises of the wind and the waves and the cries of the seagulls blanked out by sheer blind terror as I wait . . . and pray . . . and wait, not breathing . . . and it feels as if the bones in my arms will snap as I fight against the bulk of the boat and the force of the wind.

And then the world around me erupts in a flurry of movement. Davy bursts from the water on the far side of the boat, holding a lifeless bundle in his arms, shouting words I can't seem to register. There's the sound of running feet, pounding on the boards of the jetty, of voices calling, of someone issuing instructions . . . *Get the doctor!* . . . *Call the coastguard!* Hands reach for Davy, taking the bundle from him, lifting it carefully on to the boards, helping to haul him up.

I try to move forward to where Daisy lies, water pooling around her. But she is still, still, too still and more pairs of hands hold me back as Davy sinks to his knees beside her and begins – oh so gently – to try to breathe life back into her, to persuade her heart to beat again.

The small crowd that has gathered – out of nowhere, hurrying from their homes – parts slightly and I see Bridie and Mairi running towards me, their faces shocked, as white as shells. And then I hear the wild, rasping screams, over and over, like the cry of a wounded animal, on and on as if they will never stop. I look around frantically, wide-eyed, terrified, wondering where they're coming from.

It's only as Bridie reaches me and wraps her arms around me that I realise the screams are mine.

I fight to get through to where Daisy lies, needing above all to hold her. As I reach her, there's a gurgling choking sound and Davy turns her head to one side as a gush of seawater flows from her mouth. He presses a finger against her neck and looks up at me, relief flooding his face. 'There's a pulse.'

But her eyes are still shut, her damp lashes stark against the translucent, too-pale skin of her face. Tentatively, gently, I brush a strand of hair away from her forehead, where the shadow of a bruise is beginning to form. She looks so tiny, so fragile, lying there motionless, and I gasp as a sob judders through my whole being, unleashing a shaking so violent that it takes both Bridie and Mairi to hold me upright.

The crowd parts as the doctor strides to Daisy's side, crouching, setting down his bag and opening her coat to press a stethoscope to her chest.

'She fell between the boat and the jetty,' Davy tells him. 'I think she may have hit her head on the way down. She was only in the water for a minute or two, but she looked to be unconscious when I reached her. She wasn't breathing and there was no pulse. I did CPR, she's vomited up some water and there's a breath and a pulse now.' He sounds businesslike, clinical, telling the doctor the things he needs to know, but it panics me even more that they're talking over my daughter like this, like it's just an empty body, a shell, not my living, laughing Daisy any more.

The doctor nods. 'We'll not move her. There may be injuries to her head or her neck. The helicopter's on its way.'

He swivels on his heels, turning to look at me. 'Don't worry, Lexie, we'll get her to the hospital just as quick as we can. You can go with her. Davy here's done all the right things.' He notices the trembling that wracks my body, making my teeth chatter. 'She's in shock,' he tells Bridie. 'Can someone lend her a coat?' he calls.

A jacket is draped over my shoulders and Mairi pulls me close, letting the warm solidity of her body support mine. Someone else has brought blankets and they are wrapped around Davy's shoulders because he is shivering, too. One is laid gently, softly, over Daisy as I kneel at her side, clutching one of her tiny hands, willing the fingers to curl around mine. But they don't respond. And in my head all I can hear is please . . . please . . . please. Until, after an age, the noise of the helicopter's blades chops the air above us into a million pieces and they seem to flutter down around us like dying leaves.

Our arrival at the hospital is a blur of half-remembered impressions: the kindness of the medic in the helicopter who held my hand on the surprisingly short journey as we flew over the hills and sea lochs; Daisy looking so tiny and fragile, her unmoving body strapped into a cradle that they lifted out and placed on a trolley as if it were as weightless as a feather; the team of doctors and nurses who surrounded her as we hurried through the warren of brightly lit corridors; watching, helpless, as they took her away for X-rays; the waiting; the not-daring-to-breathe minutes – which felt like hours – as I sat with my arms wrapped around myself, trying not to fall apart, as I waited and waited and then waited some more.

And then, at last, the moment when the doctor came through and she had a smile on her face as she held my hand in hers and told me that they were cautiously optimistic. Davy's quick actions had undoubtedly saved Daisy's life. 'She has no broken bones and there doesn't seem to be any damage to her spine. But she has a severe concussion and hasn't regained consciousness yet. We'll just have to wait and see how she is when she comes around . . . If need be, we can arrange for her to be taken from Yorkhill to one of the other Glasgow hospitals where there's a scanner that can look into her brain. But it's too early to tell if there's any lasting brain damage yet.'

I struggled to swallow the panic that choked me when I heard those last words. 'Can I see her?' I managed to croak.

'Of course. We're just getting her settled into a side room where we can keep a close eye on her. You can come through now.'

In the twilight of watching and waiting, sitting in a plastic-covered armchair beside Daisy's cot, I've lost track of time, of whether it's day or night. Kindly nurses come and go, bringing me occasional cups of tea and plates of food. Sleep creeps up on me now and then, but mostly I just sit watching over her beneath the glare of the fluorescent lights, holding her hand, careful not to touch the tubes and drips keeping her alive while she is lost to me, drifting in the darkness beyond my reach. And through it all, to keep her there with me and to keep myself from losing it, I hum and sing every song I can think of to her, calling her back from wherever it is she's gone.

A nurse pops her head round the door. 'That's me off now. The night shift's just finishing. Just thought I'd check up on wee Daisy one more time before I go.'

I force a smile, my lips cracked and dry. 'No change. But I think she may have moved her fingers a bit more a while ago.'

The nurse nods. 'I'll get them to bring you some tea. A bowl of porridge, maybe? You need to keep up your strength.'

My voice is hoarse, despite the sip of tea, as I sing the words of the 'Eriskay Love Lilt' one more time:

'*In the morning when I go*
To the white and shining sea,
In the calling of the seals
Thy soft calling to me . . .'

And then her eyelashes flutter and her beautiful eyes open and smile at me and she says, as clear as anything, 'Seals? Go bat?'

And I'm laughing through my tears as I hug her and hug her, feeling as if my heart will burst with the joy and the relief.

Flora, 1942

As she waved Alec off on the next convoy to take on the Murmansk run, Flora tried hard to ignore the sense of foreboding that had settled itself in the base of her stomach. It felt like a lead weight that had dragged at her spirits even while she and Alec had spent his last evening ashore together. He'd made an effort to seem cheerful, but she could sense that he was distracted as they'd sat in the crowded hall watching an Abbot and Costello film. In fact, the audience's laughter had sounded a little forced to Flora's ears, as if many of those sitting around them also had half their thoughts elsewhere. This convoy had the number thirteen and it was hard to set superstition to one side.

It was March, and the first lambs were wobbling about the fields on unsteady legs as they ran bleating to huddle close to their mothers, seeking shelter from the cruel-edged, unpredictable wind. That same wind would be redoubled beyond the mouth of the loch as the convoy emerged the next day, sailing once more into the dark waters. Flora knew that the crews would keep themselves busy, fending off the boredom and the constant anxiety with the strict routine that Alec had described. He'd told her how the days on board passed in a continuous cycle of eating, sleeping, maintenance and cleaning. The men had coined the phrase 'the three Ts' to describe the mood that dominated the Arctic run: tedium, tiredness and terror. Every so often there would be a training exercise to keep them alert and battle-ready, during which they'd scramble to action stations and rattle off rounds of ack-ack at passing ice floes. Those surges of adrenalin kept the men's wits sharp, when otherwise they felt they might drown in the grey monotony that stretched from horizon to horizon as the ships ploughed their pitching, rolling way through the relentless waves.

Perhaps this time it was purely the knowledge of what took place that put her on edge. But just as the whispering of the wind foretells rain on the way, long before the first drops begin to fall, she knew that Alec could sense the gathering resolve of the Nazi forces now that they'd become aware of the convoys stealing past their Norwegian bases to keep the Russian war machine fed and fuelled. She imagined the wolf packs of U-boats must be hungry for the hunt.

She turned away, unable to bear watching the long tail of ships leaving the safety of the harbour, telling herself that he would come back to her. That she simply needed to keep herself busy for the next month or so. That with a fair wind and a bit of luck, he'd be home in time for Easter.

But the lead weight tugged at her guts again, insistent as the brisk breeze that pulled at her hair, teasing strands loose from beneath her cap and whipping them against her tear-damp cheeks.

Flora and Bridie were helping Mairi and two of her little sisters gather dulse from the rocks at low tide, carefully picking the translucent, dark red fronds and placing them in a colander whose enamel was chipped from years of use. Rationing had limited many of the usual staples, but the crofters living around the loch were long used to supplementing their diet with ingredients from the woods and the shore, which were still plentiful. With so many mouths to feed, the Macleods knew better than anyone the best spots to gather wild pickings.

Stuart and Davy Laverock appeared, scrambling over the rocks, their catapults in hand.

'Whit're you doing?' Stuart asked.

Flora straightened up and held out the handful of seaweed she'd picked for them to inspect. 'Collecting this. It's good to eat, especially if you put a dab of butter on it after you've cooked it.'

'C'n we help?' asked Davy.

'Of course. Pick the nice fresh bits like this, see?'

After a few minutes, the boys grew bored of seaweed-hunting and began firing pebbles at a piece of wood floating in a rock pool, pretending it was a German U-boat.

'Good shot, you got him! Now he's a goner,' Stuart shouted, before launching another stick into the pool.

At the sight of Hamish McTaggart passing along the road on his bike, they all paused, watching where he was heading. Since he'd been demobbed, after losing an eye to a piece of shrapnel while fighting the Italians in North Africa, he'd been employed by Miss Cameron to deliver the telegrams that had started arriving more frequently now. Very few of them ever contained any good news. He raised a hand in greeting, but cycled on past the end of the village until the bend in the road hid him from view.

Mairi sighed, shaking her head. 'It'll be someone from over at Poolewe then. Another poor soul injured or worse.'

'Our mammy was in the air raids in Glasgow, Mrs C says,' Davy announced. 'But she was fine 'cause they built a massive shelter in Port Glasgow and she slept in there when the bombers came over.'

'Wheesht, Davy, that was ages ago, there's no more air raids there now. The Jerries're too busy fighting everyone else these days,'

Stuart said, picking up a stone and chucking it out into the water with the nonchalance of youth.

'How's Mrs Carmichael doing?' Flora asked the boys.

Stuart shrugged. 'She's okay. She always keeps Matthew's bedroom door shut. We're not allowed in there now. We used to go and look at his stamps – he's got this massive collection, from all over the world – but his things are too precious to touch now he's dead. Sometimes she goes in there and doesn't come out for ages.'

'That's 'cause she's greetin',' chipped in Davy. 'I've heard her. Sometimes she doesn't come out even when it's time to cook the tea. Mr C tried to make mince once, but it was all burned and he had to chuck out the pan in the end. So on those days now we just have some more bread and dripping.'

'The poor thing,' said Flora, shaking her head.

The boys ran off, having spotted some of their friends heading for the post office, hopeful that someone might have a sweet coupon that could be exchanged for a stick of liquorice to be shared around.

'It's amazing how she keeps up appearances in public,' Bridie said. 'She still has all the ladies in the Rural shaking in their shoes.'

'It probably does her good to have that distraction,' said Mairi. 'I feel sorry for them all – those wee boys too.' She shook the colander gently, settling the heap of dulse, which now reached the rim. 'That's enough, I should think. C'mon, let's take this home and get it cooked. Dad'll be in from the milking soon enough.'

Flora said goodbye to Bridie at her gate. 'Any word from Hal?' she asked.

Bridie beamed and pulled a dog-eared postcard from her pocket. 'From New York. He says they'll be back just as soon as there's another cargo of gifts for Uncle Joe Stalin. And he says he'll bring me a bottle of perfume from Macy's, which is a huge great shop they have over there.'

'That's good news.' Flora smiled.

Bridie shoved the card back into her pocket. 'And Alec will be back, too, before you know it. I know the weeks must drag while he's out there, but surely there'll soon be news that they've made it to Murmansk at least.'

Flora nodded. 'I hope so. Any day now.' But this time her smile didn't quite reach her eyes as she turned and headed for home.

Easter arrived, but the advent of spring failed to lift Flora's spirits. The news of the unlucky thirteenth convoy had reached the crofting community and spread quickly through the fields and cottages, where the words were muttered in low voices, with downcast eyes and a shaking of heads. Flora had heard the communiqués at the base: five merchant ships lost with all hands, sunk by torpedoes from below and bombs from above. Just south of Bear Island, heavy weather had scattered the fleet over a wide area, and the naval escorts had been unable to defend the whole convoy. Separated from the pack, the stragglers became easy prey for the German U-boats and aircraft.

The remaining vessels had limped into Murmansk after three fraught weeks at sea. One of the escorts, which had been hit by one of its own torpedoes when its gyroscope froze in the icy conditions, would be laid up for repairs in the Russian port for a while, along with several more of the merchant ships that had sustained damage in the attacks.

As Flora's voice joined the others in the kirk to sing the Easter Sunday hymns, she knew that the convoy's cargo must have been offloaded by now and so Alec's ship would be heading back into those treacherous waters for the return run. She bowed her head over her clasped hands as the community prayed for the safe return of ships and men, her lashes darkened by tears when she opened her eyes again at last.

At the kirk gate, the congregation split into smaller groups and stood in the sunshine discussing the news with grave expressions, shaking their heads as they looked out across the impossibly blue waters of the loch to the darker horizon beyond. The Macleods and the Macdonalds joined the Gordons. Mairi and Bridie hugged Flora, sharing in her anguish. She imagined they were quietly relieved that the Gustavsen brothers had been too late to volunteer for this latest convoy, but at the same time they knew that Roy and Hal were still trying to gain passage on the next one to cross the Atlantic. The loss of any sailor's life affected them all, and they felt for the families and sweethearts on both sides of the ocean who would, by now, have received one of those dreaded, heartbreaking telegrams.

Flora glimpsed the Mackenzie-Grants among the throng and automatically her fingers went to the brooch that she wore pinned to her Sunday best coat, tracing the outline of the anchor and crown. Sir Charles, who was engaged in conversation with the minister, appeared not to notice them, but when Lady Helen caught sight of the Gordons she made her way over to shake hands with Iain and Ruaridh and to give Flora a quick hug.

'I'm very glad to see you wearing that,' she murmured, as she clasped Flora close for the briefest moment before hurrying back to her husband's side.

At the roadside, they caught up with the Carmichaels. This was their first Easter Day since losing Matthew, and both Johnny and Jamie were fighting in North Africa, so Flora knew it must be taking a considerable toll on them. Outwardly, though, they were maintaining a stiff upper lip and both remained as committed as ever to the community's war efforts.

'What news of Alec, dear?' Moira Carmichael was wearing her usual Sunday best, although Flora noticed that the coat, whose buttons once strained across her ample bosom, now hung a good deal looser from her determinedly squared shoulders.

Flora shook her head. 'Nothing yet. They'll be on their way back now, I suppose, so it'll be radio silence for a while longer.'

'Don't you worry, he'll come back safe and sound.' The words were supposed to reassure, but Flora heard the tremor of fear and sadness that lay beneath them as Mrs Carmichael thought of her own sons. 'Now then, where have those boys got to?' She cast around for the pair of brothers who had slipped away from her side to join some of their school friends.

'I think that's them down there on the shore, isn't it?' Flora pointed to where a gaggle of youngsters were scrambling over the rocks.

'Stuart and David Laverock, come back here this instant!' Mrs Carmichael's voice boomed across the road, stopping the boys in their tracks. 'Honestly, they really are the limit. The seawater will ruin their good shoes.' As they watched, Stuart slid down a boulder on his behind as he hurried to usher Davy back. She tutted. 'And that'll be another perfectly good pair of breeks with the seat torn out of it, I shouldn't wonder.'

With that parting lament, she strode off to shepherd her charges home for their Sunday dinner and Flora, Iain and Ruaridh walked back to Keeper's Cottage, where a shepherd's pie was keeping warm in the oven ready for their return.

Alec seemed changed when the *Isla* finally returned to port. He was distant, his thoughts elsewhere even on the evenings that Flora and he spent together, safe in the warmth of the kitchen at Keeper's

Cottage. There was no repeat of their evening at Ardtuath House. Although Alec never spoke about it, Flora sensed that Sir Charles must have refused point-blank to countenance her presence there unless it was behind the green baize door, that stark reminder of a divide that – to his lordship's mind at least – could never be crossed.

At first Alec was reluctant, too, to speak of what had happened on the convoy, but eventually Flora coaxed some of the facts from him, thinking it might make his pain a little more bearable if it were shared. He told her of the ships they'd lost sight of and never seen again, and of the men horribly burned when explosions ignited the cargo of gasoline in the hold on board the *Induna*. Those who weren't killed outright faced an impossible choice, trapped between fire and ice: stay and be burned, or jump into the icy waters where death was assured, as they'd be pulled down by the weight of their heavy woollen duffel coats and their boots, which would instantly fill with water. A lucky few managed to survive in a lifeboat, which Russian spotter planes found days later. The survivors were brought to Murmansk and treated in the military hospital there, but many were too far gone and didn't make it. Others had terrible frostbite from the days and nights spent exposed to the elements in the flimsy life craft, and several had lost hands and feet.

She watched his face as he spoke, noticing the way his features hardened, the shadows of his pain chiselling them into a stony mask. She clasped his hands in hers and held on tight, as if she were determined to keep him from sinking into the darkness by physical force. 'How long will you have this time before you go back out?'

He shrugged. 'The next few convoys are to leave from Iceland. It makes more sense to muster there, with the weather improving and the longer days. As the ice front retreats, the ships will be able to sail further north and at least that gets them out of range of strikes from the German airfields, for the most part. So I'm afraid I'll be gone for a while. I don't know when I'll be coming back . . .

although they'll have to give us a bit of leave at some point in the summer. I don't suppose I'll be based here again until the autumn, though, when they'll swap the muster point back to Loch Ewe.'

Flora tried hard not to let her fear and disappointment show. Although she was glad that the convoy route would be further from the German strike bases in Norway, the longer journey would take many more days. And every single one of those days would be filled with the lingering hours of Arctic light, making the ships more visible. She knew that Bridie and Mairi would be disappointed, too. The use of Iceland as the mustering point for the convoys lessened the likelihood that they'd see Roy and Hal back this way before the autumn either.

But the might of the Nazis threatened the whole of Europe, and with the other Axis powers now aligned, the war had spread to the furthest corners of the world. The newsreels that played in the makeshift picture house beside the remote waters of Loch Ewe spoke of RAF bombing raids in Germany and American troops on the ground in the Far East. Places that she'd never heard of before were brought to life in grainy black and white footage: Essen, Lübeck, Valletta, Leningrad, Rangoon, Darwin, Bataan . . . It seemed that nowhere remained untouched by scenes of devastation. And so she knew how vital every boatload of cargo would be in trying to help turn the tide of the war, and felt guilty that so many people were struggling and suffering when all she'd been praying for was Alec's safe return.

On the final day of his leave, he came to find her at the stable block on his way to rejoin his ship. She finished refilling the hay bag and hung it in the garron's stall, giving the pony's broad neck a pat before bolting the half-door behind her. After brushing a few stray strands of straw from her trousers, she hugged Alec.

His face was pale; she noticed the dark circles beneath his eyes and how his cheekbones seemed more sharply defined, despite the last couple of weeks' shore leave. He barely reciprocated the hug, seeming distracted, and she knew his mind was already out at sea.

For his sake, she kept her voice light, trying to stay cheerful, thinking it would make it easier for him to leave. 'Well, take care of yourself. I'll be seeing you.'

But instead of smiling as she'd expected, his face darkened, flushing with anger. And then, without warning, he lashed out, punching the render of the stable wall inches from her shoulder.

She flinched involuntarily, wincing at the sight of his bloodied knuckles, the smear of red on the whitewash.

'Alec!' she gasped, shocked and scared. 'What's wrong with you?'

In that moment she felt she hardly knew him. The kindness and gentleness of her childhood protector had disappeared and instead she glimpsed within him the possibility of terrible violence, of an anger and sadness that could overwhelm them both. It terrified her.

He covered his face with his hands, his body wracked by silent sobs.

Very gently, wary in case he lashed out again – and at her this time – she put her arms around him and drew his head on to her shoulder, holding him as he sobbed more noisily now.

'I can't . . .' he said at last, when he'd calmed enough to talk again. 'I just can't do this, Flora. I can't keep leaving you. I can't go back out there. I can't watch more ships being blasted out of the water. I can't sail past men crying out for help. I can't give more orders that I know will cause more death and more suffering.'

She soothed him, stroking his straight dark hair, smoothing it back from his forehead, searching out his eyes with her own. 'Alec. Do you remember the day I found you here at the stables? The day you were going away to for school for the first time?'

He nodded, his eyes rimmed with red, scarcely able to look her in the face.

'And do you remember what I told you then? That we'd be here waiting for you? Me, Ruaridh, the garron? Well, we will be. You will come back and I'll be here. I promise you.'

Her words were more assured than she felt. Lashing out like that, in his helpless rage, was so unlike him and it had sown a seed of doubt in her.

She could sense the distance opening up between them again as he became more unreachable, drawing away from her. The physical distance that would come between them as he went off to do his duty for his country yet again was something she knew she could endure, but he was pulling away from her emotionally, too. And that was a distance that frightened her far more. It was a distance she wasn't sure could be bridged.

She felt a twinge of guilt. Was it right to be encouraging him to go, to face again the terror and the tedium of the convoys? As a boy, his going away to school had undoubtedly had an emotional cost. Leaving to face the death and desolation of the Arctic Sea would take even more of a toll. But what was to be gained from begging him not to go? It would simply make things harder for him. She knew he couldn't, and wouldn't, desert his duties.

Once again, though, as they had done all those years ago, her words seemed to soothe and calm him. Slowly he raised his eyes to hers, the pain in them dissolving as she steadily held his gaze.

He took a deep breath and the shaking of his body slowly quietened as he regained control. She nodded, wordlessly reassuring him.

'Sorry,' he whispered. 'It's just unbearable sometimes.'

She raised his bloodied knuckles to her lips and kissed them gently.

From the loch, the sound of a ship's whistle sounded, borne to them on the wind.

He squared his shoulders, pulling himself up to his full height, and she could see him steeling himself to go.

'Come and say goodbye to Ruaridh and Dad first? We can clean up your poor hand as well.'

He nodded, shouldering his duffel bag, and she took his hand in hers, walking with him through the pines to Keeper's Cottage, hoping that he'd gain strength from a few last moments with them all.

After he'd taken his leave of Iain and Ruaridh, he held Flora in his arms at the door and they stayed like that, in silence because there were no words to be said, as the final moments ticked away with the beating of their hearts. She wore the brooch he'd given her, pinned to her gansey. And she thought it might just be the only thing that was holding her heart together, stopping it from splintering into a thousand pieces as she watched him walk away.

Lexie, 1978

I hesitate before pushing open the door of the hall. It's the first time Daisy and I have come back to the playgroup since her accident and I wonder how she'll cope with the noise and the excitement. We've been home for about ten days now, but everyone's been giving us time and space to recover. I've not seen anyone, apart from Bridie and Mairi who've been to deliver bread and milk and a large pot of home-made stew.

If I'm honest, I'm also feeling a twinge of defensiveness, wondering how the other mums will judge me. I can just picture them tutting, saying they'd never have let their own children run loose on the jetty like that.

But I needn't have worried on either count. Daisy wriggles in my arms, keen to be let down to join the other kids, and wee Jack immediately comes over to give her a shy hug and a tambourine, both of which she accepts with a grin.

Elspeth hurries across to envelop me in a hug of her own before the other mothers surround us, saying how much they've missed us and how glad they are to have us back. If anything, they seem more supportive than ever. Perhaps I only imagined that they'd be judging me; perhaps it was only ever my judgement of myself that I feared. Maybe Davy was right and I do need to cut myself a little slack, not be so hard on myself.

'It wasn't the same without you, Lexie,' says Elspeth. 'I did my best to fill in, but I don't remember the songs the way you do.'

'What are we going to be singing today?' asks someone else. I reach into my bag and pull out Mum's old songbook.

'I thought perhaps "The Bonnie Lass o' Fyvie-O" would be a good one.' I leaf through to find the page I've marked and then settle the music on to the piano. The children gather round expectantly and their mothers hand out the instruments we've cobbled together between us, which range from the makeshift (plastic jars filled with macaroni that can be shaken to make a satisfying rattle, and saucepans that can be bashed with wooden spoons), to the more conventional (several xylophones and a triangle). Elspeth settles Daisy on her lap and I smile my gratitude as I begin to pick out the notes. It feels good to be back with the group, after all, and there's not a hint of condemnation from the others. Instead, I feel their support surrounding me, welcoming us. Our voices meld together, mingling to fill the room with the music handed down to us by our parents and their parents before them, as we begin to sing the songs that bind us to our shared past and to our children's future.

After the session, I help Elspeth carry some of the paraphernalia back to her house, hanging a bag of instruments from the back of Daisy's pushchair. She rescued it all from the jetty when I abandoned it there on the day of the accident and it makes more sense for her to continue to store it at her house, where there's more space than in the cottage, and it's nearer to the hall.

'Will you come in for a bite of lunch?' she says when we reach the yellow door. But Daisy is looking worn out after the morning's excitement, so I tell her we'd best be getting back so I can feed her and put her down for a nap.

Elspeth nods. 'The sunshine and fresh air will do her good on the walk home, put the roses back in her cheeks again. Take care of yourself, Lexie. We'll be seeing you again soon.'

Daisy waves a chubby hand and I turn the pushchair, heading back in the direction of Keeper's Cottage. As we go, I sing to try and keep her awake, not wanting her to be lulled off to sleep before I've given her lunch, and she joins in here and there, happily kicking up her feet when we get to the chorus.

When we reach the house by the jetty, our voices are joined by the sound of whistling, the tune tone-perfect and each note as clear as birdsong. Daisy stops singing and chuckles instead as Davy's head pops up from behind the tangle of honeysuckle that scrambles over the fence in front of his house. He's on his hands and knees, picking wild raspberries from the canes that have woven themselves into the hedge.

Our meeting is a little awkward, as we haven't seen each other since the accident. Perhaps he's been avoiding me. Or perhaps I've been avoiding him. I've been intending to call to thank him properly, but haven't quite got around to it yet.

'Hello, you two,' he says, getting to his feet and brushing the earth from his knees. 'Jings, it's grand to see the pair of you back safe and out and about again. Been busy making music, have you?'

I reach over the hedge and hug him tight, lost for words for a moment. 'Davy, I . . . Thank you. Thank you so much for what you did.'

He smiles at me, the corners of his eyes crinkling, and shakes his head, making light of my gratitude. 'I'm so sorry it happened. I should have been watching more carefully.'

'It was my responsibility to watch her, not yours.'

'Well, I'm very glad she's none the worse for it now.' He reaches out a finger and strokes her cheek.

'Go bat?' says Daisy, pointing hopefully towards the jetty. Her accident doesn't seem to have dampened her enthusiasm for the sea one little bit.

'I've already been out this morning,' he tells her, offering her the bowl of raspberries. She takes one and looks at it thoughtfully before putting it in her mouth. 'Took the *Bonnie Stuart* out beyond the point and caught a lovely wild salmon.'

'Sam,' replies Daisy approvingly.

'But we'll go out in the boat again one of these days, shall we, when the wind's a bit quieter? It's still a bit fresh today.'

'That'd be great,' I reply, as Daisy is too busy reaching for another raspberry to answer herself.

I fish a tissue out of my pocket and wipe the wine-coloured juice from Daisy's fingers. 'And now I'd better be getting this one home for her lunch. Sorry, though, she seems to have polished off most of your pudding already.'

'Bye, Daisy,' he says, shaking her sticky hand in his. 'Be seeing you, Lexie.'

I turn the pushchair towards home. 'Okay.' And I smile. 'Be seeing you, Davy.'

And as we head on our way along the road, the wind carries with us the faint strains of someone whistling 'The Bonnie Lass o' Fyvie-O'.

Flora, 1942

The Scottish summer never usually seemed to last long enough, but that year it felt interminable to Flora, Mairi and Bridie. They tried hard to be thankful for the calmer weather and longer days, knowing that these were things that would make life on board ship a little easier for Alec, Roy and Hal and the thousands of others who sailed the restless northern seas. But when the three of them were together, they could confide in one another the secret longing they shared for the summer to end so that the winds of autumn would bring their men back to Loch Ewe.

Flora was thankful that her duties kept her so busy. She and Mairi had been selected to be given some additional basic medical training and they were spending more time driving the ambulance that they'd been allocated, working as a team. They knew the roads around the loch like the backs of their hands and made almost daily runs ferrying the ill and the injured back and forth between the sick bay in the base at Mellon Charles and the hospital at Gairloch.

'I can't get over how much it's all changed,' Flora commented. They'd been sent to pick up a Polish officer from his billet in Poolewe who needed treatment for an abscess on a tooth. He'd chatted with them on the way, describing how he'd escaped from Warsaw when the Germans invaded and how determined he and his comrades were to win back their country from the Nazis. They dropped him at the hospital and he saluted smartly as they drove off. 'Who'd ever have imagined we'd be doing this?' She patted the steering wheel of the ambulance.

'I know, it's strange, isn't it? But at the same time, it feels so familiar now. I can't imagine going back to how I was before, just helping with the farm and the bairns. Do you think our lives will ever be the same again?'

Flora shrugged. 'The war will end one day. But you're right: I think when it does we'll find it has changed our lives forever – for better or worse, I suppose.'

Mairi turned to face her friend. 'Did you hear? They're wanting to organise some concert parties to help entertain the troops. I saw a notice in the canteen asking for volunteers. You should sing for them, Flora. They'd snap you up in a second.'

'Oh, I'm not sure I'd have the courage to sing in front of an audience like that.' Flora shook her head slowly. She was torn. She'd love to sing at a concert, really, but she could just picture what Sir Charles would make of it if he found out. It'd be another black mark against her – engaging in such frivolities while Alec was off at sea. He'd certainly disapprove. And her confidence wobbled a little as she wondered whether Alec mightn't disapprove as well. His outburst of rage had sown a seed of doubt in her. She couldn't quite put her finger on why it had unnerved her so, but in that moment she'd felt he'd become someone else, not the Alec she thought she knew.

'Flora Gordon, are you a woman or a mouse? You've never been afraid to sing before. And with your voice, it'd be a crime not to share it with those poor men and women who are stuck here so far from their homes and longing for a little entertainment of an evening.'

Flora laughed. 'Are you daring me, Mairi Macleod? Because you know fine that you have a perfectly good singing voice, too, so I could say the same to you.'

'I most certainly am daring you if that's what it takes! But YOU know fine that I don't have your voice. Although I suppose Bridie and I could back you, if you're really not sure about singing on your own in front of such a big audience. In fact, Bridie would love that! Go on, let's give it a try.'

And so it was that the trio of friends became the Aultbea Songbirds, a regular and very popular act at the weekly concerts in the hall. Surely Alec couldn't object, Flora told herself, if she was part of a group, doing her bit to keep morale high. And if she began to imagine where her singing might take her, she never shared those dreams with anyone, not even Mairi and Bridie, despite being told on many an occasion that she had a voice anyone would pay good money to hear.

Away from the fun and the laughter and the applause of the concert hall, on the long summer evenings once supper was cleared away and she was free, Flora would hike on her own up the hill to the lochan. Sometimes she'd fish for the brown trout that glided between the stems of the waterlilies; but more often she would sit, lost in her thoughts as she gazed out at the distant sea, imagining Alec away there, somewhere, and wondering whether the waves that met the rocks at the mouth of the loch might have encountered his ship as they rolled towards Scotland's northern shores. As she sat beside the silvered pool cupped in the palm of the hills, the deer kept watch, silent and still, from the heights above her and, higher still, the song of the skylarks floated on the evening air.

At last, in late August, the fronds of bracken began to turn to bronze and the branches of the rowans hung heavy with clusters of scarlet berries. When the first skeins of geese appeared in the skies above the loch, their hoarse cries announcing the end of summer, the boom nets were drawn aside to allow three merchant ships through as the next Arctic convoy began to muster. Ruaridh was a useful source of information, monitoring the latest arrivals from his post at the signal station on the hill, and he kept Flora, Mairi and Bridie informed.

'They're British ships so far, come up the east coast from Tilbury and Hull. But they say there's another Atlantic convoy on the way and some of the American Merchant Marine are carrying supplies for Russia. So we may well see Roy and Hal before too long.'

Bridie and Mairi had received no postcards from the brothers for a couple of weeks now. They had a feeling that this was either very good news or very bad, and so they scanned the horizon even more frequently than usual with a mixture of anticipation and dread. Flora had heard from Alec that he was still on patrolling duties off the coast of Iceland, but she, too, waited impatiently for the *Isla* to return.

As the sun rose above the hills, Flora and Mairi were preparing their ambulance for the day, going through their routine checks. Mairi made sure they had the necessary supplies in the first-aid kit, while Flora wiped away the heavy condensation that the chill of the night had deposited on the windscreen. They had orders to run a patient over to the hospital and to pick up two soldiers who were being discharged, dropping them back at their camp on the return journey.

It was one of those calm days of early autumn when the land and sea seemed to have been given a fresh coat of paint: the water was the purest aquamarine and the green of the hills was splashed here and there with the gold of turning larches. Even so, the two soldiers – who had turned out to be from the Indian regiment encamped above Mellangaun – looked a little miserable as the girls dropped them off.

'I feel so sorry for them,' Mairi said. 'It must be a terrible shock to their systems, having to live in tents up here in the wilds. They'll be used to the heat and the dust, not the rain and the mud. And as for the food – well, it's no wonder that pair ended up with such bad stomach pains. Not that the hospital food will have made them feel any better.'

'I know,' Flora agreed. 'But even so, their spirits haven't been crushed enough to stop them proposing to us on the drive back from Gairloch.'

'Right enough,' conceded Mairi. 'The weather doesn't seem to have dampened their romantic notions. But they're probably just lonely . . .' She broke off abruptly, distracted by the sight of a ship that had just appeared around the point. Shielding her eyes against the sunlight, she leaned forward in her seat, straining to make out the ensign being raised above the deck. It unfurled itself slowly in the insistent tugging of the light breeze, revealing the unmistakable stars and stripes of the American flag.

Flora pulled the truck to a halt on the roadside above the bay where the British merchantmen lay at anchor. The girls watched as the tugs manoeuvred to open the boom nets, allowing the ship to slip into the safe haven of Loch Ewe.

And then all at once Mairi leapt from the cab, waving her WRNS cap above her head. And the autumn sunlight glinted on the blond hair of the two sailors who waved back at her, equally enthusiastically, from their stations on deck beside the flagstaff.

The far side of the loch was crowded with merchant ships now, and the naval escort had gathered in the bay at Mellon Charles. Next week, the first convoy of the season would depart from Loch Ewe, but for now the water could hardly be seen between the vessels of the densely packed flotilla.

The hall at Aultbea was equally packed out for the Friday night dance when Flora, Mairi and Bridie walked in with their own escorts, Alec, Roy and Hal. By popular demand, the Aultbea Songbirds would be singing a couple of numbers later on, but first they took to the floor as the band struck up, determined to make the most of their few days together.

When Alec had arrived back from his duties, Flora had felt awkward in his company. The flash of temper she'd witnessed in him – so unlike his usual gentleness – had continued to unnerve her. She'd tried to put it out of her mind, telling herself it was just the stress of the convoys and the thought of being away at sea again for so many. But she'd come to realise that in the moment when he'd smashed his fist into the wall she'd recognised something else in him, something that made her physically recoil: a likeness to his father. She couldn't push the thought away, nor the memory of the bruises that she'd glimpsed on the underside of Lady Helen's wrist that evening when she'd helped with the dinner.

His absence had left a vacuum that doubts and fears could easily fill. And perhaps that was why she'd purposely kept herself so busy. As well as the evening concerts, she'd thrown herself into her work by day, taking on extra duties by volunteering to help maintain the engines on the smaller boats in addition to the ambulances at the base. She'd quickly discovered an aptitude for coaxing even the most reluctant of salt-scoured, waterlogged motors back into life. The distractions of her singing and her work – and the camaraderie of the other Wrens as well as the naval ratings she worked alongside – had helped the time to pass while Alec was away. More than that, she was also developing a new sense of fulfilment: a sense of her own self and her own voice. But would Alec like this new side to her? Flora thought of Lady Helen, who always seemed such a shadow of the woman she might really be. Would Flora, too, begin to disappear if she married Alec?

Despite her worries, when he appeared in the doorway of Keeper's Cottage again she had the sense that Alec had grown more tentative, had lost something of his old self-assurance, just as she had become stronger, more confident in her work. He'd hesitated, as if unsure of his welcome, and she had quickly reached out and put her arms around him, closing the distance between them, reassuring him with her kiss that all was well and that she still loved him. It just needed a bit of time for them both to readjust to being back together, she'd told herself. She tried again to brush aside the image of his face darkened with anger when he'd punched the stable wall. Whenever she thought of it now, it was Sir Charles's face she pictured, and that image unsettled her more than Alec's rage.

Their old closeness came flooding back, though, as they spent time together walking along the shore or into the hills above Ardtuath House. It was easier, too, when they were with Mairi and Roy and Bridie and Hal, whose happiness was infectious.

Earlier that day, before the dance, the three couples had hiked over the hills to Slaggan Bay and sprawled on picnic rugs spread over the hummocks of marram grass at the edge of the crescent of golden sand. From that angle, the ships moored in the loch were hidden by the shoulder of land that enclosed the beach, allowing them to forget the convoy's impending departure for an hour or two.

Roy and Hal told stories of the Atlantic crossings they'd taken part in since they were last at Aultbea, which had taken them to Portsmouth and Liverpool.

'It was kinda frustrating being so near and yet so far,' Roy said.

Hal grinned. 'We tried to get a shore pass and see if we could jump on a train to get up here, even just for a day. But we didn't have any travel papers so we got turned back before we'd even managed to get out of the port.'

They were proud to be crewing the *Patrick Henry*, one of the newly built Liberty ships, which the Americans were turning out in record time to replace vessels lost to enemy attacks.

'She was launched by FDR himself,' Hal told them.

'It's funny to call a ship "she" when it's got a man's name,' Bridie said, picking a blade of grass and chewing on it thoughtfully. 'Who is Patrick Henry, anyway?'

'He was the guy who said, "Give me liberty or give me death." These new-style ships are going to bring liberty to Europe.' Hal reached over and handed her a sprig of sea thrift that he'd plucked from the machair that grew around the crescent of the beach. 'For you, my lady.'

She laughed as she tucked the flower into her dark curls, the pink petals highlighting the rosiness of her cheeks, flushed by the wind and the sun.

She looks so pretty, Flora thought, *because she's so happy. We all are, today.* But then she glanced down at Alec's face. He lay sprawled beside her on the tartan rug, resting on his elbows as he watched the sunlight play on the water of the bay. Even at rest, there was a darkness in him, running like a deep current beneath the surface of his smile as he caught her watching him.

The destroyer he'd been on had just returned from patrolling the northern passage between the Orkneys and Shetland.

'What was it like up there?' Roy asked him.

Alec was silent for a few moments, reluctant to allow the reality of war to cast a shadow across their day. But then he described the otherworldly landscapes he'd seen: the scattered, low-lying Orkney Islands with their pale beaches and green fields; the rugged cliffs of the Shetlands that rose from the waves like a fortress, stark and forbidding; and of Iceland with its strange black sand beaches and ice-capped volcanoes. He spoke quietly of the last Arctic convoy that had sailed from Reykjavik in early summer. 'It was huge, nearly forty ships, and the run was longer, too – all the way round to Archangel this time. We knew it was a risk, but we hoped the more northerly passage would make a difference.' He fell silent for a moment, looking unseeingly at the waves washing gently on to the sand. 'It was a disaster. The convoy was spotted and the Germans came at us in force. We were up for the fight, but then the command came through from the Admiralty in London, telling the naval escort to turn back. I still can't fathom their reasoning. Every man out there was convinced it was the wrong decision. Abandoning those merchantmen was one of the worst moments of my life. We knew once we'd gone the U-Boats and the Luftwaffe would close in for the kill.'

His turned his head away from the others, but not before Flora noticed how his face contorted in pain, the memories too hard to bear. She reached for his hand and interwove her fingers with his, drawing him away from the darkness of his thoughts and back into the mellow autumn sunlight that bathed him with its healing glow.

With an effort, he pulled himself together, giving her hand a grateful squeeze. He shook his head, as though trying to rid it of images that had imprinted themselves in his mind's eye. 'We lost twenty-seven ships and hundreds of men to German planes and U-boats. In the end, only eleven made it to Archangel. That was when they decided to suspend the runs for the rest of the summer. So, instead, we've spent the last few months patrolling the westerly reaches of the Arctic Sea, trying to stop German vessels slipping through from the east to attack the Atlantic convoys. We know they have the *Tirpitz* hidden in one of the Norwegian fjords – she's one of their biggest battleships – and we didn't want to risk her getting through.'

'Appreciate that, buddy,' said Hal. 'When we were out there on the crossing it was good to know you navy guys had got our backs.'

The others tactfully changed the subject, sensing Alec's distress. But it seemed to Flora that the shadows around them had deepened and that if you listened carefully, the hush of the waves on the sand held mournful echoes of the cries of lost souls. She drew a little closer to Alec, trying to close the gulf that seemed to threaten to take him away from her again, and they sat in silence, letting the conversation ebb and flow around them.

That evening, at the dance, Flora held Alec tight as the accordion played the last waltz. He'd applauded as enthusiastically as the rest of the audience when she'd sung 'The Eriskay Love Lilt'. But still she could sense the toll that the losses were taking on him. She could only imagine the sights he'd witnessed during the time he'd spent with the convoys – ships set ablaze, the burned and drowned bodies they'd managed to pull from the water, the burials at sea as yet more young men were consigned to the cold, deep grave that would remain unmarked and unvisited. Even worse would have been those they'd had to leave behind in the water, sailing past the outstretched arms and the desperate, pleading cries, unable to help. And she pictured the latest wave of telegrams that would arrive at homes across Britain and America, the unwelcome knock at the door heralding the delivery of a slip of paper that was all those families had left of their fathers and their sons.

She wished with all her heart that the music would never end, that they could dance there, holding each other close, forever. Because then there would be no doubts and fears, no need for goodbyes. And she wouldn't have to watch as his ship sailed away on the morning tide, tearing them apart once again as he faced the brutal cold and the relentless dread of the next Arctic run.

The rain was falling steadily and the larches wept golden tears on the day that Hamish McTaggart slowly cycled the short distance from the post office to the house at the end of the jetty once again. And this time the telegram he carried, addressed to Mr and Mrs Archibald Carmichael, weighed down his leather satchel more heavily than any other he'd had to deliver in the last year. He'd been there when Miss Cameron had carefully transcribed the words and handed it to him with a shake of her head.

DEEPLY REGRET TO INFORM YOU OF THE DEATHS OF YOUR SONS JOHN ARCHIBALD CARMICHAEL AND JAMES ROSS CARMICHAEL WHILE ON WAR SERVICE AT EL ALAMEIN. LETTER FOLLOWS.

Lexie, 1978

'What was it like, being sent to Aultbea as an evacuee?' I ask Davy.

He's sitting in the kitchen, having accepted my offer of a cup of tea when he dropped by to see whether Daisy and I would like some of his day's catch for our supper.

He spoons sugar into his mug and stirs, considering my question. 'I was so wee, I don't really have any clear memories of the day we arrived. I think I remember the bus journey a bit – the feeling of nerves at being sent away from our home, mixed with excitement at seeing the seaside. That's where our mammy told us we were going, Stuart said. To live at the seaside. I remember my coat smelling of sick because I'd boaked and there was nothing on the bus to clean it up with. And I think I remember sitting at a trestle table with the other kids and being given a dish of mince and tatties, but that might just be something Stuart told me about later on. The first things I definitely do remember are a starfish I found in a rock pool one day and the way the teacher's chalk used to screech against the blackboard in the schoolroom. I must have been about six by then, I guess. And I remember the days the telegrams came for the Carmichaels. First the one saying Matthew was missing believed dead in the Far East, and then the one about Johnny and Jamie at El Alamein.'

He falls silent and turns his face towards the window, looking out at the loch. But I get the impression he doesn't see the way the water gleams like molten silver in the sunshine against the backdrop of purple hills beyond, nor does he hear the calling of the gulls overhead. Instead, he's seeing the pain contorting the face of Archie Carmichael and hearing Moira's anguished, high-pitched scream of a single word, wrenched from the very core of her being: '*No!*'

At last he looks down at the mug of tea clasped in his leathery, work-tanned fingers as if surprised to see it there. He takes a sip.

'It must have been terrible for you and Stuart, witnessing that,' I say gently.

'It was awful being in the house, hearing the knock at the door, peering out of our bedroom window and seeing Mr McTaggart there. Knowing what he'd brought them.' He nods. 'But it was even worse afterwards. The Carmichaels were kind, but we always had the feeling that we shouldn't have been there. That we were taking up the space where their own sons should have been. We hated being the reminders of what they'd lost, the wrong boys living beneath their roof, sleeping in the beds of their dead sons. Their boys' things were everywhere: the shelves were full of their books about World War One flying aces and *Boy's Own* annuals; their shinty sticks were in the porch at the front door; Matthew's stamp collection . . . Jamie's collection of sea glass . . . Johnny's sketches of shore birds. Their photos were in frames on the mantelpiece, the Carmichaels' pride and joy, and I could hardly bear to look at them. They seemed so full of vitality in those pictures – I couldn't believe they had died.'

As if sensing his sadness, Daisy toddles across to him, grabbing his knee to steady herself, and hands him Blue Bunny. He smiles at her then lifts her on to his lap, carefully pushing the mug of hot tea out of her reach. But I can see he's distracted, that he's still back in that too-empty house of his own childhood.

'We'd creep about, trying not to disturb Mrs C on her bad days. There were lots of them, days when she couldn't get herself out of her bed. And who could blame her? All three of her boys gone like that. It was the same for so many other families across the Highlands. And in these small crofting communities, the loss of their young men was a devastating blow.'

I think of my mum and the Carmichaels and all those other people who lost so much in the war. They were a generation who had to get used to goodbyes. I realise how fortunate I was to be born just as the war ended, into a generation that knew only the optimism of a peace-filled future.

I watch Davy as he smiles at Daisy, taking her tiny paw in his much larger one to play 'round and round the garden'. His eyes are as dark as a storm-blown sea, but as warm as the sun-warmed stones on a summer's evening, too. His face is etched with the lines of his life's story, weathered by the wind and the losses he's had to bear. Yet at the same time, he seems at peace with himself and with the world that has taken so much from him. I think of him playing with the band in the bar, how the music seems to flow from within him until it's hard to say where his arms end and the guitar begins because they are all part of the same song. Maybe his music has played a part in healing those old wounds. They've left their scars, that's for sure. But maybe playing the songs and singing the words that so many have sung before him have helped to lead him to a place where he's been able to find a way to live with the loss. Perhaps that's the only way to deal with grief. It's such a heavy load to bear alone – but knowing that there are always others to share it is a help.

My own grief has been a heavy load to bear. So heavy that I've done my very best to push it aside and ignore it, I realise.

Daisy chuckles and reaches a hand up to stroke Davy's face, urging him to play the game. ''Gain!'

And as he obliges, something seems to shift inside me, slightly thawing the cold lump of grief that's sat there for so long.

He glances up at me and catches sight of something in my expression – the broadness of my smile, perhaps, or the look of tenderness in my eyes – that makes him raise his eyes to mine, questioning. I hold his gaze, giving my answer.

He swallows, as if picking up the courage to say something, and I wait, allowing him time.

'D'you think Bridie and Mairi might be persuaded to babysit and we could go out for a meal one evening?' he asks. 'Just the two of us, maybe?'

I nod. 'I'd like that. Very much.'

'It's a date, then.' Davy smiles at me. 'Not a date-date, of course,' he adds.

I can't help but blush.

'Although,' he says, his eyes not leaving my face, 'I wonder if a date-date might in fact be a possibility at some point? What do you reckon, Lexie?'

'What?' I say, in mock astonishment. 'Are you actually asking me on a *real* date-date, Davy Laverock?'

'Well, yes, I think I am. Of course, Bridie and Mairi and everyone else in Aultbea will know exactly what we're up to and be keeping a close eye on the pair of us. So you'll have to be home before midnight or your reputation will be mud.'

I laugh. 'I've a feeling my reputation went out the window many years ago. But if you don't mind risking your own, consorting with the scarlet woman of Ardtuath, then I'd love to.'

'Okay then. How about tomorrow?'

I nod. 'Okay then,' I say, echoing the hint of relief that I detect behind his words. 'Tomorrow it is. A real date-date.'

Davy picks me up and we go to the best restaurant in town. Of course, it's also the only restaurant in town, at the hotel. It feels a bit strange not to be going into the bar for a change, and at first we're both a little self-conscious to be sitting face to face across a table set with linen napkins and glistening wine glasses. The hotel sits right down on the loch shore so at least we have the welcome distraction of the view across the water, where the setting sun has begun to paint the sky in deepening shades of coral pink.

I can't help worrying about Daisy. It's the first time I've left her since the accident, and although I know she's fine now and will be enjoying all sorts of fun and games with Bridie at the cottage, my anxiety pinches at my neck and makes my shoulders hunch. I take a breath and sit a little more upright, trying to relax.

'You look nice,' Davy says.

'So do you,' I reply, settling my napkin in my lap to distract myself from how awkward this exchange sounds.

I look up and he's smiling at me. 'You know, I really did enjoy hearing you sing again, on Elspeth's birthday. Like I was saying on the jetty that day, before Daisy's accident, if you ever want to do a bit more you'd be welcome. Your new voice suits the old songs.'

'Thanks. Maybe.' I don't admit that it feels an age ago and I think my voice may well have rusted up again.

We pause while the waiter brings us the menu and pours us glasses of water. I gulp mine thankfully.

'Funny, isn't it?' Davy says. 'Highlanders are generally a people of few words. And yet the traditional songs express the things we'd never normally say. I suppose that's why they were written originally. To say the things that matter and pass them on from generation to generation.'

I laugh. 'Well, yes, they're mostly about love and loss, though. But then I suppose that's mostly what life is about.'

He shakes his head and sighs theatrically. 'Ach, Lexie Gordon, so cynical for one so young.'

'Not that young! I'm certainly old enough to have experienced love and loss. And I bet you that for every cheerful song you can name me, I could name you three laments.'

'Yeah, well, no one ever said life was supposed to be easy, did they? And it would have been especially hard back in the day when those songs were written. But that's what binds us together, isn't it? Shared hardships and the eternal hope for better times ahead. For our children at least, if not for ourselves.'

I consider this for a moment as I pretend to examine the menu. An image of my mum floats before my eyes and in my mind I can hear the songs she used to sing. Her life was pretty tough, all things considered, but he's right: there was always hope mixed in with the sadness. And being part of the tightly woven crofting community on the shores of Loch Ewe gave her a sense of solidity, of belonging to something that was as unshakeable as the hills and as constant as the tides. The music of this place is as natural to us as the cries of the seabirds and the sound of the wind on the hills – the woodwind and string sections in the orchestra that provides the score to the songs of our lives.

As he scans the menu, Davy hums the snatch of a song under his breath and I recognise the chorus of 'The Parting Glass'.

He knows a thing or two about goodbyes, I realise. How hard it must have been for him to lose his brother so suddenly and to witness the slow, interminable death of his mother through her drinking. My mum used to sing that song, too. Perhaps she'd been thinking of all the people she lost in the war. How hard it must have been for her to let me go, when the time came for me to move to London and the promise of a new life there, and how easy it seemed for me to leave: a modern-day version of so many goodbyes that have been played out before from these crofters' cottages along the shore of the loch. The Highlands are undeniably beautiful but they can be harsh, too, just like life itself. This is a land long-used to farewells.

As if he can read my thoughts, Davy glances up from the menu and says, 'Don't look so sad, Lexie. Life is full of beginnings as well as endings.' He pours wine into our glasses from a bottle that the waiter has placed between us. 'A toast,' he proposes. 'To beginnings. And to finding new songs to sing.'

I raise my glass and echo his words: 'To finding new songs to sing.'

As we talk and eat and talk some more, I begin to relax. And something seems to nourish me besides the very good steak and chips we consume. When we've finished our meal and drained the last drops of wine from our glasses, a sense of contentment has settled over me. It's a novel feeling, not just the contentment of a full belly after a good dinner. It's more than that. It seems to have something to do with being in the company of Davy Laverock.

By the end of the evening, when he gives me a goodnight kiss at the gate of Keeper's Cottage (supposedly so that Bridie won't see us, but I'm sure I catch a glimpse of light from the corner of the sitting room curtain), I notice something. Beneath the beating of my heart and the hushing of the waves there's a current that runs through my veins that seems stronger than the tides of the ocean.

I think I recognise it from bygone times: its name is hope.

Flora, 1943

As the year went by, Flora began to grow accustomed to the cycle of arrivals and departures. The loch was seldom peaceful, with the constant to-ing and fro-ing of the navy and the busy activity of the refuelling tankers and the boom-net trawlers. After a convoy left, churning the waters to a frothing chop, there might be a day or two of relative calm. But within a few days more merchant ships would begin to gather, dropping anchor beyond the island, until thirty or forty more joined them to form a solid mass of shipping. Then they would slip into their positions, one behind the other, and set off on the next perilous journey.

But no matter how many times the gathering and the leaving were repeated, she felt she could never get used to saying goodbye to Alec. Every time he left, she'd linger in his arms, savouring the final precious moments before they would have to tell each other, 'I'll be seeing you,' and she would watch him walk away again. Try as she might, she couldn't harden her heart against the lurch of pain she felt at the sight of his broad shoulders disappearing down the path, squared determinedly as he prepared to face the Arctic seas again. It only seemed to hurt more, knowing that each time he went he'd have to endure those things that corroded his soul a little further. Sometimes she felt that they were both adrift on the cold grey waters, struggling against undercurrents that were trying to sweep them apart and might well prove too strong for their relationship to survive.

Flora knew that with the desperate struggle for Stalingrad through the cruel winter of 1942, surrounded and besieged by Hitler's forces, it had become even more critical to keep the Soviet supply lines open. Yet, for exactly the same reason, it had become even more important for the Nazis to try to stop those same supplies from getting through. She pictured Alec on board the *Isla*, trying to protect the convoys as they ran the gauntlet of the stormy, ice-strewn wastes of the Barents Sea in the darkness. The men on board never knew when the next attack might come from above or below, while they battled through gale-whipped waves that turned the decks of the ships into lopsided, top-heavy ice palaces, threatening to capsize even the heaviest vessels. They might have had anti-aircraft guns and depth charges to defend themselves against the U-boats and the Heinkel bombers, but all they had to fight back against the smothering blanket of ice were pickaxes and shovels. Somehow, though, many of the ships got through, delivering their precious cargoes of fighter planes and tanks, trucks and weapons, as well as supplies of food, ammunition and fuel oil.

At the end of the winter, the convoys had been suspended again through the summer months and Alec had been sent back out on patrol on the stretch of sea between the Northern Isles. Time and time again, Flora waited and watched as she drove her ambulance along the loch, scanning the horizon for new arrivals and searching among the flotilla of vessels at anchor in the bay for his ship.

And then, at last, her patience was rewarded. He'd been given a few days of leave, days she hoped they'd spend beachcombing along the shore and fishing in the lily-covered lochan. But his father found jobs for him to do on the estate, and she suspected Sir Charles was deliberately keeping Alec away from Keeper's Cottage.

On a warm summer's evening Flora wandered up to the stable block, having volunteered to see to the garron. As she approached, she heard the rhythmic thud of an axe on wood. Behind the stables, she found Alec. She smiled at first, watching the muscles of his back move beneath his shirt with each swing of the axe and each blow. He must have been at work for hours, she realised, noticing the split logs strewn chaotically around him, left unstacked. Then she saw how his shirt clung to his back, soaked by sweat.

'Alec,' she said softly. But he was lost in the motion of the axe, swinging it high and pounding it down on another log. The force of the movement sliced through the chunk of wood, rending it in two. She said his name again, more loudly this time. He spun around, the axe held high, and for one terrible second she thought he was about to bring it down on her head, splitting her skull as easily as he'd split the logs around his feet.

That second seemed to draw itself out as the pair of them stood, frozen, in a grotesque tableau of fury and fear. And then she saw his face. It was darkened with the same rage she'd witnessed in him before, his features contorting into those of his father. With a gasp, she caught sight of the axe handle. It was red with his blood. Consumed by his fury, he'd flayed the skin from his hands until they'd become contorted, scarlet claws.

In that moment, she hardly recognised him. He seemed completely lost in the darkness of his anger. Instinctively, Flora shrank back against the stable wall and held her breath until he slowly lowered the axe and relinquished his grip, letting it fall to the ground beside him. She swallowed her fear and went to him as his body was wracked by sobs and he gasped over and over again, 'I'm sorry! I'm so sorry!'

She held him until he was a little calmer, then led him to the cottage in silence, where she washed and bandaged his hands. 'You need to rest,' she told him. 'You're supposed to be on leave.'

He shook his head. 'I can't rest. I can't sleep,' he said. 'Every time I close my eyes, I see the waves rolling towards me, coming for me. I feel as if I'm drowning, Flora. It's better to keep busy, so that I don't have to think. So that I don't have time to remember the faces of the men we've lost.'

She held his hands wrapped in their padding of white bandages between her own, as if trying to physically prevent him from sinking into the desperation and anger that reminded her so much of Sir Charles. But she was frightened. Every time Alec sailed, she feared she might lose him. And sometimes she had the sense that he was lost to her already.

On the day of his leaving they sat together on the shore, and Flora held Alec close and spoke to him of the time when there would be no more need for goodbyes: they would take their children to fish in the peat-dark waters of the lochan and to collect shells from the rock pools beside the loch. She didn't mention the issue of Sir Charles's opposition to this rosy vision of their future: she supposed that time would resolve the impediment, one way or another. And she didn't voice the doubts she felt in her own heart about the distance between them and the dark currents of anger and pain that still flowed in Alec, just beneath the surface. Instead, she traced with her fingertips the lines of the anchor and crown on the brooch pinned to her jacket and painted her picture of the years ahead, giving them both something to hold on to.

The seasons wheeled through their ever-changing cycle and the heather-covered hills changed from green to purple to brown. Then, one morning, Flora woke to find them dusted with a capping of white. And her heart lifted as the first rays of the sun made the peaks dazzle against the blue of the winter sky, because she knew it was a sign that Alec should be returning any day now.

A week later, Flora was making the tea, humming to herself while Ruaridh sat by the kitchen window with his bowl of porridge, watching the next convoy of merchantmen begin to converge on Loch Ewe. They both wore their naval uniforms, ready for the day's duties.

Ruaridh reached for the pair of field glasses that sat on the windowsill and scanned the harbour, watching the activity. Then he turned to Flora with a smile. 'Come and have a look,' he said, holding out the binoculars for her to take.

She focused the sights and then gave a little gasp of joy as the familiar lines of the *Isla* came into view, making for the pier. And standing on the foredeck she could just make out an officer standing to attention alongside the jackstaff, who raised a hand to salute Keeper's Cottage, as a squall of wind made the surface of the loch dance.

Grabbing her overcoat and cap, Flora hurried down to the base. But to her dismay, she found she wasn't the only one who'd come to welcome Alec home. Sir Charles stood at the end of the pier with his spaniel at his feet. On seeing Flora, the dog bounded over, tail wagging, and pushed its damp nose into her hand until she caressed its soft ears and broad bony forehead.

'Corry! Heel!' Sir Charles snapped. The spaniel immediately crept back to her master's side, head lowered in fear.

'Good morning, Sir Charles,' Flora said politely. 'Isn't it good to see the *Isla* back in port again?'

He glanced at her coolly before turning back to watch the ship as it manoeuvred into position. 'Shouldn't you be going about your duties, Miss Gordon?'

She glanced at her wristwatch. 'I've another ten minutes before my shift begins, so I thought I'd come down and welcome Alec home first.'

A muscle in his jaw twitched with annoyance. 'Well, as you can see, I am here already. There's no need for a delegation. I'm sure my son will wish to come straight back to Ardtuath House to see his mother. There'll be time enough for your *welcome*' – he stressed the word with a sarcastic sneer – 'later on, when you've finished your work. His Majesty's Navy isn't paying you to loiter here, distracting the men and getting in the way of important operations.'

Flora's fingers curled around the brooch in her coat pocket, squeezing it so tightly that the point of the crown dug into the flesh of her hand. She was about to reply when he wheeled around to glare at her, his face dark with anger. She recoiled in horror, recognising again that flash of likeness between father and son.

'Would you like me to have a word with your commanding officer, Miss Gordon? Or perhaps with the camp commander, who's a personal friend of mine? You would do well to remember that. I could easily have you transferred to another base, and that brother of yours as well. I've no doubt he enjoys his nice safe position on dry land, while others like my son are off facing the perils out at sea.' He spat the words at her, little flecks of spittle gathering in the creases at the sides of his mouth.

Involuntarily, she backed away from him, feeling a mixture of horror and bewilderment at the venomous bite of his words. For a moment she was speechless as she tried to gather her thoughts. She swallowed back the stinging retort that rose in her throat, though, finding the sleeve of her coat gripped by a firm hand. Turning, blinking back the furious tears that had flooded her eyes, she found Mairi standing beside her.

'Come on, Flora,' her friend said, tugging at her arm. 'Let's go and get our orders.'

As they walked towards the semicircle of huts surrounding the parade ground, Mairi said to her, 'What was all that about? I could see from the way you recoiled that he'd said something to hurt you. He's still no more accepting about you and Alec, is he?'

Flora shook her head, biting her lip so that the tears wouldn't fall. She was determined not to give him that satisfaction.

'It doesn't matter,' she said, once she could trust her voice not to break. 'Alec is back, that's all that counts. I'll see him soon enough.' She shot Mairi a grateful glance. 'Thank you for coming along when you did. I was about to say some things that certainly wouldn't have helped the situation.'

Mairi shook her head. 'There's not much point in arguing with a man like that. He'll not hear what you say, in any case. Give it time. Everything will be different once this war is over, you'll see.'

Flora sighed. 'Even more time . . . how are you and I supposed to bear it? I feel as if our lives have been on hold for years already.'

'I know, but there's progress being made. Did you hear about the *Tirpitz*? Bridie says there's been a secret mission to Norway and they just received word yesterday that it was successful. Apparently they used midget submarines and got to her in the fjord where she's been hiding. They reckon she's been put safely out of commission for months now. So cheer up, that's one less danger for us to have to worry about when Alec and Roy are out there next, isn't it?'

Flora smiled wanly. 'You're right. Every day that goes by we're one day nearer to them coming home for good.'

'And don't you dare forget it, Flora Gordon!' Mairi gave her a quick hug. 'If you're not going to let Mr Hitler beat you, then you can't let Sir Charles do so, either. Now let's get on with doing our bit to make that day come around a little sooner.'

As the year reached its final short-lived days, Flora tucked pine branches along the top of the mirror in the entrance way so they would fill the cottage with the scent of the forest, and wove a wreath of scarlet-berried holly to hang on the front door. She felt she was going through the motions, but she needed to make an effort at some sort of cheerful normality to lift her spirits.

It had been good having Alec home for a few weeks, even though, in the times they'd been able to snatch together, she'd been a bit subdued and distracted in the wake of Sir Charles's brutal threats. She hadn't been able to bring herself to tell Alec what his father had said to her, knowing it would only put him in an even more impossible position. Alec was already at breaking point. And now he was away again, and his Christmas Day would be spent in the Arctic twilight as he looked out across the steel-grey sea, constantly on watch for enemy attacks.

Last night the Aultbea Songbirds had sung carols in the packed hall. Flora had sensed the audience of men and women were putting on a brave face, covering up their longing to be at home with their families by raising their voices together to sing the familiar words of the yuletide songs. Today, thick fog shrouded the ships anchored in the loch and Flora could feel the weight of it pressing on her lungs, as stifling as the fear that shrouded this fifth war-torn Christmas.

As she pushed the roasting tin containing the brace of pheasants into the oven, she wondered how many more Christmases this war could last. Each member of the community of Aultbea was exhorted by the posters pinned to the noticeboard outside the post office to help with the war effort: *Make Do and Mend, A Clear Plate Means a Clear Conscience (Don't Take More Than You Can Eat))*, and *Doctor Carrot – The Children's Best Friend*. Flora was thankful that the hills and the sea provided them with much-needed additions to the monotonous rations that were available in the shop: she'd made a dish of skirlie to help eke out the meat on the gamebirds, the bed of coarse-grained oatmeal soaking up the savoury juices from the pan; and while there was no dried fruit to be had to make the traditional clootie dumpling, she'd improvised an apple and honey pudding that was steaming away on the stove top. The fruit had been soaked with a tot of whisky from the precious bottle given to Iain by Lady Helen which, she hoped, would infuse it with a little festive cheer. A jug of cream sat in the larder, a gift from Mairi's family, and her mouth watered as she pictured how it would trickle over the slices of hot pudding. But even as she prepared the meal, she couldn't help wondering what Alec's Christmas fare would be. She'd given him a tin of shortbread, made with most of the month's sugar ration and tied with a tartan ribbon, to help make his shipboard diet of corned-beef sandwiches and the mugs of kye, as the sailors called their watery cocoa, a little more festive.

They were all putting a brave face on things and making the most of what they had. But everyone was exhausted by this endless war. Five Christmases. And still no end in sight.

With Alec on escort duty in the Arctic and Hal and Roy on another Atlantic run, none of the girls felt like attending the ceilidh in the hall on Boxing Day that year. All three had volunteered to be on duty that day and they were on a tea break in the canteen when Ruaridh walked in. He'd just finished his watch at the signalling station and had come in search of a cup of tea and to thaw out after hours spent in the crude concrete signal post, which offered little shelter from the biting wind that had blown away yesterday's fog.

His forehead was creased in a frown as he pulled off his cap and raked a hand through his close-cropped sandy curls.

Flora glanced up, tensing immediately at his expression. 'What is it?'

He pressed his lips together, as if loath to tell her the news he'd heard from the signalman who'd replaced him at his post. Bridie set a cup of tea down on the table before him.

'Thanks,' he said. Then he met Flora's anxious eyes. 'They've been engaged,' he said, tersely. 'By a German battleship.'

Flora froze, waiting for him to say more. There was no need to ask which ships he meant.

'But I thought the *Tirpitz* was still out of commission,' Mairi broke in, instinctively reaching over to put a hand on Flora's arm.

'It's another German battleship, the *Scharnhorst*. It was anchored in one of the fjords on the North Cape. It began heading for the convoy in the early hours, so the escort cut in.'

'*Isla*?' Flora asked, already certain of the answer.

Ruaridh nodded. 'All three destroyers. But that's all I know at the moment. The communiqué has only just come in.'

Automatically, Flora's hand went to the pocket of her coat and her fingers closed around the brooch as if, by holding it tight, she could protect Alec. It was unbearable to imagine what he might be facing at that very minute, but all they could do was wait for more news to trickle through. She felt completely helpless.

Bridie had other ideas, though. They watched as she picked up a plate of the bright yellow sponge cake and marched across to where two officers sat, hunched over their teacups, deep in conversation. They couldn't hear what was said, as the exchange was muffled by the hiss of the tea urn and the hum of noise in the canteen, which reverberated from the hut's tin roof. But a few minutes later she returned – minus the plate of cake – with a triumphant grin, and seized Flora's free hand.

'It's all right! The *Isla* is safe. They think the battle's over now and the German battleship's been sunk. The convoy is back on course for Murmansk.'

Ruaridh gazed at her in admiration. 'Bridie Macdonald, your skills are wasted in the NAAFI. They should be deploying you as a secret agent. If they turned you loose with a few slices of the Yellow Peril, who knows what intelligence you might be able to unearth?'

The four of them were able to breathe again. But their thanksgiving was muted, overshadowed by the image of more lives lost with the sinking of the enemy battleship. For they knew that the graveyard of the ocean deeps was a lonely one, with ice floes in the place of headstones and only blank-eyed sea creatures to watch over the bones of lost sailors from both sides of the divide as they were stirred by restless currents.

Alec reached for Flora's hand and pulled her the last few yards up the steep path to the old bothy beside the lochan. He'd had a few precious days ashore and this time they'd spent every minute that she had free together. On his return a storm had lashed the loch, obscuring the hills, the squalls sending sheets of rain sweeping in from the sea and keeping them indoors. He'd come down to the cottage each evening to see her, leaving his dripping jacket and boots at the door and stretching his legs towards the warmth of the stove as he asked her father about the day's stalking, or chatted with Ruaridh about the latest ships to arrive in the harbour. He opened up a little, confirming what Flora had long suspected as he confided to her that he much preferred the welcoming warmth of the Gordons' home to the chilly formality of Ardtuath House. To her relief, he seemed more like the old Alec again, calmer and more relaxed, in the homely atmosphere of Keeper's Cottage. He'd also confided that his relations with his father were even more strained. They'd fallen out again over Alec's refusal to apply for a transfer to a land-based job in the south. His mother had taken his side, and the resulting atmosphere was the worse for both of them. It went without saying that Flora's presence would be an additional thorn in Sir Charles's flesh, so she was thankful that Alec never asked her up to the house any more.

Then, at last, the wind and rain had abated and the day had dawned clear and calm.

'Make the most of it,' warned Iain. 'The deer are staying on the lee of the hill. They know when there's another storm coming in.'

As Flora and Alec climbed the path to the lochan, the wind began to pick up again, filling the sky to the west, stretching it as taut as a blue sail to where it met the horizon. From the heights they could see a pair of ships entering the loch.

'Is there to be another Arctic convoy so soon?' asked Flora, surprised.

Alec shook his head. 'Not yet. Those will have journeyed up from the south to join the muster for the next Atlantic convoy. There's one due to leave in a few days' time.'

Flora breathed a sigh of relief, knowing that she had him safe on shore for a while longer. Today was a gift. They fished for a while, but nothing was biting; then they retreated to the shelter of the bothy's walls, which offered a little protection from the teasing bluster of the wind. It had swung round to the north-east, the Arctic breath slicing through their layers of clothing. There was a small stash of dry sticks and peat in one corner, half-buried beneath some old boards, and Alec managed to coax a fire alight in the grate so they could warm their hands and toast the bannock that they'd brought with them, the butter melting into the oatmeal and dripping on to their fingers.

He pulled her close to his side and wrapped his coat around them both, cocooning them from the world beyond the bothy's walls, and she breathed in the smell of the peat smoke on his hair.

'In the summer, let's come and camp up here,' he said.

And she nodded, a wave of hope surging through her at the thought that the summer would come and he would be there. And maybe the war would be over by then, and the doubt and fear that cast such long shadows would be gone. They'd be able to plan a life without goodbyes, and the paralysing unspoken anguish that each one of those farewells might be their last. And she would hold Alec in her arms until he was healed.

At last the glow of the fire began to fade, the peats crumbling to grey dust. Alec stood, brushing crumbs from his jumper, and took her hand to help her up. Beyond the shelter of the bothy wall, the wind was like a cold blade against their cheeks.

'Looks like your father was right,' he said, glancing to the west. As the winter sun slipped towards the sea, a bank of dark clouds rose to meet it, hungrily devouring the light. 'There's another storm coming in. We'd best be getting back.'

By the time they'd reached the cottage, the darkness had enveloped the loch and the wind had turned from a tease to a bully. Drawing the blackout to shut out the threatening storm, Flora shivered a little despite the warmth of the kitchen. This was no night to be out at sea. She was thankful Alec was on shore, and thought maybe the storm would delay the departure of that next Atlantic convoy. She just hoped all the ships were now safely gathered inside the harbour.

At first, as she surfaced from her sleep, Flora thought the banging was part of the symphony of the storm, a bass beat joining the banshee howl of the wind and the rush of sleety snow being driven against the walls of the cottage. But then she realised the rhythmic, insistent knocking was someone at the door. She scrambled out of bed, hearing her father's footsteps in the corridor as he went to answer it.

It was early morning, still dark outside. Alec stepped across the threshold, quickly pulling the door shut behind him as the storm threatened to wrench it from his grasp. Rivulets of melting snow ran from his oilskins and pooled on the floor around his boots.

'There's a ship in trouble out beyond the point,' he said. 'We're going to need more hands, stretchers, ambulances. Flora and Ruaridh . . . ?'

'We're here,' said Ruaridh, already pulling on a jersey and reaching past Alec for his own waterproofs, which hung next to the door.

In her room, Flora hastily tucked her nightdress into a pair of trousers and grabbed her greatcoat. 'Drop me at the base,' she told them as they jumped into the car at the gate, its engine already running. 'I'll get the ambulance and pick up Mairi on the way past. We'll catch up with you at the end of the road.'

Alec nodded. 'It's gone on to the rocks at Furadh Mor. It's not going to be easy to reach them. Bring the ambulance along the track as far as you safely can.'

In the darkness, the truck's headlights were scarcely able to pierce the spinning eddies of snow that lashed the windscreen. Flora peered ahead, her eyes straining to pick out landmarks, driving as fast as she dared, thankful that she knew every twist and turn like the back of her hand. The gale pummelled the sides of the ambulance, making it sway and lurch, the snow rattling against the metal like machine-gun fire, and she had to fight to keep it on the road, which was slippery with melting sleet. Mairi sat beside her, white-faced and tense, gripping the sides of her seat.

Flora knew what was on her mind. Just the other day, Bridie had shown her a postcard from Hal saying that the brothers were on their way back to Loch Ewe having managed to get berths on one of the Liberty ships coming up from London, which would meet with others there before returning to America to pick up another cargo. Neither girl spoke as the ambulance battled onwards through the storm, but they both shared the same fear and each prayed silently that Hal and Roy were on some other ship, in some other port, weathering the storm.

There was already a small cluster of military vehicles parked haphazardly where the road ended, just beyond the croft houses at Cove. A door opened as a frozen, bedraggled casualty was helped inside, to where Mrs Kennedy and Mrs McKenzie were doing what they could to warm those who'd managed to make it ashore through the seething waves. Flora gingerly edged the ambulance past and manoeuvred it along the rough track, pulling up behind another truck that had already stopped at the top of the cliff, its headlights illuminating the thick veil of snow and the roiling waters beyond.

'Have you got a stretcher?' shouted a man with a captain's stripes on his coat sleeves. 'Hand it over to them' – he gesticulated to Alec and Ruaridh – 'and bring what supplies you can. There are casualties on the shore, but be careful. That cliff path is dangerous and we can't afford any more injuries.'

Flora gasped as she reached the cliff edge. Beneath them, at the bottom of the sheer rocky path, the beach was veiled by the driving snow. Over the fury of the wind, she could hear waves crashing on to the rocks with the full force of the Atlantic. She strained her eyes to see the foundering ship, but there was only sleet-swept blackness beyond the beam of the ambulance headlights. She started down first, with Mairi close on her heels, scrambling into the unknown as the storm grabbed at her coat and whipped her hair across her face, trying to pluck her from the rocks and throw her into the raging cauldron that roared somewhere beneath them.

It was chaotic on the shore. Torch beams wavered here and there as the rescue party searched for survivors. It was impossible to tell whether the oil-black, huddled shapes on the beach were rocks or bodies until you reached down to touch them, feeling for hard stone or yielding flesh. Every now and then there would be a cry of 'Over here!', the words snatched by the wind and almost lost beneath the crashing of the waves.

The crofters from the cottages at Cove had been first on the scene, summoned by the flares sent up when the ship had been beached on the rocks and by an officer who had managed to swim ashore and climb the cliff to summon help. The men had raced down to the bay, followed by the women bringing blankets and a can of hot tea. A fire had been lit and there were glimpses of huddled figures in the light of the leaping flames as they attempted to revive the survivors.

Flora and Mairi stumbled towards the faint light of one of the torches and helped get a casualty on to a stretcher. The sailor retched and choked, covered in thick black oil and coughing up seawater, exhausted from the swim to shore.

Somewhere out there, beyond the reach of the torchlight and the headlight beams of the waiting vehicles on the cliff top that illuminated the feverish dance of the snow, the vessel was being swallowed, inexorably, by the ocean. Had she sailed just a few hundred yards further on, the crew would have been able to make the turn into the safety of the loch, but in the snow-shrouded darkness they'd swung close to the shore too early and the storm had driven the ship into the rocky maw of the point. Summoned by the flares fired from the mortally wounded ship, a tug from the harbour had tried to reach the stricken vessel, firing a line across to it to pull it to safety, but the waves and the wind were too wild and had thwarted the rescue attempt.

'Do we know the name of the vessel?' Flora shouted to one of the stretcher-bearers as they were about to make the perilous journey back up the cliff path with their patient.

'It's a Yankee ship,' he yelled back. 'The *William H. Welch.*'

Anxiously, Flora turned to Mairi, about to ask her whether she knew the name of the Gustavsens' ship. But she froze as a beam of torchlight illuminated the mask of anguish on her friend's face. Following her gaze, Flora turned to see Alec and Ruaridh carrying a lifeless body between them. As the faint glimmer of light scanned over them, something pale gleamed for a fleeting moment, a glint of gold in the darkness. And then Flora realised, horrified, that what she had glimpsed was a strand of white-blond hair.

'It's Hal,' shouted Ruaridh. As they drew alongside, Flora laid her fingertips in the soft crook of his neck, feeling for a pulse. But she could see already that it was too late.

Mairi had stumbled away, calling Roy's name, her anguished screams like the cries of a seabird on the wind. They searched frantically, knowing he wouldn't have been far from his brother's side, that he must, now, be here somewhere. After an eternity they found him, washed ashore, the fronds of his hair drifting like golden weed at the water's edge. As Flora shouted for a stretcher, Mairi fell to her knees beside him, oblivious to the icy water. She laid her ear against his chest and gave a single, wrenching sob of relief as she felt the rise of a faint breath. And then Flora had pulled her away as the medics went to work, willing him to live, to breathe again, to swim hard against the current that had already swept his brother away, fighting his way back to the shores of the living.

As the storm began to abate and a grey dawn broke – at last – over the hills, Flora and Mairi climbed wearily back up the cliff path, following the stretcher-bearers carrying the last of the survivors. There weren't many – only a scant dozen of the crew of over seventy had managed to live through the brutal onslaught of the storm-whipped sea. The girls were soaked to the skin, shivering with shock and cold that they scarcely registered. Through the dark hours of that February morning, they had made the journey back and forth to the hospital at Gairloch three times, carrying survivors, each one a miracle pulled from the black water. The first of them had been Roy Gustavsen.

At the near end of the beach a long row of bodies had been laid on the damp sand, their limbs gently straightened as they were set down carefully one alongside the other. Some were heart-achingly young, boys who'd joined the Merchant Marine as they were not yet old enough for military service. In that row, Hal Gustavsen lay beside his fellow crew members, and Flora had wept hot salt tears over him, her heart leaden at the thought of having to break the news to Bridie, and of Mairi having to tell Roy. And as the feeble winter daylight won the struggle to push the night westwards, it revealed the broken carcass of the *William H. Welch*, impaled on the rocks where the hungry, scavenging waves continued to pick clean its bones.

The entire community gathered in the kirk that Sunday to say prayers and sing hymns for the souls lost in the wreck the previous day. They mourned those sons of other mothers and fathers as though they were their own, as they would wish their men to be mourned should they fall in far-off lands: because humanity has no borders.

Moira Carmichael held her head high, although strands of grey hair escaped from under her Sunday hat. Her deep contralto underpinned Lady Helen's more fragile, wavering soprano and Flora's voice that soared like the lark's, rising to the rafters above the crammed pews. And as the congregation joined in the final chorus, a shaft of February sunlight slanted in through the window, blinding her eyes with tears of molten gold as she glanced over at Bridie who sat with her head bowed by the weight of her grief, unable to stand, unable to sing, unable to speak.

Lexie, 1978

So many of the old songs from these parts tell stories of the sea taking loved ones. I suppose that's inevitable in a community of fishermen, whose womenfolk watch and wait for those who might never return. As Mairi and I park the car and walk along the track to the headland, the words of one such song play in a loop in my head.

'Hushed be thy moaning, lone bird of the sea
Thy home on the rocks is a shelter to thee
Thy home is the angry wave,
Mine but the lonely grave
Horo, Mhairi dhu, turn ye to me.'

We've come for a walk to Black Bay, where a few pitiful remnants from the wreck of the *William H. Welch* still lie scattered and rusting. The carcass of the ship itself has gone, lying submerged beneath the waters surrounding the rocks of Furadh Mor. But when we pick our way down the cliffs to the beach, I spot the twisted and broken remains of a lifeboat among the rocks. As we start to walk across the stones, I hum the plaintive tune under my breath and the wind catches the notes and flings them across the stretch of water to the treacherous, craggy island that marks the ship's grave. Here and there, scraps of rusted metal torn from the ship by the fury of the storm that night in 1944 are still visible where they have washed up among the stones. I stoop to pick one up – a bolt of some kind – and it is heavy in the palm of my hand. I rub my thumb over its salt-roughened surface and it leaves a stain of blood-brown rust on my skin. Carefully, I replace the bolt in its bed of stones. This whole beach feels like a grave, and I have the sense that nothing should be disturbed.

I dropped Daisy off at Bridie's this morning when I picked Mairi up for our drive out to the point. As we were leaving, Bridie thrust a bunch of sky-blue forget-me-nots into Mairi's hands, tied with a length of ivory ribbon. She said nothing, just turned back, holding Daisy's hand in hers, and walked slowly up the path to her door.

I glance across at Mairi. She's walked down to the water's edge and she stands with the posy in her hands, watching the waves. I stay back, letting her have her space as she remembers the night that Hal was lost and Roy was saved. At last she fumbles in a pocket for a hankie and raises it to wipe the tears from her eyes, and I walk across the shingle to stand at her side.

'Thank you for coming here with me,' she says, turning towards me with a smile. 'I've never been able to face coming back before now. But it's good to be standing here with you, remembering the ones we've lost. Your mum was amazing that night. She worked tirelessly, doing what could be done for the survivors. She took care of me, too. After we found Roy and took him to the hospital, she was the one who insisted on coming back twice more so we could keep helping with the rescue. I was shattered – seeing Hal's body and thinking we'd lost Roy as well was one of the worst moments of my life. But Flora made me keep going that night, and I knew it was the right thing. Even though we couldn't save Hal, there were others who needed our help. Some of them were boys like him, as young as eighteen. In places we had to feel our way with our hands, because in the storm and the darkness it was impossible to distinguish the oil-covered bodies from the rocks.'

It's hard to imagine that night on a summer's day like this one, with the pink heads of the sea thrift nodding in the breeze and the sun warming the stones. But if I close my eyes, I can see the rescuers stumbling blindly through the storm: crofters, soldiers and sailors alike joining in the desperate search, the scene lit from the point above us by the headlights of the vehicles parked there.

We make our way to the far end of the cove and Mairi carefully places Bridie's posy on the rocks at the water's edge. Then, with a nod, she takes my arm and we turn away. As we go, I glance back to where the waves are already reaching for the brave little bunch of flowers whose pale ribbon flutters in the wind.

We walk back in silence from the headland where Mum parked the ambulance that night, along the rough track to where I've left the car at the end of the road. Mairi gazes out one last time towards the rocks of Furadh Mor and then opens the car door.

'Right,' she says with a little more of her usual brightness and briskness, 'I don't know about you, but I could do with a cup of tea and a cuddle with wee Daisy.'

'Thank you for showing me that,' I say. 'It really helps, you know, you and Bridie telling me more about Mum's life before I was born.'

She nods. 'I know. Even though it's so painful, grief is something we have to go through sooner or later. There's no way round it, no way to avoid it. That's something we all learned in the war. You go through it. But if you have a friend or two to walk along that path beside you, it helps you to bear it.'

I absorb her words as I drive back along the shore of the loch. She's right, I realise. In their different ways, the friends I've found here are helping me shoulder the burden of my grief as we walk the path together. It helps to know they're by my side.

As we push open the door of Bridie's cottage, the sound of singing greets us.

'*Step we gladly, on we go,*
Heel for heel and toe for toe,
Arm in arm and row on row,
All for Mairi's wedding.'

Bridie's teaching Daisy the 'Lewis Bridal Song', clapping along to keep the time.

'*Oh an oh,*' sings Daisy, laughing as Bridie bounces her on her knee.

'Here they are, look, your mammy and your Auntie Mairi.'

'Mam a Ma,' agrees Daisy, reaching her hands towards me. I scoop her into my arms and give her a cuddle, but then she wriggles to be let down and toddles over to the coffee table where a large photo album lies open. I settle myself on the sofa and pick it up. There's a black and white picture of Mairi and Roy on their wedding day as they come out of the kirk. Lined up on either side of the path is a guard of honour of Wrens, standing to attention in their neat uniforms. Mairi's veil blows in the breeze and she is laughing up at Roy, whose white-blond hair gleams in the sunshine as he smiles back at his pretty bride.

Mairi comes to sit beside me and Daisy clambers on to her lap, where she's as much at home as she'd be on mine. 'Look.' Mairi points to another photo on the next page. 'That's your granny.'

Daisy contemplates the picture seriously and then points a stubby finger of her own. 'Gan,' she says.

'And Bridie, too – they were your bridesmaids,' I exclaim.

I've never seen these photos before. Mum and Bridie stand on either side of Mairi and each of the three holds a posy of flowers. I swallow hard as I realise they are forget-me-nots, tied with lengths of pale ribbon, just like the bouquet Bridie handed Mairi to leave on the beach at Black Bay. She should have been marrying Hal in this photo. She should have embarked on the biggest adventure of her life alongside her friend, heading off to make a new life on the other side of the Atlantic. Instead, the life that she should have had died on a storm-blackened beach on a February night in 1944. My heart aches for her and I think of what Mairi said in the car about grief.

I'm glad Bridie and Mum had each other as they walked along that hard and stony path together, side by side.

Flora, 1944

With the arrival of spring, Alec was reassigned to the patrols on the Western Approaches and, with a promotion to commander, he joined a new crew aboard the *Kite*. While it was hard being parted again, ever since she'd witnessed the shipwreck and the oil-blackened bodies washed up on the beach, an image of his bloodied hands on the axe had begun to haunt Flora's dreams and she couldn't help but feel a guilty sense of relief.

Mairi, who knew her so well, was astute enough to notice the change in Flora's mood and commented on it one day when they were waiting outside the hospital in the ambulance. 'How are things between you and Alec?'

'Fine,' replied Flora, but she could hear the defensive lift in her own voice. She tried for a little more nonchalance. 'Why do you ask?' She was loath to confide her doubts to her friend. After all, Bridie had lost Hal and Mairi had almost lost Roy. She ought to have felt she was the lucky one.

'Because it's strange. You almost seem happier these days with him off at sea. It never used to be that way. Are things tough with his parents again?'

Flora nodded miserably, then turned to face Mairi. 'It's that, yes. But there's more,' she admitted. 'I feel I'm losing him. It's as if everything is stacked against us, not just his father and his position in life, but the war, this latest promotion . . . Sometimes it feels as though everything is conspiring to push us apart. I don't know if I can keep fighting against it all for much longer. More to the point, I don't know that he can, either.'

'I know it's hard, being parted. The war's taking a huge toll on us all. But anyone can see how much he loves you.'

'Do you think so? Because I'm really not certain of that any more. He's struggling, Mairi. And I'm not sure being with me isn't making it harder for him.'

'Och, that's just Sir Charles's interference getting to you. Don't you dare let him win, Flora Gordon! Don't give him the satisfaction of destroying something so good.'

Their passenger appeared then, cutting short the chance to say anything more. As they drove back to the base, Flora tried to feel reassured by Mairi's words. But in her heart of hearts, the doubts remained.

Alec was to have been away until the autumn. But, as the white heads of ox-eye daisies nodded at the roadside and the dog roses bloomed pink against the grey stones of the dykes, word came, via Ruaridh, that there was a plan to risk another summer convoy, which would muster in the loch and set sail for Archangel in mid-August. And so, with a mixture of feelings, she began to watch the sea again, scanning the northern horizon for the glimpse of a smudge of grey in the deep blue of the water, which might turn out to be the *Kite* returning to the harbour.

Bridie was the first of them to hear, in the end, and she hurried across the parade ground to tell Flora as she and Mairi parked up the ambulance for the day. It was the first time in months that Flora had seen a smile on Bridie's face and while she still looked gaunt, with cheeks as pale as winter and purple shadows beneath her eyes, it was good to glimpse that brief flicker of her old cheerfulness, even if it was as short-lived as a match struck in a strong wind.

'Alec's ship is due in within the hour,' Bridie announced, a little out of breath and pressing a hand into her side where a stitch griped. She gave Flora a quick hug and then hastened back to her duties in the canteen.

'Here,' said Mairi, holding out a hand for the key of the truck. 'I'll fill the tank and get everything sorted for the morning. You go and get out of your uniform and then you can be at the pier when he arrives.'

Flora smiled her thanks. 'Say hello to Roy from me.'

Mairi nodded. He was staying on the farm, helping her father while he regained his strength. His lungs had been badly affected by the seawater on the night of the wreck and they'd very nearly lost him to a bout of pneumonia that had refused to shift, keeping him in the hospital for several weeks. He'd floated in and out of consciousness, adrift between life and death, but at last Mairi's determined grasp on his hand had pulled him back to the shores of the living. Back to her. Afterwards, she'd helped him write letters to his parents, telling them of Hal's final hours and describing to them how the brothers had joined in the desperate struggle to try to save the ship. Three times the tug from Loch Ewe had tried to fire a line across to the foundering vessel and three times the strength of the storm had seized the line, wresting it away from the *William H. Welch*. When the merchant sailors knew that all was lost, the brothers had finally plunged, together, into the waves to swim for the shore, where they could see the headlights of the ambulances on the clifftop lighting a path through the maelstrom. The force of the tempest had separated them, but the thought that Hal might have made it safely to land kept Roy struggling on, even as the bitter cold sapped the last of his strength.

They wrote about Bridie, about how happy Hal had been with her and how much he'd been looking forward to seeing her again; they told his parents how much their younger son was loved by everyone he'd met in that wild mountainous land so far from his prairie home.

And Roy promised them that one day, just as soon as they could get safe passage, he would come back to them, bringing with him the pretty Scots lass to whom he was now engaged. He told Mairi that together they would all go and lay flowers on Hal's grave: a simple white stone engraved with his name, the date of his birth and the date of the wreck – 26 February 1944 – in a churchyard at the edge of a waving sea of wheat.

Flora could tell from Alec's silence that something was preoccupying him. He walked ahead of her up the path to the lochan, carrying the pack with the things they'd need to camp in the bothy for a couple of days. The springy peat cushioned each step they took, the ground soft and damp from a recent fall of summer rain. She shifted her basket to the opposite arm, swapping the pair of fishing rods to her other hand, and adjusted her pace to walk alongside him where the track broadened enough to allow it. She was a little wary, though, alert to another sudden swing in his mood, knowing that the gathering darkness might lead to another flash of that uncontrollable rage she'd glimpsed before.

He glanced across at her and smiled apologetically. 'Sorry, I'm not very good company again today. Had another almighty row with Pa this morning.'

She didn't ask what the argument had been about, knowing that it would almost certainly have revolved around his unsuitable attachment to the gamekeeper's daughter. If Sir Charles had suspected that Alec's plan to spend a couple of days camping in the hills involved spending time with Flora, too, that would no doubt have reignited his anger. As they walked, she wondered again if they could really ever be together when the war was over. These extraordinary times had allowed barriers to break down, but what would happen when life returned to normal? Would Alec ever be able to heal? Would the old boundaries reassert themselves? Could she ever really be the mistress of Ardtuath House? Or, if forced to choose, would Alec leave his heritage behind to be with her? Which would prove stronger, she pondered, duty or love? And what of her own sense of herself, which had grown through her work and her singing? Would the voice she'd found be silenced again if they were husband and wife?

As the pair climbed higher, Flora's uncertainties weighed her down more than the basket she carried, and the silence between them was heavy with unspoken thoughts.

To break it, Flora asked, 'How's your mother?', knowing how Sir Charles's ill humour might well have had wider repercussions.

'She's all right, I think. Keeping herself busy now she's so involved with the Rural these days. It's a good thing – gets her out of the house.'

In her quiet way, seeing that help was needed, Lady Helen had stepped in to assist Mrs Carmichael, gently insisting that the status quo should be maintained with Moira as chairwoman, but that she was happy to lend a hand behind the scenes to keep the SWRI's work going. With the multitude of servicemen coming and going and rations stretched more tightly than ever, their contribution to running the canteen and to the organisation of social events had become even more essential.

At the top of the steepest part of the climb, they stopped to catch their breath and turned to look back out over the loch. Alec breathed deep and, to Flora's relief, when he smiled at her his dark eyes seemed to have regained some of their old warmth. Being out on the hill was doing him good.

Most of the merchant ships had gathered now and lay at anchor beyond the island, American Liberty ships tied up alongside British vessels. Fuel ships ran back and forth between the depot and the fleet, filling their tanks in preparation for the off and servicing a Norwegian oiler, which would accompany the convoy to refuel vessels en route. On the near side of the bay, the *Kite* rode at anchor alongside the rest of the naval escort.

'They look awfully wee from up here,' Flora commented. 'I hate to think of you so vulnerable out there, on the longer route. And it's still daylight until almost midnight up there.'

Alec put an arm around her shoulders, giving her a reassuring squeeze. 'Don't worry, there's a pair of aircraft carriers going to be joining us once we get to Scapa Flow, so we'll have Stringbag support from the Fleet Air Arm too. Those pilots are aces.'

She'd seen one of the carriers once, its immense bulk dwarfing the other naval vessels in the harbour. Ruaridh had explained to her that the Swordfish biplanes – affectionately nicknamed Stringbags – lashed to its deck might look old-fashioned, with their open cockpits and fabric-covered fuselages, but they were efficient hunters of U-boats, dropping depth charges and torpedo bombs from a height on any attackers. He'd described the skill needed by the pilots to launch themselves at full throttle from the pitching deck out over the waves to hunt down enemy submarines, then to return to the carrier and land on that same moving target, with just one chance to catch the arrester wire that would slow the plane in time and prevent it from plunging off the deck into the seething sea. Flora couldn't imagine what it must be like for those pilots, often flying blind and only emerging from the blanket of Arctic fog just a couple of hundred feet above the deck.

Even with the support of two aircraft carriers, though, she knew how vulnerable that summer convoy would be. 'Just one more push,' everyone was saying. 'It'll be over by Christmas.' Again.

She hoped that perhaps this convoy would be the last one . . . but then how many times had she sent that particular prayer up already?

They picked up their gear and continued on towards the lochan, turning their backs on the grey flotilla in the loch below.

The weather was fine, so there was no need for cover as they tied flies to their lines and began to fish for their supper. The lochan's coverlet of green lily pads offered shelter to the brown trout whose burnished scales were the same colour as the peat-infused waters of the lochan, so they cast close to the edge of the lilies, hoping to tempt the fish to the surface. Soon they had a good-sized one, and Alec cleaned it while Flora got the fire going in the hearth of the ruin. She put a dab of butter into a blackened frying pan that they'd brought with them, and set the trout fillets to fry. Before long, the skin was crisped and golden at the edges, and the flesh of the fish, basted with brown butter, turned to succulent flakes. They ate it with a few potatoes, fried in the same pan, and a handful of sweet green peas.

Alec lay with his head cushioned on Flora's lap while she leaned against the fallen stones of the bothy wall, and they talked long into the evening, about how well Roy was doing in his recovery – which had a great deal to do with the care he was receiving from Mairi and her family on the farm – and how Bridie seemed to be starting to regain her spirits just a little.

'How are Stuart and Davy getting on?' Alec asked.

The Carmichaels were still struggling with their grief and Flora had been worried that the two wee boys weren't getting much attention. So she'd suggested to Mrs Carmichael that they come and help her in the garden and give her father a hand with some of the chores on the estate. Three days a week all through the summer holidays they'd turned up at Keeper's Cottage and thrown themselves into the jobs that Iain had found for them, helping him with the pony and the dogs, digging up tatties and pulling weeds from the kitchen garden. Stuart was growing as fast as a thistle, skinny wrists and ankles protruding from the cuffs of his trousers and jacket, but the extra fish and meat the boys ate at the Gordons' table were helping him fill out a little. Braan was the boys' constant companion and Davy, especially, loved the garron, too, and would happily spend hours combing the tangles and burrs out of her long blonde mane.

'They're looking well. They're off back to school again this week, but they're going to keep coming over in the evenings to help Dad and have their tea with us. They're old enough to help with the shoots now, too. Dad says they'll make good beaters.'

'Has their mum been able to get up to see them over the summer?'

Flora shook her head. 'I know the Carmichaels invited her to come and stay, but she's not managed to get here. She said she was coming for Davy's birthday, but never turned up in the end. It was awful, seeing him try not to show his disappointment. He was so brave – told me she's too busy helping make bombs to stop the Germans to come just now, but that she'll come and bring him and his brother home just as soon as the war is over. For the time being, they're better off here, I reckon.'

Alec propped himself on one elbow and threw another peat on the fire. It wasn't cold, but the smoke helped keep the midges at bay.

'Look at that,' he sighed, settling himself against her again and reaching for her hand. 'I don't think I'll ever grow tired of watching west coast sunsets.'

Silhouetted on the crest of the hill, a herd of red deer hinds stood stock-still, facing the setting sun as it painted the western horizon in shades of crimson and vermillion. The colours grew bolder and deeper before they faded finally and night drew a blue-black curtain across the sky, obscuring the deer.

In that moment, safe in the hills, the shadows of her doubts lifted a little. Alec seemed at peace, sounding more like his old self again, and Flora felt the tension in her neck and arms relax. She wriggled closer to him, resting her head on his chest as the stars began to appear.

She knew a few of the constellations: the Plough, which wheeled around the constant point of the North Star, was an eternal feature of the night sky over the loch, a familiar friend to every crofting family and to the men who fished the treacherous waters of the Minch. And when she was wee, her father had shown her how the hunter, Orion, would appear over the hills to the south in the winter, searching for the Seven Sisters who had been placed in the sky for safety by the king of the gods.

'Tell me a story about the stars,' she said softly.

Alec settled himself more comfortably, drawing her into the crook of his arm. He pointed out one of the constellations to the north. 'You see that W shape of bright stars? It's one of my favourite constellations – Cassiopeia's Chair.'

'Who was Cassiopeia?' Flora asked, tracing the line of his cheekbone with her finger. His eyes were as dark as the night sky.

'She was a very beautiful queen, the mother of Andromeda. But she boasted to the god of the seas, Poseidon, that her daughter was more lovely than his sea nymphs. He flew into a rage and cast her up into the sky on her throne, sentencing her to spin around the North Star for eternity.'

'Poor thing, she must have to hang upside down half the time.' Flora smiled.

'Well, now that you're acquainted with her, when I'm away at sea we can each look up at her and know that the light from her stars is shining on us both. The distance between us is nothing when you think how far off those stars are. I shall like that thought when I'm on watch up there in the Arctic seas. It'll help me to know you are never really far away.' He braided her fingers with his own, binding their hands together.

As they watched, more and more stars emerged until it seemed that they lay under a blanket of black velvet that had captured a million sparkling dewdrops in its folds. And as those stars wheeled above them, describing a vast whirlpool of light across the night sky, they drew even closer until there was no distance at all between the beating of their hearts, and they melted together to become one.

Lexie, 1978

Daisy's in her bed, tucked up under her shell-pattern blanket, and Davy and I are sitting on the steps in front of Keeper's Cottage finishing off the bottle of wine we've shared over supper. I lean my head on his shoulder and watch the stars materialise as the autumn night draws its own blanket of darkness over the loch.

There's a comfortable sense of companionship between us, as if we've always known one another. Which, in a way, we have. It's a new sensation for me, this feeling of contentment, and I realise that I have never felt at home like this before.

'Tell me the names of the stars,' I say.

He points out the Plough. 'Everyone knows that, and it's a good one when you're out at sea. It always points to the Pole Star, one of the few fixed points in the night sky. Once you know where true north is, you can navigate more easily.'

'What's that one?' I ask, tracing a zigzagging line in the sky above us.

'The one shaped like a W? That's Cassiopeia's Chair. It's usually easy to spot with those five bright stars. And that one over there is Sirius, the dog star. It's the brightest one in the sky. If you spot anything brighter, it's probably a planet.'

He leans forward to look towards the south. 'At this time of year, you can just see my favourite constellation on clear nights.

Aquila, the eagle. It's harder to make out, but that brighter star just on the edge of the Milky Way is Altair and that's the eagle's head. Its wings spread out in a V shape from Altair, see?' His hand describes the sweep of the eagle's wings, sketching the shape in the darkness. 'One night, when it's flat calm like this, I'll take you out on the boat. Out on the water, away from the lights of the cottages, you can see the stars even more clearly.'

I imagine being out there, picturing the deep, black water beneath the boat that swallows the light of the moon and the stars. The thought makes me shiver a little.

'Come on,' says Davy, 'you're getting chilled. Time to go in.'

I shake my head, resisting, not wanting to break the spell of our closeness by moving.

He stands anyway. 'Well, at least let me bring out a rug.'

The warmth of him evaporates from my skin and now I realise I do feel chilled. He begins to move away and, out of nowhere, a memory of the rejection I felt in London surges over me. It's absurd, I know. He's not leaving me, he's just being thoughtful. But the wounds of Piers's abandonment must go deeper than I'd recognised.

'There you go again, still trying to look after everyone.' I mean it lightly but it comes out wrong, sounding petulant and accusing.

'And there *you* go again, frightened of letting anyone take care of you in case they hurt you,' he replies. There's an edge of irritation to his words that makes me draw back, trying to read his expression. But the shadows obscure his face and he turns away to go inside.

I sigh and stand, too, before he can return with a blanket. The thought of it makes me feel claustrophobic and his words have stung me. It's too late now; the spell has been well and truly broken. I go in and switch on the light, start clearing the supper things into the sink, running the taps, wiping the countertop.

Davy stands in the doorway, the plaid rug in his hands no longer needed. He folds it carefully over the back of one of the kitchen chairs, smoothing the creases.

'I'll be going then,' he says.

I nod, busily scrubbing a saucepan, not meeting his eyes.

He comes over and gently removes the scouring pad from my hand, then wraps me in a hug.

I don't know where this evening went wrong. Perhaps we've both got too used to living on our own. Perhaps we're just too different. Or perhaps the wall I've built around my feelings over the years is simply too much for anyone – even him – to dismantle. It all seems so complicated suddenly, letting someone else in, having to work at a relationship, and I long for the simplicity of my solitary life with Daisy, even though I know how lonely it can be.

'Sorry,' I say, burying my face against his shirt. 'But don't try and rescue me, just like you try to rescue everyone else because you couldn't rescue your mum and your brother.'

He pulls away, hurt. Then he shakes his head and picks up his jacket. He turns to go, hesitates, looks back at me, the expression in his eyes wounded.

'I'm not trying to rescue you, Lexie,' he says. 'I'm trying to love you.'

I surface through layers of troubled dreams, trying to make sense of the sounds that have woken me. There's been a week of calm weather and so the sudden storm that's blown in while I was sleeping is bewildering, howling like a banshee as it flings itself at the walls of the cottage with a fury that seems to have come out of nowhere. There's another sound, too, steadier and more insistent than the wind and rain. At last I realise it's the ringing of the telephone and a surge of alarm grips me. It's the middle of the night. Who on earth could be calling?

I bump into the door jamb, jarring my shoulder as I hurry downstairs and snatch the receiver from its cradle, sending up a quick prayer of thanks that Daisy hasn't been woken by the din.

'Lexie, is Davy there with you?' It's Bridie, her voice pitched high with panic.

'No. I haven't seen him for a few days.' Not since the night I said such hurtful things to him, but I don't tell her that.

'He went off in the boat yesterday. Said he was heading out for a couple of days' fishing while the weather was good. It was forecast to change but not this fast.'

Her panic is catching, pulling me in, and my mind starts to spin in a whirlpool of fear.

'Did he say exactly where he was going?' I ask, trying to keep calm so I can think more clearly.

'No. Just that he'd be out at sea. Oh, Lexie, what should we do?'

'I'll call the coastguard. See if they've heard anything from him on the radio. He may have gone into Gairloch or be sheltering in Gruinard Bay. If not, I'll tell them he's missing so they can put out a search. I'll phone you back as soon as I've spoken to them.'

I'm still on the phone when Bridie arrives at the front door, unable to bear waiting alone. She's soaked to the skin, having cycled through the storm, and I hand her a towel to dry her hair. She starts to shake uncontrollably.

'It's all right, Bridie,' I say, sitting her down on a kitchen chair, trying to calm her, although I feel anything but calm myself. 'They're putting out a search for the *Bonnie Stuart*. His last radio contact was from just this side of the Shiant Isles – he said he was heading for home ahead of the storm.'

I try hard to stay calm and to push from my mind an image of the Blue Men of the Minch, those malicious storm kelpies, slithering out of their caves in the cliffs along the edge of the islands, intent on snatching sailors from their boats and pulling them down to their deaths beneath the surge of the hungry waves.

I hold Bridie's hands, but can't stop their trembling. 'Something's not right,' she insists. 'I can feel it.'

Her fear is infecting me. I see Davy in my mind's eye, his grey-blue eyes clouded with hurt when he left the cottage the other night, and I hear an echo of his quiet, sad words beneath the roar of the storm: *I'm not trying to rescue you, Lexie. I'm trying to love you.* I have a sudden vision of the torn and twisted remains of the lifeboat on the beach at Black Bay, and I know I have to do something, anything. I can't sit here knowing he's out there somewhere.

'Bridie, stay and look after Daisy for me, would you? I'm going to go to the point.'

She nods, as if this is the sensible thing to do in the middle of the night with a force 10 gale blowing. But then we both know, without saying it, that if he's coming back from the Shiants he'll be heading into Loch Ewe past Furadh Mor.

'Take his Land Rover,' is all she says. 'You'll be able to get along the track. Be careful, Lexie.'

I nod, tucking my pyjama trousers into my wellies and grabbing Mum's coat from the hook. As I fasten it, my fingers brush against the sweetheart brooch which I've pinned to it, and the feel of the silver beneath my fingertips gives me a little jolt of courage, reminding me that Mum made this same journey on a storm-lashed night all those years ago.

I pull up next to Davy's Land Rover, which is parked in front of his house, the keys left in the ignition as usual. The engine splutters once, twice, then turns over and I shove the car into gear. The clutch takes a bit of getting used to and I jolt on to the road, the driving rain hammering on the metal of the roof. I wrench on the steering wheel as the wind buffets the vehicle, trying to blow it into the ditch.

Thankfully there's no one else out on the road tonight. I glance up to the heavens, wishing there was at least a glimmer of starlight to keep me company, but the storm clouds have blotted out the constellations that Davy pointed out to me the other night. Without them, how can he find true north? I just pray that the compass on the *Bonnie Stuart* will be pointing out a steady course against the wildness of the sea.

At last I reach the croft houses at Cove and the end of the road. I crawl a little more cautiously along the track, unable to see anything beyond the beam of the headlights. I'm horribly aware that the ground starts to fall away steeply to my right here, as the full force of the storm howls around me. At last I've gone as far as I dare, and I jerk to a stop, yanking on the handbrake. I dip the headlights for a moment, hunching forward over the steering wheel to wipe the condensation from the windscreen with my coat sleeve, scanning the darkness for any faint glimmer of light. And then I see it. A tiny pinprick, as faint as starlight, that appears momentarily and then disappears again as the waves overwhelm it. I wait, holding my breath, straining my eyes. And it appears again. Definitely a boat! But it's on the wrong side of Furadh Mor and it's close to the coast, turning in too soon, unable to see the vicious teeth of the headland in the darkness.

Frantically, I switch the headlights back to full beam, conscious that the light seems to peter out all too close to the car, swallowed by the darkness. But if the boatman – whether or not it's the *Bonnie Stuart* out there – glances up, he'll see the faint beam of the light and realise that there's land between him and the mouth of the loch.

I jump out of the Land Rover and the storm grabs me, almost blowing me off my feet, knocking the breath out of me. I stumble towards the cliff edge, grabbing on to handfuls of heather to anchor myself to the solid ground. And there it is again, the tiny light struggling against the waves. But it's still heading towards the rocks, and I scream and wave my arms, even though I know that I can neither be seen nor heard above the roaring of the sea.

'Turn away!' I scream. 'Turn away!'

I jump back into the car and frantically dip and raise the headlights, flashing out a warning.

The pinprick of light appears, then is swallowed once again by the waves.

And then I give a sob of relief. Because the next time it appears it's changed course, heading away from the treacherous rocks of Furadh Mor. Its progress is painfully slow as it struggles against the force of the storm. Then it disappears completely for a few interminable minutes, battling the oncoming waves and hidden from view on the far side of the island. When it reappears to the right of the headland, safely past the rocks, I gasp in air, only then discovering that I've been holding my breath as I've waited to catch a glimpse of the dot of light again, that tiny glimmer as fragile as starlight in the black expanse of the ocean.

I wait until the boat is well clear of the point and can turn to starboard, running into the mouth of Loch Ewe with the waves. And then I reverse carefully back along the track until I reach a place where I can turn. As I drive back around the shore of the loch, I crane my head at every turn in the road where it's possible to see out across the water. I'm rewarded here and there by glimpses of the light, ploughing steadily onwards now towards Aultbea. The darkness seems a little less dense, at last, and the faint gleam of dawn creeps beneath the blanket of thick storm clouds above the turbulent, pewter-dark waters of the loch.

I drive the Land Rover on to the jetty. Word has got out and there are men gathered there, waiting to catch the ropes Davy throws and help him bring the *Bonnie Stuart* into the shelter of the harbour. Hands reach to pull him ashore and he shouts his thanks above the raging of the wind. They clap him on the back, each thankful that one of their own is safe home once more, snatched back from the grasp of the storm kelpies. And then he sees me, waiting beside the stack of creels, and he strides towards me. I step forward, meeting him halfway, and hold him more tightly than I've ever held anything before.

'So,' he says, when at last he's got his breath back enough to speak, 'who's the rescuer now, might I ask, Lexie Gordon?'

Flora, 1944

As the day of Alec's departure approached, she sensed the darkness growing in him once more. The precious couple of days they'd spent camping in the old bothy had brought them closer than ever before, and for a little while she'd been able to convince herself that her love really could be enough to heal him, keeping the shadows at bay. But as the coming weeks of separation loomed, she could feel him pulling away from her again, distant and distracted. Her doubts came rushing back in to fill the gap.

She'd wanted to spend every moment she could with him, but her work at the base kept them apart. And her anxiety increased still more when he stopped coming to Keeper's Cottage for his usual evening visits to sit in the kitchen with her and her father and Ruaridh and share a dram or two of whisky.

The activity in the harbour had taken on a greater sense of urgency, signalling the imminent departure of the convoy, and Flora was struggling to concentrate on the engine she was fixing. She glanced up when she heard the crunch of boots on the shingle, pushing a stray lock of hair from her eyes with the back of one oil-streaked hand.

'Alec!' Her heart gave a bound at the sight of him.

He returned her kiss, but not her smile, and his eyes didn't quite meet hers.

'It's good to see you,' she continued. 'I was worrying you'd be off soon and we might not get a chance to say our goodbyes.' She wiped her hands on a rag and tucked the loose strand of hair back into her braid.

He looked out across the bay to where the *Kite* was anchored. 'I've come to say them now,' he said. 'We'll not be sailing until the morning, but I won't get a chance to see you again before I go.'

'Won't you be able to come to the cottage tonight, then? You know Dad and Ruaridh would love to see you.'

He shook his head. 'I'm afraid not. I've a few things to do at home. And then I have to be on board early to make ready the ship before we catch the tide.'

It was there again, the unnerving distance between them. She wrapped her arms around him, trying to reclaim a little of the closeness of that night when she'd lain in his arms beneath the stars, but it was as if he'd already left her, his mind anticipating the next brutal journey stretching ahead of him.

'Och well then, I'll be seeing you.' She hoped the familiar words would make him smile, but his expression was still serious as he stooped to kiss her one last time. And then he turned and walked away, back up the beach towards Ardtuath House.

Trying to shrug off the fear she felt – for him, for them – Flora watched him go, hoping he'd turn and smile and wave so she could tell herself that everything would be all right. But he carried on without a backward glance. As he disappeared from view, she reluctantly picked up a wrench and turned her attention back to the job in hand.

She was just finishing up for the day, returning her tools to the store at the top of the base, when she saw the car. The driver and his passenger didn't notice her standing by the corrugated tin wall of the hut, but their windows were open to make the most of the light and warmth of the summer's evening, and she saw them quite clearly.

As Alec accelerated, a lock of Diana Kingsley-Scott's blonde hair fluttered in the breeze, mocking Flora as she watched them drive away.

A surge of fury and humiliation – the culmination of all those times before when she'd felt the shame of her exclusion from Alec's world – coursed through her veins. Diana couldn't just have arrived at Ardtuath House out of the blue. She must have been there for a few days and Alec hadn't told her. Not only that, he'd been avoiding her: it explained the sudden end to his usual evening visits. He'd have been enjoying fancy dinners with his parents and Diana in the dining room of the big house. It stung so much more after the days and nights they'd spent together on the hill. What a fool she'd been, believing his protestations of innocence when Diana had been there in December for the shooting weekend. This must have been going on ever since, and all that time he'd been using her. She wouldn't be humiliated by him again though. Her fingers closed around the sweetheart brooch in her pocket, gripping it so hard its corners pierced her skin.

She pulled it out and looked at it where it lay in the palm of her hand, where the silver of the laurel wreath was tarnished with a rust-coloured bead of her blood.

She ran up the path to the house, tripping over the roots of the pines in her haste. She didn't want to see Alec so she needed to drop off the letter before he got back from wherever he'd been going with Diana. To her relief there was no sign of his car, and the outer front door stood open. She laid the envelope containing her note and the sweetheart brooch on the silver salver where the postman left the daily post, so that Alec would find it on his return. And then she turned and stumbled back down the path, thankful for the darkness beneath the trees as it swallowed her up.

After a sleepless night, Flora rose early, before the others were about. Wrapping her plaid shawl about her against the chill of the dawn dew, she tried to ignore the merchant ships that were beginning to manoeuvre into position for the convoy on the far side of the loch as she picked wild raspberries from the tangle of canes growing above the cottage.

The fruit would be a welcome addition to the breakfast table. And then she'd talk to her father about the plan she'd hatched as she'd tossed and turned in her bed. She needed to leave Ardtuath, to get away from Alec and his family. She couldn't bear the thought of his deception, of seeing him with Diana again. Her presence here would be awkward for everyone, not least for her father and brother who depended on the estate for their home. But now, she told herself firmly, she'd discovered skills she could put to good use to support herself, and a voice of her own. She would ask for a transfer to another base and that would get her away by the time Alec returned. Then, once the war was over, she'd find work somehow, wherever she ended up. She'd miss her family and friends, she knew, with a pang that made her heart constrict. And she'd miss singing with the Aultbea Songbirds. But there'd be other opportunities, other chances. Even, perhaps, another man one day, one whom she could trust and who would love her back as she loved him.

A movement in the shadows among the pines made her glance up, and she set down the bowl of berries and wiped her hands on her apron as Lady Helen approached, hurrying down the path.

'Good morning, your ladyship.'

Lady Helen brushed aside the greeting. Her ordinarily pale cheeks were flushed and she seemed a little out of breath. 'Flora! I'm so glad I've found you.' She seized Flora's arm. 'Please, you have to believe me when I tell you Alec loves you and only you.' Her words tumbled out with none of her usual reserve.

Flora looked at her in speechless astonishment.

'My husband is guilty of the most terrible interference. He considers it his right to control the lives of everyone around him. For too long I've allowed him to do so, but I cannot stand by and watch him destroy my son. Alec loves you. He told me about your letter. Yes, Diana has been staying for a few days, but at my husband's invitation once again. Alec was furious and he didn't want to tell you, knowing it would only upset you. Yesterday he had an almighty row with his father and he told Miss Kingsley-Scott in no uncertain terms that he wasn't the slightest bit interested in her. He got back late, after driving her to the train. It was then that he found your letter. He's devastated, Flora. You're the girl he loves. And now he's had to go and get on that bloody ship and sail away again, thinking you don't love him any more, and it's breaking my heart . . .'

She'd never heard Lady Helen utter so many words and in such a forceful tone. And one of them a swear word, too! As she got over her initial shock and the words sank in, Flora pressed her hand to her mouth. She spun around wildly towards the loch where the merchant ships were lined up in their positions now, waiting for the off.

'No!' she cried. 'Alec! I have to go to him! I have to tell him I got it all wrong.'

She tried to turn, to run towards the pier, but Lady Helen hadn't yet relinquished her grip. 'Here,' her ladyship said. 'Take this with you.' She pressed something into Flora's hand. 'Now go!'

Flora's feet flew down the path, across the road, along the shore. But she was too late. As she watched, gasping for breath, the *Kite* slipped into its position at the head of the convoy and began to lead the line of ships towards the mouth of the loch. She waved both arms above her head, hoping that he might glimpse her there, but knowing he was already too far away. She dashed the tears from her eyes and then opened her hand to look at the sweetheart brooch that Lady Helen had given back to her. She took it and carefully pinned it on to her shawl as she stood watching the convoy leave.

'Come back to me,' she whispered. And the breeze took her words and scattered them out across the silver waters.

It was late August, a week after Alec had left. Honeysuckle spilled from the hedgerows and the song of the skylarks drifted on the summer breeze. Flora was walking home from the base when she saw the Laverock boys jogging towards her along the road. It was one of their evenings to help Iain at Ardtuath and they'd come straight from school, their socks bunched around their ankles above scuffed shoes, knees as knobbly as pine knots. She smiled and waved, but then stopped in her tracks as she saw the look on their faces.

'What is it?' she asked, automatically reaching to smooth Stuart's fringe out of his eyes.

'We seen that postie. On his bike. He turned in at the gates to the big house.' Stuart gasped for breath, panting out the words.

'Who was it? Mr McTaggart?'

The boys nodded their heads in unison.

Flora blanched. A telegram then. Alec.

She hesitated, wanting to know but not able to march up the drive to Ardtuath House and face the Mackenzie-Grants. Sir Charles's anger would be bad enough; Lady Helen's grief might be even worse.

But the not knowing was unbearable. So she was about to steel herself to do it when she caught sight of another figure in a Wrens uniform hurrying along the road towards them from the base, arms outstretched, capless brown curls askew. And as Flora's legs gave way beneath her, Bridie reached her and grabbed her just before she fell.

Lexie, 1978

Mairi's voice is gentle as she recalls the facts of my father's death. I'd heard them before, from Mum, of course. The *Kite* was accompanying that summer convoy through the Barents Sea when she was hit by a torpedo. She went down fast, taking with her the crew of 239 men. Only nine were saved, pulled from the waves by a rescue vessel, as the rest of the ships continued on their way to Archangel.

So my father lies, like so many other sailors, in a grave that I can never visit. His name on the family memorial of the Mackenzie-Grants in the graveyard doesn't seem nearly enough, but I suppose it was all Mum had. Those wildflowers that we laid there every Sunday were all she could offer him. He left not knowing that she loved him still. She had to live with that for the rest of her life. And he never knew that she was carrying his child.

And then Bridie tells me how, after the memorial service in the kirk, Sir Charles accosted Ruaridh in front of everyone, his rage and grief spilling over, and told him he should be ashamed of himself, sitting safe in a shelter on the hill in a job that Alec had made sure of for him, while his son's bones were lying under a hundred fathoms of icy sea. Ruaridh stood there and took it, saying nothing, but his jaw was clenched, his face as pale as a ghost with his own grief at the loss of his childhood friend.

Flora begged him not to go, but the very next day Ruaridh marched down to the base and asked for a transfer to the escort ships. And, because they needed a signalman, he was given a berth on the *Cassandra*, whose name indeed turned out to be a portent of doom. Ruaridh was lost as the last-but-one convoy was returning to Loch Ewe after a safe run through to Murmansk, the ship's bows shot away by a German torpedo.

And so it was that the next time Mr McTaggart cycled along the road towards Ardtuath, he passed the gates of the estate and turned in at Keeper's Cottage with the telegram that would break – again – the hearts of Iain and Flora, just three months after they'd learned the news of Alec.

'So that was it, then,' I say, once I've digested the story that my mother's best friends have told me. The tragedy of it makes me want to weep.

No wonder Mum found it hard to talk about my father. She must have felt so guilty about writing that awful letter to him. About him sailing to his death not knowing how much he was loved.

Then the awful realisation hits me, too, that she might have felt responsible for her own brother's death. Sir Charles's fury at Alec's love for Flora must have played a part in his grief-stricken rage, detonating his outburst at Ruaridh. Both my father and my uncle were war heroes, but now I understand how complex Mum's feelings must have been about the part she imagined she'd played in their deaths.

And, in the end, what had it all been for? Could we ever really have belonged in the world of the Mackenzie-Grants? Mum's last faint hope of that ever coming to pass died with Alec. She never met anyone else. Many of the men who left their Highland homes to fight in that war never returned, so there was another generation of women, just like there'd been in the aftermath of the previous war, whose prospects of marriage were slim to none. Mum had been one of those single women, living her quiet life in the little lochside community among the hills, bringing me up in Keeper's Cottage with Grandad, until he died just after my fifth birthday.

I sit in silence for a while, mulling it all over. But at last I ask, 'What happened to the Aultbea Songbirds?'

'We never sang in public again, apart from in the kirk, after Alec and Ruaridh died.' Mairi's voice sounds softly wistful. 'But, Lexie, it meant so much to your mum when you won that scholarship to the school in London. She felt then that you were being given the opportunity she'd never had. To share your voice with the world.'

I know her words are meant kindly, but I wince, feeling even worse now that I've let them all down. And my mum in particular. She'd been careful never to put pressure on me, but now I can see how much my career must have meant to her – so much more than I'd ever realised.

I pick up the photo of Mum with the wind blowing her hair and the sun on her face, her expression full of a love that was taken from her so brutally. Then I set it back on the mantelpiece with a sigh. As I look round, I catch Bridie and Mairi exchanging a glance.

'What?' I ask.

Bridie shakes her head and presses her lips together, as if the words might escape, unbidden, unless she refuses to let them.

But Mairi reaches across and pats her hand. 'It's time she knew the full story, Bridie. So she can understand.'

'Understand what?' I say, my eyes darting from one face to the other.

Bridie's expression is wary, closed off as she tries, one last time, to keep the secret that she's held tight for so many years. Almost thirty-four years, to be precise: my lifetime. But Mairi nods, encouraging. And so, reluctantly, Bridie tells me the rest.

Flora, 1944

Iain glanced over at Flora as he finished his breakfast. 'You don't have to come, you know.'

She reached for the teapot and topped up his cup. 'I'm coming with you, Dad, and that's the end of it. You can't manage the garron as well as the guns up there with Sir Charles. You know what he's like; he has his heart set on his Christmas venison. Even if he hadn't asked you to bring me along to help with the stalking, I'd have wanted to lend you a hand.'

Her father blew the steam from his tea and looked at her over the rim of his cup. 'Are you sure you're up to it, lass? Not still feeling too wabbit?'

Automatically, Flora laid a hand on the rounding of her belly. She was only four months along, but she'd discovered that she'd not been able to button her trousers that morning. She found a belt in Ruaridh's drawers, which had still never been emptied – neither of them had had the heart yet – that would do to hold them up. 'I'll be fine, Dad, honestly. I'm not so sick these days, and I'll only be sitting quietly with the garron while you go up to the ridge.'

Neither of them needed the reminder that there was no one else now, in any case, with Alec and Ruaridh gone. The Laverock boys, though they had proven themselves dogged and determined beaters on grouse and pheasant drives, were still on the young side to have the patience and the stamina for stalking.

She stood, clearing the bowls into the sink, and then handed her father a newspaper-wrapped packet of sandwiches for his pocket. She pulled on her jacket and threw her plaid shawl over her shoulders, partly for warmth and partly to help conceal the swell of her stomach from Sir Charles. She didn't want to add to his rage and grief at the loss of his only son with the news that the gamekeeper's daughter was carrying his grandchild. She'd been tempted to tell Lady Helen, who might have been glad to know a part of Alec lived on, but the last time she had seen her at a meeting of the Rural, Flora had turned away, unconsciously shielding her belly with a protective arm, worried that the dark purple bruise on her ladyship's cheekbone might be supplemented with worse if Sir Charles's anger were to be further compounded.

They set off for the stable and worked in silence, Flora slipping the halter over the pony's head and buckling the throat strap, while her father lifted the heavy deer saddle on to its back and fastened the girth. Flora led the garron slowly up the track alongside Ardtuath House while Iain went to collect the rifles from the gun safe and let Sir Charles know that they were ready.

His lordship took his double-barrelled Purdey from her father without a word, scarcely acknowledging Flora as he strode ahead up the track. She walked steadily, if a little more slowly than usual, the pony patiently matching its pace to hers as they crossed the hills above the village. They were headed for the lochan, where Flora would wait with the garron while the two men climbed on towards the higher land where the deer would be sheltering from the blustering December wind. When the path steepened, her father turned back and glanced at her anxiously, raising his eyebrows in a question. She was breathing heavily, but gave him a reassuring nod to let him know that she could manage.

An hour later they crossed the burn just below the lochan, swollen with winter rain, and her father extended a hand to help steady her where the stones were slippery with damp moss. She'd been looking down, making sure of her footing, one hand on the leading rein and the other automatically cradling her belly, the shawl slipping back slightly on her shoulders. When she raised her head again, her eyes met those of Sir Charles. He was watching her coldly, appraisingly, from where he stood on the path above her. She froze as she saw his gaze darken and his face flush claret red with anger as realisation dawned. Then he turned abruptly away and strode on ahead, towards the waters of the lochan that were as black as his mood.

When they reached the shelter of the bothy, her father handed his rifle to Flora for safekeeping and then took his binoculars from the leather case slung at his hip, scanning the hillside.

A small group of red deer hinds, foraging for the scant pickings of the winter ground, raised their heads. They were far enough off not to be panicked by the appearance of the three humans and the white pony, but watched warily from the hill. The lead hind grew uneasy and began to walk away, picking her way along the contour line, the others following in single file behind her before she stopped again. The stalking party was concealed from the herd now by the bothy wall, and Flora let the garron crop the bleached tufts of grass that grew alongside the stones, keeping her quiet. The hind's ears pricked as she waited, unmoving, muscles tensed for flight. But when the humans didn't re-emerge from behind the ruin she settled again at last, and resumed her search among the woody twigs of a clump of bog myrtle for any last leaves.

Still watching the hinds through his binoculars, her father said quietly, 'You might get a shot from here. They're well spaced and you've the hill behind them.' His words were barely more than a murmur.

Flora glanced towards Sir Charles. But he wasn't watching the deer on the hill. He was watching her. And an icy fear gripped her when she saw the look in his eyes.

His flush of anger had gone, to be replaced by a look of cold calculation. Very deliberately, he reached into the case on his belt and took out two bullets. His eyes still fixed on Flora, he loaded his rifle. Then he stepped away from the bothy, putting space between himself and the Gordons as he raised the gun to his shoulder.

The deer began to move again, edgy now, and her father lowered the binoculars. 'They'll climb higher in a minute, I don't doubt, now they've glimpsed us. Most likely they'll make for the far corrie beyond the ridgeline.'

The garron shifted, stamping a hoof uneasily on the hard ground.

There was a soft click as Sir Charles released the safety, both barrels of his rifle primed.

At the sound, her father turned towards him, raising a hand and saying, 'You'll not get a clean chest shot now, the angle's wrong.' Then he stopped, his words left hanging, unanswered, on the winter air.

For a moment there was a quietness so profound it seemed that the earth held its breath. The three figures stood frozen in a grotesque tableau, watched only by the red deer and a single skylark that dropped its fluting notes of warning into the silence to break the spell.

And then the air shattered as a shot rang out, echoing off the hills to rebound across the dark waters of the lochan, and in a terrified scramble the deer fled, leaping upwards, away from the kill.

Sure-footed as ever, the garron picked its way down the path. The deer saddle on its back swayed with each step under the weight of the body slung across it, an ooze of blood blooming scarlet against its white flank. As they reached the lochside, the pony's hooves rang hollowly on the harder surface of the road.

The crofters emerged in silence from their cottages as Iain Gordon and his daughter led the garron through the village, making their way slowly towards the gates of Ardtuath House. As they approached the hall, a group of women emerged, and Iain and Flora stopped.

There were gasps and someone whispered, 'It's Sir Charles!'

Then every head turned towards Lady Helen, who stood frozen in the doorway.

It was Moira Carmichael who moved first, hurrying to Flora, who had begun to shiver uncontrollably beneath the folds of her woollen shawl.

Iain pulled the faded deerstalker from his head and stood before her ladyship, his eyes downcast. Then he lifted his face, and it was creased with pain.

His voice was rough with anguish, though his words were clear and firm, loud enough for all to hear. 'I'm sorry. I did it.'

Flora sank to the ground and Bridie rushed to her side, wrapping her in her arms and rocking her as she keened, her cries as wordlessly plaintive as the curlew's on the shore.

Then Lady Helen took a step towards her husband's body and Iain hung his head again, unable to look at her.

'No.' The word was spoken with a firmness that brooked no dissent. For a moment the only sound was the hush of the waves on the sand, as even the curlew fell silent.

All heads turned again towards her ladyship. 'No,' she repeated. 'There has already been enough loss. There will be no more. This was an accident, Iain. A tragic accident.'

'But . . .' he began.

'No,' she said again, silencing him. 'There were two of you there to witness it, you and Flora. His gun misfired. We all understand that, don't we?' She looked around at the small crowd that had gathered, the members of the tight-knit crofting community who shared one another's lives. The bruise on her cheekbone was a dark shadow against the whiteness of her skin. There was silence, then a few faint nods.

She reached down and held out a hand to Flora. 'Come, my dear, get up off that cold ground. You've had a terrible shock. And in your condition you need to take extra care.' Tenderly, gently, she pulled the shawl around Flora, wrapping an arm around her shoulders. 'Let's get you into my car. I'll drive you home, Iain. Bridie, you come too.'

She drew herself up to her full height and looked round commandingly at the assembled company. Her voice, usually soft and slightly hesitant, was strong. 'Mr Carmichael, Mr McTaggart, would you be so kind as to lead the pony back to Ardtuath House? And could someone tell Doctor Greig to come as soon as he can? Thank you. I shall be waiting.'

Lexie, 1979

It's a bright, blustery late spring morning and Daisy and I are visiting the churchyard to inspect the stone with its simple lettering, which is now in its place on Mum's grave. We've gathered a bunch of wildflowers from the hedgerows around Keeper's Cottage – ox-eye daisies, red campion and meadowsweet – and tied it with a twist of wool from Mum's sewing box. I think she'd like that. Daisy carries a separate little posy of her own. We set them beside the headstone, next to the one that bears the names of Mum's father, mother and baby sister. I trace the incised letters, rubbing away a little of the lichen that has begun to encrust the older stone.

Daisy toddles around busily, picking tufts of bog cotton to add to our offerings. I sit on the mossy ground and watch her play, the sunlight setting her halo of rose-gold curls aglow. Among the sombre grey stones in the little churchyard, her vitality is a welcome reminder that life continues.

I extract a few of the daisies from my makeshift bouquet and put one on my grandfather Iain's grave.

'Thank you,' I whisper. 'She and I wouldn't be here without you.'

Then I clamber to my feet and take Daisy by the hand to walk across to the Mackenzie-Grant memorial. The stone angel keeps its eyes lowered, praying for the souls of those it watches over.

'And well you might,' I tell it. 'He was a bad 'un, Sir Charles Mackenzie-Grant, even if he was my grandfather.'

Then I take another ox-eye daisy and place it next to the inscription bearing my father's name. *Alexander Mackenzie-Grant, lost at sea.* 'I wish you'd lived,' I whisper. 'I wish I'd known you.'

Now that Mum's stone is in place, his name and hers face each other across a sweep of windswept hillside above the silver loch that was their home. The place where they shared the happiest days of their lives. It's not much, but at least it's something. And I know their story will be kept safe here, among the community that nurtured them as it nurtures me and my child.

I remember Mum putting her flowers on this grave. I'd always assumed they were for Alec. But perhaps they were for Sir Charles as well. Perhaps they were her way of saying she forgave him. Iain and Sir Charles's names face each other, too, I realise, just as the two fathers faced each other up there on the hill that day for a split second, before Iain fired the shot that saved my life before it had properly begun.

Daisy hums to herself as she continues to toddle between the stones of the graveyard, laying strands of purple vetch and heads of bog cotton on each one.

I wonder where Lady Helen's memorial is – my grandmother. Mairi and Bridie have told me that she was killed at the very start of 1945, in the final months of the war. With the Allies in Europe by then, I suppose everyone assumed that London would be a safer place. But they hadn't reckoned on the final desperate acts of retaliation by the Nazis, who had developed deadly V-2 rockets that could be fired into the heart of England's capital from Germany, with devastating effects. On the morning of 3rd January, Lady Helen Mackenzie-Grant had just arrived to start work as a volunteer at the Royal Hospital in Chelsea. She was one of those killed when a rocket struck the north-east wing of the building without warning.

As I trace my father's name chiselled into the polished granite memorial, I think that Lady Helen's name should be here as well, rather than – presumably – on a headstone in a lonely graveyard somewhere in London that no one ever visits. I vow that next time we come I'll bring a proper posy to lay at the feet of the angel, in her memory. I wish I'd known her, too.

Flora, 1944

The funeral procession wound along the road, following the hearse that drove slowly from Ardtuath House to the churchyard. Dressed in their sombre Sunday best, the community watched in silence as Sir Charles's coffin was lowered into the grave at the angel's feet, the minister reciting the words that had become all too familiar to so many families these past years.

Lady Helen stood straight-backed at the graveside, her black hat and coat emphasising the whiteness of her face. As the crowd filed past her, paying their respects, Flora and her father hung back, waiting until everyone had gone, bar the gravedigger, who stood to one side, leaning on his shovel. Lady Helen stepped towards them and folded Flora into her embrace.

'Are you all right, my dear?' she asked, her dark eyes solicitous.

Flora nodded, unable to speak. Iain looked wretched, his hat in his hand, finding no words, either.

'Now then,' she said briskly, 'I've been sorting a few things out. I've had a few decisions to make, as you can imagine. I'd like to come and see you tomorrow, if I may?'

'Certainly,' said Flora, looking up in surprise. 'We could come to the house, if you prefer?'

'No, I think I'd like to come to Keeper's Cottage. I know how welcome you always made Alec feel there. It will do me good to visit. Shall we say ten o'clock tomorrow morning? No need to go to any trouble.'

The keeper and his daughter watched as her ladyship got into the gleaming black car and was driven home. Then the pair of them followed, on foot, to change out of their good clothes and get on with their work.

Lady Helen knocked at the door of Keeper's Cottage at ten o'clock sharp the next morning. She wore her black coat and a silk headscarf knotted beneath her chin.

'Please, take a seat, your ladyship.' Flora's father motioned towards the sitting room, where three chairs had been set out in a row.

'The kitchen looks far cosier, I think. Let's sit at the table instead.' She pulled off her scarf and smoothed her hair into place, shrugging her coat from her shoulders as she drew up a chair.

Flora had never seen her looking so relaxed. It was as if she'd had to carry herself carefully, self-consciously, at Ardtuath House whereas here, in the cottage, she could be at ease. Just like her son before her.

'Can I get you a cup of tea, Lady Helen?' Flora asked.

'No, thank you, dear. I've only just had one. Please, sit down.' She gazed around, taking in the range and the shelves stacked with gleaming pots and pans and floral cups and saucers, and nodded her approval. 'No wonder Alec liked spending time here. It feels so homely.' She smiled.

Iain clasped and unclasped his hands on the table before him, seemingly at a loss to know what to do with them. Flora reached over and laid one of her own hands over his, reassuring him.

Lady Helen cleared her throat. 'Now then, there's to be no mention of my husband's accident. It's behind us once and for all. Doctor Greig took care of the paperwork and the police agreed there was no need for an inquest. Everyone's far too busy with more important war work these days.' She smiled at Iain, who gave a slow nod, unable to voice his feelings of gratitude. 'I've been speaking to my lawyers. I have no desire to keep Ardtuath Estate on now, and I've known for some time that the Urquharts have wanted to buy it. It makes sense for them to combine it with their own land. They're intending to plant trees. Apparently forestry is the way forward. They'll use the house for shooting parties sometimes, but otherwise it will remain shut up. They'd like you to keep an eye on things here, Iain, although their own factor will be taking on the overall running of the land. The common grazings will be maintained for the use of the community. But I have excluded Keeper's Cottage from the sale and I am making it over to you. This will always be your home, Iain, and a home for you, Flora, and for my grandchild. My lawyer in Inverness is drawing up the papers.'

Flora and Iain looked at one another in amazement. 'But what about you, Lady Helen? Where will you go?' asked Iain.

'I've decided to move back to London. There are too many memories here – good ones of Alec, of course, but they make me sad, those reminders that he's no longer here. And I have some memories that are not so good, too.' She dropped her eyes to her lap for a moment but not before Flora had glimpsed the look of pain in them. Then she lifted her head again, arranging her features in a determined smile. 'So it will be for the best if I go back to London. Thankfully the house there escaped the Blitz undamaged, and I shall enjoy being nearer to my friends and family in the south, too. It's a lot safer now that the Allies have taken back control of so much of Europe. There's work to be done there that I can get involved with, helping with the war effort. Don't worry, though, we will stay in touch. I'll pop back to visit every now and then. I can even stay in Ardtuath House if I can persuade the Urquharts that I'll be perfectly all right on my own. And you will come and see me in London sometimes, Flora, won't you? I want to get to know my grandchild.'

She stood, pulling on her coat and picking up her headscarf. At the door she took her leave, hugging Flora tight.

'It means so much to me to know that Alec lives on through his child,' she whispered.

Then she started to tie the scarf over her head but changed her mind and stuffed it into the pocket of her coat instead.

And Flora watched her walk away up the path through the pines, the wind from the loch blowing free the silvered strands of her hair.

Lexie, 1979

Davy's come for his supper. He has Daisy in fits of giggles, chasing her round the sitting room on all fours, pretending to be a bear. She allows herself to be caught and then wraps her arms around the bear's neck before kissing him firmly on the nose.

'Weed a storwy,' she demands, and the bear obliges, settling her on his knee in the big armchair beside the fire.

Her eyelids begin to droop after just a few pages of *Where the Wild Things Are* and she snuggles into the crook of his arm, resting her hand on the sleeve of his jumper. I lean against the door jamb and watch the pair of them, my heart suddenly so full of love that I think it just might burst.

It's another new sensation for me, all this love. Something I've not allowed myself to feel before. It's as if I've been sleepwalking through life and, now that the story that Bridie and Mairi have told me has fully sunk in, I have suddenly woken up to what has been right there, all around me, all along.

This community – the village it takes to raise a child – took me into its heart long before I was born, and helped protect me by allowing my grandfather to remain so that he could support my mother and me. My grandmother decreed it, stepping up to protect her unborn grandchild, and the others readily agreed. And they have kept the secret, all these years, weaving around me their web of love.

I'm so ashamed to admit that I was foolish enough to misread it. I interpreted the strands of that web as unwanted ties, pinning me down, binding me to a place that I left as soon as I could, cutting the lines and running as far and as fast as I could go with scarcely a backward glance. But now I see it in a new light. Of course everyone in the community felt they had an interest in me. I owe each and every one of them a debt of gratitude. After all, every day that they kept my grandfather's secret they were protecting Flora as she faced the challenges of raising a baby alone. And perhaps that baby represented far more to them. Perhaps she represented hope and life to those like Moira Carmichael who had lost so much. Flora Gordon's baby would have been a flicker of light in the dark months following the loss of Alec and of Ruaridh, and of so many other young men from the small crofting community.

Everything has changed. And nothing has changed. The truth is a powerful force.

As Davy turns the final page of the book, Daisy's eyelids close, her rose-gold lashes fluttering against her cheeks. I set down my glass and step forward to lift her off his lap, the slack warmth of her heavy in my arms. I carry her through and settle her gently in her cot, drawing up the blanket her granny knitted for her and tucking it in, wrapping her in love. She stirs a little, starfish hands spreading as her fingers relax against the strands of soft wool, the drift of finely stitched seashells that will keep her safe until morning comes.

When I return, Davy is still sitting in the armchair, gazing into the orange glow of the fire. He's deep in thought.

I settle myself across from him on the sofa, lost in thoughts of my own.

He gets up and crosses to sit next to me, and I rest my head against his shoulder. But then he draws back a little and I turn so that I can see his eyes. There is something there, a look of uncertainty mixed with something else that I can't quite read.

'What is it?' I ask.

He hesitates, giving a little shake of his head, and his eyes crinkle at the corners in their usual way as he gives me a reassuring smile. But that something is still there, lurking beneath the surface, and I need to know what it is.

'Tell me,' I press him.

He sighs. And then he combs his fingers through his hair, as if trying to put his thoughts in order, and says, 'Okay.'

He shifts so that he's facing me, and I can tell from his expression that this is important.

'I know what Bridie and Mairi have told you of your mother's story. But there's one last bit that they don't know. Nobody knows. I've kept it safe for so long, and I've been battling to decide whether or not to tell you. But it is your story, Lexie Gordon, so who am I to keep it from you? Besides,' he adds, 'I don't want there to be any secrets between us, ever.'

I nod, impatient for him to get on with it. 'I'd know, in any case. I can read you like a book. Tell me.'

He takes a breath. 'Okay. Well, on the evening after Sir Charles was shot, Stuart and I heard the Carmichaels talking. They were in the sitting room beneath us, and because it was just the floorboards between us and them, we could hear everything they said. Mr C said the doctor would need to issue a death certificate and that he might have to call the local police as it had been so sudden, whether or not it was an accident. Mrs C was upset at that. "What will happen to that poor lass if she loses her father as well as her brother and her sweetheart? And what about the bairn?" she said. "It doesn't bear thinking about. Do you suppose Lady Helen will be able to persuade Dr Greig to let it go?" And then Mr C said, "It'll likely be the death penalty for Iain if she can't."

'Stuart and I were supposed to be in our beds. But we got up and crept down the stairs, past the sitting room door which was closed to keep in the heat of the fire, and out the back. We'd done it loads of times before when we wanted to go looking for night-crawlers on the beach to use as bait. We took our catapults with us and we ran all the way to Keeper's Cottage. Our plan was to defend your mum and Iain if the police came. We had our gutties loaded and ready and our pockets full of more pebbles. We were prepared to go into battle for them, after everything they'd done for us.

'We sat for ages in the dark on the steps at the front door. And while we were sat there, we heard your mum and your grandad talking.' He tails off, his eyes never leaving mine.

'What did they say?' I prompt softly.

'Well, Iain's voice was low and we couldn't catch much of what he was saying at first. But then Flora said, "No, Dad, I'm not going to let you take the responsibility for what I did." And then we did hear Iain's words, because his voice was loud and firm: "I'll not let them take you, Flora. I'll not let them take my grandchild. You saved me from his first shot. And I've no doubt the second one was to be for you." Then your mum hushed him and their voices were lowered again so we couldn't hear the rest.'

I scan his face, trying to absorb what his words mean. 'Mum . . . ?'

He nods. 'Soon after that they went off to their beds. But Stuart and I sat there as long as we could keep our eyes open, guarding the door. We nearly froze. Then finally we decided it was too late for the police to come that night so we crept back to the Carmichaels' and no one was any the wiser.'

'Did anyone else know?' I ask him. 'That it was Mum who shot Sir Charles?'

'No one, so far as I know. Stuart and I never breathed a word about what we'd heard. Everyone else took Iain's word that he was the one who'd fired the shot.'

The firelight flickers, casting its play of light and shadows over us both.

'Then, in any case, Dr Greig issued the death certificate, no questions asked. So I suppose he was in on the conspiracy, too. I imagine Lady Helen would have been very persuasive. And the doctor must have treated enough of her bruises and broken bones to know what went on behind the grand doors of Ardtuath House. So maybe he was all the more inclined to do as she asked.'

I sit in shocked silence for a while, anguish tightening my throat. I could cry for my mother, who didn't hesitate to defend her father and her unborn baby when the moment came. I could cry for the two wee boys who sat shivering at the door of this very cottage, their home-made slingshots at the ready to defend my family. And I feel an even deeper sense of shame for the way I've taken so much for granted all my life – a life that I owe to so many.

Davy wraps me in his arms and soothes me, stroking my hair. When I look at him I see that his anguish mirrors mine, and anxiety flickers in the way his lips have turned down at the corners.

'You were right to tell me. I'm glad I know now.'

At last he smiles and his sea-grey eyes hold an ocean of love so deep it takes my breath away.

'Everyone's been so kind all along,' I say. 'And I never knew. I've repaid them with bad grace and ingratitude. How can I ever thank them?'

He laughs. 'You've repaid them every day by living your life. How proud you made us all, having your name up in lights in the West End. You have no idea what satisfaction that gave everyone here, feeling like they'd played a part in it.'

'And now I've let them all down again, by losing my voice and crashing out of my career.'

'You've let no one down but yourself, Lexie,' he says gently, 'by thinking of yourself as a failure. You've actually done exactly what we all wanted in the end. You came home, bringing Daisy. And it's here that you've found a new song to sing.'

His words sink in, soothing the pain I feel, and I kiss him.

And then, with a grin, he says, 'Although of course I do take most of the credit for the singing thing.'

'Och, would you get over yerself, Davy Laverock,' I say, kissing him again.

And then, as the fire's embers fall in on themselves, sending up one last flicker of flame in the darkening room, I take him by the hand and lead him, tiptoeing past the door to Daisy's room, to bed.

Lexie, 1979

I'm pegging out the washing when the postie's little red van appears, winding its way along the lochside. Carefully making sure that Daisy's dungarees are securely fixed – the wind is always eager to snatch the clothes from the line and scatter them into the branches of the pines – I go to meet him at the gate. He hands me a small bundle of envelopes and there's a familiar sinking feeling in the pit of my stomach as I take them from him, noticing that most are brown and almost certainly contain bills. I've been living off the last of my savings and they're dwindling fast now.

'I see there's one from yon lawyers in Inverness,' he remarks cheerily.

It's the postie's prerogative to inspect the mail thoroughly as he delivers it each day, and so he's usually up on exactly who has a birthday, who's received a parcel and – in my case – who's being sent shameful, red-inked final reminders to pay their electricity bill.

The lawyer is the executor of Mum's estate, such as it is, and so this letter could be the news that everything has finally been sorted out. Not that I'm expecting much in the way of an inheritance. Mum always lived quietly, eking out her pennies with the food she grew. I always insisted on paying for her train tickets to London, conscious that I was earning good money in those days and that, although she was skilled at making ends meet, she didn't have much to spare. But maybe there'll be a little money to help get me through a month or two more at Keeper's Cottage before I have to face the inevitable and sell up.

The thought of having to move away to somewhere else dismays me far more than I'd ever have thought possible. Over the past months, as I've pieced together my family history, it's as if roots have begun to grow, slowly, quietly, beneath my feet, binding me to Keeper's Cottage. This place has become a home for me and Daisy and it hurts to think of leaving. I can't imagine saying goodbye to Bridie and Elspeth and the other mums in the toddler group. I can't imagine no longer being able to make music with the next generation of children to grow up in the crofts along the loch, passing on the traditional songs in the way they've been passed down to us over the centuries. And, most of all, I can't bear to think about leaving Davy behind. But he's managed to carve out a living for himself here, and that's something I'm going to have to seek elsewhere. Just as so many have done before, I'll have to leave Ardtuath sooner or later, go and find a job in a city to support myself and my child.

I thank the postie brightly, trying not to let my problems show, and wave him off on his way before taking the pile of letters inside. I chuck the brown envelopes on to the kitchen table, putting off opening them while I read the solicitor's letter. It's not exactly informative, just a brief note asking me to call and make an appointment to come to the offices in Inverness at my earliest convenience. I put it on top of the pile of brown envelopes and busy myself making Daisy's lunch as she pushes a tractor around my feet, humming to herself.

Once Daisy's gone down for her nap and I've finished wiping mashed potato off her high chair – she insists on feeding herself these days, and the result is often messy – I phone the lawyer's office. The nice woman who fields my call tells me she 'really couldn't say, dear' what the meeting was about, but she makes an appointment for me to go and see Mr Clelland next Monday afternoon.

Then I fetch my chequebook and with a sigh of resignation begin to open the rest of the post.

The offices of Macwhirter and Clelland Solicitors are tucked into a discreet side street behind the castle. I take a seat, perching on the slippery leather sofa and nervously smoothing my skirt over my knees. After so many months of rural living, it's been a little nerve-wracking driving into the city and finding a parking space. And I'm anxious to know what Mr Clelland has to say. In my more hopeful moments, I've imagined a life insurance policy that would allow me to stay at Ardtuath for a few more months. On the other hand, lying awake in the wee small hours of the night, I've imagined a problem with taxes or death duties that means I'll be plunged into debt.

Mr Clelland emerges at last from behind the door with his name on it and smiles at me, his eyes magnified by his thick-rimmed spectacles. 'Miss Gordon? Do come through.'

He settles himself on the other side of the leather-topped desk and picks up a sheet of official-looking paper from the pile before him. He glances at me over the top of his specs and says, 'Now then, I'll begin at the beginning, shall I?'

I'd planned to have a bit of a day out in Inverness, popping into Marks for some new clothes for Daisy (she's pretty much grown out of everything I brought with me from London now), and buying a few exotic bits and pieces for the store cupboard, like curry powder, that the local shop doesn't stock. But in the end, when Mr Clelland shows me to the door I sleepwalk back to my car and drive straight home. Along the way, I scarcely register the views of the hills and the sea in my haste to return to Keeper's Cottage and share my news with Davy, and Bridie and Mairi, and Elspeth.

I left home this morning a poverty-stricken single mum. I am returning a wealthy woman. A woman who could never have dreamed of the opportunities that lie before her now.

Lexie, 1980

Davy tops up my glass and the bubbles froth to the very brim before settling again. He raises his own glass in another toast. 'To Lady Helen Mackenzie-Grant and Flora Gordon, the women who made all this possible.'

There's a round of applause before the fiddles and flute strike up again, playing 'Flora's Waltz', the piece that the band have composed especially for my mum. The lilting melody suits her perfectly with its beautifully simple rise and fall, and as I listen I can picture her gentle smile. She is with me here tonight in the big house as we launch the Centre for Traditional Music, which I've established in her name. She could never take up her rightful place here in her lifetime, but now the empty rooms will be filled with life and laughter and music. The songs my mum used to sing will resonate from the panelled walls and the corniced ceilings and – at last – Flora Gordon will be mistress of Ardtuath House.

It's to be a place where people will come from far and wide, and everyone will be made welcome: all generations and backgrounds, beginners and experts, people who want to make their own music. People who want to find their own songs to sing.

I think my grandmother, Lady Helen, would approve, too. At the meeting in Inverness, Mr Clelland had explained to me that on her death, her entire estate – the proceeds from the sale of the house in London as well as the sale of the house and lands at Ardtuath – had been put into a carefully managed trust. She had specified that an amount was to be paid each month to Flora Gordon of Keeper's Cottage, Ardtuath, to enable her to live there and raise her child. And on Flora Gordon's death, the trust was to be dissolved and the capital made over in full to the then about-to-be-born grandchild of Lady Helen Mackenzie-Grant, who would be her sole heir.

Once Mr Clelland had gone through the legalities of Lady Helen's bequest with me, he'd then shuffled through his pile of papers and turned his attention to Mum's will. She'd left Keeper's Cottage to me, of course. But what I didn't know was that she'd put almost all of her monthly allowance from the trust into her post office savings account, preferring to live simply and quietly as her parents had done before her on the little croft. She'd sent me a small allowance when I was studying in London, and I imagine she might have used her savings to pay the fees for me to attend stage school if I hadn't won a full scholarship. But she'd always preferred to let me stand on my own two feet, proving to myself and to the world that I could make my own success, and all the while the money she'd saved had been accumulating quietly in the background.

I smile at Davy as he joins the other musicians on the stage, picking up his guitar. He has a new part-time job here now as one of the teachers when he's not out on the boat. Elspeth and I will work together running the administrative side of the centre, sharing the job and our childcare. She has little Katie now, Jack's sister, and Daisy loves spending her days with them.

I caress the gentle swell of my own belly as Davy begins to play 'The Eriskay Love Lilt'. It's still our secret, but I've no doubt that before too many more weeks have passed it will be general knowledge about these parts that Daisy Gordon is going to have her own wee brother or sister by the time the heather turns the hills purple again in the summer. My money's on Bridie Macdonald being the first to know.

As he sings the verse, he searches for me in the audience and looks straight into my eyes.

'*Thou art the music of my heart,*
Harp of joy, o cruit mo chruid,
Moon of guidance by night,
Strength and light thou art to me.'

He's the one who helped me come up with the idea for the centre. We've taken out a long lease on the house so that instead of it being shut up most of the year and only used for the occasional shooting party, it's become a focal point of the community, open to all. There'll be concerts and festivals and residential retreats on offer. And there'll be music lessons for local children, as well as the toddler's music and movement group that Elspeth and I will continue to run. We have plans to install a recording studio, too, so that the traditional songs can be preserved for posterity.

Tonight, the windows of Ardtuath House no longer look like blank, dead eyes staring out at the loch, and the oppressive atmosphere of sadness and fear that used to linger in these rooms has been exorcised. Light spills on to the lawn, pushing back the shadows, and music floats on the air, bringing the night to life. Davy once said that Keeper's Cottage had always been filled with song and good cheer, and that's another way that Flora's spirit has finally been allowed to inhabit the house where she'd once dreamed of living as Alec's wife. Although that dream was destined never to come true, perhaps Fate has a funny way of making sure things work out in the end.

Once the evening is over and the new centre has been well and truly launched, I walk from room to room, switching off lights as I go. I linger in the library and trace my fingers along the edge of the mantelpiece above the fireplace.

While I'm standing there, Davy comes into the room. 'There you are,' he says, wrapping his arms around me. 'What are you thinking about? You look so far away.'

'I'm thinking of Flora and Alec spending an evening here together, and I wish that life had been different for us all,' I reply. 'I wish that he'd survived the war and that they'd been able to marry. I wish I'd known my dad. I wish that Mum had had him by her side instead of living her life alone for so many years. I wish your mum and Stuart were alive. And I wish they could all be here now to see this and share it with us.'

He nods and kisses my hair. 'But you know, Lexie, in your way, you've made sure they live on by filling this place with the music that was the soundtrack to their world. You've taken all that loss and turned it into something that's going to benefit so many more people. If things had been different, you might never have found your own song to sing. That, above all, was what Flora wanted for you.'

I smile and turn to kiss him. 'We'll keep her songs alive and pass them on from generation to generation. We'll keep all their songs alive.' I'm thankful that he and I have had the luxury of time to sort out ourselves and our relationship, a luxury that Alec and Flora never had. I'm thankful to have found him. And I'm thankful that we have each other and the music in our souls.

I turn off the last of the lights and then we leave, closing the heavy front door behind us and turning the key in the lock before we make our way back along the path beneath the pines to Keeper's Cottage. I glance back over my shoulder at the house just before its face is obscured by the trees. And, even though the windows are darkened again, it seems to me that Ardtuath House has awakened from its long sleep and is ready to live and breathe once more.

The next day, I settle Daisy into her carrier and hoist it on to my back. Then we climb the hill to the lochan where the white lilies grow, singing as we go. As we cross the slope above Ardtuath House, the strains of a fiddle float from an open window, wafted towards us by the breeze from the loch. The notes meld naturally with the sighing of the wind in the pine branches, while the fluting calls of the larks on the hill add their own harmony over the melody.

Below us, in the little graveyard, a new bench has been placed alongside the memorial to the Mackenzie-Grant family. On it is carved a dedication to Lady Helen and the words I chose from my favourite Gaelic blessing: *Deep peace of the shining stars to you.* At last her name is remembered there, beside her beloved son's, even if neither of them lie beneath the nodding heads of the cotton grass.

Out on the water, Davy will be setting off in the *Bonnie Stuart* to check his creels. If we're lucky there'll be squatties for our supper tonight.

We reach the old bothy and I set Daisy down thankfully, out of breath with the effort of the climb. As I release her from the carrier I say, 'Soon you'll be too big for this. You'll have to walk on your own two feet because your baby will be in the carrier.'

'My baby,' she says, pointing a stubby finger at my stomach. Then she potters off to pick some wildflowers from among the stones of the fallen walls.

I lift my face to the sunshine and watch as a skylark rises from the gorse above us, soaring into the blue. Its song makes me think of Davy Laverock, who kept his secret for all those years. A secret within a secret, protecting my mum. It was his way of repaying her kindness to him and Stuart, part of the natural cycle of give and take that makes up life within a tight-knit community.

A wind-scudded cloud crosses the face of the sun, obscuring it for a few seconds. And there it is again, that trick of the light that brings the ghost ships out on the loch. I picture Alec Mackenzie-Grant, and Ruaridh Gordon, and Hal Gustavsen, and Johnny, Matthew and Jamie Carmichael, and the many other young men who gave their lives to the war. I'm glad that they all knew this place, the hidden lochan covered in white lilies in the hills above Loch Ewe. I'm glad that they heard the song of the skylark and knew how good freedom can be. So good that it's worth fighting for.

I gather Daisy to me and hug her tight, burying my face in her rose-gold curls. She's the spitting image of her granny; everyone says so.

Then I settle her back in the carrier and hoist it on to my shoulders for the walk home.

AUTHOR'S NOTE

'This is a God-fearing community and the local people are to be treated with respect.'

Winston Churchill, in an address to naval personnel on the arrival of the Home Fleet in Loch Ewe. 13th September, 1939

In writing this book, I have tried at all times to keep to Winston Churchill's directive, treating the memories of the local inhabitants and their history with the utmost respect. For the purposes of the story, all the characters are fictitious. Any similarities to particular individuals are both coincidental and unintentional.

There is no Ardtuath Estate, nor was there an Ardtuath House that could be transformed from a shooting lodge into a music school. However, I am pleased to say that a thriving traditional music scene and a resurgence in the teaching of Gaelic ensure that the old songs live on in the Highlands. The idea of a school to help promote traditional Scottish music was inspired, in part, by the National Centre of Excellence in Traditional Music at Plockton, which offers residential places for students from all across Scotland. The Traditional Music and Song Association is a good starting point for finding out more about the songs included in this book:

www.tmsa.scot

As far as possible, I have tried to stick to the historical timeline of events during World War II. I have made up or altered the names of some of the ships that Alec serves upon for the purposes of the story but again, wherever I could, I have reflected the historical facts as accurately as possible.

Three thousand men lost their lives on the Arctic convoys. Those who served, undertaking what Winston Churchill described as 'the worst journey in the world', were finally awarded a special medal – the Arctic Star – in 2012. The medal was awarded to both military personnel and merchant seamen. Arctic convoy personnel are entitled to wear a white beret, earning them the nickname 'Snowdrops'. In the garden of the Russian Arctic Convoys Museum in Aultbea, 3,000 snowdrops have been planted to commemorate those who lost their lives, re-emerging as a sea of white blooms each spring.

The vestiges of Loch Ewe's pivotal role as the muster point for the convoys can still be seen today. In 1999 a memorial was unveiled at Rubha Nan Sasan, the point overlooking the entrance to the loch, to commemorate the courage of all who took part in the convoys, which played such a vital role in the Allied victory.

When I visited the memorial, among the poppies that had been left there in memory of those who never returned to the safe harbour of Loch Ewe, a stone had been placed, painted with a single word: Спасибо.

It is the Russian word for 'thanks'.

ACKNOWLEDGMENTS

Thanks to the Russian Arctic Convoys Museum, Aultbea, a wealth of material has been preserved to keep alive the memories of those extraordinary years during World War II when that remote crofting community was suddenly transformed into a busy naval base and became home for over three thousand military personnel. The museum, staffed by welcoming and knowledgeable volunteers, is a treasure trove of information and well worth a visit. Its exhibits help to bring home just how terrible conditions were on the journeys to Murmansk and Archangel. Details of the convoys and the men who served on them are available via their website at www.racmp.co.uk.

Similarly, Steve Chadwick's book *Loch Ewe During World War II* is a wonderful reference work, recording local people's reminiscences as well as the historical facts.

All Hell Let Loose: The World at War 1939–1945 by Max Hastings has a chapter devoted to the Arctic convoys, which is a good starting point for anyone wishing to read more about their history within the wider context of the war.

I was extremely fortunate to be given access to several first-hand accounts recorded by people who served on the convoys. I am grateful to Vivienne Giacobino-Simon who shared extracts from the diaries of her father, Noel Simon, the author and African wildlife conservationist. During the war, Noel was a fighter pilot with the Fleet Air Arm, flying Wildcats from the aircraft carrier *Illustrious*, one of the escort vessels accompanying several convoys. He was mentioned in dispatches for his bravery.

Jamie Jauncey very kindly shared with me his grandfather's book, the *Random Naval Recollections* of Admiral Sir Angus Cunninghame Graham, who commanded the destroyer *Kent* on Arctic convoys at one point during his illustrious naval career.

I am also grateful to Sandra Nicholl of Tamarac, Florida, for sharing photos and memories of her parents' careers in the RAF and WRNS, including mention of the WRNS guard of honour at their Scottish wedding.

My neighbour, Ernie Carrol, told me stories of his father's army career, which helped inspire some of the scenes in the book. I hope his dog, Braan, doesn't mind me borrowing his name. I also appropriated the name of my friend Kiki Fraser's dog, Corrie, with her kind permission. And my friends Peter and Wendy Miller very generously shared information about refugee children attending a west coast school during the war years.

Jamie Elder of West Highland Marine took me out on to Loch Ewe in his boat, the *Striker,* and gave me an excellent and informative tour of World War II sites around the loch from the water. He was very well placed to do so, having fished the waters all his life, along with his father before him, and – on one occasion – having found an unexploded bomb from the war years on the seabed.

Heartfelt thanks, as always, to my agent, Madeleine Milburn, and to her brilliant team for supporting and promoting my books around the world.

A massive thank you to my editors, Sammia Hamer, Mike Jones, Gill Harvey and Monica Byles, as well as to Emma Rogers for another stunning cover design, and to the rest of the Lake Union team at Amazon Publishing. You are life-changers.

Another big, heartfelt thank you goes out to all the friends and family who encourage me and keep the hugs coming. Especially: Lesley Singers and her family; my mother, Aline Wood; my aunt, Flora Crowe; Karen and Michael Macgregor for west coast inspiration; James and Willow; Alastair and Carey.

And, finally, I am so grateful to all my readers for their support and I would like to thank you personally for reading my books. If you have enjoyed *The Skylark's Secret*, I should be very grateful if you would consider writing a review. I love getting feedback, and I know reviews have played a big part in helping other readers to discover my work.

With best wishes,

Fiona

ABOUT THE AUTHOR

Photo credit: Willow Findlay

Fiona is an acclaimed number 1 bestselling author, whose books have been translated into more than twenty different languages worldwide.

She draws inspiration from the stories of strong women, especially during the years of World War II. Her meticulous historical research enriches her writing with an evocative sense of time and place.

Fiona spent seven years living in France, having moved there from the UK in 2007, before returning to live in Scotland. Her love for both of these countries, their people and their histories, has found its way into the books she's written.